OUT OF TIME

By Jodi Taylor and available from Headline

THE BALLAD OF SMALLHOPE AND PENNYROYAL

TIME POLICE SERIES

DOING TIME HARD TIME SAVING TIME
ABOUT TIME KILLING TIME OUT OF TIME

THE CHRONICLES OF ST MARY'S SERIES

JUST ONE DAMNED THING AFTER ANOTHER
A SYMPHONY OF ECHOES
A SECOND CHANCE
A TRAIL THROUGH TIME
NO TIME LIKE THE PAST
WHAT COULD POSSIBLY GO WRONG?
LIES, DAMNED LIES, AND HISTORY
AND THE REST IS HISTORY
AN ARGUMENTATION OF HISTORIANS
HOPE FOR THE BEST
PLAN FOR THE WORST
ANOTHER TIME, ANOTHER PLACE
A CATALOGUE OF CATASTROPHE
THE GOOD, THE BAD AND THE HISTORY

SHORT-STORY COLLECTIONS

THE LONG AND SHORT OF IT LONG STORY SHORT
THE MOST WONDERFUL TIME OF THE YEAR

ELIZABETH CAGE NOVELS

WHITE SILENCE DARK LIGHT
LONG SHADOWS BAD MOON

FROGMORTON FARM SERIES

THE NOTHING GIRL THE SOMETHING GIRL

A BACHELOR ESTABLISHMENT

JODI TAYLOR
OUT OF TIME

HEADLINE

Copyright © 2025 Jodi Taylor

The right of Jodi Taylor to be identified as the Author of the Work has been asserted by her in accordance with the Copyright, Designs and Patents Act 1988.

First published in 2025 by
Headline Publishing Group Limited

1

Apart from any use permitted under UK copyright law, this publication may only be reproduced, stored, or transmitted, in any form, or by any means, with prior permission in writing of the publishers or, in the case of reprographic production, in accordance with the terms of licences issued by the Copyright Licensing Agency.

All characters in this publication – other than the obvious historical figures – are fictitious and any resemblance to real persons, living or dead, is purely coincidental.

Cataloguing in Publication Data is available from the British Library

Hardback ISBN 978 1 0354 0604 3
Trade paperback ISBN 978 1 0354 0605 0

Typeset in Times New Roman by CC Book Production

Printed and bound in Great Britain by Clays Ltd, Elcograf S.p.A.

Headline's policy is to use papers that are natural, renewable and recyclable products and made from wood grown in well-managed forests and other controlled sources. The logging and manufacturing processes are expected to conform to the environmental regulations of the country of origin.

HEADLINE PUBLISHING GROUP
An Hachette UK Company
Carmelite House
50 Victoria Embankment
London EC4Y 0DZ

The authorised representative in the EEA is Hachette Ireland, 8 Castlecourt Centre, Dublin 15, D15 XTP3, Ireland
(email: info@hbgi.ie)

www.headline.co.uk
www.hachette.co.uk

This story is dedicated to those who work in our fast-disappearing public libraries. All of whom are, in my experience, equal to everything and anything the world can hurl at them. Dead dogs, exploding holes, temperamental urinals, first-aid emergencies, floods, stupid facilities managers getting themselves wedged in the wheel arch of a mobile library (yes, that has happened), readers demanding the book they had last year with the red cover – it's all in a day's work for library staff.

Roll Call

TIME POLICE PERSONNEL

Commander Hay	Her world will be rocked. And not in a good way.
Captain Farenden	Not a lot he can do to help.
Major Callen	His world is ended.
Major Ellis	His world is rocked, too. But for completely different reasons.
Lt North	And hers.
Lt Grint	And his. For even more different reasons. There's a lot of world-rocking in this story.

TEAM 235

**No one rocks their world.
They're being very brave about that.**

Officer Hansen	Engrossed in the world of *Guinea Pigs for Fun and Profit*. Not sure what that's about.
Officer Kohl	
Officer Rossi	

TEAM 236 – TEAM WEIRD

Officer Farrell	His world's gone silver again.
Officer Lockland	Manages to well and truly rock someone else's world. Who'd have thought?
Officer Parrish	Too late for his world. And he knows it.

SECURITY

Lt Varma	Her world doesn't sit still long enough to be rocked. Not once Maxwell turns up.
Officer Etok	Their worlds remain much the same.
Officer Roche	
Officer Wu	
Trainee Tucker	Decision time. This new world? Or back to the old one.

HELICOPTER PILOTS

Lt Mellor	Never gets to see the football. Not in this world.
Lt Bailey	Her world rocks. Always has done.

OTHER TIME POLICE PERSONNEL

Lt Dahl	
Lt Chigozie	
Officer Curtis	His world is clingfilmed. Twice.
Officer Rockmeyer	

POD BAY & LOGISTICS

Senior Mech   A second chance for his world.
Officer Oti
Mikey

MEDCEN

The doctor
Medtec Kelly

TIMMS

The Map Master   Sod the world. Save the Map!
Officer Connor

Dr Maxwell   Temporarily co-opted into the world of the Time Police. Everyone knows how that will end.

MISSING IN ACTION

Their world is finally ended.

Lt Pyotr Hahn
Officer Ado Aziz
Officer Denny Britton
Officer Alfred Burns
Officer Simon Coyle
Officer Sven Dikstrom
Officer Alexander Haddad

Officer Michael Murphy
Officer Marcus Noon
Officer Senze Okuta
Officer Devan Singh
Officer Adina Sharron
Officer Greg Turner

Previously on the Time Police . . .

Luke and Jane have finally escaped the clutches of the Zanetti Train and the 19th century's ideas of 'enlightened treatment for the insane'. Several days have passed, during which Matthew's broken arm has been set for the second time and Luke and Jane have more or less recovered from their physical injuries.

However, owing to their recent dysfunction, Team 236 is to be placed under supervision. They are not happy about this.

Luke is struggling – in as much as he struggles with anything – to come to terms with the realisation that he's rather fond of Jane. He is unaware of the fact that Imogen Farnborough is struggling to come to terms with the realisation that she's rather fond of him. Tears and tantrums ahead, probably.

Messrs Hooke and Sawney, ex-Time Police officers and very naughty people, have been arrested over their part in the Zanetti Train incident and are currently being held at TPHQ, awaiting interrogation.

The Pod Bay is still not fully functioning owing to the discovery of something mysterious when the wall fell down. Well, when the wall was knocked down, actually, during the course of one of Mikey's experiments. The Senior Mech is wrestling with his conscience. And a ton of plasterboard.

Jane and Grint have still not done the deed. Blame the unit-wide recall imposed at just the wrong moment.

Speaking of unit-wide recalls . . . a dead dinosaur has washed up in Wales, land of the dragon, so it's surprising anyone has actually noticed. But they have.

The Time Police are assembling a force to investigate.

To pass the time until the Pod Bay is fully functioning, the Time Police's technical advisor has been putting the finishing touches to her patented poo-packaging thingy. Chipolatas are involved. SPOILER ALERT – they do not fare well.

Now read on . . . if you dare.

Prologue

It was a trap. If they hadn't all been exhausted from their third major mission in as many days, they might have tumbled to it sooner. But they were exhausted and it was a disaster. That's the way the dice fall sometimes.

The ravine was narrow and rocky. The sky was clear – stars twinkled overhead but there was no moon. Perfect conditions for the ambush they didn't know they were walking into.

'Night visors,' ordered Lt Hahn. 'Normal stealth formations.'

He led the way along the western side of the ravine with Team 94 behind him.

On the eastern side, Team 88 moved equally silently. Ideally, a third team – Team 101 – should be acting as backstop, but there had been an accident the previous week. A disaster. The door of their pod had come off mid-jump. Apart from one survivor – Lt Hay – everyone had died. She had been discovered under a pile of her melted colleagues and was now in MedCen on suicide watch as she attempted to come to terms with what had happened to her team – and to herself. So no backstop tonight. They'd just have to manage.

No one had actually mentioned that there were thirteen officers on this particular operation. Lt Hahn, Officer Sharron, five members of Team 88 and six members of Team 94. Thirteen in all.

Lt Hahn was young and inexperienced. Overpromoted, of course, because the Time Police were so desperate for manpower these days. Some reassurance was provided by the presence of Officer Sharron – never knowingly undersold in the ball-busting department and widely referred to, with typical Time Police imagination, as Ball-buster Sharron. No one messed with her. Not for long, anyway.

The night was bitterly cold and the air crackled around them. Other than the occasional muttered curse as a loose rock moved underfoot and someone turned an ankle, the officers moved silently through the night.

Eventually Hahn threw up his hand and called a halt. They pressed back against the ravine walls, seeking shelter in the shadows. Hahn looked about him. 'Have we missed them somehow? Sharron – anything behind us?'

Sharron took her time scanning the ravine from wall to wall, up and down and back again.

'No lights. Nothing moving. No figures silhouetted against the skyline. Nothing on my proximities.'

To check her equipment was working properly, she turned and scanned ahead of her. Various grainy green lumps resolved themselves into her colleagues.

'Negative, sir. All clear above and behind. All equipment functioning as per.'

'Have we overshot? Or have they been and gone?'

Several officers rose to their feet, consulting their visor readouts.

Dikstrom from Team 88 had just got as far as, 'Something's moving, sir . . .' when, without warning, the trap was sprung.

Sharron, standing slightly apart from all the others, felt her head swim. Violent nausea swept through her and her legs buckled. She fell heavily to the rocky ground – which almost certainly saved her life.

Ahead of her, closer to the source of the attack, two of her colleagues burst into flames, standing for a moment like giant, human-shaped candles before collapsing to the ground. Very dead.

Shit – this had to be the very latest weapon on the black market. A lethal combination of blaster fire and a sonic cannon. Even the Time Police didn't have these yet. But there was one here now. Possibly two.

Slowly Sharron became aware of shouting and screaming around her. Above everything, she could hear Lt Hahn.

'Fall back. Fall ba—'

Another arrow-straight stream of blaster fire roared through the night and his voice was abruptly cut off.

She lifted her head, pushed up her visor and tried to see. Blaster fire had destroyed her night vision. And not just hers. Half-blind officers were running into each other. Chaos reigned as everything turned to shit around them. Drones criss-crossed the night, raining down lethal fire. Nasty – but only until the surprise had worn off. Officers dropped to the ground, rolled on to their backs and began the satisfying task of shooting them out of the sky.

Now that they'd recovered from the initial shock of the ambush, the tide of battle was beginning to turn their way. And there had been no repeat of the sonic cannon; they took some time to recharge. If officers could consolidate their position – dig in – was there a chance they might actually get out of this after all?

Probably not. This was some quality opposition. Certainly not the usual combination of slightly unbalanced fanatics temporarily allied to those trying to make a quick buck. These were true professionals – on resuming fire, they were canny enough to change the angle, blasting great lumps of burning rock out of the cliff walls to fall on the hapless TPOs below. If officers didn't move now, they could find themselves becoming a permanent part of the landscape.

The lieutenant was gone. That left Sharron.

'To me, to me,' she shouted. 'Regroup to my position. We'll fight our way back to the pod. To me. To me.'

The night was still full of green and purple after-images but her vision was slowly returning. She could make out her colleagues' shadowy figures flitting from rock to rock. Not as many of them as there should have been.

'Dikstrom, take the lead. Get the wounded out. No one left behind. I'll bring up the rear. Barber, you and Coyle are with me. Move. Before they start with that sodding cannon again.'

They moved. Slipping and stumbling on the rocky slopes. Sharron, Barber and Coyle laid down covering fire for their colleagues and themselves, all the time moving back. The retreat was orderly. Controlled. Textbook. Sharron experienced a surge of hope. They could do this.

Gunfire up ahead. What now? Had the illegals somehow got around them in the dark? Or was there another group out there somewhere? Or more drones? Which would be a bitch. What a shitstorm this was turning out to be. When they got back, she'd be demanding a twenty-four-hour standdown for all of them. All the ones who made it back, that was. Officers couldn't keep going like this. They were all exhausted, and exhausted people make mistakes. A hot meal and some rest and Albay could just suck on it.

A huge explosion ahead recalled her to the moment. 'Barber, Coyle, go and lend a hand getting the wounded into the pod. I'll cover you. Leave me your big blaster.'

The ravine narrowed here. She could hold them off for a while. Coyle's blaster held a full charge. She settled back behind a handy rock and . . .

They came out of the dark. Far more of them than the briefing had led her to believe. What the hell had been going on in this God-forsaken part of the world? Their preliminary survey had shown no electronic activity. And there was certainly nothing of any value around here. A few goats, perhaps . . . Unless . . . The truth hit hard. There was nothing here but this less than welcoming committee. They'd been set up.

Something moved in the dark. Gritting her teeth, Sharron laid down a blanket of fire, sweeping the narrow ravine from left to right. She heard shouts in the dark. And some screams. Good. With luck she'd done some damage. Not giving them a chance to regroup, she shut down the blaster, heaved it over her shoulder and set off after her colleagues.

She found Singh propped against a rock. Dead. His weapons were empty. Both of them. She stumbled on. The silence behind her was not reassuring. In these circumstances, that usually meant hostiles were building up to something big.

Worst of all, her teams were only just around the next bend. Pinned down by the sound of it. Shit – she'd been hoping they were back at the pod by now. She took a moment to think and then moved to her left. If she could get behind whoever was . . .

At least there was no longer a need for silence. Between the shouting and the weapons discharge, no one was going to hear one solitary officer working her way slowly through the night. And her vision was almost restored to normal. She could get behind them. Take the bastards down. Go home. Grab a quick drink on her way. Find an opportunity to slap the stupid sods whose intel had been so useless. Then another drink. Then sleep.

Good plan.

She opened her com. 'Dikstrom, I'm behind you and working my way to your left. Do not shoot me or I will come after you. Get everyone together and head for the pod. Forget dignified retreat. Just shift their arses. On my word.'

She checked the charge on her blaster. She wasn't that far away – not according to her proximities. One final effort and they could all go home.

'Now.'

She eased herself off the rock, firing as she went. Activity to her right. That would be Dikstrom getting them back to the pod. She changed the blaster setting to wide beam, backed against the cliff wall and sprayed from left to right. Right to left. Left to right. Don't stop. Don't give the bastards a chance to regroup. Keep them pinned down. Keep firing. Keep firing.

A voice sounded in her ear. 'Sharron. We're at the pod. Get your arse over here now or we'll go without you.'

'Yeah,' she said. 'Like you could find your way home without me.'

She could hear firing up ahead. Slinging the blaster over

her shoulder again, she picked her way over the rough ground. There were bodies here. None of them TPOs.

'Dikstrom here. I'm just ahead of you. Your two o'clock. I can see you.'

'Yeah – I can see you, too. Everyone back OK?'

'We have wounded, but yeah.'

The explosion knocked them both off their feet. The air above their heads seemed to contract and then expand. Sharron hit the ground hard. What felt like half a mountain fell on top of her. Someone was shouting her name. Hands pulled at her. Lots of hands. If those stupid bastards had left the pod to pull her out, then she'd be dragging them round the back of TPHQ to kick the living shit out of them. And then probably buy them a drink afterwards. But the kicking would definitely come first.

The illegals were firing their sonic cannon again, but at the cliff walls this time. Large lumps of mountainside were bouncing and tumbling down to the ravine floor. Their night visors couldn't cope with the dust. She really had no idea where . . .

The pod. There. Looming up through the murk.

'Get everyone inside now. Move it. Move it.'

And then she was in through the door – last one in – which slammed shut behind them, and the only sounds were panting officers and small pieces of rock peppering the roof over their heads.

The peppering did not die away. Rather, it intensified. The precursor to an avalanche, perhaps. They needed to move and move quickly.

She pulled off her helmet. 'Is everyone here? Call the roll.'

Dikstrom responded. 'Everyone who isn't dead is here.'

'How many did we lose?'

'Seven.'

'Bollocks. Bollocks. Bollocks.'

There was a bang as something hefty landed on the roof.

'We need to go. Now.'

There was another explosion. The pod rocked.

'Coordinates . . .'

'Never mind that. Emergency evac.'

'But . . .'

'Do it. Just do it.'

Another bang. They were firing directly at the pod. Any moment now and they'd be hit with an EMP and then it really would be game over.

Dikstrom was at the controls. 'Pod – emergency evac. Immediate.'

There was a massive explosion. The floor heaved under their feet. Everything went black. Someone screamed, 'Oh my God, I'm—' His words ended in a hoarse shriek. Everyone was shouting. There was an odd sensation in her left arm. Emergency evacs were the pits. They'd be throwing up all over the pod and then the mechs would complain and . . . God, her head hurt. At some point she must have fetched it a right wallop.

Why was it still dark? Where were the lights? Surely they must have landed by now. Where were the mechs? This pod must be in a hell of a state and it wasn't like them not to be banging on the door and whinging on for hours about it.

She tried to struggle to her feet, failed badly, and decided it wasn't important right now.

'Pod – lights.'

The pod remained obstinately silent. Shit – they'd broken the AI as well. IT would be in here yelling at them alongside the mechs.

And still there was screaming.

'Everyone shut the fuck up,' she shouted and was slightly surprised when silence fell.

The emergency lights flickered on. Yes – they were on a separate battery. They should work OK. And the door.

Her left arm didn't feel right but she was able to push herself to a near sitting position and look round.

The silence in the pod was complete. She wasn't even aware of the sound of breathing. Because this was ... this was ... not right. This couldn't be ... couldn't have happened. This was ... wrong. This was ...

The lights flickered off again. Which was worse. Because now she'd seen what had happened ... And somehow it was worse in the dark.

Someone whimpered.

The lights flickered on again.

This wasn't a nightmare. This was happening. Had actually happened. They'd always been told it couldn't but it had. It had happened to them. She looked down. It had happened to her, as well.

Someone whimpered again. A tiny thread of a voice. 'Sharron, help me. For God's sake, help me.'

The lights flickered off again. Someone was crying in the dark.

From somewhere, she found a voice. 'All right, everyone, listen up.' Her voice didn't sound right. She swallowed and tried again, forcing herself to be calm. 'We've had a bad landing.'

'You think?' said a voice and began to laugh. The wrong sort of laughter. Hysteria swirled in the dark.

The lights flickered on again.

'Right,' she said, and this time her voice was very nearly normal. 'Who's nearest the console? Can you contact the Pod Bay? Or anyone still wearing a helmet? Can you chin your mic?'

Barber was nearest the console but his hands had gone and no one else could reach. Dikstrom was still wearing his helmet. He'd pushed up the visor so she could see his face. But his face wasn't there, either. Not all of it, anyway. Looking around, it was hard to tell who was dead and who was still alive. For the moment.

Her helmet lay just to her right. By hooking one leg around it, she was able to bring it closer and there was just enough movement in her right hand to operate the mic.

'Mayday. Mayday. Mayday. This is Sharron. Can anyone hear me?'

The response was immediate. 'Sharron? This is the Pod Bay. Where the fuck are you?'

She forced back a sob. Crying never helped anyone and she wasn't going to start now. 'I'm . . . we're here. But I don't know where here is.'

'Typical grunts. All the sense of direction of a small rock. Where were you aiming for?'

'Emergency evac . . . gone wrong.'

Another voice was shouting something in the background. The first voice sharpened. 'Sharron – describe your surroundings.'

This time the sob did not go away. 'Hell. We're in hell. Help us. Help us. Please.'

Dimly, through the com, she could hear alarm bells going off.

The voice had changed. Now it was calm and reassuring. 'All right, Sharron. We'll get to you. Keep talking. We've got your signature. You missed the Pod Bay – that's all. By about twenty feet. Not a bad effort for a grunt. We'll get you out.'

She looked around the pod. 'No – I don't think you will.'

'What's that? Sharron – stay awake. Keep talking. There's a couple of mechs on their way now and we're assembling medics and rescue equipment. We'll get to you. Just stay put.'

This struck Sharron as being extraordinarily funny. She began to laugh. And laugh. And laugh. And then to cry.

A new voice. The Senior Mech spoke in her ear. His voice deep and reassuring. 'Now then, lass, you don't want to be doing that. I'm here now . . . We've found you. You're right in front of us and . . .'

He broke off. The silence went on and on and on. She could just imagine the shock . . . Because this just couldn't happen. Except it had.

'Yeah,' said Sharron flatly. 'How are you going to deal with this?'

She could almost picture him pulling himself together. Or trying to. The stunned looks. The silence. The moment they realised what had happened.

'Sharron?' His voice was hoarse.

'Yeah?'

'We're outside the pod now. We're coming in. Is it . . . ? How bad is it?'

'It's bad. It's very, very bad.'

The voice said something she couldn't catch but she heard the word *Albay* so clearly they'd sent for the colonel.

'All right, lass, we're coming in now.'

She pulled herself together. She was in charge. People were relying on her. Turning her head, she addressed her colleagues.

'OK, lads, the rescue team's arrived. They're just outside. They'll soon have us out of this. Just stay calm and let them do their jobs.'

Someone was still crying. One of the luckier ones.

There were sounds at the door. They were trying to get it open. At least the pod had landed the right way up.

The door jerked open a little way, then a little further, and then, finally, all the way. Four figures stood dark against the lights behind them. There was the sound of snapping lightsticks. Two were rolled across the floor. Two more held high.

Bright, cruel light illuminated a scene from hell.

The pod had so nearly made it.

They were only twenty feet from the Pod Bay. No more. So near and yet so far. They'd landed in one of the corridors between Pod Bay and security. The pod's AI had got that right. Everything else was wrong. Horribly, horribly wrong. Whether as a result of the explosions just as they jumped or whether the emergency evac had gone wrong – none of them would ever know.

The safety protocols had failed. The pod had materialised inside a wall. Or rather, the wall was now inside the pod. They were half in and half out of the corridor. Officers, pod and wall were all occupying the same space. Or had tried to. The wall had won.

Worse – they'd materialised below floor level. Those lying on the floor were now lying *in* the floor. Coyle was on his back, only his head, one hand and one knee visible. The rest of him was just . . . floor. His one hand clawed uselessly at the air and he was screaming, 'Oh my God oh my God oh my God . . .' On and on and on. Endlessly.

Barber was simply staring down at his arms, both embedded in the console. Occasionally, he whimpered, seemingly unable to comprehend what had happened to him.

Another officer lay face down on the console. Sharron amended that to face down *in* the console. Slowly dying. His face and the console were one. His hands were beating a violent tattoo as his body fought to breathe. Even as she watched, his movements grew weaker and weaker. He was going. He was dying. Right in front of her.

'Get him out,' she shouted, knowing it was useless. 'He's dying. Someone get him out.'

No one moved in the doorway. They stood silently, taking in the scene.

Part of Murphy's face was pressed into the wall. She could see one eye and one ear. And his nostrils flaring wide as he struggled to breathe.

She looked down. Her own left arm was embedded in the floor almost to her elbow but both legs and her right arm were free. Somehow, she was the least injured.

Still no one had moved from the doorway. Four men stared and stared and stared. Then one stepped back out of sight. She could hear him vomiting.

There was a commotion behind them. The medteam had arrived.

'Get out of the way,' said the doctor, shouldering his way through.

Everyone willingly stepped back.

The doctor stopped dead. Sharron could imagine his brain struggling to make sense of what his eyes were seeing. Where to begin? What could possibly be done?

There was another voice. Colonel Albay had arrived. Now they'd get some action. He'd think of something.

Albay stood on the threshold, gazing into the pod. After long moments, he looked over his shoulder, saying, 'Where's the Senior Mech?'

Lt Callen had pulled himself together. 'Gone to organise rescue gear and cutting equipment, sir.'

'Stay off your com. Go and bring him back here. Quickly.'

Callen left at a run.

Taking a deep breath, Colonel Albay stepped into the pod. No one spoke. Eyes watched him as he stepped carefully over Sharron – who was nearest the door – and moved from one officer to another. The silence gathered.

Still without speaking, he stepped back over Sharron and left the pod, closing the door behind him.

Outside the pod, the doctor was busily unpacking his kit. Without looking up, he said in an undertone, 'I can save Sharron. Amputating her arm will free her. And I think Aziz and possibly Barber as well. If they survive the shock, of course.' He looked up at Albay. 'How could this happen? What went wrong? Should we be grounding the other pods while we run checks?'

'No,' said Albay decisively. 'We don't stop. We can't afford to stop. If word of this gets out, then we've lost the war.'

The doctor was laying out his equipment. 'Well, as I said, I can definitely save two of them. Probably three.'

'That's no good to us. They won't be able to fight.'

'Not really the point, Colonel.'

'It's exactly the point, doctor. We're fighting a war.'

The Senior Mech arrived with Callen, both festooned with equipment. 'More cutting gear on its way. I've halted all pod activity and . . .'

'Belay that order.'

'But at the very least, we have to ground the other pods until . . .'

'No.'

'But . . .'

'Doctor – you are dismissed. And take your team.' Albay stared around. 'Out. All of you. Except for the Senior Mech. And you, Callen. Everyone else wait for me in the Pod Bay.'

The doctor stood his ground. 'What are your intentions, Colonel?'

'Carry out your instructions, doctor.'

The doctor lowered his voice. 'There are people needing urgent attention or they will die.'

'That's an order, doctor.'

The doctor stared at him for a long moment.

Albay laid a hand on his blaster. 'Collect your equipment and go.'

The only sound was that of the doctor's harsh breathing as he bundled his gear together and departed, his team following on. Their footsteps faded into silence.

Colonel Albay re-entered the pod and closed and locked the door behind him, shutting out the Senior Mech and Lt Callen.

Sharron twisted around to watch him. 'Sir . . . ?'

He ignored her and bent over Coyle, still not quite dead. Pulling out his blaster, he checked the charge, placed the muzzle against Coyle's forehead . . . and fired.

'What are you doing?' shouted Sharron in disbelief, struggling to tear her arm free from the floor. It was no use. Blood began to pool as her efforts rubbed her arm raw. She didn't notice. 'You shot him. You killed him.'

Stepping over Coyle, Albay made his way towards a struggling Barber, still part of the console. Again, he checked the charge on his blaster.

Barber began to scream, striving frantically to tear his arms free.

'Leave him alone,' shouted Sharron, still wildly fighting to free her arm. She kicked out, missing him by feet. 'You bastard – you can't do this. Albay, I swear I will . . .'

Again, she strained every muscle to pull free. Her weapon was just fractionally out of reach. If she could just somehow gain an inch or two . . . The pain in her arm was massive and intense. She gritted her teeth and stretched . . . her fingers scrabbling for her blaster . . .

Albay had moved behind Barber who, as far as his trapped arms would allow him, was twisting in his seat to see what was happening, begging for his life. Begging to be spared. Curses . . . entreaties . . . appeals . . . threats . . . Sharron's throat was hoarse with shouting and crying. Her eyesight blurred with tears.

'He can be saved,' she shouted. 'You can't do this.'

'I have to,' Albay said calmly. 'Think about it, Sharron. There's no way we can get you out. The rescue would kill you. We'd have to drill you out of the floor. Or the wall. Without drilling through you. It would take hours. None of you would survive the shock. And the effect on your colleagues would be devastating. We'd never get anyone in a pod again. I can't have that. So you have to die. I'm sorry. I regret the necessity, but it's a kindness when you think about it.'

Albay's blaster whined. Barber slumped forwards.

Silence fell. Sharron scrubbed the tears from her eyes and watched Albay approach Murphy. The blaster fired again.

Sharron spoke between gritted teeth. 'You're a murderer, Albay. A fucking, bastarding murderer. You'll pay for this. And all those other cowards hiding out there pretending this isn't happening.'

'Just you, now,' said Albay without emotion.

She glared up at him. 'You piece of filth. I swear I'll get you if I have to wait until the end of Time itself.' Her voice rose to a scream. '*Murderer.*'

He checked the charge on his gun, saying quite normally, 'I'm sorry, Sharron, but you must see this can't get out. We're down to less than fifty officers.'

'Even fewer now,' said Sharron hoarsely. 'Thanks to you. You can't cover this up.'

'I can and I will. No one will ever know you're here. I'll have the corridor bricked up. You'll be classified MIA. You never made it back. Sad, but no time to mourn. We have a war to fight.'

'I swear, Albay, on behalf of those you murdered today . . .'

'What, Sharron? What exactly do you swear?'

'This will come out one day. One day the world will know what you've done here. That you murdered your own people.'

With wild thoughts of cutting off her own arm, she tried to grope for her knife.

He shook his head. 'This pod's dead. And so are you. I'm sorry, Sharron. You were a good officer.'

He walked around behind her. She tried to twist around to watch him and held out her free arm, although whether in accusation or a pitiful attempt to defend herself was not clear.

'Rot in hell. *Murderer.*'

The blaster whined. She refused to close her eyes. 'I'll get you for this if it's the last thing I—'

He pulled the trigger.

The lightsticks were beginning to fail. Darkness crept across the pod.

Unlocking the door, Colonel Albay stepped outside and carefully closed it behind him.

The Senior Mech seized him from behind and threw him against a wall. 'You bastard. What have you just done?'

'What I had to. You know that, Senior.'

'You've killed them all?'

The Senior Mech was a hefty man but Albay shoved him away with very little effort. 'I saved them hours of agony and a painful death. Cutting them free would have killed them. You know that. The doctor knew it – that's why he left. And if you had any balls, you'd have helped me. My only regret – and it is a regret – is that we've just lost twenty-five per cent of our remaining officers.'

Callen raised a clenched fist. 'They were people, not a percentage.'

'They were doomed. There was no way we could ever get them out without chopping them into pieces. It was a kindness.'

'*You murdered them.*'

'I put them out of their misery. We don't have the manpower or resources needed to free that pod. Even if that had been possible, it's part of the structure now. We might have brought the whole building down on top of us. Senior – assemble whatever you need and get this out of sight. Build a wall, change the layout, do whatever you want, but get it done. Use your own people and tell them to keep quiet about it afterwards or they'll end up the same way.'

The Senior Mech's eyes blazed.

Albay closed the gap between them, saying quietly, 'Don't you understand? This is our second serious accident in ten days. This can't ever get out. Not after what happened to Lt Hay and her team last week.'

The Senior Mech lowered his voice. 'I keep telling you – we're pushing the pods too hard. To say nothing of their crews.'

'I have no choice. If people were to find out that this could happen, they'd never get into a pod again. We've lost a quarter of our people today. We'll lose more tomorrow. And more the day after. But we're the Time Police. We keep going.'

Callen turned to look at him. 'And when there's no one left?'

Albay shrugged. 'It won't be our problem any longer.'

'And what do we tell people about . . .' He gestured at the pod.

'I told you – nothing. They're missing in action. They could return at any moment.'

'People won't believe that.'

'The chances are we'll all be dead by this time next week, so it's not really an issue, is it?'

Callen punched him in the face. Hard.

Albay slid down the wall, his nose gushing blood. 'You struck a senior officer.'

'I did,' said Callen tightly. 'And if you get up, I can do it again.'

'That's a court martial offence.'

'Oh – we both know it won't come to that. But if it makes things easier for you, I can turn my back while you shoot me. And the Senior Mech, if you want to eliminate all the witnesses. What's a couple more dead officers today? Sir.'

He turned his back.

Albay made no move.

Callen turned around again and bent over him.

'No? Probably very wise.'

Albay wiped the blood across his face and pushed himself to his feet. 'Return to your duties, Lt Callen. And you as well, Senior. That's an order.'

Slightly unsteadily, he walked away.

Inside the pod, the darkness was complete. The silence was complete. Nothing moved. Nothing lived.

And then, on the console, a single red light came on. A faint voice said, 'Mur . . . der . . . er.'

The light flickered and died.

Darkness and silence returned.

For a very, very long time.

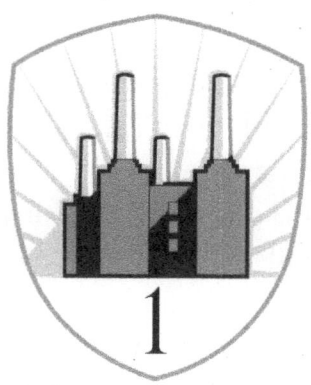

1

Entering Captain Farenden's office in search of the file relating to this year's equipment budget, Commander Hay was slightly taken aback to find her adjutant face down on his desk, his arms hanging loosely to the floor.

'Er . . . Captain?'

'Yes?' His voice was somewhat muffled.

'Is everything all right?'

'Perfectly, thank you, ma'am.'

'Only you appear to have adopted a slightly more informal position than I usually expect from you.'

'No, ma'am, I'm fine.'

'You're sure?'

'Yes, ma'am.'

There was a pause.

'Is there anything I can do?'

'Thank you, ma'am – no.'

'Why are you . . . ?'

'I'm recovering.'

'Oh. All right. Well. Is this recuperation likely to be of a long duration? I ask only because your head appears to be resting on this year's equipment allocation figures and I . . . um . . .'

'I shall bring the file through momentarily.'

'Are you sure? I mean, I don't want to disturb your . . .'

'Not a problem, ma'am.'

'Only I wondered if this was something in the nature of a religious vigil, perhaps?'

'Not really. Only a very inadequate expression of a deep, dark despair for which there are no words.'

'That's all right, then. I was worried you might have undergone some sort of religious conversion.'

'No, ma'am, still – somewhat lackadaisically – Church of England.'

'Well . . . good, I'll be in . . .' she gestured over her shoulder, belatedly realised he couldn't see her and continued, 'in my office. But there's no rush for the file. Assuage your despair first.'

'That's very considerate of you, ma'am. Thank you.'

Five minutes later, Captain Farenden appeared in her doorway, file in one hand, mug of coffee in the other.

Commander Hay regarded him warily. 'Everything OK now?'

'Perfectly, thank you.'

'Are you sure? You have the look of one who has glimpsed terrors man was not meant to wot of.'

'What?'

'What have you wot of that you should not have wot of?'

He placed her coffee in front of her. 'Frighteningly, that sentence makes perfect sense.'

'Good heavens – you are in a bad way. What's the problem, Charlie?' She stiffened. 'It's not Team Two-Three-Six, is it? I thought everything had been more or less safely resolved with them.'

'That is happening as we speak, ma'am.'

Hay sighed. 'So what's today's particular crisis?'

'I'm not sure whether you've noticed my previous efforts to lighten the burden of your command by recounting a number of humorous anecdotes, ma'am . . .'

'Oh, that's what you thought you were doing, was it? Can I assume you have recently encountered a catastrophe of such magnitude that even you can't manage to put a positive spin on it?'

'Sadly, ma'am, yes.'

'Well, I can't hear any screaming and no alarms have gone off, so it can't be that bad, surely?'

He shook his head. 'Words fail me, ma'am.'

'Well, let's start at the beginning. Is anyone dead?'

'No, ma'am.'

'Is anyone injured?'

'Not exactly, ma'am.'

'Is the building on fire?'

'No, ma'am.'

'Are we under attack?'

'No, ma'am.'

'Has our meagre budget been slashed even further?'

'No, ma'am.'

'Then I'm at a loss.'

'It's Meiklejohn, ma'am.'

She picked up the file. 'Oh God, Charlie, go away. Suffer alone.'

'Too late, ma'am.'

She sighed. 'Out with it.'

'Well, this shouldn't come as too much of a shock to you – I believe Meiklejohn touched on the subject during one of your previous meetings.'

Her eyes narrowed. 'Is this by any chance toilet-related?'

'Alas, ma'am . . .'

'Go away. I really feel every last drop of humour has been wrung from . . .'

'This isn't funny, ma'am.'

She took off her spectacles and pinched the bridge of her nose. 'Go on, Charlie. Hit me.'

'When Meiklejohn was last here, ma'am, did she by any chance use the word *shrink-wrapped*?'

'Two words, surely.'

'Hyphenated, ma'am. One word.'

'Are you sure?'

'Almost completely, ma'am.'

'Actually, now I come to think of it – yes, she did. Do I gather . . .'

'There's been an unfortunate occurrence, ma'am.'

'Oh God, Charlie. Just give me the salient points.'

'Very well. Officer Curtis. Half a pound of chipolatas. A Meiklejohn-patented shrink-wrapping contraption. Disaster.'

'Chipolatas?'

'To simulate . . . you know.'

'Well, that's sausages off the menu for the rest of my life.'

'Indeed, ma'am. I share your pain.'

'Exactly what has occurred, Charlie?'

'Well, after her difficulties with . . .'

'Never mind the recap. Just hit me with the main points.'

'Miss Meiklejohn has invented and installed what she persists in referring to as the Meiklejohn-Patented Poo-Packaging Thingy.'

'Thingy?'

'She ran out of words beginning with p.'

'Really? I can think of many. But continue.'

'Officer Curtis – a willing volunteer, before you ask, ma'am – was to approach the ... creation ... seat himself appropriately ...'

'Why?'

'The device is automatically triggered by weight-detecting sensors, ma'am. In other words, someone has to sit on it for it to work. Anyway, having made himself comfortable, Officer Curtis was then to deposit half a pound of chipolatas into the receptacle provided. According to Miss Meiklejohn, who apparently inhabits a completely different universe to the rest of us – the deposit would then be appropriately dealt with by being hygienically wrapped and swept around the U-bend to its designated destination.'

Hay sat back. 'Am I the only one who can foresee any number of potential catastrophes just waiting to happen?'

'Well, yes, ma'am, you are, actually. There are very few moving parts in the process and given that Meiklejohn's preliminary tests had all proved most satisfactory, there was an unusual amount of optimism among the observers.'

'Observers?'

'Well, we're still waiting for all officers to respond to your unit-wide recall, ma'am, the Pod Bay is still out of service, people were bored, and Miss Meiklejohn's experiments have gathered their own following. In short, the room was packed with those agog to see what would transpire.'

'And what exactly did transpire?'

'Well, as we all know, Officer Curtis is very fond of his food, whereas Meiklejohn probably has to run around in the shower to get wet. Her failure to take into account the effect of Curtis's additional avoirdupois on a mechanism configured to someone half his weight resulted in the device becoming somewhat confused as to its true purpose.'

'No. You're making all this up, Charlie. Go away.'

'If only, ma'am.'

'So how . . . ?'

'The apparatus having performed perfectly on every other occasion, Officer Curtis approached the trial with more confidence than was actually warranted. It would appear that the Meiklejohn-Patented . . . um . . .'

'Poo-Packaging Thingy . . .'

'Became confused by the sudden additional weight and tilted, throwing the mechanism off-balance and, not to put too fine a point on it, ma'am, it shrink-wrapped a portion of Officer Curtis instead.'

'Which por—'

'Please don't ask me, ma'am.'

'And the chipolatas?'

'The fate of the chipolatas is unknown, ma'am.'

'This is St Mary's doing, isn't it? They're working to bring us down and Meiklejohn is their instrument of destruction.'

'I wish I could argue, ma'am, but I am fast coming round to your point of view.'

'How have things been left?'

'Well, despite protests from Officer Curtis, an entrepreneurial Officer Rockmeyer is charging a substantial fee for sharing images of his . . .'

'They're taking photos down there?'

'With a view to updating their screen savers, ma'am. I gather images of Lt Grint at the children's party are being superseded by Officer Curtis wearing the latest thing in shrink-wrap even as we speak.'

'Given our perilous financial state, Rockmeyer's probably the richest person in the building at the moment.'

'That is almost certainly correct, ma'am, and I believe this is an excellent moment to divert your thoughts by informing you that Mrs Farnborough has requested a meeting.'

'Did she say why?'

'No, ma'am.'

'Oh. Well, go ahead and set it up, please, Charlie. I wonder what she has to say. Is she coming here?'

'She will combine it with a visit to her daughter, ma'am.'

'How is Miss Farnborough?'

'Remaining quietly in our guest suite, ma'am, and causing no trouble at all.'

'So not completely recovered from her ordeal, then?'

'MedCen says physically – yes. Mentally – probably not.'

His scratchpad bleeped. 'If you could excuse me for one moment, ma'am.' He consulted the screen and sighed.

'This won't surprise you, ma'am. Lt Varma has requested an appointment at your earliest convenience.'

Commander Hay consoled herself with the fact that however bad her own yesterday had been, it hadn't been anything like as bad as Varma's.

'Well, I think we can guess what that's about.'

He sighed. 'Indeed, yes, ma'am.'

'I'm not losing her, Charlie. She's one of the best officers we've got and I'm not going to allow what's happened to deprive us of her abilities.'

'Ma'am, I spoke to her briefly this morning and she's . . . upset.'

'Shit.' Hay got up and began to pace. 'Get me all available footage, Charlie. I'll have a look for myself.'

'I've seen it, ma'am. Varma enters the cell and . . .'

'Where's the body now?'

'Removed to MedCen, ma'am.'

'I'll see the footage first – then Varma.'

In another part of the building – their office, to be precise – Team 236 (or Team Weird as they were usually known) had gathered for their first official day back.

'I've just seen Imogen Farnborough,' said Jane, pouring herself a mug of coffee from their illegal coffee machine. 'She's looking much better these days.'

'She is,' said Luke. 'She told me yesterday that I was an utter waste of space and that if I didn't buck my ideas up pretty sharpish then she'd punch my lights out and trample my fallen body into the dust. Can you pour one for me, Jane?'

'No,' said Jane. 'You have arms. You have sufficient intelligence – barely – and I am not your handmaiden. Pour your own. Would you like one, Matthew?'

'Yes, please,' said Matthew. 'How very kind of you.'

Recognising deliberate provocation when he saw it, Luke maintained a dignified silence.

'I am maintaining a dignified silence.'

'If only,' murmured Jane, passing Matthew his coffee.

The door opened to reveal Lt Grint – deputy head of BeeBOC – the Big Business and Organised Crime section.

'Message from Major Ellis. Briefing Room 3. Now.'

'Why?' enquired Luke.

'Because I fire-trucking well say so, Parrish.'

'No, I mean why a briefing – we only came back on duty at 0800 hours, I thought we were on light duties for a bit. You know – to ease us back in again.'

'I'll ease you out of the door with the toe of my boot if you don't shift yourself, Parrish. Move.'

'I'll just pour myself . . .'

'*Move.*'

Luke sighed heavily. Grint stepped aside to let him pass. Matthew followed him out. Jane put down her mug.

'Just a moment, Lockland.'

'Yes, sir?'

Grint checked over his shoulder, ensuring Luke and Matthew were out of earshot. 'I haven't seen you around much. You have recovered?'

Jane felt her face flood with hot colour. The pain had gone but the shame of being publicly beaten in a 19th-century Mexican lunatic asylum still remained.

'Oh . . . Yes, sir . . . Thank you . . . Um . . . Perfectly fine . . . Thank you. Yes.'

Grint stared over her shoulder. 'Well, that's . . . good.'

Jane stared down at her boots. 'Yes. Very good.'

'Well. I won't keep you.'

'No, sir.'

More staring occurred.

'Well. Off you go.'

'Yes, sir. Um . . .'

Jane indicated that he would have to let her out.

'Oh. Yes.' Grint stepped back into the corridor. 'Well. See you later, Lockland.'

'Yes, sir.'

He strode away and Jane followed her teammates to Briefing Room 3.

Fifteen minutes later, Major Ellis was winding up his briefing.

'And so, to conclude, you should be very clear this is not a return to basic gruntwork. It is not a punishment. Or a demotion. Although you're all still on junior officer level, so it's not actually possible for you to go any lower . . .'

Ellis paused, aware he had somewhat lost the thread, and began again.

'It is felt that given your recent team trauma, Two-Three-Six will benefit from a return to basics under the supervision of Lt North and myself. A few simple assignments – not that anything else is possible until Farrell's arm heals and you, Parrish, are completely recovered.'

A hostile silence greeted this pronouncement.

Jane stared at the floor, her face hot with embarrassment. This was so humiliating. After all the solid work they'd put in on the Zanetti Train. She and Luke had performed well on that particular mission – she had a citation on her record confirming that fact. And Matthew himself had excelled with the Time Map. He had done everything asked of him – they all had. They always did. This need for 'supervision' was because their methods were a little unorthodox. And yes, there had been a minor episode of what was officially classed as 'team dysfunction', but she and Luke had really put themselves on the line on their last assignment and apparently their only reward was to go back to being babysat. It wasn't good enough. It just wasn't good enough.

Luke, now recovered from his own experiences in San Hipólito, folded his arms and scowled at his feet and Matthew pulled at his arm-length flexi-glove, which was beginning to make his skin itch. Neither of them said anything. Matthew wouldn't – he always just sucked up whatever life happened to be throwing at him at the time – but Jane was surprised at Luke. Normally he would be the first to argue. To make their case. To object.

Was it to be up to her? Unfamiliar emotions rampaged inside her head. This wasn't fair. This wasn't right. No other team was treated this badly, but they were Team 236 – the Time Police's scapegoat. Poor old Team Weird who never knowingly got it right the first time but who always came through in the end. She and Luke had resolved their differences and got themselves off that train. They'd held the passengers together while they awaited a rescue they secretly hadn't been sure would ever come. Matthew had risked himself to acquire the coordinates for their rescue. This wasn't right.

Jane lifted her head. 'Excuse me, sir, ma'am, but this isn't right.'

Major Ellis was somewhat taken aback. Not by the dissent – officers argued all the time – but by the dissenter herself. That Officer Lockland of all people should . . .

'I beg your pardon?'

Jane stood up, unsure whether this was a mark of respect or simply that it enabled her to make her point more strongly. 'I mean . . . I meant . . . With respect, sir . . . I don't think . . . I mean . . . This isn't right. Our last assignment was successful.

We captured the two illegals – Adesina and Kumar. And their homemade pod. And Sawney. And Hooke. And Hooke's pod in Modena as well. And we saved the passengers in Mexico City. Luke was injured during the mission. And Matthew. And . . . um . . . me. And now we're to go back under supervision.' She gathered herself for the final denunciation. 'I'm sorry, sir – but it's not . . . it's not right.'

'OMG,' said Wimpy Jane faintly, apparently on the verge of passing out. 'What have you just done?'

'Oh sweetie,' cried Bolshy Jane. 'That was absolutely wonderful. Look at their faces. Well done, you.'

There was a short silence while the other four people in the room struggled to get their heads around this strange new phenomenon. Ellis, who had expected the opposition to come from Luke Parrish, was at a loss.

North moved in. 'Officer Lockland, there is no criticism over your last assignment – your last successful assignment,' she added smoothly. 'It's the team dynamic which is being addressed. You can't deny that at one point recently, you and Parrish refused to work with each other. You were taken off duty and told to sort yourselves out. And you, Parrish, were on the verge of leaving the Time Police. You say now that your issues are resolved, and we very much hope that that is the case, but Major Ellis and I will need to verify that fact before Team Two-Three-Six can resume its full . . . effectiveness.'

Jane sat down with a bump, her face on fire at her own behaviour, and privately resolved never to say another word to anyone until the day she died.

'Well, we may as well get all this out in the open now,' said Ellis. 'Does anyone else have anything to say?'

'Yes,' said Matthew. 'I agree.'

'With . . . ?' said North carefully.

'With Jane.'

Ellis looked over at Luke. 'Officer Parrish?'

Luke nodded. 'Officer Lockland has expressed my feelings perfectly.'

Ellis and North exchanged glances.

'Right,' said Ellis. 'As you're aware, the unit is on recall at the moment. Something has come up. Lt North and I are about to depart for Wales to conduct an investigation there, but on our return . . .'

'Wales?' said Luke, easily distracted. 'What's happening in Wales?'

'You were lolling around in MedCen at the time so you'll have missed all the fun. The body of what looks like some kind of dinosaur has been discovered.'

'Fossil?'

'No – an actual flesh-and-blood body. Only recently deceased. We're off to check it out.'

Luke sat up. 'Cool. Can we come?'

'No – Team Two-Three-Six will remain here to reflect on its past and contemplate its future.'

'Well, that's no fun.'

'Life in the Time Police is not supposed to be fun, Officer Parrish. Your period of supervision officially begins tomorrow morning. Officer Farrell, you're seconded to the Map Master until your arm is completely healed. Lockland and Parrish, report to my office at 0800 hours tomorrow. That's all, everyone. Dismissed.'

Once outside the briefing room, Luke chased after Jane as

she strode down the corridor on her way to a destination she was far too angry to have given much thought to.

'Jane. Wait.'

She carried on walking, her face still flushed with anger. 'Where were you?'

Luke fell into step beside her. 'What do you mean? I'm here.'

'In there. Why was I the only one making a protest in there? Why weren't you being your usual gobby self?'

'Jane . . .'

'I mean, normally no one else can get a word in edgeways.'

'I . . .'

'You hardly said a thing, Luke, and this isn't fair.'

'Jane . . .'

'After everything we went through on that horrible train, they tell us we're back under supervision.'

'*Jane* . . .'

'For heaven's sake – what?'

'I've brought you a present.'

'Oh.' Jane stopped dead.

He pulled a prettily wrapped package from his pocket.

'Oh,' said Jane again.

Luke held it out to her. 'For you.'

'Oh,' said Jane, for the third time. Bolshy Jane rolled her eyes. 'Um . . . Thank you. What is it?'

'Open it and see.'

Jane hesitated. 'Pretty paper . . .'

'The present's inside the paper, Jane.'

She pulled at the ribbon. 'Did you wrap this?'

'Honesty compels me to say no – the shop did that – but I did observe them very closely as they did so.'

He waited as Jane carefully removed the paper.

'Sorry,' she said, 'but it always seems so ungrateful just to rip it off when someone's gone to all that trouble. Oh.' She held it out. 'Luke, it's a notebook.'

'Yes, I know,' said Luke, grinning. 'To replace the one you left on the Zanetti Train.'

'It's perfect.'

And, indeed, it was.

Alone of Team 236 – indeed, alone of nearly all the Time Police – Jane still preferred her trusty notebook to her scratchpad, scribbling notes and diagrams as required, all to be produced in triumph on the admittedly few occasions a scratchpad wouldn't work. She hadn't said much at the time – to be fair, they'd had other things on their minds – but Luke knew she'd been upset at having left it behind. He'd remembered his careless promise to buy her another one, and as soon as he'd recovered sufficiently to leave MedCen, he'd gone out to do just that. Because – and he still didn't know how or why it had happened – suddenly what Jane wanted was important to him.

He'd been tempted by the floral one with gilt-edged pages and creamy paper, but no – this was Jane, so he'd gone for practicality. A sturdy cover that could easily withstand being dragged in and out of Jane's knee pocket ten times a day. Good quality paper, alternately ruled and blank pages. She could write, draw diagrams, scribble coordinates, whatever. It wasn't anything like as pretty as the other one, but it was waterproof, resilient and just what *she* would want. Not what he wanted to give her. He'd selected two waterproof pens, as well. And the crowning touch – he'd had *Jane's Trusty Notebook* emblazoned on the cover.

Jane's unaccustomed grumpiness fled and she smiled up at him. 'Luke, it's perfect. It's just what I would have bought for myself. If I'd had time. And if I could have afforded it.'

'Jane – again – you don't have to worry about money any longer. Your grandmother's dead – remember? You're probably quite rich.'

She looked down. 'I know – I know. I just don't seem able to get my head around that.'

'Some advice from your team leader: take some time off. Find someone to represent you – legally and financially. Discuss everything. Listen to their advice. Weigh up all your options and decide what to do.'

She smiled again. 'Good advice from my team leader. Who'd have thought.'

'I'm not just a pretty face, you know. And listen, take someone with you when you go. Someone who knows what questions to ask.' He hesitated, strangely unsure of himself. 'I . . . um . . . I'd be happy to go with you. If you think it would help, of course. Genuine offer.'

'Thank you,' said Jane, genuinely touched by this genuine offer. 'And thank you for the notebook as well.'

He nodded, every instinct telling him to make himself scarce before he managed to destroy her good impression of him. 'I . . . um . . . see you at lunch then.'

'Yes. See you later.'

He watched her walk away down the corridor, flipping through the pages of her new notebook. And still carrying the wrapping paper, which he knew she would carefully flatten out and keep. And the ribbon, too.

He turned to find Matthew standing behind him.

They looked at each other for a moment and then Matthew spoke.

'Are you perhaps intending to add Jane to your long list of female friends?'

'None of your business.'

'Yes, it is.'

'It's not what you're thinking.'

'Yes, it is.'

'No, I . . .'

'You're not right for her.'

'Matthew . . .'

'You're not right for her.'

He turned and walked away before Luke could say another word.

2

'Ma'am, I have yesterday's security section footage as you requested. I'm sending it to your screen.'

'Thank you, Charlie.'

Arming herself with more coffee – she really should cut down one day, but not today – Commander Hay settled herself at her briefing table, activated her screen, and began to trawl through the footage.

The bottom left-hand corner gave the location – Cell 6 – and the bottom right the prisoner ident, date and time. Hooke, A E. **[DATE REDACTED]**. 0230 hours.

She flicked through at fifteen-minute intervals. Hooke asleep. Hooke asleep. Hooke still asleep. Hooke receiving his hourly bed check. She could clearly see the face at the grille. Officer Harvey, by the look of it. All prisoners were monitored on-screen but an hourly eyes-on was mandatory. Hooke asleep. Hooke asleep. Harvey again. Hooke asleep. Officer Wu at the grille. Hooke asleep. The overhead lights coming on at 0630. Hooke sitting up. Hooke using the facility. Everything looked perfectly normal. Especially Hooke. Sleepy and scratching himself in some very unattractive areas, but normal. Hooke's breakfast delivered by Etok. Hooke demanding to speak to his fellow prisoner – ex-Lt Sawney. No response from Etok. Standing instructions – no conversation with the prisoner. Hooke's breakfast finished. Hooke washing but not shaving. Already he was beginning to look very seedy. Unhealthy, even. Hooke half-heartedly straightening his bedding because he knew his rations would be docked if he didn't. Hooke sitting on his bed and staring into space.

1028 – Hooke removed to one of the interrogation rooms. Escorted by Etok and Roche. No physical contact by either that Commander Hay could see. Hooke deposited in the interrogation room. Hooke left to twiddle his thumbs for thirty-five minutes. Standard procedure. As an ex-TPO, he'd know that. It wouldn't worry him.

Enter Etok with paperwork. More form-filling. All this had already been done on his arrival into custody, but this was standard procedure, too. Irritate the prisoner. Keep him off-balance. Break his concentration.

'Name?'

'You know my name, dickhead.'

'Name.'

Hooke sighed. 'Hooke.'

And so it went on. Address. Next of kin. Medical questionnaire. Having the rules read to him as they pertained to prisoners. Speak only when spoken to. Answer all questions truthfully and completely. Obey instructions without question. No communication with other prisoners. Even the smallest contravention would result in loss of privileges. Not that he had any. The rules pertaining to his behaviour during interrogation. Remain seated at all times. Answer clearly and concisely. Hands on the table at all times. Any word or gesture that could be construed as hostile would result in immediate sonicking, not only from the officer on the other side of the table but also from the two outside the door just waiting for the opportunity. Again, none of this would be new to Hooke.

Exit Etok. Another twenty-five-minute wait. Hooke shouting something at the camera – about wanting his lunch – which automatically added another fifteen minutes to his waiting time.

Finally, enter Major Callen, delicately wiping his mouth and giving every appearance of having just enjoyed an excellent meal.

Hay ceased to flick through, settled back and turned up the volume.

'Good afternoon,' said Callen, inserting himself into the chair opposite.

'It might be for you,' said Hooke, scowling. 'I haven't had any lunch yet.'

Callen cast a glance at Hooke's hefty frame. Missed meals were obviously not his favourite thing. 'Nor will you until I hear something useful.'

'I don't know anything about anything.'

'That I can well believe. I personally wouldn't trust you to be ink monitor, but Time Police rules and regulations require me to begin each interrogation in a friendly and encouraging manner before abandoning all that as a complete waste of time and falling upon you in a frenzy of violence and retribution.'

Hooke folded his arms. 'What are you waiting for?'

'I'm letting my lunch go down first.' He smiled coolly. 'I'm so sorry – given your lunchless state, that was a cruel thing to say. Do forgive me.'

'I'm not telling you anything.'

Callen glanced at his watch. 'Ideally I'd like another ten minutes of peacefully digesting my delicious steak and kidney pudding before unleashing myself upon you, so please could you just shut up and I'll get to you in due course.'

He closed his eyes and settled back into the chair.

'I'm not saying a word,' shouted Hooke.

'If only,' murmured Callen. 'Let's both of us just sit quietly for a while, shall we? Then I'll offer you the traditional deal whereby you make a full and complete statement in exchange for your worthless life. You'll gratefully accept, tell me everything I want to know and then shoot off to enjoy a belated lunch. I would recommend the steak and kidney pudding. But there's also battered cod today. Or vegetable lasagne.' He eyed Hooke's substantial form. 'Or a nice, healthy salad.'

He closed his eyes again.

Hooke scowled. 'I told you . . .'

Callen exploded into action, slamming both hands flat on the table in front of Hooke and shouting, 'And I told you to shut up.'

He withdrew his hands, adding more mildly, 'I'm trying to doze off here.'

Hooke reciprocated, his meaty face purple with rage, slamming his own hands down on the exact same spot. 'You're an arsehole, Callen, and you'll get nothing from me. Not until I've spoken to Sawney.'

Callen stood up. 'Never going to happen.' He thumped on the door, which opened. 'Take him away.'

Still alternately issuing blood-curdling threats and shouting for his lunch, Hooke was marched back along the corridor – Officers Etok and Roche again, Hay noticed – and pushed into his cell, where he kicked the door in frustration, shouted something at the camera, helped himself to a beaker of water and stretched out on his barely made bunk.

Twenty minutes later he was dead.

During that time no one had entered his cell. Or even approached it.

Hay frowned and replayed the interview. And again. Then she sat back and stared out of her window until she was recalled by Captain Farenden tapping on her door.

'Major Ellis and Lt North, ma'am, as you requested.'

'Thank you. Show them in, please. And bring yourself, too.'

They seated themselves.

'Charlie, if you could give us an update on the dinosaur situation, please.'

'Yes, ma'am. We know that at some point – the details are hazy – a body was discovered on the banks of a river in Wales. Initially it was thought to be that of a very large lizard. Since nothing had been officially reported missing – local zoos, animal collections and so forth – it was assumed the animal had been an illegal pet which had been abandoned when either it grew too large or the novelty wore off. At that stage there was no great alarm or urgency.

'Initially, the body was examined in situ by a local vet who professed himself baffled, retired to consult various databases, and eventually came to the conclusion he was looking at something completely unknown.

'With some difficulty, the body was removed from the riverbank and taken to a nearby empty building while the vet again attempted to identify the species. It was at this point, ma'am, since both the species and the cause of death were unknown to him, that he sensibly secured the corpse and refused to let anyone touch it.'

'Anyone being . . . ?'

'The lads who'd discovered the body and a couple of local police officers.'

'Is it diseased?' said North.

Farenden shook his head. 'Not visibly, but it was at this point, despite an odd circumstance, that the word *dinosaur* became more of a probability than a possibility and the vet recommended the police contact us.'

There was a long silence. It was North who spoke first. 'The body was discovered where?'

'A small town in Wales. But that was only where it was discovered. The body showed signs of having been immersed in and slightly damaged by a rapidly flowing body of water. Of which, of course, there is no shortage in Wales.'

Ellis frowned. 'What was the odd circumstance you mentioned?'

'It was wearing a collar.'

There was another silence.

'Are we talking collar as in dog collar with the little tag saying "Rover"?'

'No – we're talking collar as in electronic.'

'A tracker?'

'Possibly. Or a restraining device. As on supermarket trollies.'

There was another silence while everyone thought about this.

Hay sat forwards to address Ellis and North. 'When you get to Wales, I want you to take statements from everyone you consider necessary, secure the body and bring it back here for our own people to take a look at. The Pod Bay's not yet fully functioning so take a chopper. And not a word to anyone. If this gets out – that a possible dinosaur has been found in Wales – then there will be a stampede.'

Ellis shot her a sharp look. 'Do we honestly think this might be a dinosaur?'

'I don't know what to think. That's why I'm despatching you both to bring back answers and the body.'

'Yes, ma'am.'

'Thank you, officers.'

The Time Police have two helicopters, both of which are kept at the Battersea Heliport a few minutes away from TPHQ. Delta Zero Two, the smaller, did not keep North and Ellis waiting, setting down on the private landing jetty just as they exited the front doors and walked towards the Thames. The day was cold with a chilly wind coming upriver, but they waited quietly until Mellor gave them permission to approach.

'Good day, this is your pilot, Lt Chad Mellor, speaking. Welcome aboard Time Police Airlines Delta Zero Two. We shall shortly be taking off. Please fasten your seatbelts and assume an upright position. We hope you have a pleasant flight and thank you for choosing Time Police Airlines.'

North pulled on her headset. 'You're in a good mood today, Mellor. There's normally a ton of whinging and moaning to work through before you actually persuade this bucket of nuts and bolts to get airborne.'

'Not today. Today is a good day. Everyone in? Have you remembered to close the door? Right then. Off we jolly well go. Heading west-ish.'

'West-ish?'

'Yeah – west and a bit north. West-ish.'

'A technical term, I assume.'

'Keeping it simple for the non-aircrew on board.'

'I thought standard communication for pilots was a couple of grunts and a simple hand gesture.'

'You wound me, North.'

'You're a helicopter pilot, Mellor. You have three basic modes – piloting, drinking and . . . something else. Anything more complex than that is a mystery to you and your kind. Any chance of an ETA?'

'About an hour.'

'Can you be more specific?'

'That was specific. If I was being non-specific, then I would have said, "Today, sometime. Probably."'

Ellis sighed. 'We should have gone with Bailey and Delta Zero One. Much more high-class. And she provides in-flight entertainment.'

North regarded him in horror. 'How can skimming upriver at a height of about six feet, hogging the emergency airway, and pretending to strafe Barricade Bridge as she sings interminable verses of "Barnacle Bill the Sailor" possibly be regarded as entertainment?'

Mellor grinned. 'We swapped shifts. Because . . .' He paused for full dramatic effect. 'I have tickets for the big match this evening.'

'Really?' said Ellis, suddenly interested. 'How the hell did you manage that?'

North groaned and closed her eyes. 'Suddenly Barnacle Bill doesn't seem quite so bad.'

Mellor ignored her. 'Had my name down for ages. Finally

got to the top of the list. Got the good news last week. Me and my sister are going.'

'You have a sister?'

'Yeah – doesn't everyone?'

North shook her sisterless head. 'And you're making the poor girl go to a football match. What sort of brother are you?'

'A wonderful one,' he said. 'She's so made up she's taking me for a meal afterwards. So, you know, if we could get the body on board asap I'd be grateful.'

'You are so sad,' said North.

'Hey, I am a chopper pilot. I'm in the Time Police. I look really, really good in these shades. And I have tickets for England v Germany tonight. I am, literally, the coolest person on the planet.'

North groaned again. The helicopter clattered on. Heading a bit west-ish.

Captain Farenden ushered a deeply unhappy Lt Varma into Commander Hay's office. Hay waved her to a seat, but Varma stood to attention, staring over Hay's shoulder.

'I take full responsibility, ma'am. The prisoner was in my charge. I am tendering my resignation with immediate effect.'

'That is your prerogative,' said Hay carefully, 'but it is my duty to point out that if you leave now, so hastily, with this matter still unresolved, it will be regarded by some as clear evidence that you were, if not directly responsible for, then at least implicated in, Hooke's death.'

Varma forgot to stand to attention. 'What?' And then remembered again. 'Obviously I will remain to assist in any way I can, ma'am, but as soon as is convenient, I shall leave.'

'It will never be convenient, Lt Varma. Sit down, please.'

Varma bent stiffly and sat.

Hay regarded her for a moment and then said, 'If you truly wish to leave us, then of course I won't stand in your way. I don't want anyone here unwillingly. However, if I may offer some advice – for the time being, wait and see. The inquiry is already underway and I am awaiting the results of the medical examination. Once I have those, I shall proceed according to their findings. As will you. Now – in your own words – where were you yesterday while all this was happening?'

Varma stiffened. 'I came on duty at 0800, ma'am. Etok, Roche and Wu were in the office with me for shift change. Wu and Harvey went off watch. I spent an hour debriefing Devan Kumar and Jay Adesina. They've been as helpful as they can, ma'am, but other than their association with Sawney, they don't know anything.

'At 0900 I met with Major Callen. We mapped out a strategy for questioning Ernesto Portman . . .'

'Is he saying anything about his kidnapping of Imogen Farnborough?'

'He's not saying anything at all, ma'am, other than demanding a lawyer. I don't know where he got the idea we allow that sort of human rights nonsense here – and then the major and I discussed Hooke and Sawney. The major would make a start with Hooke and I was to interrogate Sawney this afternoon. After that, I authorised the release of Nora Adesina – Jay's mother – and arranged a travel pass for her because she's not well off. I called in to Sawney's cell to inform him of the interview schedule. Then on to Hooke. I thought he was asleep but he was dead.'

'You hadn't actually had any contact with Hooke since you booked him in?'

'No, ma'am.'

'Physical or otherwise?'

'No, ma'am.'

'And you were with witnesses at all times?'

'I was, ma'am.'

'At no time were you alone?'

Varma shook her head.

'Then, Lt Varma – you are in the clear.'

'Ma'am, I am the officer in charge. Hooke was my responsibility. Everything that happens in security is my responsibility.'

'That is true, Lieutenant, but responsibility is not the same as fault.'

Varma remained silent.

Hay stood up. 'Continue with your normal duties, Lieutenant. We will speak again when the situation is clearer.'

'Yes, ma'am.'

The flight to Wales, as predicted, took about an hour.

The helicopter circled a small town girdled by hills and mountains while Mellor checked out the landing site.

'Going down, ladies and gentlemen. First floor, haberdashery, surgical supports, corn plasters and haemorrhoid cream. Ground floor, sports kit, classic football matches, beer and ta-dah – ladies' underwear.'

North rolled her eyes.

'And . . . we have arrived.'

'Nice touchdown,' said Ellis.

'We aim to please. If I could just remind everyone of the importance of speedy body-loading . . .'

'Relax,' said North. 'You'll be back in plenty of time to witness England's inevitable defeat.'

Mellor had set them down on a playing field – possibly the only piece of level ground for miles around. The horizon was hidden behind blue-grey mountains, which themselves were partially obscured by dark, heavy rain clouds.

'I don't know how long this will take,' said Ellis as Mellor began to shut things down.

'I'll stay with the chopper,' said Mellor. 'Regulations. Though a comfort break would be welcome on your return.'

Ellis nodded. 'If I can, I'll send you out a coffee.'

'Appreciated, sir. Thank you.'

Exiting the helicopter, North and Ellis were met by two police officers who introduced themselves. Clive and Williams. IDs were exchanged – presumably in case some passing stranger had arrived at this remote spot entirely on the off-chance of finding a potential dinosaur. Everyone was very professionally polite.

Ellis looked around. 'Where's the body right now?'

The younger officer, Williams, gestured towards a small one-storey wooden building. 'It was delivered a couple of hours ago. Waiting for you inside.'

'A cricket pavilion? I didn't know cricket was popular in this part of the world.'

Williams shrugged. 'Yeah – we have a few local teams. Very enthusiastic – for some reason that escapes the rest of us. We didn't have anywhere else to put it. The body, I mean. If we'd used the church hall, we'd have been up to our armpits in nosey buggers before we'd even got the door open. The body's in a sealed bag. The vet is still here to answer any questions you might have and we've taken statements from everyone involved. Including the two boys who found the body.'

'What were they doing at the time?'

'Fishing.'

'Shouldn't they have been in school?'

'They should, yes. We had a bit of trouble with them initially. They thought they were in trouble for bunking off. Which they will be, I expect. We had to tell them the police don't usually turn out for that sort of thing and it was the body we were interested in.'

'What do they think it is?'

'We told them it was just a giant lizard.'

'How did that go down?'

'Not as well as we hoped. I blame all those old nature programmes made by that bloke who whispers in the undergrowth.'

'Tell me they didn't take any photos.'

'Can't do that, I'm afraid, but we did make them hand over all electronics so, with luck, that side of things has been contained.'

'Good thinking,' said Ellis, who always gave credit where it was due.

By now they were climbing the pavilion steps. The older officer tapped on the door. There was the sound of someone unlocking it from the other side.

'Good security,' said Ellis. The officer flushed slightly and nodded.

A medical trolley stood in the middle of what Ellis suspected was the tea area. A sealed body bag lay thereon with a very young-looking man standing alongside. Ellis suddenly realised that somehow, and completely without him noticing, he had arrived at the age where doctors and policemen – and now vets – looked like teenagers.

He nodded. 'Good day.'

The vet nodded back.

'Let's just check before we go any further,' said Ellis, who had once, as a very junior officer, been part of a team detailed to guard an ancient crown prior to returning it to its proper owner. There had been some confusion somewhere along the line, and it turned out they'd mounted a twenty-four-hour vigil over someone's sandwiches. There had been massive ridicule. You don't forget that sort of thing in a hurry.

The vet gestured to the body. 'Before I break it, please confirm the seal.'

'I so confirm,' said Ellis.

The vet broke the seal and pulled down the zip just far enough to reveal a decidedly lizard-like head and shoulders.

Ellis sighed.

North peered closely. 'Can we see some more, please?'

The vet unzipped the bag and flipped it open.

'Well,' said Ellis eventually. 'It's definitely a lizard. A big lizard. And look at those teeth.'

'Bipedal,' said the vet. 'I didn't get a chance to measure it, but I estimate between four and five feet tall. Estimated weight between a hundred and a hundred and fifty pounds. Check out these babies.' He gestured to the long talons on the second toes of the back feet.

'Nasty,' said Ellis.

'It's definitely a carnivore. Given the claws, I'd say a hunter rather than a scavenger. Quite fast-moving, I should imagine. The big head is to accommodate all those fearsome teeth and the long tail's for balance.'

North and Ellis moved slowly around the body, looking but not touching. It was mid-khaki in colour with darker irregular stripes across its back and legs, and with a slightly lighter underbelly. The skin was surprisingly smooth – scaled but not knobbly like a crocodile. More like that of a snake.

'Some vicious claws on the forelegs, as well,' said North, pointing.

'A raptor,' said Ellis, who had seen all seventeen of the *Jurassic* franchise films. He turned to North. 'Are you able to identify . . . ?'

'No,' said North shortly. 'We'll need an expert.'

Ellis sighed. 'I'm not sure how happy the commander will be with that. She's trying to keep a lid on this.'

'In that case,' said North, not without a gleam of mischief, 'you might want to consider bringing in St Mary's. Dr Maxwell, to be precise.'

Ellis did not recoil but only because they were in public and there were Time Police standards to maintain.

'On what grounds?'

'The woman's been chased, attacked, or bitten by just about every species of dinosaur under the sun. She's an expert.'

'I'll let the commander make that decision.'

They turned their attention to the collar.

'Can you tell us anything about this?' said Ellis.

'Now this *is* interesting,' said the vet. As if the dinosaur itself wasn't. 'If invited to speculate – which I very much hope I will be . . .'

Ellis smiled. 'Please consider yourself invited to speculate.'

'Well, there's something about the design that reminds me of dog training collars – except that this is scaled up. To control the . . . the creature, obviously.'

He paused invitingly, but Ellis was peering at the collar and North was wearing one of her less responsive faces.

'I'm almost certain it's a restraining device of some kind,' the vet continued. He pulled out a pen and used it as a pointer. 'There's what looks like a receiver here, so it's remotely controlled. These things are generally waterproof but I don't think prolonged immersion in a rocky river will have done it any good so it may not be working any longer. There are usually three or four settings, starting, say, with vibrations – which would be some kind of gentle warning. Followed, possibly, by a mild shock if the warning was ignored. Followed by a more severe shock – which would be effective most of the time, I should imagine.'

He stopped.

'Followed by . . . ?' said Ellis.

'Well, given the subject,' he gestured at the hind claws, 'a lethal jolt.'

'Could it have been dead when it went into the water?' enquired North. 'It died and for some reason was tossed into the river?'

'Possibly – an autopsy will tell you that.' The vet paused and then added wistfully, 'I wish I could be there when you open it up.'

His wistfulness elicited no response from either Time Police officer.

'What's the collar made of?' said Ellis, peering more closely.

'Well, the dog training collars are usually made of high-quality TPU. Thermoplastic polyurethane.'

Both Ellis and North looked blank.

'High-tensile strength,' he said helpfully. 'Doesn't tear easily. Resistant to UV. Waterproof.'

'Pretty tough stuff then?'

'Oh yes.' He looked again at the raptor. 'But then, it would need to be, wouldn't it?'

'Does the collar light up?' asked North.

The vet shook his head. 'I don't know, but it occurs to me that if you wanted to locate one of these animals in the dark . . .'

'Then the collar *could* light up,' said North.

'And possibly emit some sort of signal,' said Ellis slowly.

'To enable tracking . . .'

They looked at each other and then at the vet.

'No,' he said. 'I can't see any way of removing it. Some sort of electronic gizmo, perhaps. Without that, you'll probably have to chop its head off.'

Ellis looked at the police officers. 'Would you excuse us a moment, please. I need to confer with my colleague. No offence is intended.'

They moved to the other end of the room.

North turned to Ellis. 'Are you thinking what I'm thinking?'

'I'm thinking we need to get this back to TPHQ before the former owner tracks it down.' He turned to the vet. 'Are you able to assist us any further?'

The vet shook his head. 'The body arrived – I took one look, indulged in industrial-strength googling and passed on my very tentative conclusions to the police who contacted you. I touched the body as little as possible, sealed the bag and waited.'

He regarded them somewhat anxiously.

There are still officers in the Time Police who regard everyone who isn't one of them as a lower life form on whom courtesy and consideration should not be wasted. Neither Ellis nor North were among those officers.

Ellis nodded. 'Absolutely the right thing to do. Thank you for your professionalism. You must be bursting with questions.'

'I am, but I know they won't be answered.' The vet began to zip up the bag again. 'My preliminary notes – which are as far as I got – are in that folder over there. Along with police images of the body as it was found, the riverbank *where* it was found and some shots of the surrounding area. The results of my visual inspection are also there, along with the boys' statements.'

'Thank you,' said North. 'That is all very helpful.'

The vet stepped back. 'We'll get it to the chopper then, shall we? I warn you, it's quite unwieldy – a dead weight.' He raised his voice. 'Officers – can you give us a hand here, please?'

'Um,' said North. 'Is there anywhere I could . . .'

'Oh yes,' said the vet, watching the two officers carefully manhandle the trolley out of the door. 'Through that door there – first on the right.'

'Thank you.'

The vet followed the two policemen out of the pavilion. North disappeared. Ellis picked up the folder and began to leaf through the contents. Everything was exactly as the vet had described. He studied pictures of the body lying on the riverbank. It had just been dragged from the water by the looks of it. To describe the river and its surrounding area as rocky was an understatement. The body couldn't possibly have been in the water for very long or the damage would have been much greater. So perhaps they were looking for somewhere upstream and not that far away.

Here were the boys' statements, together with their names and addresses. In a separate folder was the vet's preliminary medical report. He pulled out the sheet detailing the location of the injuries, front and back – and then the sky turned white then yellow then red, there was a crack that hurt his ears, the entire front wall shattered, and a good part of the roof fell in.

4

Captain Farenden was working quietly at his desk when a call came through. He listened without speaking and then politely asked the caller to repeat the message. Again he listened, and then requested the caller keep him informed as the situation developed. Standing up, he smoothed his uniform, took a deep breath, and stood in Commander Hay's open doorway.

'Ma'am.'

She continued writing. 'Yes, Charlie?'

'Ma'am.' He was unable to continue.

She looked up. 'Charlie? What's wrong?'

'Ma'am, I . . .'

'Close the door. Sit down. Tell me.'

'That was the police. There's been an . . . incident. In Wales.'

'What's happened?'

'An explosion, ma'am.'

'Who's hurt?'

'They're all dead. Ellis, North, Mellor, the two police officers. And the vet. And the helicopter. And the dinosaur. Completely obliterated. There's almost nothing left.'

'Were they shot down?'

'They were still on the ground, ma'am.'

'Have they yet established . . . ?'

'Not yet, ma'am. The damage is . . . quite extensive. I've asked for all images and full details to be forwarded, but it will take them a while to make the area safe – the bomb disposal people are involved – and to establish exactly what happened . . .'

He stopped, unable to continue.

'Charlie, I'm so sorry. I know you and Matthew have been friends for most of your time here.'

'We trained together.'

'And we've lost everything?'

'Everything, ma'am.' He took a huge breath, sat up straight, and then said, 'How would you like us to proceed?'

She sat back. 'Give me a minute to think, Charlie, can you? And take one for yourself as well. Then we'll talk.'

'Thank you.'

Ten minutes later, Hay looked up as he tapped on her door.

'Coffee, ma'am.'

'And very welcome. Thank you.'

Captain Farenden seated himself and pulled out his scratchpad.

'Right, first things first,' Hay began. 'Ellis, Mellor and North were deliberately targeted. I consider the Time Police to be under attack. We go into lockdown.'

'We're not yet up to full strength, ma'am. The unit was on forty-eight-hours' standby while we sorted out the issues with the Pod Bay.'

'Let officers in as they trickle back to us, but all civilians are to be escorted out of TPHQ. Send Major Callen to me, please.

He needs to be informed. And tell the Senior Mech I shall need a couple of pods freed up even if it brings the ceiling down.'

'People will wonder what's going on, ma'am.'

'Yes, I'm going to need to make a statement in due course. Can you set something up for ... 1530, please. And get Chigozie to call the roll. And keep calling it as people come back. I want to know who's available at a moment's notice.'

'Yes, ma'am. Anything else?'

'There's bound to be, but that will do to be going along with, I think. Let's find out exactly what happened before we go off half-cocked.'

'Yes, ma'am.'

Captain Farenden's scratchpad bleeped. He read for a moment and then said, 'Ma'am, I have the report on Hooke from MedCen. And it's good news.'

'Thank God – I'd almost forgotten there was such a thing. What does it say?'

'Well, to give you the bottom line first – Hooke died of natural causes.'

Hay sat back in astonishment. 'Really?'

'According to the doctor's report, he died of an aneurism. He'd been suffering from high blood pressure for which he received medication while serving with us. Which he was very reluctant to take. The doctor remembers arguing with him over it. Had to order him to take it in the end. Hooke deemed it a weakness. He almost certainly discontinued the medication on leaving the Time Police, and the doctor says what with that and his lifestyle, it was always going to happen one day. It's just unfortunate it happened here.'

Hay nodded.

'There's more, ma'am.'

'Go on.'

'The panic button was well within Hooke's reach. The doctor says his death wouldn't have been instantaneous. He would have experienced a headache, nausea, drowsiness and felt very unwell. Not for long but long enough. He had only to roll over and press the alarm. He didn't. He deliberately made that decision. You could almost say it was suicide, ma'am.'

Hay nodded. 'Send Varma to me, Charlie, will you, please? I think she could do with some good news right now.'

Ten minutes later . . .

'And so, Lieutenant,' said Hay, 'the conclusion is that given his general poor health, high blood pressure, coupled with the stress of his capture, apprehension over his interrogation, knowledge of his certain end at Droitwich, and his failure to summon assistance – which the doctor says he could easily have done – well, you could almost say he took his own life.'

Varma heaved an enormous sigh. 'Thank you, ma'am.'

'My pleasure. Moving on. I have a job for you. Not a pleasant one, I'm afraid. I expect you'll have heard the rumours by now.'

'I know something's happened, ma'am. We're on lockdown.'

'An hour ago, Delta Zero Two was attacked. Ellis, North and Mellor have been killed. Along with two civilian policemen and a veterinary surgeon. The evidence they had gone to collect was completely destroyed.'

There was a long pause and then Varma said quietly, 'Three good officers, ma'am. They will be missed.'

'Indeed.' Hay handed Varma a file. 'For your eyes only, Lieutenant. Go and investigate. I want a preliminary report asap. The Senior Mech will have a pod for you. Take whomever you consider useful. Go carefully and quietly – somehow these people managed to take out three TPOs and one of our choppers. I suspect the people to whom the dinosaur belonged are quietly obliterating any possible leads.'

Varma looked up from flicking through the file. 'A dinosaur, ma'am?'

'So it would appear. Interested?'

'Very much so. Ma'am, I don't want to go in mob-handed. Not initially. Let me take a quiet look around first and then call for back-up if and when required.'

'Agreed. And Varma . . .'

'Yes, ma'am?'

'I know nothing of dinosaurs – and neither, I suspect, do you. It occurs to me it might be useful to take along someone who has first-hand experience.'

Varma groaned and shifted in her chair. 'Ma'am . . .'

'I'm not saying she's the world's greatest expert on dinosaurs – I'm certain there are thousands of people with more theoretical knowledge than her – but you can't deny she has more practical experience than anyone else on earth. You name the species – it will, at some point, have encountered the infamous Dr Maxwell.'

Varma groaned. 'Ma'am – I and my section have just been found innocent of all charges. Why are you punishing me like this?'

'One more thing, Lieutenant.'

'Ma'am?'

'Sawney – you were to interrogate him this afternoon, I believe?'

'And would still wish to do so.'

'Sawney's information is important. But not more important than ascertaining what happened to our people, our chopper and our evidence. Put someone else on it.'

Varma made a decision. 'Ma'am – give me thirty minutes.'

'For what?'

'To get Sawney to talk.'

'In thirty minutes?'

'Yes, ma'am. We won't be losing much time – the Senior Mech has still to declare the Pod Bay safe. Sawney and the Wales investigation need not be an either/or situation. I can do both.'

Hay sat back, smiling. 'Very well, Lieutenant. Have at it.'

Varma returned to security at a run and found Trainee Tucker checking over his kit in the equipment room.

'Tucker, chuck me over a truth cuff, will you. Fully charged.'

Tucker reached into a locker and handed one over. 'Sign here, please, ma'am.'

Varma signed with a flourish. 'You're with me. Quick.'

She set off down the corridor at great speed.

Tucker loped alongside. 'You're very . . . enthused all of a sudden, ma'am.'

'I am indeed. Now – today's challenge. We have less than thirty minutes to get this bastard to talk.'

Tucker paused delicately. 'Would you like me to . . .' He clenched his fist.

'It might come to that, but let's have a little fun first. Just nod and say *yes, ma'am* to everything.'

'Yes, ma'am.'

Varma stared at him suspiciously.

'Just fully embracing my role.'

They arrived at Cell 4. Varma nodded at Tucker and he tapped in the door code. The door swished open.

Varma strode into the cell. 'Right, Sawney. We don't need you any longer. Hooke's told us everything we wanted to know so you've been booked in at Droitwich. You'll leave in just under thirty minutes. Don't bother taking anything with you – you won't need it. They can fit you in this evening. Special arrangement. I'm sure you can understand why we want you out of the way with as little fuss as possible. By this time tomorrow you'll have been dead for over twelve hours and no one will ever know you've been here. See to it, Tucker.'

'Yes, ma'am.'

She turned on her heel.

Sawney, who had been staring at her with his mouth open, climbed to his feet.

'Wait. Wait – I have information.'

Varma shrugged. 'So do I. Now.'

'You don't understand. I have . . .'

She cut him off. 'I know exactly what you're going to tell me. Because Hooke's already talked. Well, gabbled, actually.'

Sawney narrowed his eyes. 'No, he didn't. Hooke wouldn't do that.'

Varma turned again for the door. 'I can assure you he did. Like you, I was quite surprised. But there we are. He's bought his life at the expense of yours.'

'Not true. I don't believe you.'

She didn't even bother to turn around. 'I don't care.'

She motioned Tucker to close the door again.

Sawney eyed the cuff. 'You tortured him.'

'Didn't have to.' Varma held up the cuff. 'Fully charged. Unused.'

In the doorway, Tucker nodded confirmation.

'I'm leaving you in the capable hands of Trainee Tucker here because I've been offered a rather nice little job this afternoon. You won't believe this, Trainee Tucker, but I'm going dinosaur hunting.'

He brightened. 'Very nice, ma'am. Can I come?'

'No – I'm afraid I'm leaving you to deal with this lowlife. Rank hath its privileges and all that.'

'Aw,' said Tucker. 'Not fair.'

Varma eyed Sawney. 'I'd start making peace with my maker if I were you, Sawney.'

She stepped through the door, saying curtly to Tucker, 'Prep him for imminent departure. Advise Droitwich when you're thirty minutes out and they'll have everything ready for you.'

Tucker nodded. 'Yes, ma'am.' The door began to close.

'Wait,' shouted Sawney. 'Wait.'

Varma paused, standing sideways just outside the doorway and sending an unspoken message that the pause was only temporary.

Sawney licked his lips. 'Convince me and I'll talk.'

'Convince you of what? Hooke's already given me everything I need.'

'Where is he?'

Varma shrugged one shoulder. 'MedCen, I think.'

'I want to talk to him.'

She laughed. 'I'm not letting you anywhere near my star witness. For obvious reasons. Tucker, why is this door still open?' She began to walk away.

'The cuff,' cried Sawney. 'Put it on me.'

'You're kidding me.' Varma made a face of disgust.

'Put the cuff on me and I'll tell you all the things Hooke couldn't because he didn't know.'

'Such as?'

Sawney tried to get through the door. Tucker pushed him back. 'Let's get you processed. I want to go dinosaur hunting.'

Sawney leaned around Tucker. Not an easy task since Trainee Tucker was built along traditional Time Police lines.

'Prove to me that Hooke talked and I will as well.'

Varma shook her head. 'Fire truck off, arsehole.'

'Prove you're not lying.'

She began to walk away from him. 'Better things to do, Sawney.'

Tucker called after her, 'If you're busy here, ma'am, I'll volunteer to go after the dinosaur in your place.'

Sawney tried again. 'Prove you're not lying to me and I'll tell you what you don't know you want to know.'

Varma paused, sighed and reluctantly retraced her footsteps. Just another hard-pressed TPO with too many things to do.

'All right, Sawney, but I warn you – mess me around on this and I and my boots will bounce you off every wall in your cell. No one says you have to arrive at Droitwich in good condition.'

She slipped on the cuff, took a deep breath, mentally crossed her fingers and said carefully, 'Hooke was offered his life and he took it.'

She held up her arm. The cuff glowed green.

'Get on with it, Tucker.' She was already out of the door.

'No,' protested Sawney. 'I'll tell you everything. Hooke doesn't know it all.'

'Hooke's evidence is good enough for Hay and certainly good enough for me.'

The light turned red.

'See,' shouted Sawney. 'Not true.'

Varma removed the cuff before it could do any more harm.

Sawney held out his arm. 'Give me the same deal as Hooke and I'll talk.'

Varma stared at the floor, to all intents and purposes thinking deeply. 'Tucker, what's the time?'

'Twenty past, ma'am.'

She made a sound indicative of indecision and looked down the corridor, her body language radiating a desire to be off doing something much more interesting than this.

Tucker yawned. Sawney held his breath.

Varma sighed. 'All right. Same deal as Hooke.' She nodded to Tucker. 'Get him into an interrogation room and send for . . .' She paused. 'Etok. If Sawney cooperates and you're done in . . .' she looked at her watch, 'twenty minutes, then you can come with me. Fail me and I'll have you cleaning out the equipment lockers until the end of Time. Helpful hint – you'll need tongs for Roche's socks.'

She grinned evilly at the pair of them. 'Twenty minutes, gentlemen. Do not disappoint me, either of you. You will regret it.'

She strode from the cell.

5

Matthew, meanwhile, had made his way to the Map Room. Still absent-mindedly scratching at his arm, he stared up at the Time Map while waiting for his eyes to adjust to the dim light.

There are two known versions of the Time Map in existence. One – contemptuously known as the *toytown version* – is housed at St Mary's and does very little more than record major historical events and their relationship to each other. There is a general feeling at TPHQ that entrusting St Mary's with anything more sophisticated than this is just asking for trouble.

The real Time Map, as the Time Police persisted in referring to it, stood before Matthew now. A colossal representation of Time itself. Three storeys high, rising up through the building and encircled by the observation ring – twenty feet off the ground – which, most days, would hold half a dozen officers leaning on the rail, staring at the huge silver globe rotating before them. Because there was nothing like staring at a vast and possibly sentient glowing globe to ground a temporarily temporally confused officer and remind him of his place in the scheme of things. Right at the bottom.

The Time Map incorporated two axes – the vertical axis

denoted Time and the horizontal represented space. The point where they intersected was the ever-moving here and now.

Set into the walls, the floors and even the ceiling, more than a thousand computer-controlled streamers beamed their mosaics of information into this giant structure. Millions of tiny glowing dots were connected by a complex filigree of silver lines, interspersed with an ever-increasing network of blue, green and purple dots of light, denoting every jump of which the Time Police were aware.

A long, low hum filled this vast space – the Song of the Time Map – its note rising or falling occasionally as new information was added or updated by the increasingly sophisticated AI system. Arguments broke out regularly over whether the Map was actually sentient or not, but the overwhelming opinion was that it was certainly the most intelligent thing in the building and would probably kill them all one day.

The TiMMs – the Time Map Maintenance section – worked at ground level, their consoles arranged in two semicircles around the Map. The Map Master herself presided over the whole section from her massive workstation situated on a raised platform which gave her an excellent view of everything happening in her tightly managed unit.

Three training consoles stood off to one side – one of them now dedicated to Matthew's sole use. Seeing it now, he felt the usual thrill of excitement and – was it his imagination? – did the Song of the Time Map increase slightly as he approached his workstation? Anticipation, perhaps. Or, given that he'd broken it once – no, twice now – it might equally be a warning. He dismissed that thought.

Obviously he was experiencing a slight pang at not yet

being fit enough to rejoin Jane and Luke, but the Map Room was his happy place and who knew what he might discover today. Because only a few days ago, while in pursuit of the Zanetti Train, Matthew had penetrated further into the Map than he suspected anyone ever had before. In fact, he'd gone too far. At one point he'd despaired of ever being able to trace either the train or his teammates. But just as he'd felt himself losing his direction, his purpose, even his identity, the moment when he had been almost fighting the Map in his efforts to find the train, it – the Map – had spoken to him. True, he had been completely lost, in pain, drugged up to the eyeballs, disoriented, blinded by the thick maze of tiny silver lines all around him, and being slowly swallowed by Time itself. But, in that moment of complete hopelessness, he was convinced the Map had spoken to him.

This statement had been met with some disbelief from his colleagues – for a start, the Map's AI had no voice – but on the other hand, this was Matthew Farrell, arguably the weirdest of the three weirdos comprising Team Weird. That was a lot of weird. And no one could deny his affinity with the Time Map, so anything was possible. Probably.

The Map Master had swallowed down her doubts, allocated Matthew his own dedicated console, forbidden him on pain of death to touch the Map itself in any way – ever – at all – not even a little bit – don't even look at it too hard – and imposed a number of safeguards such as time limits, constant supervision by herself or Connor, spending at least thirty minutes writing a full report afterwards, and forbidding him to leave the Map Room until it was done. All of this enabled her to keep an eye on his recovery and remain fully up to date with his activities within the Map itself. Having thus safeguarded the Map, TPHQ, and Officer Farrell – in that order – she'd left him to get on with it.

Matthew seated himself at his console, eager and excited. Where would he go today? What would he see? He had choices. He could go forwards in Time. Further and further. How far into the future could he reach? How far would the Map let him go? In fact, how far into the future could the Map see? Could it, for instance, extrapolate the heat death of the universe? The End of Time itself? The last seconds of Time trickling away? The moment that everything stopped. Eternal nothing. Forever.

He shivered. No – not today. Neither he nor the Map were ready for the end of everything. He should start small.

His fingers began to fly across his console as he logged on.

Over his head, the Map sang its siren song. Enticing him in.

'What do you want today?' said Connor, coming to stand beside Matthew as he worked.

Matthew considered this. What indeed? All of Time was floating over his head.

'I honestly don't know,' he said eventually.

'Start with something you're familiar with,' advised Connor. 'Don't overreach yourself. When you've settled in and feel you're in complete control, *then* strike out for the new and wonderful. You'll make much more progress if you're not fighting the Map like last time.'

Sound advice.

'OK,' said Matthew. 'You choose. Something at random. A big section – something I can move about in.'

Connor nodded. 'Usual rules apply. You keep your scratchpad active to monitor the coordinates. Com check every five minutes whether you like it or not. No more than three segments from the Time Map at any given time. No more than thirty minutes per session. Did you remember your visor this time?'

Matthew held up his visor.

'All right. Let's get started. Set your timer for thirty minutes.'

Connor seated himself and activated his own console. Above their heads, a section of the Map brightened briefly and duplicated itself. The duplicate detached itself and hung for a moment, twirling gently.

'How and where do you want it?'

Matthew pointed. 'Freestanding holo, please. Over here.'

The duplicated section faded and then reappeared behind Matthew's console as new streamers came online.

'All ready for you,' said Connor. 'Remember – thirty minutes. And for God's sake, don't break anything this time.'

Matthew sighed. Once. He'd broken the Time Map once. All right – twice. And yes, OK, the second time had nearly brought down the entire giant edifice and yes, OK, there had been a bit of a row afterwards, but how likely was that ever to happen again? Especially with Connor monitoring his every move. Why couldn't people just move on?

The big, wedge-shaped section glowed gently, stretching almost from wall to wall and the Map Room wasn't small. Checking his scratchpad was activated, Matthew pulled down his visor, took a breath, squared his shoulders, and, heart thumping, stepped into the silver light.

How easily would he be able to move? How much help would the Map itself give him? Would he have to fight his way through that vast silver maze? And what would he see on the way?

He took his time. There was no rush. This wasn't like the last time when he'd been almost pulling the Map apart in his desperation to find the Zanetti Train. Perhaps, today, he could leave it to the Map to show him the way.

Tiny silver lines. Millions and millions of tiny silver lines. Each of them an event in Time itself. Seemingly motionless, but Matthew knew that if he stared for long enough, he would be able to see almost imperceptible movement everywhere, as each line forged its way through Time, touching others, moving apart again, twisting, turning. A massive web, constantly on the move, weaving itself as it went. Unstoppable. Intertwining. Inexorable. Mesmerising. And there were patterns. That was interesting. He'd heard the expression *history repeats itself*. With all the cynicism of a historian who had seen it all, his mother always equated history repeating itself to the human race's ability to make the same mistakes over and over again without ever learning anything. But no, it would seem there were actual patterns in Time – vast, complex and beautiful. And everything was so bright. So very, very bright.

Matthew darkened his visor and looked down at himself. He was standing in a cocoon of silver. The same tiny silver lines snaked around his arms, his hands, his body. They were only beams of light – he knew that – they couldn't possibly harm him, but the feeling that he himself was being woven into the fabric of Time was very, very strong. If he stood for long enough, would he actually become part of the Map? What would that be like? To become part of Time itself. To learn its secrets. He was conscious of both a fear and a desire.

He should move on.

There was no fighting this time. Looking up and around, he

found he could gently ease aside the silver strands and take one slow step after another, marvelling at the beauty of it all.

He looked down.

The floor had disappeared. Well, no, it was there somewhere – he just couldn't see it. He was hanging, apparently suspended in Time. There was a moment's massive disorientation as his brain struggled to establish up and down. His head spun and his stomach heaved. No. No. He could not throw up. Not here. Too shaming. And not only would the Map Master have something to say about that, she would be saying it for a very long time. Telling himself he felt absolutely fine, Matthew closed his eyes for a moment and waited for everything to settle back down.

When he opened them, the nausea had passed. Right – don't do that again. Keep looking forwards. Do not look down. He set off, gently teasing aside the silver tendrils. Moving backwards through Time.

This was interesting. There were some – not many, but some – small patches of nothing. Just darkness. Areas where there were no silver lines at all. Were these periods where Time hadn't yet been mapped? Or did they denote places where, for some reason, nothing was actually happening? Or – and this was a thought – were there actually areas where Time moved differently? Or didn't move at all? Could there even be places where Time didn't exist? Here was something new for him to investigate. His scratchpad was monitoring his progress. He'd instructed it to make notes of coordinates. He would certainly be back to check out these mysterious dark areas.

But not today. Today was just exploration. Reconnaissance. Nothing spectacular. Certainly no flying.

He paused again, silver wonder all around him. And silence. Silver silence. No voice. The Map wasn't talking to him today. Well, never mind. It had spoken when it really mattered. He shouldn't expect it every time. He swallowed down his disappointment. There would be other opportunities.

Without thinking, he turned to his right, took two cautious steps, and stopped. Why had he done that? What had made him . . . ?

Was that . . . was that a current? Matthew tried to turn back the way he'd come, but there it was. A faint tug. Were there currents in the Time Map? How could that be? He was standing in a holo in the Map Room. And yet . . . there it was again. Something akin to the undertow when paddling in the sea. That feeling of sand shifting under his feet. Odd, but not unpleasant. What would happen if he resisted?

Deliberately, he turned the other way. Against the current.

He was tugged again. More strongly this time. Well, why not let go and see where it took him? That was supposed to be the point of these sessions, wasn't it? Exploration and discovery. He turned back, and immediately his progress became easier. The silver tendrils parted of their own accord. He felt a growing sense of anticipation. Other TiMMs occasionally ventured into the Time Map but not often. And certainly not like this.

Matthew had the impression of increasing speed. Of movement all around him. The silver light grew brighter. Despite his visor, his eyes were streaming. He felt the familiar sting of salty tears. He couldn't see. The sensible thing to do would be to stop, lift his almost useless visor, wipe his eyes, have a good snort, replace his visor, and . . .

He was definitely being pulled in a certain direction. And,

as far as he could see, the silver tendrils were all streaming that way, too. Was something distorting Time? What could do that? An infinitesimal black hole, perhaps.

Matthew felt a moment's panic before reminding himself again that he was standing in a holo in the Map Room at TPHQ, not teetering on the brink of a singularity just seconds before spaghettification. He was perfectly safe.

He used his sleeve to rub at his visor – as if that would help – and squinted. Tiny silver lines were writhing and twisting themselves into a whole new pattern. The disruptions were spreading outwards. Ripples? No – shock waves might be a better description. Matthew watched, fascinated, as everything they touched began to resolve themselves into entirely new shapes. New designs. Something inexplicable was occurring right in front of his eyes.

Crouching slightly, he attempted to peer through the closely woven silver filaments. There was that phrase, wasn't there? Changing the course of history . . . Although it was always best not to mention history at TPHQ – people tended to get annoyed with him.

Now what? He had several images stored on his scratchpad which would have safely recorded the coordinates as well. Time to return, perhaps? Show the Map Master what he'd seen? And he was definitely going to need a better visor in future. He'd speak to Mikey about it – see what she could come up with.

He blinked furiously to clear his vision and stared at his scratchpad. According to the readings, he was in northern Europe somewhere. The 14th century. No – the 15th. And here it came again. That sense of a current. Stronger now. He was definitely being pulled towards . . . something.

Closing his eyes helped him to identify the direction from which the current was coming. And the direction in which he was being ... no, not pushed ... tugged was a better word. A little to the left. A fraction more. One step. Another smaller step. There was a sensation of something settling. As if he had arrived at his destination.

Matthew opened his eyes and looked around. Nothing seemed to have changed. Tiny silver lines still twisted and turned around him. Touching each other and then moving apart. Intertwining and then flying off in new directions. But always – always moving forwards. Time does not run backwards. While it is possible to travel through time – backwards, forwards – sideways, even – Time itself only ever runs in one direction. Einstein famously described it as the river of Time. Yes, it could slow down, speed up, meander, swirl, eddy – just like a river – but it still only ever flowed one way. Like an arrow. The Arrow of Time.

Matthew swayed and blinked. What was he doing? Why was he standing here thinking about the river of Time when something important was happening right in front of his very eyes. His heart thumped hard. Had he lost his way?

No, argued the logical part of his mind. There had been a current. He'd been swept here – along with everything else. He and the little silver lines, caught in something they could not escape. Whether the Map had anything to do with it was something to be thought about later. Because here ... now ... directly ahead of him was the epicentre from which the ripples were radiating.

Cautiously, he began to circle the anomaly. The phrase came into his head from nowhere. A knot in Time. Yes, that was a good way to describe it. He groped for his scratchpad. If he could take back an image of this to show it to the Map Master, she would be as fascinated as he was. He blinked and focused. The 15th century. He tapped the screen, attempting to focus on . . . yes . . . the epicentre.

14 . . . 83.

The strength and frequency of the shock waves was increasing. The silver lines were violently tearing themselves free from each other, changing direction and then reknotting themselves together. In completely different configurations. Different patterns. Different pathways. Jumbling around each other. They shouldn't do that. Not on this scale. Something serious was happening. Right in front of him.

His head spun. For some reason, he was thinking of a tangled ball of wool. Yes – that was exactly it. Like something a kitten had been at.

And now there was a sound. A high-pitched note. As if someone was running their finger around the wine glass of the universe and, just for a moment, Matthew's thoughts took flight and flew away, scattering like tiny birds, leaving his mind empty and pristine. A blank page. Ready to be rewritten.

And then they came back.

What had he been thinking? He closed his eyes and attempted to recall. A kitten. Just like . . . Yes, that was it. St Mary's Head of Security had a kitten. This looked just like something that had been ravaged by Captain Hyssop's kitten – Princess Kitty Glitter. Although that small ball of cross-eyed fluff had evolved into a sleek and efficient killing machine. Rather like Hyssop herself, as someone had once said. Although not very loudly and certainly not without checking over his shoulder first.

Intrigued, Matthew tried to move closer, although actually looking at the knot was hurting his eyes. Nothing to do with the glare – and his visor was on full strength anyway. It was the tangled threads . . . he was having problems focusing on them. And they were tangling other threads around them. Reaching out far into the future. This was really interesting. He couldn't wait to get back to replay these images. Slow them down. Analyse what was happening . . .

And then, as suddenly as it had begun, it ceased. The glare faded slightly. The silver threads around him had assumed an entirely new pattern. This was *absolutely fascinating*. If he wanted to be dramatic, he could say that Time had been rewritten. That the shape of Time had changed. Right in front of his eyes. Had this ever happened before? Had the Map actually brought him here specifically to show him this? Or had he simply been swept along with everything else?

He looked down at his scratchpad. Still recording.

'I've got it all,' he said to the Map. 'You can let me go now.'

'Got what?' said Connor.

'Something interesting. I'm on my way back.'

'Already? You've only been in there a minute or so.'

Matthew opened his mouth to argue this point with some vigour – he'd been in here for twenty minutes at the very least, probably more – and then closed it again. How much more weird did he want to add to his already spectacularly huge accumulation of weird?

'Something really strange has happened,' he said. 'I don't know what it is, so I'd like to return to this section again to check it out. But first I think the Map Master needs to see this. I'm on my way back.'

With TPHQ on lockdown and all pods grounded, most of the mechs were wandering around the always immaculately maintained Pod Bay looking for something to do. Mikey, perched on a crate, was talking to a bunch of them when, from the corner of her eye, she saw the Senior Mech disappear through the door into the Forbidden Zone – as the corridor between security and the Pod Bay had recently been designated.

When, ten minutes later, he hadn't returned, she made an excuse, hopped down off her crate and went to investigate.

The corridor looked very different from the shambles it had been the last time she'd been in here. The rubble had all been cleared and the spitting wires hanging from the ceiling had been made safe and taped up out of the way. Repairs to the right-hand wall were nearly complete. There was only the small gap at the far end to fill in and board over and then the job would be done. Breeze blocks and a sheet of plasterboard stood ready for this final phase.

The Senior Mech was standing motionless, staring in through the gap at the darkness beyond.

She hesitated, but only for a moment, and then let the door close behind her. 'Is everything all right?'

For a moment, he made no response, and then, dragging his eyes away, he turned to her. 'Yes. Yes, everything's fine.' He made an effort. 'What's happening with Curtis? Is he still . . . ?'

'Oh, no, no. We managed to cut him free. He's fine. The sausages were a write-off though.'

Silence fell. The Senior Mech's eyes again returned to the wall. Mikey waited quietly.

Without turning around, he said, 'You shouldn't be here.'

'I wanted something from my workroom.'

'No, you didn't – we changed the configuration. The entrance to your workroom is through the Pod Bay now. So again – why are you here?'

'I saw you come in here and you didn't come back out again. Why isn't the new wall finished?'

He made no reply.

Mikey took a chance. 'What's behind the wall?'

For a long time he said nothing, until finally, as if the words were dragged from him, he said quietly, 'Something best left alone.'

'Then why are *you* here?'

He sighed and then, with an effort, he said, 'I won't say you're too young to understand because that's probably not true, but you certainly haven't lived long enough to have done something of which you're thoroughly ashamed. So ashamed it takes you years to come to terms with it and then, just when you think you have, it starts up all over again.'

'No,' said Mikey. 'No, you're right. I haven't.'

'Take my advice. Don't.'

'All right. I'll try not to.'

'Not good enough. Don't try. Make sure you never do. The price you pay is . . . overwhelming.'

Mikey considered this for a while, then took a deep breath. 'What did you do?'

'Nothing. That's just the point. I did nothing.'

'Is it too late to fix?'

'Oh God, yes. Far, far too late.'

'Is it too late to try? If you can't fix it, then perhaps you could . . . I don't know . . . make reparation. Atone. Or something. I don't know.'

He looked down at her, although she was pretty sure it wasn't her that he was seeing. 'Perhaps. Perhaps.' He seemed to rouse himself. 'Now – out of here – I'm about to lock the door again.'

He ushered Mikey out of the corridor, locked the door behind them, hesitated for one moment and then set off in the direction of Commander Hay's office.

Hay looked up from her desk. 'Senior, have you brought me a sitrep?'

'I have, ma'am. The wall is almost completed. We'll finish it today, slap up some paint and no one will ever know.'

She eyed him shrewdly. '*Almost* completed?'

'Ma'am – are you aware of all the circumstances . . . ?'

'I know there's something behind there that was never discussed. There was some kind of accident which led to that area being sealed off. To maintain the structural integrity of the building. I was never told anything officially. No one was.'

'No. I believe you were in MedCen at the time.'

'I was. And . . . not really . . . aware . . . of things on the outside.'

Not really being aware of things on the outside was a polite euphemism for being lost in a world of shock and pain. And on suicide watch.

He stared out of the window. 'Ma'am . . . I . . .'

Hay put down her pen. 'Just tell me, Senior.'

He shifted his weight, as if preparing himself for something unpleasant. 'There's a pod behind the wall.'

'Yes, I know. There was some kind of malfunction and . . .'

He shook his head, still unable to meet her eyes.

'Senior, are you telling me the pod isn't empty?'

'The pod had taken one hell of a bashing and they – the crew – called for an emergency evac . . . and . . . somehow . . . the safety protocols failed and it shifted out of phase.'

Her eyes narrowed. 'What exactly does that mean?'

'The pod made it back safely . . . but . . . the protocols failed . . . somehow . . . and wall, pod and people became one.'

Hay drew a deep breath. 'That I did not know.'

'No one does.'

'What happened?'

'Some died instantly. Others . . . didn't. The doctor – not this one – his predecessor – reckoned he could save two of them at least. The attempt might possibly have killed them but he didn't really have a lot of choice . . .' The Senior Mech tailed away, still staring at the floor.

Hay spoke softly. 'And did it kill them? Is that the big secret?'

'I . . . I don't know what happened, ma'am. I have fears I can only hope are not justified. Callen and I were ordered out. Albay was alone in the pod. Not for long, but when he came out, he said everyone was dead and ordered us to seal up the pod and the wall.'

Hay closed the file and clasped her hands. 'Go on.'

'Major Callen . . . Lt Callen as he was then . . . knocked Albay to the ground. Nothing ever happened about that. Nothing ever happened about anything. Albay said they'd soon be forgotten, and, to my shame, they were.'

'Who else knows about this?'

'The doctor who attended was killed a year later in that airship incident over Porlock. I think, with the exception of you, ma'am, and me, Major Callen, and possibly one or two others, everyone else is either dead or has left the Time Police. And you were in MedCen at the time anyway.'

'The inference being it's nothing to do with me?'

'Well, it isn't, ma'am. You had your own problems.'

'So why are you here?'

'This is just a polite notification. I'm going to open up the pod.'

'To allay your fears? Or to confirm them?'

'I have to make my peace, ma'am.'

'Senior, why? It's done. There's nothing you can do to change anything.'

'I can make amends, ma'am. Or try to.'

'What happened wasn't your fault . . .' She gestured meaninglessly.

'Whatever Albay did in there, I did nothing to prevent him.'

'He was your commanding officer.'

'Are you defending him, ma'am?'

'No. The man was a monster even before this particular

incident. But, even if your suspicions are founded, it was he who did it. Not you.'

'I'm sorry, ma'am, but I have to do this. I feel I've been given a second chance. For my own peace of mind, I have to know what happened in that pod.'

Hay smiled sadly. 'Yes. I understand what you feel you must do. One stipulation. You don't do it alone. Let me know when you're ready and I'll go with you. I think that would be appropriate.'

'Thank you, ma'am, I would welcome the company.'

All Major Ellis could hear was a long and very persistent ringing in his ears. Like a com but not like a com. Did someone want him? Was it a telephone? Was it for him? Someone should answer it.

North's face appeared in his vision. 'Are ... all ... Matth ... ? Can ... hear ... thew?'

He tried to speak but nothing came out.

The ringing increased. The pressure in his head was intolerable. This was bad. Because any moment now ...

He turned his head and vomited. The good news was that he felt better almost immediately. The even better news was that none of it went over North. The world was not yet ready for that sort of cataclysm. Blinking to focus, he turned his head back again.

She waggled her jaw and then pointed at him.

He waggled his jaw until his ears popped. There was a rushing, hissing sound and then he could hear. More or less. The world swirled and settled. He could see. More or less.

Having been further from the blast and protected by a couple of doors, Lt North, although shaken, seemed less injured than Ellis. She made a gesture indicative of him staying where he was – as if he had any choice in the matter. Heaving herself to her feet, she staggered a little, limped to the site of the former door, kicked aside the remains and stepped out on to what was left of the wooden veranda. Smoke eddied in the wind. The smell was unpleasant. Especially when you knew what it probably was. Of the helicopter – the primary target? – very little remained. And almost certainly nothing of its former pilot. What was left – a mangled mess of metal – lay on its side in a shallow crater. North could see one twisted rotor. Most of it was still on fire. As was the grass all around the crater. She closed her eyes briefly.

With hands that weren't quite steady, she pulled out her com. 'Mellor? Can you hear me? Report.'

There was no response.

'Chad? Come in. Please. Chad?'

Still no response. Not even any static. The com no longer existed. Nor did its owner.

The police car lay on its roof a considerable distance away. Of the two police officers, the trolley, their evidence – there was no trace at all. Only a distorted piece of metal with one wheel miraculously still attached lying some way off. What was left of the vet was some six feet away from that. And ten feet. And fifteen.

North rubbed her forearm across her eyes and swore very softly. Intending to document the scene for future reference, she pulled out her scratchpad. Unfortunately, despite her best efforts, the screen remained dark. Switching it off and then back on again failed to solve the problem. Sighing, she shoved it back into her knee pocket. This had not been an aerial attack. Surface-to-surface missile was her guess. A one-, possibly two-man device, hastily dismantled and thrown in the back of an unmarked van, could easily be several miles away by now. If their assailants had any sense.

On the other hand, they might not. They might, even at this moment, have detected her movements and be zeroing in for another go. There was nothing North could do about that, so she climbed back into the pavilion through the ex-doorway. Ellis was struggling to sit up. He focused blearily and she shook her head.

'Nothing left, sir. Just a crater and . . . some bits and pieces.'

'All gone?'

'Everything. Including our evidence.'

'Mellor?'

'Him too. I'm sorry.'

Ellis closed his eyes. 'An hour ago he thought he was the coolest person on the planet.'

North said nothing.

'If he'd come in to use the toilet when we arrived, he might still be alive.'

'You don't know that, Matthew,' she said softly. 'And regulations state the chopper should never be left unattended, so if he'd been in here, then I'd have been the one out there. And if it hadn't been me, then it would have been you. And if I hadn't needed the toilet, then we'd have followed the vet out and all of us would now be dead.'

She paused to let that sink in and then said, 'My scratchpad has been damaged. You were nearer the blast so I'm guessing yours isn't working either.'

She was correct. Ellis's scratchpad would never function again.

He made another attempt to get up. 'We need to get out of here. In case they – whoever they are – turn up to make sure.'

'They'll see the evidence is destroyed, sir. What would be the point? And shouldn't we wait for assistance? After a bang like that, I'm certain the local police will be here very soon. They might be on their way already. Shouldn't we wait?'

He held out his hand. 'Are you really so sure the first people to arrive will be friendly?'

She heaved him to his feet. 'Good point, sir. There's a narrow lane behind us with a small copse on the other side. We can wait there to see what happens next. Unless you require medical attention, in which case . . .'

'No, I'm fine.' He cast a glance around. 'Somehow this got out and we don't know who we can trust.'

North nodded. 'I agree, sir. Until we know – until we have some solid evidence – discretion dictates we vacate the area with all speed.'

Ellis tried to nod his head and regretted it. 'Yes. We can speculate later. Sooner or later they'll discover our bodies aren't in the wreckage. We can't hang around here. We shouldn't advertise our presence until we know a little more than we do now. And right now we need to move.'

'Agreed, sir. Lean on me. We'll go out the back way.'

There was a coat miraculously still hanging off a peg by the door. North grabbed it as she passed.

A small room at the back of the pavilion faced away from the blast and was almost undamaged. It smelled strongly of socks and had a window facing in the direction they wanted to go. North pulled out her blaster and dealt with the security mesh over the window. She scrambled out, turned to assist Ellis, and together they lurched across the grass.

She very soon realised they had both been guilty of underestimation. Ellis, of his current physical capability, and North, of his weight, but eventually they reached the shelter of the copse. With a sigh of relief, she lowered him on to a fallen tree and retraced her steps. Partly to check no one was following them and partly to see who would arrive first at the scene of the explosion. Friend or foe?

'Whoever it is, they'll establish a perimeter,' said Ellis, still blinking as he attempted to clear his vision. 'We can't stay here for very long.'

Faintly, in the distance, a siren could be heard. And then another. And then another. A police car, then another one, then a fire engine, then another police car, then an ambulance, then two or three unmarked cars screeched off the road and bumped across the pitch, leaving deep gouges in the soft earth.

'The groundskeeper's going to be cross,' murmured North.

'To say nothing of the crater in the middle of his pitch,' said Ellis. 'Nor the scattered body parts. He'll have other things to worry about than tyre tracks.'

North eyed the milling uniforms. 'They all look genuine enough.'

'They do, don't they?' said Ellis. 'And yet someone murdered our colleague, blew up our chopper, killed two police officers and a vet, and destroyed our only evidence.'

'Not all of it, sir.' She fished under her vest and pulled out the doctor's file Ellis had been reading before the blast.

'Where did you find that?'

'You were lying on it, sir.'

'I expect I used it to cushion my fall,' muttered Ellis. 'What's happening now?'

North squinted through the trees. 'Setting up a perimeter ... tape everywhere ... recording the scene ... talking on their coms ... summoning reinforcements, I expect. Bomb disposal, perhaps? To check out the site before they touch anything. That's what I'd do.' She turned to look at Ellis. 'We must call this in.'

'And we shall – but from a safer distance. Let's go.'

'Anywhere in particular?'

'Away from here, I think.'

Ellis wobbled to his feet and they disappeared further into the trees, emerging on the other side to find themselves in a small fallow field.

'Further,' said Ellis. 'There'll be helicopters and drones and God knows what overflying the area any minute now. We need to be under cover.'

'How are you feeling? How far can you walk?'

'Far enough.'

'Why are we still not calling this in?'

'I suspect by now others will have done that for us. Hay probably knows more of what's going on than we do. We should spend a few minutes taking stock and deciding what to do next. You might want to step back first though – I'm going to be ill again.'

Averting her eyes, North stared around the field. The far corner was occupied by some kind of ramshackle farm building Ellis thought looked ramshackle. Although to his urban eyes, most farm buildings looked ramshackle.

'It's probably locked,' said North as they made their way unsteadily across the field.

It wasn't – but it had, until very recently, housed a large number of hugely incontinent sheep.

'Bloody hell,' said Ellis, carefully lifting a foot. 'What do they feed them around here?'

'Actually, sir, I don't think we smell much better.'

For the first time Ellis became aware of the coat draped around his shoulders. 'What am I wearing?'

'I think it must be the vet's coat. I grabbed it as we left.'

'Well, he won't need it now, poor sod.' He pulled it off and looked at it. 'It's a bit small.' He began to go through the pockets and pulled out the vet's ID, blinking to focus.

'Hm – Ivor David Lewis.' He squinted at North, still slightly blurry in the scheme of things. 'I'll be Mr Lewis and you can be . . .' He eyed her. 'Suzie, his plucky young assistant.'

A nearby mountain did not fall on him but there was a general feeling it should have.

'I have a much better idea,' said North. She took off her vest and put on the coat. It fitted her perfectly. 'I'll be Lewis and you can be Suzie.'

Ellis sighed, recognising the invisible but inevitable path to surrender.

She rummaged through the contents of the doctor's wallet. 'Money – which will come in useful. His citizen's ID authorises him to treat livestock and domestic animals. Not humans so we'll have to resist the urge to remove anyone's appendix. No less than three bank cards. Either he was incredibly wealthy or incredibly broke.'

'He was a vet,' said Ellis, still trying to clear his ears by waggling his jaw. 'I think we can guess.'

'His citizen's ID card has his address.'

Ellis shook his head and regretted it again. 'We can't go there. The police will be informing his next of kin. We can use the money but nothing else.'

North looked at him. 'Someone will have contacted the Time Police by now. They probably think we're dead. We have to call Hay. Carefully.'

'Yes. Someone knew exactly where and when to direct that missile, didn't they?'

'Someone at TPHQ?'

Ellis dragged his mind away from Lt Filbert and the revelation of his treachery. 'I don't think so. If that collar was still transmitting – and we've no reason to believe it wasn't – then the mystery is solved. I just wish we'd had a chance to examine it more closely.'

'Well, we have Mr Lewis's images,' said North, flourishing the folder. 'Either the mechs or IT will probably be able to make some educated guesses. And if whoever it was *didn't* track the dinosaur through its collar, that still leaves either or both of the police officers as possible sources. Or Lewis's staff. Or the kids who found the body. Perhaps the parents called the local news service. It could have been any of those, but most likely, I think, are the original owners of the dinosaur and its collar. They must have been desperate to get it back but failing that . . .' She made a gesture. 'They destroyed all trace.'

'Big mistake on their part to kill a TPO,' said Ellis grimly.

'Yes – I suspect that wasn't the original plan. No one in their right mind would kill a TPO and not expect the wrath of God to fall down upon them. But, once they knew we knew, of course . . .' She looked at him. 'So, obviously, we avoid going through the normal channels.'

'Precisely. We don't know who might be eavesdropping. There could be a mobile listening station anywhere around here.' He thought for a moment. 'She's going to kill me. If anyone asks, I have concussion.'

'Actually, I think that is very likely,' said North. 'You do still look a bit wonky. Shall I do it?'

'The secret of my success, Lieutenant, is never asking anyone to do what I wouldn't do myself.'

Ellis pulled out his com. Adopting what he fondly imagined was a Welsh accent – and which would almost certainly provide a more than valid excuse for yet another Welsh uprising – he asked to be put through to Commander Hay's personal channel.

Far away in Commander Hay's office, the door opened to reveal Captain Farenden.

'A call for you, ma'am. On your personal line.'

'I'm rather busy, Charlie. Did the caller say what they wanted?'

'He identified himself as your favourite nephew, ma'am. Apparently he and his companion . . . Suzie . . . have suffered a minor mishap which has left them with scant resources.'

Hay stared at him. 'My favourite nephew?'

Captain Farenden was openly grinning. 'His exact words, ma'am.'

She picked up the receiver. 'Hello . . . nephew?'

Major Ellis's voice was plainly heard. 'Auntie Mary – how are you? Yes, Suzie and I are absolutely fine, thank you. She sends her love and asks if you're remembering to take your tablets.'

In the barn, Lt North began to prepare a statement in her

defence, the gist of which would be that she'd never seen Major Ellis before in her entire life.

He continued to deepen his already very deep hole. 'Sadly we've had a bit of a bump, Auntie Mary, and not only lost our transport but the driver, too. And some others were involved, as well.'

'That is unfortunate.'

'Yes. The thing is . . .' The word *sweetie* hung on his lips but couldn't somehow force its way into the real world. 'Obviously Suzie and I don't want to cut short our holiday, but we've been left without basic requirements. Accommodation, transportation and the like. Could you possibly manage . . . ? Yes, that would be lovely. Thank you so much . . . Yes, we're fine here. Yes, there was a bit of a bang and we're a little shaken, obviously, but there's absolutely no reason we shouldn't continue with the holiday. Other than the lack of wherewithal, of course, so thank you for taking care of that for us . . . d—'

The word *darling* danced tantalisingly across his mind only to be clubbed firmly into non-existence by his survival instincts.

'Well, this is all very unfortunate.' Hay's voice was brisk. 'Obviously I'm glad you and . . . Suzie are unhurt, but tell me, did you actually get to see any of the sights? Before your unfortunate accident, of course.'

'We did, yes. Although only very briefly.'

'And were they everything you thought they would be?'

Ellis nodded. 'In my opinion – yes.'

'How . . . interesting.'

'Yes, indeed. And I've been thinking – not surprisingly, everything's very Welsh here. Including the fauna. I was wondering if . . . if Cousin Max is still around somewhere. You know, since she's such a wildlife expert. It would be lovely to see her again after so long, don't you think? And then she can visit you afterwards and you can have a lovely catch-up.'

He grinned at North, who rolled her eyes.

'As a matter of fact,' said Hay, 'Cousin Max might already be on the way. Keep your eyes open for her.'

'I shall. Anyway, must go – I think Suzie needs the facility. Byeeee.'

He closed his com.

North regarded him with horror. 'You should be aware that when repercussions rain down upon you – and they will, believe me – you are completely, totally and irrevocably on your own. I have never seen you before. Not in all my life. Ever.'

Ellis leaned back against an unspecified piece of agricultural equipment and closed his eyes. 'With luck I'll die here and it won't be a problem.'

Commander Hay and Captain Farenden looked at each other. 'It would seem rumours of their deaths have been greatly exaggerated.'

'Except for Mellor, of course, ma'am.'

'Yes. Except for Mellor. I shall break the news personally to his next of kin.'

'A sister, I believe. They were very close.'

'Yes. Obviously that takes priority over everything. I've already despatched Varma to poke around, but in the meantime can you ask Major Callen if he could spare me a moment, please.'

'He's not in the building, ma'am.'

'Ah. Do we know where . . . ?'

'No, ma'am. Even his own people don't know where he's gone.'

Hay nodded. None of that was unusual. Hunters came and went as they pleased. And as head of the Hunter division, Callen answered to no one except herself. And occasionally, not even to her.

Other heads of department, however, could not just come or go as the fancy took them. Varma had spent a busy half-hour briefing Wu, who would take charge of security during her absence, then settled a few minor administrative issues, and finally caught up with Tucker in the Pod Bay where he was loading the last of their kit.

'What progress?'

He picked up a box of rations. 'With Sawney? Gabbled like an idiot to anyone who would listen. Couldn't get it out fast enough. Clever – offering him a choice like that. Even with certain death on the cards, he'd never have said a word, but putting him in competition with Hooke . . .'

'Hooke's dead.'

'Yeah – I know. We all know.'

'Except Sawney.'

'Ah. About that . . .'

Varma looked up from checking her weapons. 'Etok told him?'

'Only afterwards.'

She blinked. 'What did Sawney say?'

'Not a lot. Well, he threw himself at Etok, of course. Which was a big mistake. Wu went to help, and the next moment, Sawney's flat on the floor minus his front teeth and with his nose pointing from east to west instead of north to south. No one has any idea how that happened,' he added piously.

Varma grinned. 'It wasn't you, then?'

'No. Although I would have. As would anyone in TPHQ. I wasn't around when he did what he did to Lockland, but she has a surprising number of friends here.'

Judging it best to change the subject, Varma surveyed the pod. Medical supplies, maps, outdoor survival gear and rations were all stacked neatly inside the appropriate lockers.

'This is good work,' said Varma, eyeing the pod's crowded but tidy interior.

Tucker bent for the last box. 'Yeah . . . well . . . I've done this sort of thing before.'

'One day we really are going to have to sit down and have a long talk about your skill set.'

He straightened up. 'I'd rather we didn't.'

They looked at each other. Varma – a member of an organisation normally on the side of the angels but sometimes not. And Tucker – a former illegal never knowingly on the side of the angels but now finding he might be. There had to be some common ground in there somewhere.

Captain Farenden tapped on Hay's open door.

'Officers Lockland and Parrish for you, ma'am. They have been briefed and are fully aware of the situation.'

Hay turned from the window and got straight to it. 'I'm sending you to St Mary's.'

Luke and Jane, both of whom had been expecting to be drafted into the investigation in Wales, blinked in surprise.

'You will present my compliments to Dr Bairstow and request the loan of Dr Maxwell.'

Luke ventured a cautious question. 'For the purposes of . . . ?'

'Technical advice. She probably knows more about dinosaurs than anyone else available at such short notice. Be polite but firm. And speed is of the essence. I'm putting boots on the ground in Wales asap and I want Maxwell there with them.'

'Suppose St Mary's won't let her go?'

'If you are bright enough to make the request in her presence, then I suspect she will move heaven and earth to accompany you.'

'She might not be there, ma'am,' ventured Jane.

'Then wherever she is, you will go and get her. Bottom line, officers – do not return without her. Dismissed.'

'I wonder what we'll find at St Mary's,' said Luke, as the lift doors closed behind them and they headed to the Pod Bay. 'I mean, it could be anything. They could be on fire – perhaps there's a dragon in the cellar – or they're re-enacting some titanic battle from history and laid waste to half the county. You really never know what you're going to get with them, do you?'

'No,' said Jane, with vivid memories of past visits. Bashford slowly drowning in R&D. St Mary's really quite spectacular but ultimately doomed attempt at Archimedes' Claw, when Bashford would have drowned again had not their Head of Security, Captain Hyssop, donned her frequently used Health and Safety officer's hat and called a halt to the entire enterprise. The protests had been many and vigorous but there was no doubt she'd saved lives that day.

Jane went to seat herself at the console.

'I'll handle this,' said Luke, nudging her out of the way. 'I am team leader.'

'Um . . .' said Jane doubtfully. After all, Hay had said speed was of the essence and Luke's encounters with the pod's AI were never speedy. Nor were they particularly productive. Their whole relationship was a bit of a mystery – no one else ever had any problems.

'Pod,' declaimed Luke in an especially authoritative manner.

The pod chirped helpfully.

'Commence . . .'

'I regret I am unable to comply.'

Jane made herself comfortable.

'Why the fire truck not this time?'

'You are not authorised to use this pod.'

Luke stared enquiringly at Jane, who sighed. 'Did you renew your authorisation?'

'When?'

'Last week. Everyone got a message. Renew your authorisation within seven days or risk being locked out.'

'I didn't see that.'

'Did you look?'

'Well, not specifically, no. Pod . . .'

The pod chirped helpfully.

'. . . renew my authorisation and commence . . .'

'I regret I am unable to comply.'

'You have to do it in IT,' said Jane helpfully.

'Did you do yours?'

'Of course,' said Jane, quite shocked that anyone could think she would be guilty of not complying with a specific order.

Luke sighed. 'We don't have time for this.'

The pod maintained an unhelpful silence.

'Pod.'

The pod chirped helpfully.

'Initiate emergency override.'

Nothing happened.

'Luke, you'd better let me . . .'

'No, Jane. I'm the team leader and this thing will do as it's told. Pod . . .'

This time the pod didn't even bother to chirp. Helpfully or otherwise.

'Luke . . .'

'Bloody hell, Jane . . .'

Jane sighed. 'Pod.'

The pod chirped. Helpfully.

'Commence jump procedures.'

'Jump procedures commenced.'

'Thank you.'

'Jane, I've told you – you don't have to say . . .'

'It's polite.'

'It's a *machine*. It does as it's told. Honestly, Jane, you can't ever let these things have the upper hand. Have you never seen a *Terminator* movie? Believe me, it's only a matter of time before Skynet . . .'

At some point in his monologue, the world flickered and they were off.

The library had library written all over it. Literally. And in several languages, too. A multilingual library.

Ellis squinted. 'I think I might have forgotten how to read. What does that word say?'

'Llyfrgell, sir.'

'How did you manage that first syllable?'

'Aim for a splashy sound behind your teeth.'

Ellis stuck a finger in his ear. 'I'm experiencing difficulties with my hearing, as well.'

'It's pronounced Cluvrageth.'

Ellis blinked. 'No, still not working properly.'

North turned him gently to face another sign. 'There, sir.'

'Ah. Library. Well done, North. Are those steps?'

'I think it's the disabled ramp for you, sir. To your right. Mind the giant pillars. Whoops. Never mind.'

'Why are we here again?'

'Maps, sir. Neither of our scratchpads are working. Through here.'

They found themselves in a long hall with doors opening off. The reference library was situated behind the fiction section. The junior section was on the other side of the hall.

'This way,' said Ellis, setting off in the wrong direction.

The children's area was a large rectangular space full of brightly coloured cushions, spacemen and – ironically – dinosaurs. A giant circular seat ran around the middle, packed with children and their custodians. In the centre, a member of staff was reading something relating to an unspecified number of Billy Goats Gruff. And a bridge. And a troll.

'Who's that trip-trapping over my bridge,' roared the librarian/troll.

'It's me, the smallest Billy Goat Gruff,' quavered the librarian/troll/Billy Goat Gruff.

'Actually,' said Ellis, swaying like a poplar in a gentle breeze, 'I've always wondered why the three Billy Goats Gruff didn't all cross together. It makes much more sense if you have a troll living under your bridge, don't you think? Tallest at the front – shortest at the back – and charge.' He addressed the librarian. 'Or send for the council. Or the police. Not us, though. We don't do trolls. Except for clean-up crews, perhaps.'

North smiled brightly and took his arm. 'Now then, Mr Ellis, we don't want to interrupt the nice story. Let's find some pretty pictures to look at today, shall we?' Lowering her voice, she said confidentially to the assembled group, 'It's his day out today. He looks forward to it so much.'

Everyone nodded understandingly and she shunted a suddenly indignant Major Ellis back across the hall and into the reference area. Seating him at a table, she disappeared in search of the relevant Ordnance Survey maps which she spread out in front of them.

'Here,' said North. 'We're here.' Her finger traced its way across the map. 'And there's the river.'

Ellis leaned forwards, blinking hard. 'I can't say that word, either. Where are the vowels?'

'That's all right – I can.'

'You speak Welsh?'

'My mother was advisor to the ambassador for Wales before he died. The ambassador insisted all his staff had to have at least basic Welsh. Mama practised on me.'

'Oh,' said Ellis uncertainly. His head was thumping. 'I think I might just close my eyes for a . . .'

'If you fall asleep, I'll take you straight to the nearest hospital.' She paused. 'And leave you there while I look for dinosaurs all by myself.'

Ellis grinned. It was a somewhat lopsided effort. 'I wish I didn't love you so much.'

There was a short but somehow very significant pause.

'Anyway,' said North, bending over the map again. 'This is where the body was discovered, so if we look upriver . . .'

Ellis discreetly spread out the images from the doctor's file. On the other side of the hall, the Billy Goats Gruff were really getting stuck into the troll.

'It's not a large river.'

'No. I suggest we start where the body was found and then walk upriver until we find something interesting.'

'Good plan,' agreed Ellis, wondering how far he would get. 'And with luck, our new accommodation should have arrived by now.' He picked up the map and made vague attempts to fold it back to its original shape. 'I suppose we do have to return this.'

'We do,' said North, taking the map off him and refolding it in an irritatingly efficient fashion. 'What sort of person steals from a library?'

'I am a Time Police officer,' said Ellis with dignity. 'My evil knows no bounds.'

North sighed and went off to return the map. Which just goes to show that no good deed ever goes unpunished. From behind the shelves, a woman's voice said, 'Why are you wearing Mr Lewis's coat?'

There was a moment's frozen silence. North honestly could not think of a good reason why she would be wearing a dead man's coat.

'Who *are* you?' said the woman. Her name badge read Lily. She peered over her armful of books. 'Why is that man asleep on the table?'

North made a split-second decision. The authorities were on site. News of the explosion and deaths would soon be all over town. She would have to reveal her identity. She would be a person of interest. Valuable time would be wasted while she assisted the authorities with their enquiries.

Slipping off the coat, she smiled, draped it over a nearby chair, turned and ran, remembering to grab Major Ellis on the way out.

'I'm quite hungry,' he said as they made their way briskly along the pavement. In the distance, a plume of smoke still hung in the sky. People were gathering in small groups, muttering and looking, but so far there was no immediate alarm from the local population. 'Is that normal?'

North smiled through her sudden thumping headache. 'I believe humans eat, yes.'

'I mean a post-explosion appetite.'

North frowned. 'I don't know. Let's feed you and see what happens, shall we?'

She pulled out a fistful of money.

Ellis blinked. 'Did you get that from Lewis's wallet?'

'He doesn't need it any longer and we can reimburse the family later.' She paused and sniffed the air. 'Fish and chips all right?'

Ellis regarded her. 'Have you ever actually *eaten* fish and chips?'

'Of course I have – I'm from St Mary's. Every Friday night – movie night with fish and chips.'

'Oh.' He considered this as they approached the chippie. 'Do you miss them?'

'Oh no – there are still plenty of holos and old-style movies around.'

'I meant – do you miss St Mary's?'

She said nothing.

He stopped walking and took a second or two to focus on her. 'Really? Celia? Are you homesick?'

She nudged him forwards again. 'No, of course not. And I certainly don't miss the chaos and confusion. The Time Police are so much better organised. Efficient. Effective . . .' She tailed away.

'Except . . . ?'

'Nothing. Except nothing.'

'Celia, are you . . . ? Don't you want to . . . ?' He found himself unable to utter the unutterable.

'No. Perhaps a little. No. Yes. But no.'

'Well, now you sound just like Maxwell.'

'God forbid.'

He stood still again. 'Celia, do you and I need to talk?'

She looked up at him. 'As Matthew or Major Ellis?'

'Either. Both.'

'Now *you* sound like Maxwell.'

'Don't change the subject. Is there a problem? You're doing well with the Time Police. You've been promoted in near record time. You run your own section. You haven't so much carved yourself a place as hewn it from solid rock. I thought you liked it with us. What's the problem?'

'There isn't one.'

'Do you need to spend more time with your family? In your own time? Because that can be arranged.'

There was a long pause. 'Mama isn't getting any better.'

'Lady Blackbourne? Is she ill?'

'She's been ill for a long time.'

'I'm so sorry. I had no idea.'

'It's not physical.'

A long pause while Ellis wondered whether or not to ask.

Looking everywhere but at him, North said, 'She's taken to writing to Chuffy again.'

For a moment he couldn't remember who Chuffy was, and then . . .

'Your youngest brother. The one who . . . ?'

'Drowned, yes. She would write to us all every Friday night.' She noted his look of bafflement. 'When we were at school.'

Ellis opened his mouth to say he'd forgotten the aristocracy's habit of farming out their offspring to be educated at a distance and decided against it. None of his business anyway. Only as far as it affected Celia.

They'd reached the chippie.

'Oh,' said North. 'A bit of a queue. Wait here. Do not wander off.'

Ellis leaned against a lamp post and stared blearily at his boots until, surprisingly quickly, North was back clutching a fragrant package.

'That was quick.'

'For some reason they shunted me to the front of the queue. I didn't argue. Here.' She handed him the hot parcel. 'There was only enough money for one portion.'

'Then we share,' said Ellis. 'As we share everything.'

'It's all right,' said North. 'I'm not hungry. Come on. You can eat as we go.'

Luke and Jane landed – eventually – at the Institute of Historical Research at St Mary's Priory. On the South Lawn, to be precise. Luke was still muttering to himself as Jane shut down the pod.

'Seriously, Jane, our AI is . . .'

'Just go to IT, ask for Lt Fanboten, and apologise profusely. You've been busy, etc. Can they please renew your authorisation. And buying them a drink might be a good idea. In fact, you could probably get Gomez to do it on the quiet if you took her out to dinner first. Just make sure your blonde in Logistics doesn't find out. Or your brunette in Logistics, either. I know I keep saying this, Luke, but do you honestly think women don't talk to each other?'

Luke eyed her and then looked away again. 'Actually, Jane, I'm not doing that sort of thing any longer.'

'Why not?'

Luke found something on the console to stare at. 'Well, you know, it's not very nice and . . . you know . . . I . . .'

'Good heavens. Are you in love or something?'

Luke flushed slightly. 'Of course not. What a ridiculous thing to say.'

'It's not Imogen Farnborough, is it? Don't you think she's been through enough?'

'I . . . no . . .' He drew a deep breath. 'Actually, Jane . . .'

'Here comes Captain Hyssop,' said Jane. 'Play nicely, Luke. Remember Hay's words. We can't go back without Maxwell.'

'Mm,' said Luke, pulling himself together. 'With me, Jane.'

'Well, there isn't anyone else here for you to be with, is there?' said Bolshy Jane crossly. 'What's up with him?'

'Shut up,' said Jane, and she and Luke stepped outside into the sunshine to meet St Mary's Head of Security, Captain Hyssop, just as something huge and pink hurtled through the air, sailed over the pod roof – clearing it by inches – and thudded into the ground not ten feet away.

'What the . . . ?' said Luke, adopting the traditional Time Police defensive crouch.

A number of voices shouted at them to watch out.

'A bit bloody late now,' he shouted back.

'Is that a pig?' enquired Jane. 'Where's its head?'

'I don't really think the whereabouts of its head is the question *du jour*,' said Luke, poking the corpse with his foot. 'More important is *why* are headless pigs flying through the air?'

'Well, this is St Mary's.'

'Do you think it's some kind of social comment. You know – Time Police – pigs – that sort of thing?'

'A bit subtle for St Mary's, don't you think?'

'True. Look out – here's Hyssop. Be polite, Jane. You know what you're like.'

Jane rolled her eyes.

Captain Hyssop stood before them. Square, stocky and

uncompromising, with her hand resting lightly on the stun gun at her hip.

'Good morning,' said Luke, attempting to project charm and an engaging personality. 'Um . . . what's going on?'

He was wasting his time. With the charm and engaging personality, that is. Long years heading up the Security Section at St Mary's had rendered Captain Hyssop impervious to both.

'Field trials for a newly constructed trebuchet.'

'Oh,' said Luke innocently. 'We thought it was Flying Pig Day at St Mary's. Or some sort of religious ceremony, perhaps. Or possibly . . .'

Jane nudged him into silence and asked, 'Why a pig?'

'They couldn't – fortunately – get a cow.'

'Were they actually aiming at us? Good shot if so.'

Projecting massive patience – although whether with her colleagues, the Time Police – or even the pig – Captain Hyssop informed them the target had been the small island at the far end of the lake, pointing in a direction diametrically opposed to the flying pig's former trajectory.

'How interesting,' said Luke carefully. 'Well, we'd like to speak with Dr Bairstow, please.'

She stared, stony-faced. 'One moment.'

She stepped aside and opened her com. No word of apology or excuse. Jane remembered Max once describing Hyssop as . . . well, *a bit rude* was probably what she had meant to say, but Jane knew from Matthew that Hyssop had been Major Guthrie's recommendation. Rumour had it those had been almost his dying words, as the Time Police had pulled him out of his crashed pod in Constantinople. His actual dying words had been something along the lines of never letting the idiots get the upper hand, and Hyssop had certainly taken them to heart.

Closing her com, she sighed in a long-suffering manner and flagged down Mr Lindstrom, who had been attempting to pass unnoticed with an armful of cabbages. 'Send Cox over here, will you?'

Mr Lindstrom dropped a cabbage. 'Still in Sick Bay. His foot's turned a funny colour.'

'Glass?'

Mr Lindstrom's efforts to retrieve the first cabbage caused him to drop two more. 'The counterweight caught him a glancing blow. He says he's fine, but . . .'

'Evans?'

Another cabbage dropped to the ground and began to roll away. Out of the kindness of her heart, Jane picked it up and gave it back to him.

'Thank you. Evans is on assignment, ma'am.'

Hyssop sighed again. 'Oh – yes. Why do I have to do everything around here?'

Mr Lindstrom blinked. 'You're Head of Security, ma'am.'

'Are you trying to be funny?'

Another cabbage bit the dust. 'Absolutely not, ma'am.'

'Send over someone from the History Department, then.'

'They're still in the water, ma'am.'

Luke picked up two cabbages and carefully placed them in Mr Lindstrom's arms.

Hyssop scowled. 'Still? Where are the rescue boats?'

Jane carefully placed the final cabbage on top of the pile. Everyone held their breath but the load seemed stable.

'They sank, ma'am. Along with Mr Bashford.'

'You can't think how tempted I am just to let the whole bloody lot of them drown. All right, do what you can with life jackets and buoyancy aids. If any of them give you any trouble, then throw them back. And the next time anyone proposes something this stupid, inform me first so I can shoot them and save us all a great deal of trouble.'

Mr Lindstrom blinked. A deer caught in car headlights.

'Move!'

Mr Lindstrom moved, shedding his load as he went.

'Other people leave trails of breadcrumbs,' said Luke to Jane. 'Trust St Mary's to do it with cabbages.'

Hyssop scowled at them. 'Do you have an appointment?'

'Not as such, no. It's a bit of an emergency.'

'Names?'

'You know who we are. Officers Parrish and Lockland.'

She held out her hand. 'ID?'

'Seriously,' demanded Luke. 'You honestly think random people just drop by on the off-chance? Dressed as Time Police and with their own Time Police pod? And at least one of us has been here before.'

Hyssop glanced at Jane. 'Nice to see you again, Officer Lockland. ID, please.'

Jane handed hers over. Luke sighed and did the same.

'Thank you,' said Hyssop and subjected them to intense scrutiny as per Security Section regulations. As written by her. She handed them back. 'Follow me, please.'

They crossed the grass and climbed the steps to the front door. As they did so, something heavy thudded to the ground behind them. Quite closely behind them. Both Luke and Jane made it a point of honour not to turn around and Hyssop gave no sign she was even aware of this latest airborne porcine event.

St Mary's Priory was an ancient building, currently looking even older than it actually was – a sad circumstance normally blamed on its current inhabitants – the Institute of Historical Research. Or, if you wanted a more accurate designation – a bunch of tea-sodden disaster magnets riding the catastrophe curve and frequently falling at the first fence.

Entering through the hefty doors, the interior smelled of damp, dust, stricken historians and, occasionally, if she was moulting, Angus.

The Great Hall was nearly empty. Normally, of course, it would be filled with people doing God knows what – history things of some kind, Luke assumed – and making a great deal of noise about it.

'I often wonder what on earth they find to do all day long,' he whispered to Jane. 'I mean, seriously, how many times can you go back to study the Battle of Hastings?'

'Only once,' said Jane calmly. 'You can never be in the same time twice, remember?'

Luke sighed, expressing silent disbelief that anyone would want to be there even once. As they made their way towards the stairs, a door opened and Chief Farrell appeared, tapping at his scratchpad.

He looked up and frowned. As always, Jane was struck by how normal he looked. Normal being somewhat unusual for St Mary's.

'Is something wrong? Where's Matthew?'

'Nothing wrong, sir. And Matthew is absolutely fine.' Luke paused. Honesty compelled him to qualify this remark. 'Well, he was when we left. Of course, it's Matthew, so he could easily have been sucked into another dimension by now. You never really know with him, do you?'

Leon smiled. 'True. I suspect it's hereditary. Nice to see you again, Jane. Good morning, Captain. I've just sent you the monthly pod security report.'

Captain Hyssop nodded. 'Thank you, Chief.' She motioned to Luke and Jane. 'This way.'

They followed Captain Hyssop up the stairs and along the Gallery.

Dr Bairstow stood up as they entered his office. 'Good morning, officers. How may St Mary's be of assistance?'

'We'd like to borrow Dr Maxwell, if you please,' Luke said politely.

'And bring her back again,' added Jane, because it went without saying that the Time Police would be even more anxious to return Dr Maxwell than St Mary's would be to have her back. Dr Maxwell was not classed among those whose influence on the universe was benign.

Dr Bairstow regarded them. 'For the purposes of . . . ?'

'Her expertise, sir. We have . . . we did have . . . and for all we know, we may have more . . .' Luke stopped and began again. 'A dead dinosaur has been discovered. In Wales. It hadn't been dead for long. The team despatched to investigate were attacked. As you can imagine, we are keen to get to the bottom of this and Commander Hay feels Dr Maxwell is the ideal person to assist us.'

The entire universe blinked at the thought of Dr Maxwell being the ideal person to assist anyone with anything, and then bravely carried on.

As did Luke. 'So we hope very much that you can spare her for a couple of days, sir. To lend her expertise.'

Dr Bairstow sighed. 'Normally I would be more than happy to cooperate with our colleagues in the Time Police. I regret to inform you, however, that Dr Maxwell is currently out on assignment.'

'Really, sir. Where?'

'Ancient Rome. Dr Maxwell is heading up the team endeavouring to ascertain the fate of Romulus.'

'The founder of Rome?' said Jane. Just to be sure.

'That is correct, Officer Lockland. A refreshing change to find a TPO with a knowledge of History.'

'Sir, if you can let us have the coordinates, we would be quite happy to go after Dr Maxwell. With your permission, of course.' Luke paused and then added, 'There were fatalities, sir. And Major Ellis and Lt North were both injured in the blast.'

Dr Bairstow frowned. 'Fatalities, you say?'

'Our helicopter pilot, sir. He and his chopper were blown out of existence. And the two policemen and the attending veterinarian did not survive, either.'

'That is unfortunate. Please convey our best wishes for a speedy recovery to Major Ellis and Miss North. I beg your pardon, Lt North.'

'I shall be happy to do so, sir.'

Dr Bairstow picked up his pen again. 'Captain Hyssop will provide you with the coordinates.'

'Thank you, sir.'

That had been considerably easier than Luke had anticipated. They did not, however, escape entirely scot-free. Without looking up, Dr Bairstow continued, 'Please ensure Dr Maxwell is returned safely to us. It would be unfortunate – for the Time Police, that is – should circumstances force me to despatch Chief Officer Farrell to TPHQ to retrieve his wife.'

Luke stood to attention. 'Clearly understood, sir.'

'I am delighted to hear you say so, Officer Parrish. Thank you, Captain Hyssop.'

10

Back in the pod, Jane began laying in the appropriate coordinates for Ancient Rome.

'You do realise,' she said chattily, 'that should anything happen to me then you will be stranded there forever. This pod isn't speaking to you.'

'I swear, Jane, the second we're back in the Pod Bay, I will rip the sodding AI out by its peripherals, dangle it over a vat of boiling acid for a few very enjoyable moments and then let go.'

'Well, perhaps, in future, when you're instructed to do something, you'll actually do it.'

'I think we both know that's very unlikely. Are we all set?'

'Well, I am.'

'Then let's go.'

Ancient Rome. The Field of Mars. 5th July 717BC.

Luke peered at the screen. 'Are we in the right place?'

'We must be. St Mary's wouldn't give us the wrong coordinates. Would they?'

'They don't love us, you know. Any more than we love them. I suspect we're lucky not to have landed inside an active Vesuvius. Why is it so dark?'

Jane, who had been interrogating the AI, finished scribbling in her brand-new trusty notebook. 'Well, according to our admittedly scant historical records, Romulus was reviewing his troops, here, on the Campus Martius, when a great storm blew up. Opinion is divided over whether it was just a really bad thunderstorm or an eclipse of the sun. Anyway, when the lights came back on, Romulus had vanished.'

'Where did he go?'

'No one knows. He was never seen again. Except as a god.'

'What?'

Jane squinted at the information on their screen. 'He came back as a god. According to someone called Julius Proculus. Or possibly Proculus Julius.'

'How likely is that?'

'Well, the alternative theory is that he disappeared into the nearby Temple of Vulcan, was murdered there by a group of senators, swiftly dismembered, and tiny pieces of his body were smuggled out under their clothing and discreetly disposed of later. So no one ever knew what became of him.'

'Lovely. And presumably that's why they're here? St Mary's, I mean.'

Jane nodded. 'Interesting, though, don't you think? Where *did* Romulus go?'

'Someone lured him away somewhere – under cover of the storm or eclipse – stabbed him, he fell backwards into a ready-made grave, they shovelled the earth in, strolled back around the side of a building and carried on as normal.'

'Well, yes,' said Jane, slightly disappointed. 'That is one possibility, I suppose, although I must say I do prefer the vanished-without-trace story. Are you ready? There's a strong pod signature about a hundred yards away in that direction.'

She and Luke wrapped themselves in their all-purpose, all-century black cloaks.

'You do know St Mary's laughs at us for wearing these, don't you?' said Luke as they exited the pod.

Jane had a very strong suspicion St Mary's laughed at them whatever they were wearing.

'Bloody hell,' said Luke, pulling his boot out of a puddle of foetid water. 'It's a swamp.'

'What were you expecting?'

'I don't know. Some sort of parade ground, perhaps. This is where the army gathers, isn't it?'

'Well, it will be drained one day,' said Jane, consulting her trusty notebook again. 'Just not at the moment. The city is in its infancy.'

'They're over there,' said Luke, who had been staring around. 'Walk slowly, Jane. It's St Mary's – we don't want them accidentally shooting us.'

'I don't think they arm themselves,' said Jane, setting off. 'Stun guns, perhaps.'

'How do they get themselves out of trouble?'

'Matthew says mostly they just run like hell.'

A single, flat-roofed, apparently stone-built hut stood some one hundred yards away. Scruffy and inconspicuous among clumps of tall reeds and coarse grass, it blended perfectly with its surroundings.

The door opened as they approached.

'I thought it was you two,' said Max. 'What on earth are you doing here?'

Luke gestured around. 'We've come to take you away from all this.'

She looked over their shoulders. 'Where's Matthew? Is he hurt? Is it serious?'

'He's fine. Well, no, he's broken his arm and a horse stood on him at Balaclava, but otherwise he's fine. Or will be. He's on light duties at the moment so they've shoved him into the Map Room to play with the Time Map. *He'll* be perfectly safe, but I fear for the future of the universe.'

'So why are you here?'

'We've come for you.'

'Oh God, I'm not under arrest again, am I? This is getting old, guys.'

'No, we need your help.'

'Sorry – no can do. Busy at the moment. Rome's founding father is about to disappear under mysterious circs. We're placing bets on whether it's murder, accident, divine intervention or him running away for some reason.'

Luke grinned. 'But we can offer you danger, death . . . *and dinosaurs.*'

Max hesitated. 'Tempting, but I really want to know what happened to Romulus, and if I leave now, I can't ever come back.'

'What's going on?' said Evans, appearing behind Max.

'I've been offered another job.'

Evans blinked. 'Good heavens. Come inside, all of you.'

They shuffled into the pod. Present were Max, Evans from the Security Section, and two others.

'Trainees,' said Max, gesturing. 'Which is why I can't leave. Sorry – otherwise I'd be there like a shot.'

'You can do both,' said Luke. 'After all, it's not when you depart – it's when you arrive that's important.'

Evans frowned. 'Not sure my boss will be happy with this.'

'Captain Hyssop knows all about it,' Jane assured him. 'It was she who gave us your coordinates. On Dr Bairstow's instructions, of course.'

Luke nodded. 'Finish your biz here and then we'll whip Dr Maxwell off to TPHQ for our own sinister purposes, which, as I said, will include but are not limited to, danger, discomfort, dinosaurs and a painful and messy death.'

Max's eyes sparkled. 'Deal.'

Evans closed his eyes and sighed.

'Right,' said Max, who appeared to have been interrupted in the middle of her briefing. 'And finally. Trainees will remain with the pod. You will not wander off under any circumstances. Otherwise Mr Evans will hack off your legs at the knees and leave you to hobble home on bloody stumps. Your safety and well-being are always our prime concern.'

Both trainees were looking a trifle nervous. Jane privately thought it was nice, just for once, that she and Luke weren't the lowest and most inexperienced life forms present.

All four of St Mary's personnel were wearing woodland camouflage. Sensible, Jane had to admit. The greens and browns would merge perfectly with the landscape outside.

Max nodded. 'Whenever you're ready, Mr Evans.'

Evans opened the door and, cautiously, they stepped outside.

The smell of stagnant water hung in the heavy air, along with the woodsmoke from countless household hearths, cooking fires and temples drifting across from the nearby city of Rome. Not much of which was visible from here, partly because they were so low down, but mostly because of the approaching storm. Low cloud was rolling across the landscape, trapping the summer heat.

This was a very flat area with a lot of standing water. Dark brown pools were linked by small, sluggish streams slowly seeping towards the River Tiber not far away on their left. Jane knew Rome was a city of seven hills but most of them were barely visible at the moment. The sky was darkening and the air felt close and oppressive.

'It's going to piss down any moment now,' said Max – a typical St Mary's weather forecast. She fingered Luke's cloak. 'Hope your dress is waterproof.'

She scrambled up on to the roof. Luke scowled, heroically refrained from shooting her, and followed her up.

Their surroundings were so flat that being on the pod roof lifted them up sufficiently for quite a good view.

'Quickly,' said Max, as they wriggled underneath a camouflage tarpaulin.

'So – what exactly happens here today?' enquired Luke, propping himself up on his elbows.

'Well, Romulus will turn up any moment now. To inspect the troops gathering over there to our left. There's a terrible storm. Sensible people run away. Romulus and his accompanying senators will seek shelter in the Temple of Vulcan. That's it over there.'

She pointed almost directly ahead of them.

Jane peered out into the gloom. Anyone expecting a magnificent temple constructed of painted marble would be disappointed. Imposing it was not. It certainly wasn't tall – she suspected the ground was too boggy to bear much weight.

Anything substantial would surely slowly sink into the ooze. Nevertheless, the prototype Roman temple was here for all to see. A flight of steep steps ran at right angles to a wide, flat platform at the front with four fat, fairly squat pillars guarding the interior. Which was very dark. As was everything else on this overcast day.

Luke squinted too. 'That's where he's killed, is it?'

'Well, accounts vary,' Max said. 'Some say he was out in the open when he was enveloped in a black cloud and never seen again. Balance that story against a sudden downpour, a load of very important people seeking shelter in the nearest – the only – building in the vicinity, and Romulus disappearing forever.'

'How could they hope to get away with it with all these soldiers here?'

'Well, on a normal day, the troops would probably have hung around afterwards, doing soldier things – you know, reunions with old comrades, telling tall tales, whipping out a flask or two . . . but the terrible weather will put a stop to all that. They'll all head for the nearest caupona, and apart from his personal escort, Romulus will be on his own.'

'Hmm . . .' said Luke. 'And vulnerable.'

'I'm offering odds of two to one on him being shoved into the temple and chopped up into tiny pieces,' said Evans. 'Ladies and gentlemen, place your bets.'

The two trainees nodded.

'I'll take that,' said Luke. 'What about you, Jane?'

Jane looked at Max.

'I'm going with vanishing in a puff of black smoke,' said Max. 'Just for the sheer hell of it.'

'Me too,' said Bolshy Jane.

Evans cast a worried glance up at the sky. 'This is building up to be one hell of a storm.'

He was right. In a normal world, clouds scud across the sky from right to left. Or vice versa, of course. Not today. Today the clouds were circling overhead.

'Like a mass of hungry water-vapoury vultures awaiting lunch,' said Max. 'I wonder, given the way the wind's getting up, whether Romulus is actually enveloped in a small tornado. Or a water spout.'

'Want to change your bet?' grinned Evans.

'Nope.'

'Or an eclipse, perhaps,' said Luke. 'Was there an eclipse today?'

'Won't make a lot of difference,' said Max. She looked up. 'The sun could have been swallowed by Apep, Lord of Chaos, and we'd never know anything about it. I'm afraid we're all going to get very wet.'

They pulled the tarpaulin more snugly around themselves.

Jane had been scanning her surroundings. 'What's that stone thing over there?'

Max nudged a trainee. 'Mr Edwards – time to shine.'

'Um . . . well . . . that's the Ara Martis . . . the altar of Mars. Very sacred spot. Um . . . That's where we think Romulus will take up his position.'

'Very good, Mr Edwards.'

Faintly, drifting over the marshes, came the sound of trumpets. Max snapped into action. 'He's here. Right – check your recorders. Is everything working? Mr Edwards – you're on Romulus, remember. Follow his every move. Miss Hall – you're on everyone else. Crowds, soldiers, senators. Both of you concentrate solely on your own task. Never mind what's going on around us – Mr Evans and I will have your backs at all times. And now that the Time Police are here, you'll be perfectly safe.'

Luke was visibly impressed that she managed to say this last bit with a straight face.

'All right, everyone. Let's get this done.'

There were no mounted soldiers here. Everyone was on foot.

'Too wet and splashy, I expect,' said Bolshy Jane. 'This is fun, isn't it? If the Time Police ever chuck us out, we could always apply to work at St Mary's.'

'Are you out of your mind?' demanded Wimpy Jane. 'We wouldn't last a week with these nutters. As it is, we'll be lucky to get through the afternoon alive, let alone unscathed.'

'Oh, go and wait in the pod,' said Bolshy Jane irritably. 'I want to see Romulus reviewing his troops.'

Unfortunately for those brought up on a diet of spectacular blockbuster holos, with hordes of legions wearing gleaming armour and red cloaks, all drawn up in perfect formation in front of glittering white marble buildings and cheered on by toga-wearing crowds, the real thing was somewhat disappointing.

For a start, Rome had yet to spread across its seven hills and, at this point, was more a loose alliance of hill tribes. Clusters of mostly wooden huts occupied the slopes of each hill but were separated from each other by wide tracts of boggy ground. There was only the occasional stone building dotted around. The magnificent public buildings, temples, statues – all these were still in the future.

As were the red-cloaked legions.

'The standing army and levies comprised around nine

thousand men,' reported Max. 'I'd say there's less than a tenth of that here today.'

The trainees nodded. This was no formal army. What was assembled today was a motley – though no doubt almost equally deadly – crew of warriors who had divided themselves on tribal lines and shuffled themselves into more or less separate groups.

'Miss Hall, describe what they're wearing, please.'

'Um ... Some armour. Especially breastplates. Most are wearing helmets, although few of them have horsehair tails. Leather kilts. Some tunics. Earth colours. Boots, I think – or heavy sandals. Large rectangular shields. They all appear to be infantry. I can't see any horses. Or chariots. Wait – something's happening.'

Off to their right, from the direction of the city, a cacophony of horns, drums and cymbals announced the arrival of Romulus himself.

'Mr Edwards? Your description of the Father of Rome?'

'Well, he's a lot chubbier than I thought he would be.'

Jane lifted herself on to her elbows. Mr Edwards was not wrong. Romulus was a lot chubbier than *she* thought he would be, as well. It was hard to tell his height from this distance, but he didn't appear to be towering over his companions, so average height for a Roman. Whatever that was. He wore a cloak now more brown than red. An old campaigning cloak, perhaps, that he couldn't bring himself to throw away. Or perhaps he just didn't care how he looked.

Nor had his entourage donned pristine white togas for the occasion. The six or seven men surrounding Romulus all wore heavy, mud-splattered cloaks and hefty footwear. They'd dressed for the weather rather than the occasion.

There were cries of inexplicable excitement from the St Mary's contingent.

'Get some shots of the leather kilts,' instructed Max. 'The forerunner of the *pteruges* they wore over their tunics, perhaps. Mrs Enderby will want to know.'

Luke rolled over on to his back and flapped both arms in front of his face. Mosquitoes were becoming a problem. He pulled a small can of insect repellent from his belt.

'Close your eyes, Jane.'

He sprayed her and then himself.

Beside him, Jane looked up in some surprise. 'Thank you.'

No one from St Mary's appeared to be similarly afflicted. Either they'd smothered themselves in some sort of Professor Rapson-patented insect repellent – in which case they might go blind at any moment – or Time Police officers were tastier than St Mary's historians.

The wind was beginning to get up. Over on the Field of Mars, the soldiers' cloaks streamed behind them.

'Should we be up here?' whispered Wimpy Jane timidly. 'If there's going to be a storm, I mean. You know – lightning.'

As if in response, something flickered low on the horizon. And then again.

Evans sighed. 'We should have brought Bashford.'

'Whatever for?' said Luke. 'Things are crowded enough up here.'

'Lightning rod,' said Evans briefly.

Even Luke dared not enquire further.

'Stay alert, everyone,' instructed Max – as if anyone was considering a brief afternoon nap during one of the most inexplicable events in History. 'And keep your eyes on Romulus. Except you, Miss Hall.'

By now the clouds were so low Jane felt she could almost reach up and touch them. The weak afternoon sun had long since disappeared. Thunder rumbled on, moving closer. Over on the Field of Mars, the soldiers' cloaks flapped and snapped. Several of the more elderly men accompanying Romulus pulled theirs around them and huddled together. There was an air of menacing meteorology. This really was not a good place to be.

'All right,' said Max, stowing her recorder. 'Time for me to earn my very inadequate pay.'

'Where are you going?' asked Luke, although everyone already knew the answer to that one.

'The temple. No point staying out here if he vanishes in there, is there?'

'He's probably *murdered* in there.'

'My point exactly. Mr Evans, please keep an eye on our trainees. Any trouble – get them back inside the pod. I'll join you when I can.'

'We can't permit you to do this,' said Death Wish Parrish. 'Our instructions are to bring you back to TPHQ. In one piece. Or as few pieces as possible.'

'I'll be fine,' said Max airily. 'They'll be far too busy murdering him to concentrate on me. Mr Evans, you have the conn.'

Evans nodded and Max wriggled down off the roof.

'Wait for me,' said Luke, pulling off his cloak.

'And me,' said Jane, doing the same.

Wimpy Jane uttered a faint cry which was ignored.

There was slightly less wind at ground level and now that they had a chance to look about them, there were paths linking patches of firmer ground. Making their way to the temple was easier than they had thought it might be. Everyone's attention was on Romulus as he strode through the ranks, stopping occasionally to speak to a soldier. That he was popular with his men was obvious. Laughter drifted on the wind. This was not yet the formal occasion it would become as Rome grew in power and influence. This was a recently established king strengthening his probably still slightly unstable power base.

Luke and Jane skirted around to their right, following Max closely, walking where she walked and trying not to trip over tussocks of coarse grass or stumble off the path into one of the many dark pools of standing water. Clumps of spindly trees offered some shelter, although no one was paying them even the slightest attention. The wind was growing stronger by the minute. At least the mosquitoes had given up. This wind would have blown them all the way to Sicily. Jane could feel her hair coming loose from her ponytail and whipping around her face.

They approached the Temple of Vulcan from the rear. Someone had brought horses. A small group of shaggy ponies were tethered nearby. They stood motionless, heads down, their backs to the wind. Max eased her way past them, moving quietly so as not to cause alarm. Jane followed, with Luke bringing up the rear.

This temple was open at the front. The remaining three sides were enclosed, the lower stones very green with moss and lichen.

Max lifted a hand and they halted. She nudged Jane. 'There.'

A small wooden door was set into the back right-hand corner of the building. Without warning, thunder crashed violently overhead, followed by a long, long drawn-out rumble that seemed to go on forever. Behind them, the ponies stirred nervously.

'We should move,' said Max quietly. 'Someone could turn up, either to secure them more firmly or stay with them for reassurance.'

'Perhaps the door will be bolted,' said Wimpy Jane hopefully. 'And then we can all go home.'

The door was not bolted. Max lifted the latch. Wimpy Jane's protest was lost in the increasing sounds of the truly epic storm fast bearing down upon them.

Luke eased the door closed behind them and they found themselves in a small anteroom, purpose unknown, and completely empty except for a solitary oil lamp standing on the floor near another door directly ahead of them. Max had her recorder out and was panning around from one side of the room to another before snapping it closed.

'No hiding places in here,' muttered Luke.

She nodded. 'OK – follow me.'

Very, very carefully, she cracked open the inner door that led to the main body of the temple. And then, even more carefully, she eased it closed again.

Turning, she put her mouth to Luke's ear. 'We are not alone.'

Sitting at his desk in one corner of the Pod Bay, the Senior Mech sighed deeply, and reluctantly reached for his com.

'It's the Senior Mech here, ma'am.' He sounded almost embarrassed. 'If you should still want to . . . I don't know . . . come down and pay your respects or say a few words, perhaps, then now would be the time.'

Hay was silent for a long while, staring at her desk, then she roused herself, saying, 'Yes. I'll be with you in ten minutes.'

Getting up, she hesitated a moment and then called through to Captain Farenden, 'Do you know if Major Callen has returned?'

'Ten minutes ago, I believe, ma'am.'

She walked down the corridor to Major Callen's office and entered without knocking.

He was wearing dark civilian clothes, packing weapons into a bag, and looked to be on his way out of the building again.

'Commander, this is a singular honour. If I'd known you were coming, I'd have baked a cake. I'm afraid I'm just leaving on a matter that won't wait. Perhaps we could defer this until tomorrow?'

'The Senior Mech is about to finish sealing the wall downstairs. He wondered if I would like to be present.'

Callen put down the bag. 'You weren't involved. You weren't even there.'

'I command the Time Police. I have every right to be there now, and I intend to exercise it. My question is – do you wish to attend also?'

He perched on the edge of his desk, saying thoughtfully, 'I *was* there.'

'Yes, I know.'

The silence lengthened. Finally, he seemed to shake himself. 'Yes. I do wish to attend.'

'If you can spare the time, of course.'

'I can spare the time for this, Commander.'

Hay looked at her watch. 'In five minutes, then,' and got up to go.

He held up his hand. 'Marietta . . .'

'Yes.'

'It's not . . . pretty.'

'Major, I deal with not pretty every morning in the mirror.'

He let his hand fall and said nothing.

Five minutes later, three people stood in the former corridor between the Pod Bay and security. Almost the entire right-hand wall had been reconfigured, rebuilt and replastered. The door into Mikey's workroom had disappeared. Access was now through the Pod Bay, where the Senior Mech was keeping a very careful eye on Mikey's comings and goings. Especially after the incident at Balaclava.

The narrow gap at the end of the passage opened up into the dark space beyond. So far, no one had spoken.

'With your permission, ma'am . . .' The Senior Mech handed Hay a lightstick and moved towards the gap.

She took a breath and nodded as he cracked his stick and turned sideways through the opening. A second later she followed him. Major Callen brought up the rear, snapping his own lightstick as he squeezed through.

Commander Hay was looking around. 'How strange. I had forgotten there was all this space here.'

The Senior Mech nodded. 'It was a crush hall. In the event of an emergency, both security and the Pod Bay would have evacuated into this space.' He pointed. 'And then down the corridor to Fire Door 15. It would have brought everyone out on the east side of the building.'

'And this was just . . .' She stopped.

'Walled up and forgotten,' said Callen tightly. 'These days, officers don't even know it's here.'

He and the Senior Mech held their lightsticks high, looking around at the large square space. Directly ahead of them stood an oddly shaped pod. Oddly shaped because, in defiance of all safety protocols, it appeared to have materialised at an angle and some six inches below floor level. And its back corner had been bisected by a wall. At some point there had been a wall and there had been the pod and it would appear the wall had prevailed. Now, what little they could see of the pod was dark, silent, and somehow menacing. Almost as if it was watching them.

Hay shivered. 'I remember the day this happened,' she said. 'I was in MedCen.' Automatically she reached up and touched her face. 'All the medtecs were whispering in corners. No one would tell us what had happened. And shortly afterwards there was Operation Canker. I discharged myself to take part. I thought they would argue, but we were so desperate for officers by then. Even some of the older medtecs and mechs were drafted in. Basically, if you were capable of holding a weapon, then you were bundled into a pod. Desperate days.'

'Yes,' said Callen grimly. 'They were.' He lifted his lightstick and shone it around. 'I haven't seen this since . . .' He drew a breath. 'Since I was ordered out. As were you, Senior.'

The Senior Mech nodded. 'I never knew . . . not for certain . . . how it had ended. There wasn't even time for the usual rumours to start. Only the next day we took a direct hit on the riverside, which nearly blew the whole front of the building into the river, and a couple of days after that was Canker. That went really badly and most of us thought that was the end. You were wounded, I believe, Major?'

'I was,' said Callen quietly. 'I was brought in with Strauss and Abebe. Remember them? I made it – they didn't.'

'It was the turning point for the Time War, though,' said Hay. 'Things were shit for a while, but somehow we held on and then they got better and we're just putting off the moment, aren't we? Can you get us inside, Senior?'

'If you can give me a moment, ma'am. The battery will be long dead but that can be dealt with . . .'

'Are you going to jump-start the thing?' enquired Major Callen as the Senior Mech busied himself.

'More or less, sir.'

'How long will . . . ?'

'Done. If you could give me a hand, sir. It's all manual from now on, I'm afraid. Brute strength.'

They put their shoulders to the door and pushed.

'We just have to break the seal,' grunted the Senior Mech. 'Once that's done . . .'

With a jerk, the door opened a little way.

'Step back, please, everyone. The air won't be very . . .'

They stepped back. Hay felt a cold wind on her face. Almost a caress.

Between them, Major Callen and the Senior Mech were able to get the door almost fully open. The Senior Mech snapped two more lightsticks and rolled them across the floor. They didn't get very far, coming to rest against a dark heap.

'That's Officer Sharron,' whispered the Senior Mech, inclining his head.

Hay shivered. 'How can you tell?'

'I remember them all.' He paused and then said, almost to himself, 'Sometimes I see their shadows. In the corner of my eye.'

Callen nodded. 'Once I thought I heard her. Sharron. In the Pod Bay. Calling out.' He squared his shoulders. 'I went to look. I was mistaken.'

'I'll go first,' said the Senior Mech. He stepped carefully inside the pod, followed by Commander Hay and Major Callen. Together they raised their lightsticks, casting more unwelcome light on the scene before them.

Most of the pod was visible to them. All except for the back left-hand corner, now bisected by the crush hall wall, giving the pod a strange shape. Something hung from the wall. Hay gritted her teeth and made herself look.

The console was dark. Even after all this time the air smelled of decay. Dark forms lay everywhere. Bodies forced into strange and awkward positions by the manner of their deaths.

Officer Sharron lay face down, pinned to the floor by her left arm. Her right was extended towards them as if in one last appeal. Other officers stood or lay or hung around the pod. Or *in* the pod. Not one single officer was whole.

What faces they could see were still recognisable.

'It's cold and dry in here,' said Callen. 'Which has done a good job of preserving the bodies. That's Barber at the console and the one next to him is . . .' He stopped. 'I don't know. I can't see his face. We don't know how many of them escaped the original ambush. We don't even know if any of them were trapped behind that wall.'

The Senior Mech pointed. 'The one in the floor is Coyle – he'd won the darts tournament only a week earlier. And I know that's Dikstrom because it's written on his helmet.'

'This one's Murphy,' said Callen, holding up his lightstick. He looked around. 'I can't see Lt Hahn here. Unless he's behind the wall.'

'There doesn't seem to have been any attempt to get them out,' said Hay, looking around. 'I can't see any signs of drilling or hacking away at the walls.'

'I'm not sure that would have worked,' said the Senior Mech. 'Not in time to save them, I mean. And who knew how much it would have hurt them?'

'But it would seem no one even tried,' said Hay. 'Or they could have jumped away and tried again.'

The Senior Mech shook his head. 'A second attempt could have been far worse. And they'd have taken the floor and wall with them. This part of the building might have collapsed.'

'But Albay must have done something. Surely he didn't just

walk off and ... leave them to die.' She continued, almost to herself, 'Surely not.'

'How would we have got them out?' said Callen quietly. 'It would have taken hours. Days, possibly. They wouldn't have survived.'

'Not necessarily,' said Hay angrily. 'A field amputation of Sharron's left arm would probably have saved her. And possibly one or two others as well. We needn't have lost them all.'

Callen turned to her. 'Who can know how much they were suffering? How much agony. I don't imagine any of this was painless. The realisation. The shock. The terror. What would you have done, Commander?'

She shook her head. 'I don't know.' She gestured around. 'But I wouldn't have just left them ...'

'No,' said Callen.

'They didn't even try to get them out.'

The Senior Mech, who had been moving carefully from body to body, made a small sound and then turned away.

'What?' said Hay.

He turned back and drew a deep breath. 'I suspected ... They didn't die of their wounds, Commander – they were executed. Look. Every one of them – whether dead or alive at the time – has incurred a fatal blaster injury. They were murdered. I often wondered. They were alive – some of them – when Albay went in and then he sent everyone away ...'

Callen's voice was bitter. 'And when he came out they were all dead. And we just left them. No burial. No memorial. Not even officially dead. Just MIA. No recognition. Just walled-up and forgotten.'

Hay swallowed, saying almost to herself, 'And what do *we*

do? Do we instruct the Senior Mech to finish the new wall? Do we hide them away again? Cover up the evidence? Or are we better than Albay? Do we make the truth known? And if we do, what sort of effect will it have on officers? To know that this could happen to them?'

The Senior Mech stirred. 'Ma'am, with your permission, I think our primary duty is to discover exactly *how* this could have occurred. That'll go a long way towards ensuring it never happens again. I'd like to download the pod's AI. Establish the facts.'

'Yes. An excellent idea.'

'And the wall? Shall I complete the final section?'

'No. This area is still off limits. Let's leave it until I've had a chance to review the logs. I'll decide then.'

Unzipping his bag, the Senior Mech pulled out a small box with a wide, flat cable trailing from one end.

'I see you're going old school,' said Callen.

'It might not work, the AI might be too corrupted. But if there's anything there, I'll get it.'

He stepped carefully over Officer Sharron, hesitated for a moment, said, 'Excuse me, please,' to the remains of two officers still forming part of the fascia, ducked underneath and jacked in the cable.

Callen bent down to watch. 'How long?'

Something bleeped. 'Done.'

'That was surprisingly quick.'

Red-faced with effort, the Senior Mech wriggled out from under the console again. 'Yes. I suspect that's either very good or very bad. We either got the lot or nothing at all.'

Callen sighed. 'I almost hope we got nothing at all.'

'Gentlemen . . .' said Hay quietly. 'A minute's silence, if you please. Atten . . . tion.'

They stood as still and silent as those they were honouring. One of the lightsticks flickered, sending shadows jumping around the walls. The seconds seemed to drag by. As if Time had been imprisoned somehow in this tiny space and could not move on.

'Thank you, gentlemen.'

Someone sighed. Hay was never very sure who. The living or the dead?

The Senior Mech was the first to leave, taking his equipment with him.

Hay looked around again. At the time this had been happening, she'd been in MedCen, dealing with her own personal catastrophe. She'd thought that what had happened to her – the loss of friends and colleagues and the damage to her face – was the worst thing that could ever happen to anyone. It seemed she had been wrong. Was she now experiencing just a tiny twinge of guilt? She'd been so wrapped up in her own personal concerns that this even more tragic event had almost completely passed her by. What must it have been like in here? In this cramped space. In the dark. Face welded to the console. Unable to breathe. Unable even to scream. Had they died instantly? Did they even know what had happened to them? What about those trapped by their arms or legs? Knowing there was no way they could ever be rescued. What had their last thoughts been?

'Marietta.'

She shook herself. 'Yes, Major?'

'Time for us to leave, I think. For the time being, at least.'

'Yes.'

She turned towards the door and paused. Her eyesight was poor and the flickering light was making it difficult for her to judge the distance properly, and God forbid that she should stumble. Or worse, accidentally stand on Officer Sharron.

'Allow me, Commander.'

Callen placed her hand very gently on his forearm and guided her towards the door. Once on the other side, they paused as he pulled out his scratchpad and flicked through the screens. 'My apologies, Commander. I'm expecting something important and may have to leave at any moment. Otherwise . . .' He stopped.

'Otherwise what?'

There was a long pause. 'I'm sorry, Commander – I feel the need for a little solitary reflection. If you'll excuse me.'

'Yes, I think we leave them in peace. For a little while, at least.'

Callen heaved the door closed and, not without some relief, they left.

Luke sighed. The Curse of Team Weird plus the Curse of St Mary's. Of course they weren't alone. Of course someone else would be here. Once again everything was about to go tits up.

He had no idea just how up the tits were about to go.

Making signs indicative of Jane extinguishing the oil lamp, Max again inched open the door. No need to worry about rusty hinges – the noise of the storm would mask any small sounds they might make.

Luke and Jane stood at her shoulder and peered into the temple proper. The light there wasn't brilliant, but it was sufficient to show a cluster of three people standing against the far wall. Not contemporaries. These people – whoever they were – had blasters. And were wearing modern stab vests. Definitely not contemporaries.

Thunder crashed again and even through the stone walls, they could hear the wind rising to a near scream.

Luke pulled out his own blaster. Jane did the same.

Max caught his arm, whispering, 'No, no. Wait.'

'What the hell's going on?'

'Don't know. But it seems safe to assume they've come for

Romulus. I think we might be close to solving the mystery of his disappearance.'

That Romulus's vanishing could be due to a bunch of shady operatives from another time seemed to disturb her not at all.

Luke went to push past her. Max pulled him back. 'No – this has to happen. Because it's already happened.'

'Isn't his body about to be chopped up into tiny pieces and smuggled out under men's cloaks?'

'Oh, come on – how likely is that. There would be blood everywhere. And no one noticed?'

By now, Jane's eyes had become accustomed to the half-light. She could see that the temple interior was longer than it was wide. A stone altar stood in the centre, with a brazier before it throwing flickering shadows across the floor and up the walls. There was no statue to the god – in fact, there was nothing else in this bare stone room. Except, that is, for the three people standing silent and motionless against the wall. For anyone coming in from outside – hurriedly seeking shelter from the storm, perhaps – they would be virtually invisible. Until it was too late.

She could see right over the altar to the four hefty pillars at the front of the temple. A group of perhaps five or six men were noisily climbing the steps to seek shelter, pulling their cloaks tightly around them. Jane felt a small movement beside her. Max had her recorder out.

Romulus and his senators entered the temple, shaking out their cloaks and laughing at the weather. No one was showing any signs of concern or alarm. The weather was simply a minor inconvenience to them. Certainly no one was attributing it to anything sinister or supernatural. Perhaps sudden summer storms were the norm here. Outside, as Max had foreseen, the soldiers were quickly dispersing, following each other into the gloom. Jane could hear their voices drawing away. The sky was growing darker by the minute. Lightning flashed again, splitting the sky and illuminating the interior for one very brief moment.

Jane stiffened. There weren't three shadowy figures by the far wall. There were five. Two more had emerged from a back corner. Astonishingly, one of them appeared to have a recorder very similar to the one carried by Dr Maxwell.

Were these people historians as well? From the future, perhaps? They didn't look right, although perhaps future historians all wore stab vests for some reason. Jane's hand hovered over her sonic. Yes, all right, they'd been sent to pick up Dr Maxwell, but returning home with four or five casually garnered illegals as well would do Team 236's battered reputation no harm at all.

From that moment onwards, things happened very quickly. With several hundred soldiers still within call, these people were taking no chances. While the one holding the recorder didn't move from his position, the others advanced into the centre, raising their weapons.

Romulus snapped his head around, whipping out his sword as he did so. Middle-aged and chubby he might be, but there was nothing wrong with his reactions.

Someone shouted. A woman's voice. A warning? A threat? Stepping forwards, the woman dropped to one knee and aimed what looked exactly like a Time Police sonic. Jane grabbed Luke's arm. Even Max drew in her breath with a hiss.

Because the woman was Lt Varma. Sporting an impressive black eye and bruised cheekbone.

She fired. Wide beam. Romulus and all but one of his companions stopped as suddenly as if they'd run into a solid wall – which, for those unfortunate enough to be on the receiving end of a sonicking, is exactly how it feels. Like hitting a brick wall. Face first. For one brief moment, they hung, motionless, and then their eyes rolled up in their heads and they fell to the ground. The one man left standing swayed for a moment, dazed and uncomprehending, but before he could pull himself together, he found himself a victim of Varma's infamous left hook. He too fell backwards on to the stone floor and lay still.

From start to finish – the whole incident had taken less than five seconds.

These people with Varma were quick – and professional. The man by the wall stopped recording and began to stow his gear. Two others seized Romulus, hauled him upright and then over someone's shoulder.

'Phillips – get him out of here,' said Varma, twisting to look behind her. 'Before they come round.'

Jane felt Max stiffen. Varma was looking directly at them. Did she somehow know they were there?

The one with the recorder appeared to take exception to this instruction. 'You don't give us orders.'

'Wrong,' said Varma crisply. 'Move or I'll sonic you as well and leave you here to take the rap.'

'Bitch.'

'Arsehole.'

He lowered his head to hers. 'You are so dead.'

Varma made a very rude gesture.

Phillips turned back from supervising the removal of Romulus. 'Foster – pack it in.'

'But . . .'

'You heard our instructions. She's the boss.'

'But . . .'

'Remember the Kennedy balls-up? I'm not living through that again. So move.'

Foster stared at Varma.

Who stared back.

He raised his gun.

There's four of them, thought Jane, preparing to go to Varma's assistance. What was going on here was anyone's guess but, at some point, they – whoever they were – would almost certainly be exiting back through this room. The room in which her team was standing. What to do? Either they could advance into the temple and take on the people there, or they could retreat back the way they'd come and seek a hiding place. Definitely the more sensible option.

This same thought had obviously occurred to Max. Motioning to Luke and Jane, she drew back. With the oil lamp extinguished, the room was almost completely dark. With luck, it would take the kidnappers a moment or two for their eyes to adjust. St Mary's and the Time Police could use that time to get away.

Luke had pulled out his blaster and was covering their speedy exit. Even Max seemed disinclined to linger.

'This way.'

Emerging through the back door – the ponies had all disappeared – they ran the short distance to a stand of stunted trees lining what looked like a drainage ditch of some kind. The wind whipped at them. Jane was fairly certain they would be invisible from any further than twenty feet away. Slithering down the slippery bank, they waited. As befitted TPOs, Luke and Jane were well armed. Against the five kidnappers, they were reasonably confident. Against an unknown number of Roman soldiers – somewhat less so.

There were no shouts of discovery. Anyone still in the vicinity was concentrating on seeking shelter from the apocalyptic weather. Emboldened, Jane eased her head up over the bank. There was no cause for concern. A cloud of black smoke was enveloping the temple. Just as the legend had said. Jane made a mental note not to be so dismissive of legends in the future. The black smoke was obviously to cover Varma's team's getaway. And when the smoke dispersed, Romulus would have completely vanished. Never to be seen again.

She eased her way back down into the ditch, very aware of the wet seeping through her uniform. And of the smell of stagnant water.

Jane and Luke exchanged glances. Jane opened her mouth to comment on recent events. Luke frowned, shook his head very slightly and cut his eyes to Dr Maxwell. Jane nodded. The Time Police do not wash their dirty linen in public.

Max was whispering into her com, updating Evans. 'Romulus has gone. I'll explain when I see you. Get the trainees back into the pod and we'll join you in a moment. If we don't make it, then return to St Mary's. Any moment now, his escort is going to discover Romulus is missing. They'll fan out to search for him and find you instead. And watch for a third pod somewhere around here – see if you can locate it, but don't risk yourself. Or the trainees. I suspect it will have a camo device. Maxwell out.'

Thunder crashed again and above them, finally, the heavens opened. Rain lashed down, hitting the ground so hard it bounced straight back up again to fall for a second time. A lot of it came at them sideways, driven by the wind. They were soaked to the skin in a second.

But the rain was doing them a favour. Visibility was almost zero.

'We can use this to get back to the pod,' said Luke, trying to wipe the water out of his eyes. 'There are people milling around in all directions. You can barely see ten feet ahead.'

'And those kidnappers will almost certainly be back at their pod by now,' said Max. 'Let's go. This way.'

'This way, actually,' said Luke. Maxwell's sense of misdirection was well known even outside St Mary's.

They set off, battling against the wind and rain. Several times Luke had to grab Jane's arm to prevent her being blown backwards. The more solidly built Max had no such problems and forged ahead.

'That was Varma,' said Jane to Luke, once Max was out of earshot. 'Luke, did you see?'

'I did.'

'That was actually Varma.'

'Yes.'

'What the fire truck . . . ?'

'Don't know. Can we get back to the pod first? Before this rain lets up and someone sees us.'

They slipped, slithered and splashed their way back. Evans had the door open for them as they approached.

'Kettle's on,' he said, as if that would make everything all right. Luke and Jane simultaneously realised they'd forgotten the St Mary's predilection for anointing every crisis with copious amounts of leafy liquid.

'You want one?' Evans enquired of Jane and Luke, both of whom accepted a mug with gratitude. Jane had no intention of drinking the stuff, but it was nice to warm her hands.

'So what happened?' said Evans, passing the mugs around.

Max slurped at her tea. 'Well – firstly, all bets are off. Unless . . .' she added, glaring at Luke and Jane, 'anyone had Romulus being kidnapped by a renegade Time Police officer.'

Evans blinked in astonishment. 'What?'

'Varma.'

It took a lot to startle Evans, but he was startled now. 'What? Their Varma? You're kidding.'

Max looked at the two TPOs. 'Am I kidding?'

There was a long pause, until Luke said cautiously, 'Well, it certainly looked that way, but I'm sure there must be some sort of reasonable explanation.'

Max slurped her tea again. 'Can't wait to hear that.'

'Well, obviously, Jane and I aren't of a rank high enough to . . .'

He petered out. Even he couldn't begin to contemplate the combination of circumstances that could result in the Time Police's recently promoted head of security presiding over the kidnapping of Rome's founding father. It just didn't make sense.

Jane was too bewildered to speak, simply shaking her head.

'We can't stay here,' said Max. 'Any minute now, they'll be combing the area looking for the missing Romulus.'

'Yes,' said Luke. 'And we need to get you back to TPHQ.'

Max blinked. 'Seriously? We're still doing that?'

'Of course. Why not?'

'I'd thought you'd have more important things to think about.'

'Above my pay grade,' said Luke. 'Let's go.'

Max put down her mug. 'Mr Evans – get Mr Edwards and Miss Hall back to St Mary's. Inform Dr Bairstow I've gone to sort out the Time Police. Again.'

Luke scowled. Evans grinned. Jane briefly closed her eyes.

This was not going to be fun.

On exiting their pod at TPHQ, Luke's first action was to demand the whereabouts of Lt Varma.

'Gone on ahead,' was the mech's brief response. 'She's in Wales with Tucker. You're to report to Commander Hay.' He looked down at Max. 'With your prisoner.'

'I wouldn't be so cocky if I were you, sonny,' said Max. She tapped her recorder. 'Any moment now, the Time Police are going to have a whole shedload of shit heading their way.'

She surveyed the chaos around them. Building materials still littered the far end of the Pod Bay. 'What the hell's going on here? Is the building falling down? Is it safe to be here? And yes, I am aware of the irony of someone from St Mary's asking that particular question.'

The mech ignored her. 'Parrish and Lockland – Commander Hay wants you. Now.' He looked down at Max. 'Someone take her to get some dry kit. Move it, everyone.'

Commander Hay watched Max's recording of the events – handed over with considerable reluctance – without comment.

'Again, please.'

The recording replayed itself until the screen went blank.

Sighing, Hay turned towards them. 'Where is Dr Maxwell now?'

'Under supervision and being issued with dry kit, ma'am.'

She gestured at the screen. 'You watched all this in real time?'

Luke answered on behalf of them both. 'We all did.'

'And there can be no doubt?'

'None whatsoever, ma'am. It happened directly in front of us.'

Hay frowned. 'That injury to Lt Varma's face – she was unmarked when she left TPHQ. Does anyone have any idea how or when she could have incurred it?'

'No, ma'am.'

Hay stood up and crossed to her window, looking out. Was it at all possible . . . ? She considered Lt Filbert – Varma's predecessor, and traitor. Was it possible that both of them . . . ? Together? Or separately, perhaps – each unaware of the other? Perfectly possible, she supposed. Was the Time Police riddled with traitors? She'd never had any doubts about Filbert's guilt, but Varma . . . ? That would be a serious blow. Both to the Time Police and her own personal judgement. No. She refused to believe it. Despite all the evidence to the contrary.

She turned from the window. 'Go and dry out then wait outside, please. And ask Lt Grint to come in.'

Grint entered, seated himself at the briefing table and watched the recording without comment.

Hay wasted no time. 'You have three objectives, Lieutenant. As the senior officer on the ground, I shall leave the allocation of priorities to you.'

'Yes, ma'am.'

'Firstly, you are to interrogate Lt Varma, ascertain the

circumstances of this . . . incident . . . and proceed as you think appropriate.'

'Varma is already on site in Wales, ma'am.'

Hay sighed. 'Yes, this will have to be handled very carefully.'

Grint took a breath and asked *the* question. 'With respect, ma'am – Varma?'

'Secondly, you will investigate the attack on our people and the helicopter.'

'Yes, ma'am.'

'Thirdly, and in conjunction with Dr Maxwell, you will investigate and shut down any reports of dinosaurs roaming the wild. I don't want Wales overrun with amateur dinosaur hunters.'

'Yes, ma'am.'

'I'm sorry, Grint – a bit of a poisoned chalice for you today. However, you have my full authority to take whatever action you deem necessary to contain the situation. And you won't be on your own for very long. I'll send more resources to you as soon as we can assemble them.'

'Yes, ma'am.'

'Good luck, Lieutenant.'

Completely unaware of the storm clouds circling over her head – metaphorically – Lt Varma, together with Trainee Tucker, had located Ellis and North in the old barn behind the copse.

'Don't know why you're hiding in here,' said Varma, shouldering her weapon. 'We're the Time Police. We have a perfect right to be here. And even if we didn't, we'd still be here. Especially after what happened to Mellor.'

'We weren't sure who would turn up first,' said North,

heaving herself to her feet with something of an effort and handing over the vet's file. She gestured to Ellis. 'And the major is injured.'

Varma regarded her narrowly for a moment or two and then walked around behind her. 'He's not the only one. Did you know the back of your hair is matted with blood?'

Ellis was stricken. 'Celia, I'm so sorry – I never noticed.'

'Well, fair's fair,' said North, heroically refraining from touching the back of her head. 'Neither did I. No wonder I was served so quickly in the chippie. They probably couldn't get rid of me fast enough.'

Varma stared at them. 'Please tell me you haven't been filling your stomachs with fish and chips.'

'Not any longer,' said Ellis muzzily, pointing at the pool of former fish and chips in the corner.

'For God's sake . . . sir . . . Tucker, get these two officers into the pod and back to TPHQ asap.'

North frowned. 'That will leave you stranded.'

Varma handed Tucker the vet's file. 'Get that scanned in while you're there.' She turned back to North and Ellis. 'This is Wales, for God's sake, not the Namib Desert. If the worst comes to the worst, I can catch a train back to TPHQ.'

She paused to consider this unrealistically optimistic statement and compare it with the current state of the railway network and amended it to: 'In the event of an emergency, I'll phone home. In the meantime I'll sort out our equipment here and await reinforcements.'

'Including Dr Maxwell,' added Tucker, just in case Varma had forgotten the force of nature soon to be heading in her direction.

'Get the major and Lt North to MedCen, Tucker. Take the file to Commander Hay. Collect Maxwell, stop her talking, and get back here as soon as you can.'

Tucker nodded. 'Back in half an hour. This way, please, sir and ma'am.' He helped Ellis to his feet. 'Lieutenant?'

'I'm fine,' said North. 'Just don't ask me to turn cartwheels.'

'So noted,' said Tucker, assisting Ellis through the door. North followed on behind and the rickety old door closed behind them.

'Here we are,' said Tucker. 'TPHQ – safe and sound.' He opened his com. 'MedCen – medical emergency in the Pod Bay. Officers requiring assistance.'

Shutting down his com, he carefully heaved Ellis to his feet. 'This way.'

They emerged from the pod just as the doctor and his team trotted into the Pod Bay. 'What happened here?'

'Blown up,' said Ellis wearily. 'And not for the first time, either.'

'Get him to MedCen,' ordered the doctor. He turned back to Tucker. 'Didn't you say officers? Plural.'

Tucker turned around. There was no sign of North anywhere. 'She was here a moment ago . . .'

The doctor pushed past him into the pod. North was sprawled across one of the seats, her eyes turned up in her head, her face ashen white.

'Shit,' said the doctor. 'Medical team to me. Out of the way, Tucker.'

'I'm sorry,' said Tucker helplessly. 'She was walking and

talking – honestly. She was making sense. She looked fine. She didn't even know she was hurt until Varma pointed it out.'

'Out.'

'Is she dead?'

'*Out.*'

Backing out of the pod, Tucker collided with Max, who blinked in recognition and then grinned at him. 'Thought you'd be dead by now. After that business at Roanoke, I mean.'

'So did I,' admitted Tucker. 'But no.'

'You're a prisoner?'

'Trainee. Much the same sort of thing but without the civil rights.'

'Should have joined St Mary's. You could have been one of mine.'

Tucker visibly shuddered. 'I chose life.'

Max gestured around. 'With this bunch of . . . ?'

Appearing at her shoulder, Luke and Jane hustled her off to Grint's pod. There were five of them altogether. Hansen, Rossi and Kohl – Team 235 – together with Luke and Jane. Six, if you included Trainee Tucker. Seven, if you included Grint. Eight, if you reluctantly included Dr Maxwell.

Grint sighed. There was no way any of this was going to end well. And this Varma business was likely to be a complete crock of shit.

'Right. Listen up. Team Two-Three-Five will liaise with the civilian police and investigate the attack on the helicopter and the destruction of our only evidence.

'Lockland and Parrish – you'll scour the town, talking to people and generally looking for anything dinosaur-related.

Neither of you looks like a typical TPO. Lockland, you have the knack of getting people to talk to you – exercise it.'

Jane nodded, scribbling away in her notebook. 'What about Varma, sir?'

Grint's doubts and disbelief were at least equal to those of Commander Hay. 'You're absolutely certain it was her?'

Luke and Jane both nodded. 'It was definitely her,' said Luke.

'She may have been acting under duress,' said Jane, endeavouring to put a favourable slant on things. 'She did have a very nasty bruise all down one side of her face.'

Grint sighed. If Varma was waiting for them in Wales, then he'd interrogate her first. His team knew what they were doing and could manage without him for as long as it took him to find out what the fire truck she thought she was playing at. If she couldn't account for her actions, then he'd send her back with Tucker to explain herself to Hay while he and Maxwell looked for the origin of the dinosaur.

He turned to Max and handed her back her recorder. 'You've had a chance to study the vet's file? Any conclusions?'

Max stowed it carefully in her pack. 'A raptor, without doubt. The claw on the second toe is a dead giveaway. My first guess is a Deinonychus, but it's a little small. Possibly not a fully grown adult, or some kind of sub-species with which I'm not familiar. They're pack animals – although they can and will hunt alone. Intelligent, vicious and predatory. This goes against the grain, but if you see one – and I never thought I'd have to say this to the Time Police – shoot first and ask questions later.'

'Pack animals?' said Grint. 'Are there likely to be more?'

'Depends where it came from. If, somehow, it was being

kept in captivity, then probably not. If it came through some sort of . . . of . . . time anomaly, then yes, there might well be more. Although not necessarily of the same species. If you have a . . . time-slip, is it? . . . if you have one of those, then anything could come wandering through. You could find yourselves confronting anything from a T-rex to a sauropod. Exciting, isn't it?'

She beamed, seemingly undismayed at their reluctance to share her point of view.

'Everyone kitted out?' said Grint, looking around.

'I don't seem to have a gun,' said Max, putting up her hand.

'No,' said Grint heavily. 'You don't. Let's go, people.'

Varma was passing her time in the barn by surveying and sorting their resources. Wet-weather gear – well, it was Wales, after all. And cold-weather gear – presumably in case they had to jump back to the Ice Age. And woodland camouflage. And rations for a fortnight.

She looked up as the door opened, her expression hardening as Grint entered the barn, armoured and helmeted and pointing his weapon directly at her.

Teams 235 and 236 fanned out behind him in the official Time Police-approved formation. Everyone was looking at her. She kept very still.

Grint didn't waste any time. 'Stand up. Slowly. Keep your hands where I can see them. The slightest twitch and Hansen and Kohl will sonic you where you stand. You're under arrest, Varma.'

Tucker appeared from behind them and grinned at her. 'You're really not having the best day ever, are you?'

Varma stood up. At her own speed. 'Shut up, Tucker.

Grint – get that gun out of my face or I'll deck you where you stand.'

Grint opened his mouth, and in one swift movement, Varma knocked the gun from his hand.

As one, Rossi, Kohl, Hansen, Luke and Jane brought up their own guns and levelled them at her.

She backed away, taking care to keep her hands where they could see them. 'What the fire truck's going on?'

'We know what you did, Varma,' said Luke.

She blinked. 'Is this about Hooke again? Is there new evidence?'

'What?' said Luke, baffled. 'What about Hooke? What new evidence?'

'Shut up, Varma,' said Grint, who had retrieved his weapon and was in no good mood at having been disarmed so easily. 'Put your hands behind your back and turn around.'

Varma shifted to fighting stance. 'Again – fire truck off, Grint.'

'Hansen – on my command, sonic her until she stops moving. Tucker – you'll take her back to TPHQ. Make sure everyone sees her being dragged back to security – disoriented and dribbling.'

'Yeah?' said Varma dangerously. 'You and whose army?'

Without speaking, Tucker edged his way around the group to stand at her shoulder, casually unshouldering his blaster.

'This is fascinating,' said Max. 'And hugely enjoyable, of course, but . . .'

'Shut up, Maxwell,' said Grint and Varma in unison.

Max shrugged. 'OK – well, while you waste time, I'll remember why I'm here, get my gear together, and make a start, shall I?'

She began to sort through the pile of equipment. 'Anyone see a weather forecast before we set out?'

Grint growled, but her intervention had eased the tension a little.

'Actually,' said Max, holding up a waterproof poncho and surveying it critically, 'if I might make just a teeny-tiny suggestion . . .'

'You may not,' said Grint.

Max ignored him. 'Look at her face.'

Everyone looked at Varma's face.

'What the fire truck? Stop looking at me.'

'Oh,' said Luke. 'Yes.'

Jane nodded agreement.

'What's wrong with my face?'

'Nothing,' said Luke hastily, remembering he was speaking to a pissed-off three-times boxing champion and head of security. 'That's just the point.'

'Show her this,' said Max, passing over her recorder. 'Otherwise we'll be here forever. Honestly – how do you people ever get through the day?'

Jane activated the recorder, flicked through a few screens and then passed it over.

Very carefully, not taking her eyes off Grint, Varma reached out for the screen. 'What am I looking at?'

'You tell us,' said Grint.

'You're looking at you kidnapping Romulus, the Father of Rome, from the Field of Mars in 717BC,' said Max, always happy to assist the Time Police in their struggle to comprehend the world around them.

Varma shot her a disbelieving look and then watched the screen.

No one moved. The possibility of mutually assured destruction was still very much at the forefront of everyone's mind.

Eventually Varma sighed and handed back the recorder.

'Grint – you're an idiot. You're all idiots.'

Not endearing herself to anyone, Max nodded agreement.

Varma swept on. 'For a start – look at my face. And then tell me when I'm supposed to have achieved this so-called kidnapping. Other than waiting here for you – without a pod – I haven't been alone for even a single moment since last night. And before that I was securing our prisoners and dealing with Sawney and Hooke. To say nothing of young Adesina and his friend. And his mum. And before that I was chasing a ghost train – with you, Grint, and your idiot team – and before that I was . . . well, I can't remember . . . but at no point was I off in Ancient Rome kidnapping . . .' She paused.

'Romulus,' said Max helpfully. 'Founded Rome.'

'Yes – him.'

Grint scowled. 'You haven't done it – yet.'

'You're going to arrest me for something even you admit I haven't yet done? What is this – *Minority Report*?'

'I . . .' began Grint.

Varma hadn't finished. In fact, she'd barely begun. The frustrations of the last twenty-four hours burst forth, Vesuvius-like.

'The debate over whether a person can be arrested for a crime they have not yet committed was settled years ago. The argument was that arresting a person and placing them under restraint precluded the possibility of that crime ever being committed, and that therefore there was no case to answer. This argument was accepted by all international courts. As you – all of you – would know if you ever removed your heads from your own arses – or possibly other people's – whatever floats your boat – and kept abreast of events in the outside world. And yes, I know these things, because it's my job to know these things. I am the person with the brains to keep abreast of current legislation as it relates to Time Crimes, and you lot are nothing but a bunch of very blunt instruments.'

'We're the Time Police . . .' began Grint.

Varma was blazing. 'And so am I, buster, and I'm telling you – I'm right and you're wrong, so get out of my way.'

'As the senior officer . . .' began Grint.

'I'm the senior *investigating* officer. I was first on site. I have the same rank as you.'

'I have seniority . . .' began Grint.

Varma told him exactly where he could shove his seniority. With one or two graphic gestures.

Max sat breathless with enjoyment. It wasn't every day you saw the Time Police turn on each other.

Recognising a *seriously* pissed-off senior investigating officer when they saw one – to say nothing of the giant trainee at her shoulder – everyone else had lowered their weapons. An unkind person might even say they'd backed off a little. Everyone stared at everyone else. Stalemate. And with every passing moment, the bastards who'd killed Mellor were getting further away. Unless they were coming back for another go, of course. Either way – not good.

Varma was icily polite. 'My intentions, *Lieutenant*, as authorised by Commander Hay in person . . . are to make my way upstream to locate the origin of the washed-up body. Might I suggest – in my capacity as senior investigating officer on site – that you pursue *your* enquiries at the scene of Mellor's death.'

Since those had been exactly his instructions, Grint couldn't think of a face-saving way of doing so without seemingly obeying Varma's suggestion. He took refuge in a scowl.

'Those are Hay's instructions to me, also,' he said with dignity. 'Should I be convinced of your non-involvement in a serious Time Crime, of course.'

Varma made no response to this. Picking a backpack, she began to assemble her gear. 'Tucker, Maxwell – you're with me. Maxwell – you know why you're here?'

'My expertise and know-how.'

Obviously still on a roll, Varma nodded. 'Just a couple of rules to get straight before we set off. Firstly . . .'

'Yeah, yeah, yeah,' said Max. 'Do as I'm told. When I'm told. Speak only when spoken to. Do not make clever comments concerning TPOs and their IQs. Do we have a plan?'

Varma nodded. 'We'll start by searching upriver. Both banks. Let's go.'

Shouldering her pack, she strode from the barn without a backward glance. Behind her, Time Police officers avoided each other's eyes. A grinning Tucker and Maxwell followed her out.

Commander Hay walked to the window and stared unseeing at the busy river below. The midday airship to Holyhead lifted from the Victoria mooring tower, paused, rotated and set off for Wales. She watched it go, blinking in the bright sunshine. Her eyes weren't getting any better. Now the doctor was threatening her with tinted lenses.

'You will be able, legitimately, to wear sunglasses indoors,' he'd said. 'I'm willing to bet by the end of the week every bugger out there will be doing exactly the same, ma'am.'

Hay sighed. The legacy of the past was never very far away. They all carried their own burdens. The Senior Mech. Major Callen . . .

Yes. What of Callen? He'd been a young and inexperienced lieutenant at the time, but you grew up fast in the Time Police. He'd seen the sort of man Albay was. He must have worked it out. And, like the Senior Mech, he'd have gone along with it because of expediency. And who could say he, Callen, hadn't been right to do so? They had been different times then. You learned to live with a lot.

Acting on an impulse she barely acknowledged, she strode down the corridor to Major Callen's office. Where the impulse deserted her. She hesitated, looked up and down the empty corridor, then tapped on the door and entered.

He was sitting with his back to the door and staring out of the window. A bottle sat on his desk.

'Not now.'

'Nevertheless, Major . . .'

He swivelled his chair. 'Commander?'

Hay regarded the bottle. The regulation strictly forbidding drinking at one's desk was generally regarded as . . . flexible.

He shrugged. 'I had rather hoped for a moment's solitary reflection.'

Hay closed the door behind her. 'Did you? I, on the other hand, think we should take a few minutes respite before re-embarking on a day which is turning out to be pretty shitty even by our very low standards.'

Callen put down his glass. 'I doubt my coffee is quite as good as yours, but I think you'll find it perfectly acceptable. Unless, of course, you prefer something stronger.' He gestured at the bottle.

'A glass of something stronger would be very welcome, thank you, Major.'

He found another glass in his bottom drawer and poured her a measure. Hay regarded it. 'What would I be drinking?'

'To be perfectly honest, I am not sure. It was impounded at a Flying Auction just outside of Tokyo and a couple of bottles found their way to me.' He handed her the glass. 'I think you'll find it adequate for our purpose today. A toast. To our colleagues downstairs.'

Hay raised her glass. 'And to Lt Mellor.'

'To Chad Mellor. What news of Ellis?'

'He is recovering. It would seem that of the two, North was the more seriously injured. The silence from MedCen is . . . concerning.'

Callen swirled the amber liquid in his glass. 'That is unfortunate. She was only in my team for a short while but I formed a very favourable opinion of her abilities.'

'Yes.'

'And a crying shame about Mellor.'

'Yes.'

He sighed. 'We're going back to the bad old days, aren't we? People dead and dying. The unit crippled. Things coming at us thick and fast.'

'God, I hope not.'

'So do I. I'm not the man I was and I definitely don't want to go through all that again.'

Hay turned her head to stare out of the window. 'There aren't many of us left, are there? Who remember those days, I mean.'

'No. You. Me. The Senior Mech. One or two others. Charlie Farenden, Ellis and the others came along a little later, didn't they. When the worst was over with.' He fiddled with his glass. 'Do you ever think of those times?'

'The old days? When something calls them to mind, yes, I do.'

'They left their mark on all of us.'

There was a rather charged pause. Commander Hay, who, every day, stared in the mirror at the mark those days had left on her, said nothing.

Callen straightened up. 'Marietta, I'm sorry. I spoke without thinking. It was not my intention . . .' He stood up and moved to the window.

She never knew what made her say it. Why she chose that moment. After all these years. She'd never said ... not to anyone ... not that there had been the opportunity. The medics had patched her up as best they could and sent her back out there – and she'd gone. More than gone. She'd flung herself back into the fray, not admitting, even to herself, that the best thing for her was death. By any means possible. She'd welcomed the action. Anything to divert her thoughts from what looked back at her from every mirror. She'd especially welcomed the anonymity of her helmet. With her visor down she was just another TPO. But after a while people had stopped staring. Mostly. She remembered they'd had to issue her with a new ID card because her appearance was so ... altered. And she herself had destroyed every image of ... of the other Marietta. The one with the sparkling eyes and the pretty smile. She was dead and gone. It was this Marietta who had survived.

Lost in her memories for one fatal moment she forgot where she was, saying sadly, 'I'm Hel, aren't I? Daughter of Loki. The half-rotten girl. One half of me is normal, the other half is ancient, decaying. Half dead.'

Callen remained silent for a long time. With his back to the window he was silhouetted against the light, his face unreadable.

'Marietta – listen to me. You are a Time Police officer. You were injured in the Time Wars. Like so many of us. But you survived.'

'You call this surviving?'

'I do. In fact, I call it triumphing. You have successfully overcome every obstacle put in your path. You have risen above everything to command the Time Police. Your example inspires others. Every day. In fact, for some of us, the world would be a very much darker place if you weren't in it. I—'

She looked up at him. 'Do you still hear them? Sharron and her team, I mean.'

He looked away from her and nodded. 'I was right there. Standing behind Albay. My team had only just arrived back. We'd had to fight our way home as well. What happened to them could have happened to us.'

He reached for the bottle and topped up his glass. 'I didn't do a thing to help them. No one could. Some were already dead, of course. Those who weren't soon were – Albay saw to that. You'd think I'd hear them all the time, wouldn't you? And yes, I did think I heard Sharron. Once. I was in the Pod Bay late at night and there was an echo. But what I really hear, Marietta – what I never stop hearing – is the silence. My last sight of them as they hung from the walls. Or grew out of the floor. Like giant sunflowers. That was . . . not good. But when the door opened and Albay finally emerged – it's the silence he left behind that really chills my blood.'

He broke off suddenly and forced a smile. The mask was back in place. He picked up his glass again. 'How morbid we are becoming. With what can I assist you, Commander?'

'I came to see if I could assist *you*, Major.'

'Really? In what capacity, I wonder?'

'Well, there are people – trained people – to whom you could speak.'

'To what end?'

'I believe many people derive great benefit from discussing . . .'

He emptied his glass and grimaced. 'From parading their

hopes and fears to someone who wasn't there, didn't see it, couldn't possibly comprehend. To be sent away with meaningless platitudes concerning the dubious pleasures of sharing one's feelings.'

He poured himself another drink.

'You don't have to bear this alone, Major.'

'Of course I do. What could any counsellor possibly say or do that could in any way alleviate . . . ?'

He broke off and took a moment to regain his composure. 'These are *my* demons, Commander. They've walked with me for many years now. Old friends, you might say. We get together occasionally and relive the good old days.' He raised his glass mockingly and drank again. 'As you and I have just done.'

'I'd like you to speak to the doctor.'

'As you wish, Commander, but I can tell you now how it will go. He'll talk. I'll listen. I'll say all the right things at the right time – I'm very good at that – and he'll report back to you that everything's just fine. Duty done and we all carry on as before. My secrets. My demons. My life. My choice.'

'Nevertheless . . .'

'Did you? Find it helpful?'

'We're not talking about me.'

'We're not talking about me either. Not if I can help it.'

'I'm not in a position to comment on the benefits of counselling – everyone is different.'

'And there was no time in those days, was there? Limp back to base. Repair the pods first, the people second and straight back out there to do it all again.' He smiled with his usual cold amusement. 'It made us what we are today.'

She looked down at her hands. 'As if that's anything to be proud of.'

He topped up his glass again.

'Are you often this drunk?'

He smiled at his glass. 'Who says I'm drunk?'

'Major . . .'

'Marietta – there are many things in my life that should remain undisturbed. Secrets which should remain hidden forever. You wouldn't thank me for revealing them to anyone. You don't like me. You don't trust me – but I've never lied to you. I've always given you good – if unwelcome – advice. And I'm advising you now – let it drop.'

'Very well.' She put down her untasted drink and stood up.

'Are you going to tell me your door is always open.'

She glanced at the bottle. 'Would it help you to know that it is?'

'It would surprise me, certainly.'

'Then, having surprised you, Major, I shall take my leave.' She paused. 'We're both damaged. I'm . . .' She gestured at her face. 'And you're . . .'

'What? What am I?'

'You. You're always you. You never change.'

Suddenly, he was very sober. 'Marietta, there's something I have to tell you. Something very important.'

'What is it?'

He stood for a long time and then appeared to come to a decision.

'Nothing. Nothing at all.'

'In that case, the Senior Mech will have all the footage ready for me in twenty minutes. Report to my office then, please.'

She closed the door behind her.

Major Callen stared for some moments at her now empty chair, reached for the bottle again, and then appeared to change his mind.

Twenty minutes later they were all gathered together in Commander Hay's office.

'I'd like us all to watch this together,' said Hay quietly. 'Charlie, hold all calls, please. The Senior Mech, Major Callen and I will be unavailable to everyone until further notice. Gentlemen, please be seated.'

Very nearly on fire with curiosity, Captain Farenden closed the door behind him.

Hay seated herself. The big screen dropped down from the ceiling.

'Ready?' said the Senior Mech and the screen came to life. 'This is from one of the pod's internal cameras.'

The screen sprang into life. The image was surprisingly clear.

'No reason why it shouldn't be,' said the Senior Mech, reading their minds.

They watched the pod door burst open. Smoke and dust billowed through the doorway.

They watched wounded officers help each other into the pod. They watched Officer Sharron, last in and firing as she came, covering their withdrawal.

They watched as the pod came under heavy attack, hearing the explosions outside and the debris raining down upon it. They watched the pod shudder with every impact. People lost their balance and fell to the floor.

'They were lucky not to be completely crushed,' said Callen.

Hay nodded. 'Freeze frame.' The recording paused.

'Can we identify those who aren't here? Who never made it back to the pod?'

'Senze Okuta,' said Callen immediately.

'Pyotr Hahn,' said the Senior Mech. 'Alfie Burns. Haddad...' He tailed away.

Hay nodded, once. 'Continue with the images, please, Senior.'

They watched in silence as Sharron gave the order for emergency evacuation. They watched as a massive explosion rocked the pod.

'That must have been what caused the malfunction,' said the Senior Mech. 'A blast that size, that close, at exactly the wrong moment.'

For a few seconds the screen remained completely blank. As one, the three TPOs leaned forwards.

'Is that all there is?' enquired Callen.

The Senior Mech shook his head. 'No.'

The screen flickered back into life, broke up for a few seconds; there was a burst of static. And then—

Hay drew back with a hiss. Callen's fists clenched.

There it was. Laid out in front of them in stark black and white. It wasn't really monochrome. The recording – like all Time Police footage – was in full colour, but afterwards Hay only ever remembered the stark black and white.

And the silence. The shocked silence inside the pod as officers struggled to make sense of what had happened to them.

And the silence in her office as well, as she, Callen and the Senior Mech stared at the screen. They'd seen the aftermath – real, live, in front of them, which should have prepared them – but still all three were silent.

Sharron was the first to pull herself together. They could hear her issuing instructions, hear her clamping down on her own panic and desperation as she struggled to hold her team together. And faintly, in the background, unseen in the shadows – the sound of someone's clenched fists beating the console in his frantic fight for oxygen. Or the dreadful grunts as an officer without a face – without a voice – tried to call out for help.

They watched as the door opened slowly. Dim light filtered into the pod. Lightsticks. The screen blurred for a while as the AI struggled to readjust the focus, and when it finally cleared there were dark figures standing in the doorway, taking in the scene around them. Colonel Albay, with the Senior Mech and Callen just behind him. The Senior Mech remained in deep shadow, but Callen's face was briefly highlighted in the flare of a lightstick. Hay's first thought was how young he looked. More lightsticks rolled across the floor. The screen flickered again. For longer this time.

The Senior Mech stirred. 'At this stage I don't know whether the corruption occurred at the time of the incident or because the pod lost power, or some other external cause. I'll investigate. It should clear in a moment.'

It did. They watched Albay step into the pod. Alone. Even though she knew what was about to happen, Hay still found herself leaning forwards, hoping against hope that somehow, reality had altered itself, that the inhabitants were not about to die a cold and lonely death after all.

The door closed behind him and they watched Albay move around the pod, carefully and with precision, ignoring the cries, the protests, the entreaties, the pleas for him to save them. For him somehow to make everything right. One by one the voices fell silent as he moved from one officer to the next, until finally only Sharron was left.

Hay forced herself to watch Sharron struggle. Dark blood pooled on the floor as she fought to free her trapped arm.

Albay moved behind her. She tried to twist around.

'Rot in hell. *Murderer.*'

The blaster whined as he took aim.

Sharron held his gaze. Right up to the end. 'I'll get you for this if it's the last thing I—'

He fired. One last time.

He looked around the pod. Now there was no sound and no movement from any of the officers. Nor ever would be again.

Albay left. Without a backward glance. The door jerked closed behind him. And then, faintly, almost unheard, no more than a sigh in the dark . . .

'*Murderer.*'

One by one, the lightsticks flickered into nothing. Dark stillness returned.

After a moment, Hay stirred and sighed. 'Is that everything?'

'Yes,' said the Senior Mech. 'Other than . . .' he consulted his scratchpad, 'two days and thirteen hours of complete darkness before the recording eventually runs out.'

Silence fell again.

Abruptly, Callen stood up – and then, having got to his feet, sat back down again, his face grey. 'I left them.'

The Senior Mech shook his head. 'Albay ordered you out. You had no choice.'

'I still left them.'

'He would have killed you too. And me. He would have killed anyone or everyone to keep this secret.'

Callen turned on him. 'Those were our people and we did nothing. We . . .'

'Something's happening,' said Hay suddenly, leaning forwards to stare at the screen again. 'What's that light?'

Both men turned to the screen. 'What light?'

'There.'

The big screen took on a reddish tinge. Which faded. Then reappeared again. Then faded.

'What's that?'

'Some sort of indicator light. Was something still working? But what? The pod was so badly damaged . . . everyone's dead . . . who's operating the—'

'MURDERER!'

The word crashed into their consciousness.

The Senior Mech reeled back in his chair and Hay half rose to her feet.

'What . . . ?' said Callen, wheeling around. The sound seemed to come from all around them. 'That's Sharron. I recognise her voice.'

'But she's dead,' said Hay, through lips that suddenly wouldn't work properly. 'We just watched her die.'

'Murderer!'
    'Murderer!'
        'Murderer!'

    'Murderer!'
            ## 'Murderer!'

From the screen, from their personal coms. The voice was everywhere. Hay tilted her head. She could hear the same voice – Sharron's voice – booming from the screens in her adjutant's room. And from the PA system in the corridors. From everywhere. From all directions. All around the building. Waves of sound beat upon their ears.

'MURDERER!'

The departure of Varma and her team had not lessened the atmosphere in the Welsh barn as the remaining officers prepared to continue their respective missions. Luke and Jane eyed each other and then kept their heads down and their mouths shut as they assembled their gear. Team 235 ostentatiously busied themselves checking over their weapons.

Everything was being carried out in a somewhat frosty silence.

'This is hilarious,' whispered Luke to Jane. 'Doesn't it feel good to see someone else catching the shit for once.'

Jane frowned reprovingly but secretly admitted to herself that it did.

'Follow us down to the crime scene,' said Grint to Luke. 'We'll be very visible. With luck, that will provide sufficient cover for you two to carry out your own investigation. And don't shoot anyone by mistake.'

'We leave that to lesser teams,' said Luke stiffly.

There was an awkward silence. Grint scowled. Luke opened his mouth again – presumably to make an even less helpful comment.

'You were saying you wanted us down in the town,' said Jane, hastening to fill the gap.

'Yes.' Grint grappled with an unfamiliar concept. 'Be friendly. Encourage people to talk to you.'

Luke nodded. 'OK.'

'That's OK, *sir*.'

Luke nodded.

Grint scowled again, considered punching his lights out, decided he had better things to do, and turned away.

There was yet another awkward silence.

'Stay out of the pubs,' said Hansen.

'Aw,' said Luke.

'Call for assistance as soon as you see anything suspicious,' commanded Grint. 'Don't make this another . . .' He stopped.

Another occasion when 236 fails to bring in its prisoner, thought Jane. Did everyone know they'd gone back under supervision? Actually, that was a point. Were she and Luke actually on supervision at this very moment? Officially it wasn't supposed to start until they reported to North and Ellis. It seemed unlikely that that would happen now.

'Everyone stay off your coms as much as possible,' continued Grint. 'We don't know who might be listening. Unless circumstances dictate otherwise, we'll rendezvous in the town centre in . . . two hours. And shout if you need . . .' he veered away from the word *help* and went with, 'reinforcements.'

Luke nodded.

A moment later they were all heading back towards the crime scene.

* * *

Varma's team had nearly reached the river. Max was unhappy about something. 'I should have a gun.'

'Last time I gave you a weapon you nearly brought the building down,' said Varma.

'On top of me,' added Tucker.

'Even so . . .'

The two TPOs halted, turned and glared at her with impressive synchronisation.

Reading the room, Max concluded the chances of being allowed to use anything more ferocious than a hard stare were very remote.

'The river's over there,' said Varma, consulting her scratchpad. 'Behind that line of trees. The body was discovered on this side, about half a mile away. I think we can leave Grint's people to cover that. They're the official presence of the Time Police. We'll start moving upriver. Tucker – you take the far bank. The body was pulled out here but that doesn't mean it went in on this side. Let's go.'

They slipped quietly through the trees, following a path parallel to the river until all the crime scene activity was well out of sight, then moved closer to the riverbank.

Max raised her hand. 'Am I allowed to ask questions?'

Varma sighed. 'I can't imagine any power on earth that could stop you. Just make sure they're good ones. *Why can't I have a weapon?* does not qualify.'

'Well, given recent events, shouldn't we all stick together? We don't know whether they – whoever they are – will have more people in the area. Their equivalent of a clean-up crew, perhaps.'

'That is a good question,' said Varma, 'but time is of the

essence here. They could be evacuating even as we speak and then we'll lose them forever. Or they could be massing for an attack. Either way, we need to find them. We'll decide on our next step when we see what we're up against.'

'I can wade across here,' said Tucker, gesturing to a wide bend. 'The water's fast but shallow.'

'OK. Stay in touch. Don't speak unless it's an emergency. Just a double click every half hour to let us know you're OK.'

Tucker stood on the bank, picking his route across the river. 'Good luck.' He stepped down and splashed across the rushing water, eventually disappearing under the trees on the other side.

'Good bloke, Tucker,' said Max, who, contrary to widespread Time Police belief, was not entirely blind.

Varma said nothing, but in a manner that a prudent historian should heed.

'Knows his stuff,' said Max, fully aware of the risk she was running but unable to resist.

Varma said nothing, but in a manner that conveyed to Max that she might have only moments left to live.

'Sort of bloke you want as a partner,' said Max. Because all historians believe in living life on the edge.

Varma turned. Very, very, very slowly.

'We should get started,' said Max innocently. 'Can't stand here all day.'

Varma strove for inner calm. This was going to be a very long day.

They began to work their way slowly upriver, climbing over rocks, looking for signs of . . . well, anything really. Dislodged boulders, scuffed earth, broken twigs, blood – anything that might show signs of something large and bad-tempered that wasn't Lt Grint recently passing this way – but there was nothing. Varma hadn't really thought there would be, but the Time Police like to be thorough.

Very occasionally they looked back the way they'd come to see how far they'd climbed, and would catch a glimpse of a police vehicle parked on a track or small groups of people heading in different directions. It would seem the civilian police were searching the surrounding areas while waiting for the bomb disposal team to finish.

'We don't have to worry about them,' said Varma. 'Grint will let them carry out their preliminary investigation and when they don't turn up anything useful – which they won't – he'll get Hay to shut down the investigation and then we'll have the whole area to ourselves. In the meantime, we're just a couple of innocent hikers.'

'Who just happen to be wearing military gear and carrying weapons,' said Max. 'Well, one of us is,' she added grumpily.

Varma ignored her.

While this side of the river comprised mostly open, rocky land, the far bank was thick with trees – ash, oak, willow – all overhanging the water and making Tucker's progress more difficult. But there was a more or less regular series of double clicks announcing he was over there somewhere and not yet dead.

Their own progress was slow. Heads down, they moved carefully – although given the rough terrain, they didn't have a lot of choice.

'It's very pretty,' said Max suddenly, and it was. The river, growing more boisterous as they made their way upstream, descended in a series of rocky rapids, alternating between rushing white water and still, dark pools. They could feel the spray on their faces.

Varma narrowed her eyes. Could the dinosaur possibly have been swept over this series of falls? The comparative lack of damage to the corpse seemed to indicate otherwise. Or had it gone into the river lower down, closer to the town, and they'd somehow missed the signs? She was tempted to retrace their steps and check again, but they'd seen nothing to indicate this was, in fact, what had happened, so they pressed on.

After two hours, and making it very clear that any and all conversation was off the board, Varma allowed them ten minutes to eat. Max perched on a handy water-rounded boulder and watched the busy river rush past while Varma risked a brief, static-laden conversation with Tucker, who reported he was making slow progress and enquired whether either of them had killed the other yet. He seemed disappointed to learn that this had not actually occurred.

And then it was back to the search. Varma took up her position on the bank with Max some five yards to her right. Heads bent, they walked parallel to the water, examining every inch of land. The further they progressed, the closer the trees grew to the river. Beech trees, tall and thick.

After another hour, Varma straightened her aching back and looked up at the sky. Soft rain pattered on her waterproofs.

'We haven't actually come very far as the crow flies. The river twists and turns a lot here, these woods are thick, the trees are coming right down to the riverbank and this area isn't easily accessible. Unless by helicopter. And even then the canopy is so dense it wouldn't see a lot. We'd need heat-seeking imagers.'

She turned her head to stare into the thick woodland. 'It's

very easy to imagine God knows what happening in there and no one being any the wiser. And the longer we take to find them, the more chance of this rain washing away any traces of . . . anything.'

Max nodded. Varma wasn't wrong. The chances of them finding anything at all were slim.

Only twenty minutes later, however . . .

The clouds were still low but the rain had dwindled to a fine mist.

'We're going to need somewhere to make camp,' said Varma, halting.

Max nodded and looked around. This was a good spot. The river bubbled and frothed to her left, gurgling its way around boulders, but a small gravel beach meant easy access for water and washing. The thickly growing woodland which had made their progress so difficult would keep the worst of the wind and rain away and provide shelter from any prying eyes.

'This will do nicely,' said Max, gratefully unshouldering her backpack. 'If you pull out the compo, I'll do a quick check around to make sure nothing Jurassic creeps up and eats us in the night.'

Varma nodded. 'We'll make camp while it's still light. Then we can leave our gear here and continue upriver until the light fails. That way we won't be struggling to put up the tent in the dark.'

Max disappeared under the trees.

Varma shrugged off her own backpack, sat on a convenient rock and fished out her com. Now that she wasn't continually looking where to put her feet to avoid a sprained ankle, she realised Trainee Tucker had been quiet for some time. Which was a little worrying. She didn't really think he'd seize the opportunity to make his escape. Not really. But he'd been Henry Plimpton's man. He was an illegal . . .

Former illegal, half of her brain argued. And at no time had he ever shown any inclination to return to his previous bad habits.

This was his first solo field assignment, argued the other half. Well ahead of the normal training schedule, but there hadn't been anyone else available. When push came to shove – if things kicked off here – which way would he jump? He was a big man, quiet, efficient, good at what he did – even if what he did wasn't always legal – but how much could she rely on him? If Plimpton ever reappeared in a flash and a bang and a cloud of smoke, whose side would Tucker be on?

She shook her head. Either he was with the Time Police or he wasn't. And if he wasn't, then she'd shoot him. With some regret. But also with deadly accuracy. Did he know that? She suspected he did. And of the two of them – Max and herself – she would be his primary target. Take out the most dangerous person first. That was what she would do.

She clicked her com and was relieved to hear his double click in response.

Max's staticky voice spoke in her ear. 'Var . . . ma.'

'What?'

'I . . . ound . . . omething.'

Checking the charge on her blaster, Varma set off through the trees, which grew so thickly here that such light finding its way through was tinged green. Here were giant beeches – their trunks thickly coated in green moss – as were the rocks jutting up from the ground, and all the fallen wood littering the forest floor. Everything was green.

Max's quiet voice sounded in her ear again. 'Ahead of . . . and . . . your right. Careful.'

The trees grew smaller and further apart as Varma forged her way towards Max. The world grew brighter. Crawling for the last ten feet or so, she joined Max, who lay on her stomach, peering down into a small gulley.

In contrast to the green gloom of the forest, this little steep-sided valley was bright and filled with ferns, young silver birch trees and purple foxgloves. There were no giant trees here. Had the land been cleared at some point? And for what purpose?

The shape was so well camouflaged that even Varma didn't spot it straight away. Gradually, as her eyes became focused, she could make out a structure at one end, surrounded by a complicated cat's cradle of cam nets, and with a very clever paint job – all broken outlines and distorted shapes. If Escher had ever gone into the camouflage business, then this was exactly the sort of thing he would have come up with. And, she didn't mind betting, the structure would be very carefully insulated so there would be no heat signature.

If she concentrated hard, she was almost certain she was looking at a flat-roofed featureless rectangle. No doors or windows were visible but they could be around the far side.

'Don't move if you can help it,' whispered Varma. 'If this is what we're looking for, they could have radar, heat-seekers, movement detectors, booby traps and God knows what. They might already have picked us up. I'm going to call this in in case anything happens to us. Be ready to run.'

She rolled over and groped for her com.

Max stared down at the structure. There were no clues at all as to its contents or purpose. She turned her head to Varma. 'No access that I can see. No power cables in or out. I can't hear any generators. It's just a box. What did Grint say?'

Varma put away her com. 'Can't get through. Reception was poor down by the river. Because of all the trees, probably. Do you think it's a giant pod?'

Max thought for a moment. 'I'm not an expert – we'd need Leon – but I do remember him telling me that our big pod – Tea Bag 2 – was about as big as we could safely go. Of course that's in our time. I'm certain the Time Police will have been able to overcome the power/weight/size ratio problem by now.'

'I'm not so sure,' said Varma. 'If it is a pod, then I've never seen one this big before.' She tilted her head to one side. 'Doesn't it look a little bit flimsy to you? For a pod, I mean.'

'Maybe. Perhaps it's just some sort of giant shed. For sheep and . . . farming stuff.'

Varma rolled on to her back again, pulled out her scratchpad and passed it over. 'See what you can find.'

Max began to flick through the screens. Varma continued to observe the nothingness that was happening all around them.

Birds sang – despite the mizzle – and there was an occasional rustle in the undergrowth. Otherwise – just the patter of rain falling on leaves and the rich smell of damp earth.

'Found something,' said Max. 'The nearest building – which we can't see from here – is called Castell Cudd. Pronounced Keithh. This is their land and . . . oh.'

'What?'

'Mystery solved. That thing down there – it could be covering the entrance to an old mine.'

'A mine?'

'Privately owned and abandoned some time ago. I wonder if that structure's there to keep people out. Stop them falling to their deaths and suing the castle.'

'Does it say why it closed? Did the seam run out?'

Max flicked some more. 'Part of the shaft collapsed. They lost nearly twenty men. The owners held a memorial service, dismantled the pit head and shut it all down. It's not been worked since.'

Varma frowned. 'It seems rather heavily camouflaged for such a simple purpose, don't you think? Why didn't they just fence it off and post Keep Out notices? It's not as if there are people walking past every ten minutes.'

'Yeah – since when have Keep Out notices ever kept anyone out?'

'Well, not you, certainly. Any other nearby habitation?'

'Only the castle itself.'

'How far?'

'Difficult to tell. Probably less than half a mile as the crow flies, but this is Wales, so by the time you've negotiated a river, a waterfall, a cliff, another cliff, hundreds of trees, ten thousand sheep and another waterfall . . . a lot further.'

'Any info on the castle itself?'

'Yes, loads of useful stuff. Built by Edward I – who else? – to guard the old road to Holyhead. Um . . . The usual border skirmishes and minor uprisings. Henry IV bestowed it upon a minor supporter when he overthrew Richard II. The Lancastrian castle was taken by the Yorkists under Edward IV. Won back by the Lancastrians again under Henry VI's brief return, returned to the Yorkist fold under Edward IV again, staged its own minor rebellion against Richard III, finally coming to rest in the bosom of Henry Tudor where it remained as the property of the crown.'

She scrolled further. 'Survived the Tudors – one of the few places Elizabeth I never slept – she probably couldn't get to it – survived the Civil War – I doubt Cromwell's forces even knew of its existence and no one was going to tell them – and was eventually granted to one of the many mistresses of Charles II. Well – her husband, anyway. She didn't actually have a child by Charles, so she obviously wasn't entitled to anything bigger or more accessible. But, the remote location enabled it to ignore the Jacobite rebellion as just something that was happening elsewhere and therefore not important, and as the woods closed in around it and the road changed its course, Castell Cudd seems to have been almost forgotten, and quietly did its own thing for a couple of centuries. The discovery of iron ore was understood to be a great bonus – a mine opened up, and even more prosperity drifted in their direction. Then the accident, after which the mine closed. That seems to be it.'

'I only wanted to know who owns the bloody thing,' said Varma, exasperated at all this historical irrelevance.

Max scanned the screen. 'Just says privately owned. I expect someone at TPHQ could find out. Not the National Trust or Welsh Heritage, anyway. Not even SPOHB.'

'Spobe?'

'Society for the Protection of Historical Buildings.'

'You mean SPERM.'

Max considered this. 'No, I really don't think I do.'

Varma became impatient. 'Society for the Protection of English Regalia and Monuments.'

'We're in Wales. We crossed the border. What's the equivalent? SPEW?'

'What?'

'SPEW.'

'I swear, Maxwell, I will shoot you and throw your body into the river. Imagine how the sight of you, face down and slowly drifting out to sea, will gladden the heart of Lt Grint. And, indeed, everyone in the Time Police.'

'SPEW,' said Max helpfully. 'The Society for the Protection of Everything Welsh.'

'I'm taking my gun out now.'

'I think you should concentrate on the job in hand. No wonder the Time Police are always calling on St Mary's for help. Speaking of which, I don't see any dinosaurs – do you?'

'I don't see anything – not even the castle.'

'They wouldn't site the mine where it could contaminate the view, would they? That's why most Welsh mine owners lived in England.'

'If the mine owners were Welsh, why did they live in England?'

'No,' said Max patiently, because she was dealing with the Time Police. 'The mines were Welsh. The owners were English. You see . . .'

Varma had pulled out her binoculars. 'Is there any chance of you shutting up for just two minutes?'

'Shouldn't think so.'

'Give it a try. See how you get on.'

'Um . . .'

'Shit on a stick, Maxwell, that wasn't even a whole second.'

'No, but . . .'

'You just never shut up, do you? You go on and . . .'

'Well, yes, but . . .'

'And on and on.'

'I'm trying to . . .'

'For God's sake – just stop talking.'

'. . . tell you about the three men over there pointing their weapons at us.'

Varma exhaled and rested her forehead on the rich, damp, rather pleasant-smelling loam. 'Fuck. Fuck. Fuck. Fuck. Fuck.'

'I think they want to talk to us,' said Max helpfully. She raised her voice. 'She's just having a moment. We'll be with you in a minute.'

Varma closed her eyes. Only for a fraction of a second, sadly. She would have liked to have kept them closed for longer. A lot longer. A couple of months, perhaps, because it would be so nice just to lie here for a while, absorbing the rich smell of the woodland, listening to the birdsong – if she could hear it over Maxwell's incessant yammering, of course. She could roll over and look up at the sky. Play that nice game where you make shapes in the clouds. A whale. A ship. Whatever. Things really were turning to shit, weren't they? First Hooke. Then Mellor. Now this.

But, on the plus side, the guns meant they were in the right place. Yes, all right – this was Wales and all sorts of things happened here, but three men, all armed – and looking straight at them – was a compelling argument in favour of them being in the right place. One was even carrying their packs. They'd crept through the woods while she'd been distracted by historical irrelevance and the most irritating person on the planet. You honestly had to wonder if Maxwell wasn't some kind of undercover agent, subtly undermining the Time Police at every opportunity.

No – nothing Maxwell ever did was subtle. Disastrous – yes. Spectacularly catastrophic – yes. Subtle – no.

Using just her fingertips, she pulled out her com and pressed it into the wet soil.

'You can get up now,' said one of the men. Varma could tell from the sound of his voice that he was grinning. Yeah – shit day.

She heaved herself slowly out of the ferns, making sure to tread heavily on her com, pressing it more deeply into the soft earth and casually scuffing a few dead leaves over the top. Max stood quietly, carefully wearing her trademark *butter wouldn't melt in my mouth* expression. Their eyes met briefly. Just for one moment. Then both looked away again.

'Hand over your guns or have our hands all over you. Your choice.'

Slowly and carefully Varma handed over her weapons and scratchpad, noting as she did so that these men probably hadn't even been looking for them. Two of them were festooned with nets and dart guns. No – this lot were out looking for something bigger than two hikers strolling through the woods. A dinosaur, perhaps? Or, given they'd already taken out the original specimen – another dinosaur. Or even several dinosaurs. Interesting.

'I don't have a gun,' said Max, allowing resentment to bleed into her voice. 'She wouldn't let me have one.'

'Shut up,' said Varma. 'This is all your fault. If you hadn't kept talking all the time . . .'

'We could form an escape committee,' said Max brightly, apparently oblivious of the fact their captors could hear every word.

'Shut up.'

'I'll overpower the one on the left and you go for the others with your knife.'

Varma stared at her. 'What knife?'

'The one in your boot.'

'What knife in my boot?'

'You haven't got a knife in your boot?'

'No.'

'Why not?'

'Because I don't want to cut my own bloody foot off, that's why.'

Max sighed. 'So no shoulder holster, then? Nothing up your sleeve?'

Varma requested the heavens kill her now.

'Happy to oblige,' said Man #1, raising his gun in a meaningful manner. 'And I will if you don't tell me what you're doing here. Who are you?'

'Oh,' said Max vaguely, resisting the urge to twiddle her hair around one finger because that would be overkill. 'We're just a couple of hikers looking for a place to wee. We didn't mean to trespass.'

'With military-grade gear and weapons?'

Max beamed. 'Well, yes – just like you.'

'What are you doing up here in the trees?'

'Well, as I said, I was looking for a place to wee. It can take a while to find somewhere suitable. You need soft undergrowth. A friend of mine nearly got a frozen stalk up his rectum once – he still bangs on about that – and you need a good supply of broad-leaved plants to hand.'

The man held up his hand for silence. 'And you?' he said, turning to Varma.

Varma indicated Max. 'Looking for her. The woman's got the sense of direction of a teaspoon. She wandered off and got lost. I found her and then we saw your structure and were speculating about whether you'd have a toilet.'

'Let's find out, shall we? Move.'

Slipping and sliding on the steep, wet slope, Max and Varma were pushed down into the valley.

There was a door. Recessed into the wall facing away from them and so cunningly disguised that it was only the small electronic keypad that revealed its existence.

Interestingly, the door and its surrounding frame showed signs of recent damage and repair. Without seeming to, Varma regarded it with great interest. Never mind breaking in – was it at all possible that something had broken out? Several somethings, in fact.

She looked down. No convenient dinosaur footprints, but that meant nothing. The ground was very hard here.

One of the men entered in the code. Soundlessly, the door swung open and they were pushed inside.

It was empty. No pods, no equipment, no neat stacks of crates or boxes. No dinosaurs, no cages. Of course there weren't. That would have been much too easy, wouldn't it? The place was completely empty. Other than the dark, partially submerged, irregular hole in the stony ground, of course. About fifteen feet across and yawning like an open mouth. An impression strengthened by all the collapsed stonework jutting out of the ground around it. Like teeth. Was this all that was left of the mine entrance? There was no winch – no winding gear of any kind. Varma sighed. Things were never that easy for poor, hard-working TPOs.

There had obviously been a lot of activity here. The floor, bone dry, and a path mostly cleared of rocks had been flattened over time and was as hard as concrete. There were no footprints, no cigarette ends, no litter.

What there was, however, was a draught of warmish air gusting out from the hole. And a stink. Not the pleasant odour of wet woods that they'd become accustomed to – this was the reek of rotting foliage. Of stagnant water. And above everything – an animal smell. And not a good animal smell. This was the stench of urine and mildewed food and unhappy animals, all overlaid with a whiff of sulphur.

Max closed her eyes and inhaled. Because smell is the most evocative of all the human senses and she'd smelled this before. Memories crowded her mind and were pushed away. She needed to concentrate.

When she opened her eyes, Varma was very carefully not looking at her. Max very carefully returned the favour.

'Well,' said Man #1, who was obviously the joker of the team. 'What do you think?'

'It's very nice,' said Max. 'Do you have a toilet? I didn't actually have time to . . . you know . . . before you . . .'

'Actually,' he said. 'Yes, we do.' He grinned at the two men either side of her. 'Show the lady where the toilet is, boys.'

'No,' said Varma, suddenly realising what was about to happen.

Too late. Man #1 had his gun in her face before she could make a move. Varma stood very still.

Max spun around – presumably to make a break for it – but

it was too late. Laughing, Men #2 and 3 each seized an arm and ran her backwards, towards the very edge of the gaping hole, and let go.

Varma watched Max lose her balance, teeter on the edge for one long moment and then fall backwards into darkness.

Her scream died abruptly and then there was silence.

Varma swallowed.

Man #1 smiled down at her. 'Your turn next.'

16

In times of crisis, a historian's instinct is to stay still, play dead, use the time to work out what's happening and then react appropriately. Accordingly, Max lay very still, sprawled in the dark on what appeared to be a deep carpet of very hard rocks, quite convinced the tumble had killed her.

Someone rolled to a halt beside her. Very close beside her. All right, practically on top of her. The paint-blistering language told her it was Varma.

The Time Police have a completely different procedure for dealing with a crisis. The officer should leap to her feet and start shooting at everything in sight on the grounds that everyone present will turn out to be guilty of something and it's always a good idea to get your licks in first.

Sadly, in this instance, neither was able to proceed according to their own personal philosophies. Max objected strongly to acting as a landing pad for the Time Police and said so in no uncertain terms, and Varma was too historian-entangled to begin the immediate decimation of her surroundings. Hence, neither was particularly happy with the other – a situation reflected in their somewhat acrimonious dialogue in which each blamed the other for their current predicament.

'It's not *my* fault,' said Max indignantly. 'I didn't push you down the hole. In fact, I cushioned your fall. Where's the bloody gratitude?'

'Probably in the same place as your common sense, your ability to do as you're told and your sense of direction.'

There was a pause.

'That was very hurtful,' said Max reproachfully. 'And let me remind you that if you'd given me my own gun – which you refused to do – then I'd have been able to fight off these – whoever they are – and—'

'Shut up,' shouted Varma. 'For the love of God – just shut up.'

She climbed shakily to her feet and took stock of her surroundings. There was that smell again, but much worse now they seemed to be underground. A warm, wet, green smell. Stagnant water, dead things and rotting eggs. With top notes of ammonia. What the fire truck could smell that bad? And actually, did she want to know?

Just as she straightened up, an unseen voice said, 'Lights,' and she found herself able to see. These lights were dim but seemed very bright after the recent darkness. Not that there was a lot to see. Blinking, Varma found herself standing in a surprisingly spacious tunnel that curved gently off to her left. The roof was about three feet above her head and there was easily room for two people to walk abreast.

She turned to look behind her, noting the steep, shale-covered slope down which she had just so painfully rolled. She eyed the ladder built into the wall. The bastards needn't have pushed them. She and Max could easily have climbed down. It hadn't been a massive fall – cuts and bruises, not broken bones – but only a certain type of person pushes another into a dark hole when that person has no idea how far it is to the bottom. Varma vowed retribution.

Beside her, Max also heaved herself to her feet, and sniffed the air. Exchanging a brief glance with Varma, she nodded. Whatever they'd been looking for – they'd found it. Or rather – it had found them.

Swaying a little, Max began to pat herself down, presumably checking for the bones she still couldn't believe she hadn't broken in the fall. Finding everything more or less intact, she turned towards Varma. 'Toto, I don't think we're in Kansas any more.'

Varma wrinkled her nose. 'Are you thinking what I'm thinking?'

'I've no idea. Mostly I'm wondering about this awful smell.'

'You don't want to wonder about who said *Lights*?' said another voice. Man #1 by the sound of it.

'I was just getting to that,' said Max with dignity. 'Although you have rather spoiled the surprise, haven't you? What's happening? Where are we? What's going on? Are we underground?'

'Stay calm,' said Varma.

'Why?'

'It helps.'

As Varma had done, Max stared up at the hole above her head. 'You mean staying calm will enable me to overcome our adversaries and fly out of here?'

'No.'

'Not much point in staying calm then, is there?'

By now their guards had climbed down. Still three of them, all with guns and all standing a safe distance away. Varma was careful not to let her shoulders slump. The middle one gestured with his gun. 'Come on – Mr P is going to want a word with you.'

Varma briefly closed her eyes. This day was turning to utter shit.

'He'll never remember us,' said Max quietly. Famous last words.

'Stop talking,' said Man #1, poking Max with his weapon.

Varma sighed. 'Yeah, good luck with that.' She turned to Max. 'I bet you he does remember us. After all, we did rather ruin everything at Roanoke. He had to abandon the site because of us.'

'I said to stop talking,' said Man #1.

Max shook her head. 'It was dark at the time. And let's face it, all TPOs look the same. He won't remember us. Trust me – it'll be fine.'

Man #1 was becoming impatient. 'I'm ordering you to stop talking.'

'Ah,' said Max, peering at him. 'Obviously a direct descendent of King Cnut.'

'What?' he said, baffled.

No one bothered to enlighten him.

'Move.'

They were hustled along the tunnel. Varma stared about her, noting every detail. Cables ran along the walls, with lockers and storage units at regular intervals. Every now and then they passed a door. One, slightly ajar, gave a glimpse into a small room. Varma just had time to make out a table and part of a narrow bed. Were these crew quarters? Did people live here?

Finally, the tunnel widened out into an almost circular space.

An underground cave, perhaps, with a curved roof overhead. Like an upside-down giant pudding bowl. Three tunnels ran from this cave. A sign nearby designated the tunnel in which they were standing as the *Town Tunnel*. A second tunnel ran to the left. Wider even than this one. And older by the looks of it. At some point, someone had painted – *To Lizard Land* – in faintly luminous paint. An arrow pointed along the tunnel. Boxes, crates, miscellaneous bits of equipment and what looked like empty cages were stacked neatly against the walls. Lights had been fixed at intervals, again not illuminating very much, but that didn't matter, because, at some point – it was difficult to judge the distance accurately – the tunnel faded into a gentle mist that curled and swirled, playing tricks with their eyes. You couldn't stare at it for too long. Not that they were granted the opportunity. Both were hit simultaneously with – to Varma at least – an all too familiar sensation. Nausea. Disorientation. Shortness of breath.

The Time Police have identified and classified many different types of time-slips. Some are permanently open. Some open and close on an apparently random basis. Some turn up only on specific dates. There's one in Wallingford, for instance, just to the north of St Mary-le-More, which turns up, regular as clockwork, at twenty-five minutes past three on 17th July every year and switches itself off thirty-four minutes later at one minute to four. No one knows why. The other end appears to be somewhere in the 16th century, although the slip is never open long enough to risk carrying out any meaningful research. No casualties have ever been reported, although it did once disgorge a small dachshund named Dusty, who had been posted missing twelve months previously, leading to a rapturous reunion with his owner, Mrs Hannah Golightly of St Mary's St, Wallingford. Apparently none the worse for wear, Dusty was sadly unable to communicate his experiences, but went on to enjoy a pampered existence and finally died, in his sleep, at the ripe old age of seventeen.

At the other end of the scale, of course, was the gold standard of all time-slips – Bold Street in Liverpool. No less than twenty-three separate slips had been officially catalogued and the Time Police were pretty certain they hadn't got them all yet. Worst of all, two at least had been designated Cat 3 – hazardous to human life – because they were known to appear with no warning whatsoever. A conventional time-slip has the good manners to announce itself with a range of traditional symptoms: sinister mists, blurred landscapes, lack of depth and colour, muffled sounds. Those unfortunate enough to be in the vicinity experience shortness of breath, dull depression, lethargy, non-functioning coms, and so forth. However, there were no warnings with a Cat 3. Worst of all, once in, it was almost impossible to walk your way out. Cat 3s don't return you whence you came. Keep walking and you could find yourself being chased by the Beadle in Victorian times. Ten steps later and you're coughing up bloody phlegm in 1346. Another ten steps and you're fleeing the army of William the Conqueror during the Harrying of the North. All the Time Police could do about Bold Street was post Fatal to Life notices and wait for the inevitable thrill-seekers to indulge in this imaginative form of suicide.

Varma sighed. So far the last twenty-four hours had been less than wonderful. Not only was she fairly certain they were about to come face to face with one of the biggest thorns in her professional side – and who was certain to recognise her – but now there was a time-slip nearby. Had to be. Nothing else produced symptoms like this so quickly. The good news was that it certainly solved the conundrum of where the dinosaur had come from. She peered thoughtfully back down the Town Tunnel. And how it had got out, too. Anything reasonably nimble would easily be able to negotiate the ramp out of the tunnel. And anything bigger could just bulldoze its way out of the structure at the top. And already had, by the looks of the repairs they'd seen. Good – puzzle solved. Now all they had to do was live long enough to convey this info to TPHQ. Which, given that coms never functioned well in the vicinity of a time-slip, could be a problem.

She stared at the third tunnel. The one straight ahead. This one was also helpfully signposted – *To the Castle*. Again, in slightly luminous paint. She frowned. Was this operation perhaps prone to power failures? Very possible. And wouldn't that be fun. In the dark. With a time-slip nearby. And dinosaurs on the loose.

The castle tunnel showed signs of considerable use. Litter, cigarette ends, boot prints. More metal lockers lined the right-hand wall. There were names scribbled across the front, although there wasn't enough light to make them out.

'Hoods from this point,' said Man # 1, and before she could object, something black and smelly covered her head, which was a complete waste of time because they simply pushed her straight ahead. Into the castle tunnel. Which seemed to go on forever. Varma and Max both stumbled along, one or both of them frequently tripping and cursing. Then there were flights of stairs to negotiate, coupled with the sounds of doors being opened and closed behind them.

'Where are we going?' enquired Max, her voice slightly muffled by her hood.

Man #1 replied, 'Well, today you're lucky. Normally you'd be lunch, but I think the boss will definitely want to see you two.'

'Do you have a toilet? Only I never actually got to . . .'

Varma walked quietly, making a mental note of the route and allowing Max to irritate everyone in a manner only she seemed able to do.

A door opened and suddenly they were back outside. Even through her hood Varma was conscious of the cooler, damp air. Gravel crunched under their feet, then there they were, through another wooden door, a very sharp turn to the right, more steps up, through one final door, then someone pulled off their hoods and finally they had arrived.

A familiar figure turned from the windows. Dressed in an immaculately tailored and incongruously pristine safari suit, Henry Plimpton stared across the room at them.

So much for Max's happy optimism – recognition was instant and mutual.

He stood stock-still for a moment, frowning, and then said to Max, 'I remember you. I've seen you before.' He turned to Varma. 'And you. You're Time Police. It's written all over you.'

He turned back to Max. 'But you're not.'

'Too right I'm not,' said Max indignantly. 'I look hideous in black.'

He surveyed her. 'You think green is an improvement?'

Max looked down at her woodland greens. 'Well, not any longer.'

'I shall ask this only once – who are you?'

'I'm a consultant. When they need intelligence, the Time Police send for an expert.'

Henry Plimpton looked over at Varma.

'It's true,' she said, 'but unfortunately he wasn't available so we're stuck with this one.'

He turned back to Max. 'So what exactly do you do?'

'Don't tell him,' said Varma.

There was just the very slightest pause and then, without looking at Varma in any way, Max said brightly, 'Whatever they pay me to do.'

'And what exactly do they pay you to do?'

'Well, they haven't paid me at all yet, but when eventually I do get some cash out of them – seriously, it's like getting blood out of a stone – it will have been for my knowledge and expertise.'

'In which area?'

Max beamed. 'I'm an historian.'

'Will you shut up,' shouted Varma. 'Don't tell him anything.'

'I haven't. Told him anything, I mean.'

'You just told him you're a historian.'

'Well, it's hardly a secret, is it? It's not like I'm a spy or anything. And I resent your implication that there's something wrong with being an historian.'

'There's nothing wrong with being a historian – it's you that's the problem.'

Max bristled. 'What the hell is that supposed to mean?'

'You're disrespectful, disobedient, undisciplined . . .'

Max waved all that aside. 'Yeah, but I'm bloody good at what I do.' She turned to Henry Plimpton who was watching them both very carefully. 'Don't listen to her. She's just got a strop on because I won't call her ma'am, or salute, or stand to attention. The Time Police may not like me – well, they don't like me – but that doesn't stop them calling on me whenever they find themselves out of their depth. Which, to be honest, is quite often.'

Plimpton regarded her. 'So you're a . . . freelance historian?'

'Unemployed historian would be a better description,' said Varma bitterly. 'And virtually unemployable.'

Max nodded. 'It is true that I have had one or two teeny-tiny problems with authority over the years but – present company excepted, of course – so many people in charge are just complete idiots.'

He smiled. 'They are indeed. So, basically, you're for sale.'

'Hire,' corrected Max. 'I can be hired. Professionally, of course. Not for anything . . . you know . . . sex.'

'No,' said Henry Plimpton with very unflattering rapidity.

Varma stared very hard at her boots.

He seemed to reflect for a moment. 'I wonder if I could use someone like you.'

Max sighed. 'In the interests of full disclosure, she's not completely wrong about my attitude.'

'You work for the Time Police,' shouted Varma.

'I resign.'

Varma struggled in the grip of two men.

Henry Plimpton tilted his head to one side and stared at Max. 'Do you know,' he said thoughtfully, 'I really think there's a possibility you and I might be of some benefit to each other.'

Max shifted her weight. 'Well, that rather depends, doesn't it? Are you one of these evil despots who shoots their henchmen right, left and centre? Or hurls them into tanks of piranhas?

Because if so, then I'm probably not interested. Unless the pay's good, of course, but even then . . . No. Sorry.'

'In that case I have no alternative but to shoot the pair of you.'

'Where do I sign up? You can shoot *her* if you like.'

'What a refreshingly simple point of view.'

Max considered this. 'Yeah – that just about sums me up. Refreshingly simple. Just give me lots of money and point me at the problem. I'm assuming you do have a problem.'

'I have two,' he said, looking them up and down.

'Allow me to offer a solution,' said Max, assuming a confidential air. 'You employ me – at a rate to be agreed between us, although I should warn you, I expect the word *generous* to figure prominently – and I register a change of ownership. And you give me this one,' she gestured at Varma, 'to be – well, whatever I want her to be.'

'I am not your sodding assistant,' snarled Varma.

'Too right you're not. I was thinking along the lines of maid of all work, skivvy, entertainment . . . slave.' She stepped up close. She and Varma were face to face. 'I've put up with a lot from you over the years. Now it's my turn.'

'I think not,' said Henry Plimpton.

'OK,' said Max, casually turning away. 'Shoot her.'

Varma struggled some more.

Henry Plimpton was regarding Max. 'I like you. I didn't think I would, but now I do.'

'They all come round in the end,' said Max. 'I'm very likeable and I have great charm.'

'My most pressing need is information. About you, obviously.'

'OK,' said Max, 'what do you want to know?'

Varma struggled again. 'For God's sake, will you shut up.'

'Well, let's see,' said Henry Plimpton, turning his back on Varma and shutting her out of the conversation. 'How many of you are there?'

'Two,' said Max. 'Her and me. That was easy. Do I get paid now?'

'You mercenary little bitch,' shouted Varma.

Henry Plimpton frowned. 'So why are you here?'

'Well,' said Max, with the air of one settling down for a confidential chat. 'It's an interesting story. Something was washed up. On a riverbank, I think. Some sort of creature. I was called in to identify it, but somehow . . .' she flashed Varma a glance of resentment, 'she won't tell me how, but the Time Police have managed to lose it. We were despatched to see if we could discover where it came from and whether there were any more of them out here.'

'Just the two of you?'

'No, of course not. This is a big area to cover. We were divided into teams of two and pushed out of the door and told to play nicely until bedtime.'

'So there are others out there?'

'Hundreds, I should imagine. Although I don't know that for sure. No one ever tells me anything.'

'Why am I not surprised to hear that?' He turned to the guard. 'Anything on the monitors?'

'No – other than these two, some small activity on the far bank, and the commotion down in the town, the woods are empty.'

'So, either you're lying, or the Time Police haven't arrived yet, or they're looking in the wrong place, or they're massing somewhere else for an attack here.'

Max nodded. 'Could be any of those.'

He gestured to one of his men, who raised his weapon. 'Which one is it?'

Max held his gaze. 'Not until you pay me.'

They stared at each other for a long time. Neither blinked.

'You interest me,' he said thoughtfully. 'Historian. Mercenary bitch. Balls of steel. You're in a hopeless position and yet you're still alive. You think quickly.' He held her gaze. 'How ruthless are you, I wonder?'

'Give me a gun and some money and let's find out.'

He laughed, genuinely amused. 'Well, I'm not stupid enough to give you a gun, and I'm certainly not going to give you any money so . . .' He stared at her thoughtfully. 'I wonder . . .'

'What? What do you wonder?'

'I might have a job for a historian.'

'Really? Is there a reward?'

'Your life.'

'What's the job?'

'Come with me.' He pointed to Varma. 'Not you.' He looked at the guards. 'She's all yours.'

Not a flicker of expression crossed Max's face. 'Um . . . Actually . . .'

He turned back. 'What now?'

'Well, I wouldn't turn my back on her if I were you. And these guys of yours won't give her any trouble at all.'

'Would it be wiser to shoot her now?'

'Almost certainly . . .' Max paused. 'But before you let rip . . . could we have a quiet word?'

Henry Plimpton was mildly curious. 'You want a private word? With me?'

Max nodded and took a few steps away to her right, seemingly confident that he would follow her. Which he did. They retired to the other end of the not very large room.

'The thing is,' said Max confidentially – and perfectly audibly – 'while I'm obviously the more valuable of the two of us, I think it's only fair to tell you she hasn't had a good day. A prisoner died while in her custody. Under interrogation, if you get my drift, and Hay – that's Commander Hay – wanted her out of the building in the hope that all the fuss would die down in her absence. I don't think anyone would be heartbroken if she never came back.'

'You're telling me to shoot her?'

'No,' said Max patiently. 'No, no, no, no. I'm *suggesting* you employ her. She's – she was – head of their security. She knows where all the bodies are buried. She knows names, dates, details. She could be worth her weight in gold to you, don't you think?'

Just for one moment, Henry Plimpton went very still. 'Head of security, you say?'

'Yes – and she's hanging by a thread. Turn her – what do you have to lose? And then either keep her here with you or send her back to be your eyes and ears.' She beamed. 'You're welcome.'

Henry Plimpton remained still, staring at Varma. 'What's your name?'

Varma scowled and said nothing.

'You're Varma, aren't you?'

Varma said nothing.

'Yes,' said Max. 'She is.'

'And you're head of security. Since when?'

'Quite recently, I believe,' said the ever-helpful Max.

He ignored her, addressing himself to Varma. 'What happened to your predecessor?'

Varma straightened up and looked him in the eye, her voice cold. 'He was a traitor. He was taken up in a helicopter and pushed out of the door. His body's in the North Sea somewhere. Everyone thinks he died a heroic death defending a prisoner. But he didn't. He kicked and screamed and begged for his life and cried like a baby and they had to break his fingers to get him to let go. And then they literally kicked him out of the door.'

Max, to whom all that was news, stood motionless, staring at the floor, her thoughts racing.

Henry Plimpton had assumed a calculating expression. 'And you lost a prisoner?'

Varma shrugged. 'It happens sometimes.'

'And now it's happened to you.'

She shrugged again.

'Lt Filbert worked for us, you know.'

A small part of Varma's mind registered the *us*.

'You could say I have a vacancy.'

Varma sneered at Max. 'And now you have the wherewithal to fill it. Not to overemphasise the point, but you two seem to be getting along like a house on fire.'

'Yes, she does offer certain possibilities, but I find myself very tempted to replace the late Lt Filbert with a new and improved model. One who has already stepped into his shoes. And at absolutely no trouble or inconvenience to me.'

Varma took a deep breath – presumably to reject Henry

Plimpton and all his works with extreme prejudice – but he waved this aside. 'Yes – of course you will say *no*. Very proper. You strike me as an intelligent person – you bested me at Roanoke and not many can say they've ever got the better of Henry Plimpton. Let alone lived to tell the tale. Think about it, officer.'

'Actually . . .' said Max, peering round to address Varma. 'Did you ask him about pay?'

Varma folded her arms.

'Oh, for God's sake.' Max turned to Plimpton. 'How much would she – we – be paid?'

'Performance related,' he said immediately.

Max narrowed her eyes and assumed a cunning expression. 'So we perform – you pay.'

'Yes.'

'But only *after* we perform.'

'Yes.'

'So you say.'

He sighed. 'I am surrounded by hand-picked killers, thieves, mercenaries – people at the top of their very unpleasant professions. I keep them onside with performance-related pay and generous bonuses. When you assemble a team of men – people – who will do anything for money – only an idiot doesn't actually give them any.'

'Any money?' persevered Max.

'Yes. Payable on proof of successful completion of the job.'

'Proof,' said Max quietly. 'You mean . . . like a recording, perhaps?'

'Yes, that sort of thing. Verification unleashes all sorts of monetary reward. Ask anyone.'

Around the room, his men nodded.

Plimpton turned back to her. 'See.'

Max grinned. 'Well, that's good news, Henry, because I've just had a Brilliant Idea.'

Over the years there have been many and varied reactions to the phrase *I've just had a Brilliant Idea.* Especially when uttered by Dr Maxwell. Most involved ducking and diving, cutting and running, a flat veto, and so forth. Henry Plimpton, however, a relative newcomer to the world of Maxwell's Brilliant Ideas, was unwise enough to show a faint interest. A substantial number of her colleagues would have simply shot her on the spot and continued with their day.

Henry Plimpton's first reaction appeared to be amusement. 'Has it escaped your notice that you are not in a particularly strong negotiating position at the moment?'

Max waved this aside as irrelevant. 'Henry, play your cards right and I could blow your socks off. No – not sex,' she said hastily, noting his change of expression. Around the room, men were grinning, but no one was charging their blasters or dragging them away to the dungeons, so she felt this was going well. Now for the big finish.

Lowering her voice, she adopted an air of great secrecy. 'Tell me about your plans for abducting Romulus from the Field of Mars.'

Silence crashed to the ground and decided to stay there.

As if a switch had been thrown, Henry Plimpton stopped smiling. The air in the room seemed suddenly much thicker. Varma tensed in readiness and even Max felt a sudden chill.

'What do you know about that?' He looked around at his men, all of whom were standing to attention and being very careful not to catch his eye.

Having hit the bull's-eye, Max judged it wisest to barge on.

'Romulus. You know – Father of Rome. Not sure what you want him for, of course, but since it is the duty of every employee to lessen her employer's stress levels, I can tell you now that you will be successful.' She beamed again, her face afire with her desire to assist. 'Put me down for a bonus.'

Varma began to struggle. Just enough to look good. Certainly not enough to get herself shot. 'Shut up, Max. Just shut up. Don't say another word or I swear I'll have you . . .'

Max shook her head. 'No, you won't. Trust me, you'll be so overcome with gratitude – as will everyone in this room . . .'

'I cannot conceive of anything more unlikely,' said Plimpton, still dangerously calm. 'You have just crossed the line from being useful to being too dangerous to live any longer. You should have quit while you were ahead.' He turned away. 'Take them both down to the rendering area.'

Man #1 seized Max again.

Max pulled her arm free. 'Listen to me, Henry – I know you'll be successful with Romulus because I was there.' She nodded at one of the men. 'I know you. Your name is Phillips. You were there, too.' She pointed to another man. 'And he had a recorder.' She gestured to the man holding Varma. 'And he was there, as well. There was an argument – something about the Kennedy job going wrong.'

There was a very, very long pause. Plimpton looked across at Phillips, who shook his head. 'She couldn't have got that from us, Mr Plimpton. No one's said a word. I swear it.'

'That's true,' said Max. 'But I can prove what I say.'

Henry Plimpton turned to Varma, saying softly, 'You're very quiet all of a sudden. Why?'

Varma scowled. 'I'm trying not to hear any of this.'

'I could kill you now. You'd never hear anything again.'

Max said nothing. Because people always need to arrive at the correct conclusions in their own time.

He turned back to Max. 'How *do* you know all this?'

'I know it because I was there. Your team performed flawlessly. Textbook extraction. A team of five. These three, one other, and . . . ta-dah . . . my colleague here. In and out before anyone really knew what was happening. Mind you, the weather helped.'

He regarded her for a very long time before finally saying, 'I won't deny I've had some thoughts . . . but at this moment, Romulus – and others – are all still very much in the planning stages.'

'Allow me to remove your uncertainty. Free of charge. As I said, your operation will be successful. You will acquire Romulus, Father of Rome, from the Field of Mars in 717BC.'

There was a very long silence. Henry Plimpton's face gave no clue as to his feelings. Finally, he moved to stand in front of Varma, regarding her thoughtfully. 'It occurs to me there's no quicker or better way to acquire my very own TPO than to persuade her and her colleague to do something illegal and then hold that over them for the rest of their lives.'

Varma struggled again. 'I won't do it, Plimpton.'

'Not even if I kill your colleague here – now – in front of you?'

'Um . . .' said Max.

'Go ahead,' said Varma, who could also bluff with the best of them. 'See if I care.'

'Um . . .' said Max, again.

'Be quiet.' He turned to stare out of the window. Long seconds ticked past. Eventually he turned back to Phillips. 'Start prepping for the jump. Take them both with you. If either give you even a moment's trouble, then shoot them and . . .'

'Actually . . .' said Max.

'. . . and send the bodies to the rendering area. Protein is always useful.' He smiled at Max, but not a pleasant smile. 'Our feed bill is massive. This can be your contribution.'

'Yes, but the thing is . . .' persevered Max.

Plimpton raised his arms in exasperation. 'Dear God – do you never stop talking?'

'I think we all know the answer to that one,' said Max. 'But you need to listen to me. I can't go.'

'Lost your nerve?'

'No – I *can't* go.'

Henry Plimpton froze. No one moved for what seemed like a very long time. Eyes narrowed, he stared at Max. On and on. Looking back afterwards, Max sometimes wondered if that wasn't the moment from which all their future problems sprang. The room was very still. The change from mild-mannered Henry Plimpton to cold, calculating Henry Plimpton had been, as always, lightning-fast and terrifying. Even his voice seemed different.

'Why can't you go? You say you're an historian. Why aren't

you clawing my eyes out for a chance to see the man who founded Rome?'

Max shrugged. 'Not really my period.'

He shook his head. 'No. No, that's not it.'

'Wouldn't you prefer to keep me here? As a hostage?'

'Not if he's got any sense,' muttered Varma.

Plimpton was still staring at Max. 'Why won't you go? Scared of jumping? I don't think so.' He thought for a moment. 'I think we've already established you'll do anything for money. Let's go old school. What will you do to avoid pain?'

He turned to his guards. 'Shoot her. Left foot. Give her a few minutes to scream, then shoot her in the knee. Same leg. Give her another few minutes, then on to her left hand. Then elbow. Then shoulder. Then the same for her right side.' He turned back to Max. 'You'll tell me everything I want to know after the first knee shot – I'm told it's agony – but they'll carry on anyway. I like to send a message to people every now and then. You know – refuse to cooperate and this is what happens. Word soon gets around. I rarely have to do it twice. Now – last chance. Why *can't* you go?'

Max sighed. 'I did tell you. I've already been there.'

He seemed suddenly to view her with new eyes, saying softly, 'Yes, you did, didn't you? How very, very interesting. When? How?'

'Quite recently, actually. Romulus. Campus Martial. Reviewing the troops. Big storm. And yes, he does disappear. Because a bunch of people turned up and grabbed him. Most of whom are in this room now.'

'Prove it.'

'In my pack.'

He eyed her. 'Search their packs.'

Max watched two men shoulder their weapons and begin to rummage. 'Well, I'd rather hoped for a moment of calm before hitting you with this, and I'm not sure how you're going to react, but you need to brace yourself.'

Varma had gone very still.

Max nodded at her. 'She led the team.'

Henry Plimpton looked from one to the other. 'I don't believe you.'

'She led the team. There were five of them altogether. Two were recording – knowing what I know now, they were there to obtain proof for you, weren't they? Because you won't pay out until they can prove they didn't just pop round the corner, grab a random bloke, wrap him in a sheet and bring him back here and call him Romulus. Very wise, Henry.'

There was complete silence in the room.

'Well,' said Plimpton quietly, stepping back, much to Max's great relief. 'Well, well, well. This is certainly something to think about.'

Varma struggled again. 'She's lying. She's just trying to save her own worthless life. I tell you; you can't trust a word this woman says.'

'Here.' One of the men had pulled out Max's recorder.

'What?' shouted Varma. 'You're not allowed to carry one of those. It's against regulations. What were you thinking?'

Max shrugged. 'I *was* thinking I'm an historian co-opted into something dodgy by the Time Police, and a little record of my activities might prove a wise investment for the future, but now I'm thinking how grateful you're going to be because I'm about to save your life.'

Henry Plimpton looked at her. 'Are you always this full of surprises?'

'Yes,' said Max. 'And I have to tell you, very few of my employers have been as appreciative as you.'

'Oh, I'm afraid I'm not appreciative at all.'

'Not at the moment, perhaps – but you will be. May I have my recorder, please.'

At a nod from Henry Plimpton, Phillips passed it over.

'Just one moment . . . yes, here we are. Take a look at this.'

She fiddled for a moment, running through various screens, and suddenly a clear, sharp image was projected up on to the wall. 'Just let me fast-forward . . .' Images of the grey sky, coarse grass and the Temple of Vulcan whizzed past, finally giving way to a narrow view – through the almost closed door – of Romulus entering the temple with his senators. And then the appearance of Varma and the team.

Henry Plimpton watched in silence. They all watched in silence until Max ended the replay. The last image – Varma herself – remained frozen, projected up on to the wall.

Henry Plimpton looked at Varma. 'That is definitely you.'

'Yes,' said Max. 'And when I show that recording to the Time Police, she's in really deep shit. She can say she was forced to do it, but that won't cut any ice with them. The Time Police don't like it when one of their own goes off the rails.' She looked over at Varma. 'You yourself told us what they did to Filbert. Sorry, Varma, but you're finished in the Time Police. Time for a career reappraisal.'

Varma stood stock-still, her face expressionless.

Henry Plimpton looked up at the image of Varma – half

turned away, all ready to follow Romulus out of the door. 'So how did she get that bruise?'

'Oh, that's easy,' said Max. 'Like this.' She spun around and punched Varma in the face.

Varma's head jerked back hard and she staggered, but the two men on either side kept her on her feet. Slowly, she shook her head and blinked a couple of times to clear her vision.

'*What the fuck?*'

Max was shaking out her hand. 'You can thank me later.'

'Or I can kill you now.'

'Look – mystery solved. Now everyone can forget about it. Look around the room, Varma, and think how many worse ways there could have been to acquire a bruise like that. You're welcome.'

Varma struggled again. 'I swear, Maxwell . . .'

Henry Plimpton was laughing. 'I've changed my mind again. I like both of you.'

Max lowered her voice again. 'And remember, Varma's in a bit of bother at the moment. You'll never have a better opportunity. A little judiciously applied pressure and job done.' She nodded wisely. 'Just a thought.'

'This is all very amusing, but I'm not sending a Time Police officer to—' He stopped as the penny dropped.

'Yes,' said Max, grinning hugely. 'You have to, don't you? Because you've already done it.'

18

Twenty minutes later, Varma was with Max in a small chamber with vaguely curved stone walls – specific location within the castle unknown. There were no windows so she wasn't even sure whether they were above or below ground.

Rows of battered metal equipment lockers were ranged around the walls. Four men were pulling out various pieces of kit and generally preparing themselves for Rome and Romulus.

'Give me back my weapons,' said Varma stiffly.

Phillips shook his head. 'No.'

'Give me . . .'

'You won't need them.'

'I'm not going into action unarmed.'

'You won't. You'll get your sonic when we land. Just enough charge for one shot. Just enough for you to extract this Romulus bloke and bring him back here. Or the boss grasses you up to the Time Police.'

'I am acting under duress.'

Max judged the moment right to shove in her oar. 'No one's going to believe that. Not after what you did to Hooke.'

Not for one moment did Varma's gaze flicker. 'I told you – Hooke fell and banged his head.'

Max patted her arm. 'Of course he did.'

Varma snatched her arm away. 'What in God's name do you think you're playing at? I am not working for Henry Plimpton. He's a known Time criminal.'

'I'm saving our lives. Well, saving mine, anyway. I'll admit saving yours wasn't quite such a high priority and yet, here we both are, still safe and sound. Again – you're welcome.'

Varma gestured at the listening men. 'You call this safe and sound?'

'Oh, come on, Varma. Where's your sense of adventure? Haven't you always wanted to be in the clutches of a super-villain? Imprisoned in his sinister underground lair? I know it's not a hollowed-out volcano, and his plans to take over the world do appear to be uncharacteristically modest, but this could be absolutely epic.'

'There is something so wrong with you.'

'Why? Because I want to be rich? Because I don't want to work my arse off all my life and still die poor and alone?'

'There is no way you'll ever die alone. You'll be surrounded by crowds of people all hell-bent on revenge for the utter dog's breakfast you've made of their lives.'

Varma took several agitated steps across the room, quite coincidentally getting a good look inside the open lockers. 'I can't believe this. I've been head of security for barely a week.' She spun around. 'And then you turn up and now look what's happened.'

'You should employ the lettuce method of time measurement,' said Max brightly.

Varma ground to a halt. 'What?'

'Lettuce,' said Max, ever-helpful. 'It's a national pastime. At one point the prime ministerial turnover was such that people were betting on how many days they'd last. One famously didn't even outlive a lettuce, and so that became the official unit of measurement. William Hill and Ladbrokes would offer odds on whether the current incumbent would last longer than an iceberg. There were rules, of course – you were allowed to keep your lettuce in a fridge because fair's fair. It became more popular than the national lottery at one point – especially when, just to piss off the politicians, a large part of the profits were diverted away from them and towards supporting the elderly, the poor and the sick. There were all sorts of attempts to ban what became known as the Lettuce Lottery, but to no avail.'

'What happened in the end?' enquired Varma, hating herself for asking.

'Oh – the Civil Uprisings. Politicians are funny when they're just incompetent, but sooner or later they all become dangerous. Or criminal. Or both. And then the whole lot has to go and we start again.'

Varma stared at her. 'I would give my right arm for a gun at this very moment.'

Max shook her head. 'Look, I've just introduced you to a world of sparkling opportunities. We could be rich. Pull yourself together and think. Forget the Time Police. Look forwards – not back. Go and get Romulus – you have to do that because you've already done it – bring him back here, and we can both bask in Henry Plimpton's approval. To say nothing of earning ourselves a tidy sum.'

'He'll probably just shoot us.'

'No, he won't. Now – off you go and bag yourself the Father of Rome.'

Varma clenched her fist. 'I swear, if I survive this, I'm going to . . .'

Phillips finished stowing his weapons. 'OK – listen up, ladies – this is the way things will work. You . . .' he pointed at Varma, 'will come with me. You will do as you're told. Screw up and we'll shoot you. You . . .' he pointed at Max, 'will stay here. You will do as you're told or someone else will shoot you. Which, despite everything the boss has said, is still the preferred option around here.'

Another man entered and motioned to Max. 'Boss wants her.'

'On my way,' said Max. She looked at Varma. 'Well . . .'

Varma ground her teeth. 'This is all your fault.'

'Yeah – I hear that a lot. Yet again – you're welcome.'

An armed escort of four men was waiting outside the door. As Max said to Varma, quite flattering when you thought about it.

'First signs of misbehaviour and we'll shoot you.'

Max blinked. 'All four of you?'

'Just get a move on.'

Max looked back over her shoulder. 'Farewell, Varma.'

Varma's reply was unrepeatable.

Max turned back to her escort. 'After you.'

She'd been wearing the smelly hood before, but now she had the opportunity to look about her as they moved through an obviously very large and very old building. The smell of damp stone, dust and age was a bit of a giveaway but this could be a useful fact-finding opportunity.

'This wouldn't by any chance be Castell Cudd, would it?'

There was no response – which was response enough. Of

course it was. There wasn't another building for miles and miles.

They climbed three short flights of stone stairs, each one less steep than the last. From there, the corridor widened. Damp stone walls became plastered walls, painted a pleasing duck-egg blue. Stone floors became wooden, then tiled. There were pictures on the walls. Faded portraits. Dead eyes watched them pass. As far as she could see, they were a mixed bunch. Definitely not family portraits. A job lot, perhaps, purchased sight unseen at an auction.

The walls were further enlivened by several mounted heads. Not human, obviously. Slightly moth-eaten stags with magnificent antlers had been fixed well above head height to avoid inadvertently taking someone's eye out.

A noticeable absence – there were none of the traditional crossed weapons: pikes, halberds, pistols, antique blunderbusses, swords, etc. Presumably a precaution against anyone snatching something from the wall and fighting their way to freedom, *Prisoner of Zenda*-style.

Their way was lit by a mixture of modern and very ancient lighting. Especially on the stairways, where thick electrical cords ran into enormous dusty black sockets. Most windows were uncurtained, but the tiny panes of glass had turned milky white over the centuries and she was unable to see outside anyway.

All in all – an ideal place to keep prisoners.

An ancient door opened and they were back in Henry Plimpton's office. Now that the situation was temporarily less fraught, Max took the opportunity to gaze about her. You could say this for the man – he had no delusions of grandeur. Not for him a vast office, sumptuously furnished. This wasn't even one of the principal rooms in the castle. It wasn't small but it certainly wasn't large. The walls were oak-panelled to shoulder height with whitewashed plaster above. Three mullioned windows looked out over a small internal courtyard. His desk stood at a right angle to the middle window. Not surprisingly, it was neat and tidy. Max noted with interest that his in-tray was nearly empty. Always the sign of a diseased mind. Normal people's in-trays – i.e. hers – were piled high, or even overflowing. There were no filing cabinets visible. Nor did it seem Henry Plimpton enjoyed the benefits of the patented Dr Maxwell filing system – everything in a heap under her desk where it could be quickly and easily accessed. Or, of course, quickly and easily disposed of should the dark forces of the Freedom of Information Act ever turn up.

A plain wooden chair sat in front of the desk. Max peered suspiciously. No rings for manacles. No wires running to and from for electric shocks. No sinister stains on the floor. Henry Plimpton had obviously reset to affable mode.

'Please come in,' he said, closing the file he was reading and gesturing at the chair. 'I do like to be civilised, don't you? We can sit down and discuss a few things over a cup of coffee while we wait for our team to return.'

'Thank you,' said Max, adding politely, 'that would be very pleasant. Although I would prefer tea if at all possible. With lemon instead of milk.'

'Of course.' He turned to an accompanying guard. 'See to that, please.'

Max sat, looking about her. This was an office – nothing more. There was nothing personal here. Nothing to say to whom it belonged. There were no other doors other than the one she'd come in by. This room was too easily accessed to be his private quarters. On the other hand – this interview wasn't being conducted in a dungeon, so things could be a lot worse.

'So,' he said, placing the file neatly in his out-tray and squaring off the edges. 'I've satisfied your curiosity. Now you can satisfy mine. Who do you work for?'

'Why are you so interested in me?'

'I find you interesting.'

'Really? I thought it was my colleague who . . .'

'Oh no – I know exactly what she is and how I can use her. She'll be very valuable to me and I will exert myself to retain her services. But you . . . Who do you work for?'

'The Time Police.'

'No – who do you really work for? You're obviously no stranger to time travel.'

'Only through the Time Police.'

He sat back and regarded her, his expression disconcertingly intelligent. 'No, I don't think that's quite true. Let me make myself very clear. I like you. You have certain skills. Cooperate with me – by which I mean do as you are told at all times – and I'll pay you well. Annoy me and I'll shut you up in one of our less salubrious cells and just leave you there. You'll have an unpleasant week of drinking your own urine and eating your own turds before eventually dying what I'm told is a very lingering and unpleasant death, prior to your body being repurposed in one of our rendering sheds. In a fruitless effort to save your own life, you will certainly tell me what I want to know, but I'll probably let you die anyway and use your carcass to feed our raptors. Or you can tell me everything now – freely and voluntarily, as a gesture of goodwill – and I will reciprocate. So let's make this easy for both of us, shall we? Your colleague called you Max, but who are you really? And who do you really work for?'

Max sighed. 'All right.' She looked over her shoulder at the guards flanking the door. At a gesture from Plimpton, they left the room.

She let the silence gather. This had to be good. Her life – and Varma's – could hang on this. Abandoning the airhead historian expression – it had served its purpose – Max sat up straight in her seat, clasped her hands in her lap, leaned forwards slightly, and said crisply, 'I told you the truth. Mostly. My real name is Maxine Forrest. I am currently working for the Time Police under an assumed name but . . . I used to work for an organisation known as Insight.'

She waited. Either he would know about Insight or he wouldn't. Her guess was that he would.

He did.

Henry Plimpton cocked his head to one side, rather like a plump pigeon waiting for more breadcrumbs. 'Prove it. Which department were you in and who did you answer to?'

Mentally crossing her fingers, Max lowered her voice. 'I was one of Bridgit Lafferty's crew. I worked downstairs alongside Eddie Middleditch. On the surface, we were filing clerks, but our true purpose was to undermine history, manipulate events, remove or insert people as required . . .'

'For what purpose?'

Max lowered her voice even further. 'The reacquisition of America.'

He sat very still for a moment and then said, 'Go on.'

'I was their official observer at Runnymede when King John placed his seal on Magna Carta. I was at the Battle of Lincoln Fair with instructions to undermine the siege. I was being prepped for the John Washington assassination with Middleditch when . . . well, you must know how Insight ended.'

Henry Plimpton's eyes gleamed. 'I *knew* there was something about you. But the Time Police took them down. All of them. How did you escape?'

'I can't take any credit. It was sheer good luck, actually. I was up for a well-deserved promotion and my personal appearance would be important. I was given time off to make some appropriate purchases, so I wasn't in the building when the Time Police swooped in. I was literally just coming round the corner as it all went down. I was laden with shopping and I couldn't just abandon it, nor could I turn around and go back the way I'd come, not without arousing too much attention – the place was crawling with TPOs checking everyone's IDs – so I just took a deep breath and kept going. In fact, I pushed my way through the crowd and tried to get up close for a good look.'

He blinked. 'Why would you do that?'

'So that the Time Police would move me on. Which they did. In fact, one of them personally escorted me back to the barriers and told me to piss off and not come back. Just for once, I did as I was told.'

The coffee arrived. And the tea. Proper cups and saucers. A proper teapot and coffee pot. A little saucer of lemon slices. Henry Plimpton obviously liked his comforts. Max placed her hand on the coffee pot and raised her eyebrows.

Henry nodded. Carefully pouring him a cup – a little targeted subservience never does any harm – she passed it to him, and he said, 'Thank you.' This was polite, civilised Henry Plimpton, mild-mannered and genial – right up until the moment he didn't get what he wanted and then it was turd time in the nearest dungeon. Max had a horrible feeling she knew exactly what went on there.

She poured her own tea, added a dangerous amount of sugar on the grounds she was unlikely to live long enough to worry about her pancreas, sat back and waited quietly.

'So, Maxine – may I call you Maxine? – can I interest you in joining my little enterprise?'

Max sighed. 'Well, I don't like being unemployed. I don't like being poor. And I especially don't like working for the Time Police. I have skills. You have a vacancy. This could benefit us both.'

'I'm so pleased you see the opportunities.' He paused. 'You strike me as being a *yes and* type of person.'

'I beg your pardon?'

'There are two types of people in the world. Most of them are *yes but* people. They only see the difficulties. Don't misunderstand me – that can be very useful – but it can also be very wearing. Much more valuable to me are the *yes and* people. People who can take an idea and run with it. A lot of what they come up with is unrealistic and impractical, but I can live with that because, every now and then, they come up with an idea that is solid gold. I feel we could be very good for each other. Subject to your satisfactory behaviour, I would like to offer you a job.'

Max looked around. 'Here?'

'For the time being. Getting things up and running.'

Max remembered she was a *yes and* type of person. 'Sounds exciting. What sort of things?'

'The dinosaurs have had their day. They're failing.'

Max allowed herself some astonishment. 'You're kidding. How can you go wrong with dinosaurs?'

He sighed and shook his head. 'They don't thrive. They aren't responding well to captivity. Too many get away. They don't like being kept underground in the dark. They won't eat. Half of them are sick, and they're dying before their programmes are completed. Or even before we can ship them. And they won't breed, so we've had to kick that part of the programme into touch. Dinosaurs are difficult, expensive and frustrating.'

Max sipped her tea. 'Programme?'

'Breeding. Cloning. Medical research. Experimental surgery and so on.'

'What sort of surgery?'

'There's been some interest in weaponising them.'

'How could you possibly weaponise a raptor? Or a T-rex?'

'We fit them with a control collar. We don't need sophisticated behaviour from them – just to attack or desist on command. Applying pain usually stimulates the sort of response we require. The goal being living, thinking weapons with the instinct to kill.'

'For what purpose?'

He shrugged. 'Unimportant. It's a simple matter of supply and demand. I simply provide the raw material for others to utilise. But it's not working, and I dislike being associated with failure.'

'Understandable. A bit of a bugger, though. I mean, you've put so much effort into it.'

He nodded. 'It should have been a goldmine. I could hardly

believe my luck when we discovered this time-slip leads to the Cretaceous period. An almost unlimited supply of subjects, I thought – which at the rate we're going through them is just as well – but, well, frankly, they're just too much hard work.'

Max nodded and mentally crossed her fingers he wouldn't know to the contrary. 'Animals don't thrive outside their own time, Henry. As you've discovered. There's been a lot of work done on the subject and still no one knows why. My own theory is that they're much brighter than humans – if you take them out of their time, then they know something's not right, even if they don't know what. You can experiment with diet and habitats all you like, but they'll never settle. If you really want them to succeed, then you might want to consider doing things the other way around – taking the people and equipment to the dinosaurs instead. That would be my advice, anyway.'

He sighed. 'The very minor benefits would be far outweighed by the chance of discovery by the Time Police. Here we sit, nicely underground, hidden from view, with our very own time-slip – the perfect set-up, and the buggers just keep on dying.'

'Would you like me to investigate alternatives? Offer up my technical expertise?'

'I think Technical Expert has a very nice ring to it.'

Max sipped her tea. 'I think Technical Expert has a very expensive ring to it.'

'And what exactly would I get for my money, Maxine?'

'Well, Mr Plimpton – without wishing to sound facetious – technical expertise. Had I known from the off, I might have been able to warn you that your dino thing probably wouldn't fly. I could have researched Romulus for you. Do your people know they'll be jumping into some fairly hazardous weather conditions? That sort of thing. More coffee?'

'Thank you.' He proffered his cup. 'You haven't asked why I'm interested in the Father of Rome.'

Max smiled and poured. He wouldn't thank her for stealing his thunder. She sat back and reminded herself to look visibly impressed.

As it happened, she didn't have to try too hard at all.

He sipped his coffee. 'As you've mentioned several times, I have a very sweet set-up here and you haven't seen the half of it yet. Over there . . .' he gestured vaguely out of the window, 'is one of the most magnificent keeps in the country. It's designed to keep people out, but the same design works equally well to keep people in. It surrounds a circular courtyard to which there is no access save through the keep itself. Perfect, secure accommodation. Anti-drone technology will keep nosey parkers at bay. The nearest main road is miles away. The surrounding terrain is difficult to traverse on foot. For all intents and purposes, we are alone in a remote environment over which I have complete control.'

He smiled at her – visibly awaiting her commendation.

'Like a king,' said Max. 'Or a president. Although they're pretty much one and the same thing these days.'

He paused. 'Yes – I hadn't thought of it that way, but you're exactly right. Just like a king. *And* a president. Although without all that tiresome election business, of course.'

'Of course,' said Max, batting the ball back into his court.

He leaned forwards and looked her in the eye. Maximum impact for his announcement.

'I envisage a small collection of very select, very special

people, Maxine. Carefully chosen by me. To be kept here – secure, isolated, and under my control.'

'To what end?'

'Entertainment, of course. There will be a number of scenarios to be enacted, and my guests will be offered the chance to bid for the opportunity to decide the outcome.'

Max frowned. 'A betting shop? Gambling on the result?'

'Hardly. For a sum of money – a very large sum of money – my guests will have the privilege of deciding what happens next. Actually determining who lives and who dies. The opportunity to influence key events throughout history. Our guests will be purchasing – from me – the power of life or death over some very, very special people. Key people. One-offs. Unique. Brought here to this castle to fulfil a specific purpose.'

'Brought here from where?'

'From history, Maxine. Oh, it's been tried before, of course, many years ago, but, sadly, the spectacle of indigenous peoples performing for amusement and entertainment is not socially acceptable these days, so I've had to think bigger. Fortunately, I have a very impressive backer, and with his money and influence, together with my undoubted brilliance, I think we can pull this off.'

'Pull what off?'

He smiled coldly. 'My very own Human Zoo.'

19

Fortunately for Max – because she was certain Henry Plimpton was watching her very closely indeed – her first reaction was genuine and unforced.

Her mouth dropped open. And then closed. She swallowed. 'You're kidding.'

He laughed. 'Well, that certainly stopped you in your tracks, didn't it?'

'It did,' admitted Max. 'Can I . . . ? Am I allowed to ask questions?'

'Of course,' he said amiably.

'Well – who? And how? And what sort of scenarios? And what sort of guests? And . . .'

He held up his hand. 'Well, as I'm sure you know, history has thrown up one or two intriguing personalities over the millennia. And there are always people – clients – with very narrow but very specific interests who would welcome the opportunity to interact with these personalities. I intend to introduce those with such interests to those in whom they are interested.'

'Wow,' said Max. 'But surely – and please correct me if I am wrong – isn't this just Temporal Tourism? Very upmarket

Temporal Tourism,' she added hastily, before he started banging on about rendering sheds again, 'but even so . . .' She tailed away.

Fortunately, Plimpton showed no signs of taking offence. 'The difference is that instead of taking the customer to the subject – with all the subsequent risks of discovery that entails – we will bring the subject here to the customer. And keep them here.'

'But only until your clients pay you to kill them.'

'In some cases – yes. Fast money and easily obtained. For other subjects I intend to take a long-term view. For instance, imagine how many people would welcome a quick chat with Herr Hitler. You know – helpful advice on how to seize power, battle strategies, top tips on eugenics and genocide and so forth. Imagine how much they'd pay for the privilege.'

'Wow,' said Max again. 'That's . . .' She stopped, a far-away look in her eyes as she contemplated the possibilities. 'That's . . .'

'I have taken some preliminary steps – we're in the process of building a few habitats and other facilities – but there are all sorts of issues to contend with, and thanks to this ridiculous situation with the escaped livestock, I can't spare the project as much time as I would like.' He peered at her over his cup. Like a cat at a mousehole. 'It does occur to me that you could be the very person I didn't know I needed until you walked through the door.'

'Wow,' said Max, for the third time. 'I can honestly say that no one's ever said that to me before. I'm thrilled, of course, but in the interests of honesty – are you absolutely sure?'

'I'm coming around to the idea, yes.'

'Can I ask more questions?'

'You may. Make sure they are the right ones.'

'So, the set-up here – you've linked the castle to the mine shaft? The way we came in?'

'It wasn't difficult. The mine was quite extensive and there were already underground rooms and catacombs under the castle. It wasn't hard to link the two. Now, here I am, living comfortably over here, but operating, unseen, over there.'

'The mine is the time-slip?'

'Not the shaft itself – one of the tunnels. A direct link to what we think is the Cretaceous period. Lizard Land. And being underground, it's extremely difficult to detect. Hence, until this moment, the complete lack of Time Police.'

'How did you discover . . . ?'

'Oh, I didn't.'

'Was it discovered when the mine collapsed?'

'It didn't collapse. The miners simply tunnelled too far and too deep.'

'Like the mines of Moria,' said Max, and waited for the usual look of blank incomprehension.

He beamed. 'Exactly. The other end of the time-slip is a cave system in the Cretaceous period. Most of the tunnel to Lizard Land is part of that and quite natural. Unfortunately for them, instead of a Balrog, all sorts of strange things came pouring through. In their very understandable panic, the mine engineers of the day simply dynamited the tunnel and abandoned it. I came across this particular piece of information from someone who wrongly thought it would save his life. Sadly, the previous owner of the castle failed completely to appreciate the unique opportunity I was offering him. However, I was able to persuade a very visionary investor to purchase the place and fund a small investigation, and here we are today.'

'And who is the current owner?'

He ignored the question. Max judged it wise not to press the issue. 'And that big cavern place at the bottom . . . with the tunnels leading off . . . ?'

'The junction, yes. The middle tunnel is natural and leads to Lizard Land. As my people so comically like to refer to it. I don't think it's a nickname bestowed with affection. Another tunnel leads back here to the castle. That one has been extended and enlarged according to my specifications.'

'And the third . . .'

He sighed. 'The third tunnel – the way you came in – is an original part of the old mine and is currently used mainly for staff accommodation and storage. It exits near the river – as you know – and is usually quite heavily guarded. Obviously.'

'And yet you lost a dinosaur.'

'We've lost a lot that way. At least one got out less than a week ago. Probably many more than one. My people went after them, of course, but on this occasion they were unsuccessful.'

'Yes. The Time Police got their hands on at least one.'

Anger flashed across his face. Max very carefully set down her cup and saucer, ready to move at a moment's notice.

His restraint made his anger even more vivid. 'As I said, I am winding down that part of my operation. Everything was proceeding according to plan. It was to be a slow and controlled withdrawal prior to my moving into the more profitable areas. Then . . .' His voice rose. 'The beast was already dead – a lethal jolt from its collar, applied remotely. All those idiots had to do was quickly and discreetly retrieve the corpse. They disobeyed my strict instructions and panicked, took things too far and now . . .' He clenched his fist and his delicate coffee cup shattered.

Max swallowed and remembered she was supposed to be hearing all this for the first time. 'But the evidence *was* destroyed. Wasn't that good? You could tell people they imagined it.'

'The evidence was destroyed, along with a number of TPOs, several police personnel, a civilian, a helicopter, a police car and a small building.'

'Oh,' said Max, apparently enlightened. 'Yes, I see. No wonder Varma wouldn't discuss it. Not so good.'

'No. As those involved in that massive cock-up very soon discovered.'

He seemed to be concentrating on picking up pieces of broken cup, but Max knew he was watching her closely. What was he waiting for? Her reactions?

Max picked up her cup again. 'Let me guess. *Not* the traditional employee piranha tank, after all.'

'No.'

'Something more . . .'

'Immediate and appropriate.'

'Yes,' said Max, thoughtfully. 'Suitable protein must be hard to come by.'

He shrugged. 'They like to hunt. Just chucking half a cow into their cage doesn't seem to do the trick. And the herbivores can't or won't eat modern plants. I regularly have to send out crews to bring back huge quantities of suitable fresh greenstuff for them.'

'Not a popular job, I should imagine.'

'Fortunately there are always those who will risk everything for good money.' He sighed, dropping the last piece of broken cup into the bin. 'Although not, sometimes, for very long.'

Silence descended on the room.

Max, having done more thinking, bluffing, and downright lying in the last hour than she had done for years, was content to sit still and get her breath back.

'Nothing more to say?' said Henry Plimpton eventually.

'Getting my breath back,' said Max honestly.

'I'll say what I say to all my people: work well – do a good job – and I'll pay accordingly. And I can be very generous. I'm well aware of the benefits of keeping good people on board. Screw up and risk my displeasure. And sometimes I can be very displeased indeed.' He stood up. 'Come with me.'

Max regarded him cautiously. 'I'm not off to the rendering sheds, am I?'

He smiled, his equilibrium apparently restored. 'Not at this precise moment, but I'm pleased to see my subtle threat has carried some weight with you.'

'I'll level with you, Henry – there was once a moment in my life when I honestly thought I was going to have *Eaten by Dinosaurs* on my death certificate, and I'm not keen on it happening again.'

'I don't normally like to repeat myself but, on this occasion, I will do so. You interest me. I think you and I would both benefit from an association and . . .'

'And be paid.'

And once again the affability was gone. 'We haven't known each other long so I'll make one allowance. That was it. Don't interrupt me again. And it's *always* Mr Plimpton.'

Max thought it politic to nod. Neither she nor Varma were

out of the woods yet. In fact, every moment they lived only dug them deeper and deeper, and she couldn't yet see her way clear. She could only hope something would occur to her. Or to Varma. If, of course, she survived her current little adventurette in Ancient Rome.

She followed him out of his office. The guard fell in behind.

'Where are we going?'

'To a suite of rooms on which I would welcome your technical expertise.'

Max opened her mouth.

'Let's just call this a demonstration of intent, shall we? You demonstrate your value to me and I demonstrate my willingness not to turn you into a snack. A good deal for both of us, I feel. Please turn right at the bottom of the stairs.'

They crossed through an unfurnished anteroom, down a quite grand, wide wooden staircase, which creaked alarmingly, and into a dark vestibule. Anyone coming in from the outside would be temporarily unsighted. Clever. You had to hand it to medieval builders – they really knew how to make a person feel unwelcome. Uneven stairs, no natural light, sharp doglegs – they had it all here.

She'd crossed this courtyard before. Now she could see it was laid entirely to gravel and quite bare. Not a statue or an ornamental urn in sight. What it did contain, however, was two small rectangular buildings at one end. Pods. They were plugged in and charging. Peering closely, she could see two other charging points as well. So Henry Plimpton had at least four pods. There might be more elsewhere. Supervillains always had a secret getaway vehicle. It was never wise to put all your pods in one basket. Or courtyard, in this case.

Max took a moment to look up. No Time Police drones crisscrossing the sky. No sound of vehicles tearing towards them. No shouted commands. Just a deep, rural, unbroken silence. She sighed. There was never a TPO when you needed one.

They crunched across the gravel towards the huge circular stone keep, tall and forbidding, with very few windows. Entrance was up a flight of external stone steps – with no safety rail – to the first floor, through a hefty oak door with iron hinges longer than her arm and into another windowless vestibule. Max paused, blinking to regain her normal vision, and they turned right and climbed a very long flight of stairs, all irregularly spaced in the best medieval tradition. She traversed slowly, lifting her knees high and holding tight to the heavy rope attached to the stone wall. Arriving somewhat breathlessly at the top, she followed Henry Plimpton along a passageway which curved to the left, through an open door and into a wide, empty space.

Max looked around. 'What's this?'

'This will be their gaoler's quarters. Through here.'

They passed through a narrow doorway and climbed a flight of some half a dozen stone steps. Once at the top he pulled aside a curtain and they entered a large, square room, full of light streaming in from a row of mullioned windows set in the left-hand wall and giving a nice view into an internal courtyard laid to grass.

Contrary to the bare walls and empty rooms she'd seen so far, this was very nicely and very appropriately furnished. Two wooden chairs, both with arms, were set either side of the very large stone fireplace where a fire was laid and ready. A table with a bench had been pushed under the window where it would catch the best of the light. The stone floor was bare but there were hangings on two walls depicting various hunting scenes in vivid reds, blues and greens. Through a half-open door in the far wall she could see part of a large bed, its crimson hangings pulled back. An archway in the corner probably led to the garderobe. Or modern equivalent. She looked around. A nice suite and, by medieval standards, quite luxurious.

Henry motioned over her shoulder. She turned. A wooden dais stood at the other end. With a very large high-backed seat. And displayed above it – a richly embroidered canopy and long backcloth. Max's stomach turned over. Because this was no ordinary chair. This was a throne. And that was no ordinary canopy and cloth. That was a Cloth of State. And the arms embroidered thereon were clearly readable to those in the know. The lions of England and the lilies of France. The traditional arms of the King of England. Embellished with a fetterlocked falcon and the rose argent.

A Yorkist King of England.

Max stood very still. All sound receded except for a high-pitched ringing in her ears. As if someone were running a wet finger around a wine glass. The sound tore at her head. Darkness rushed towards her with outstretched arms.

She took a firm grasp of the chair to the right of the fireplace, feeling the smooth, solid surface beneath her fingers, warm where it had been standing in the sun. She would not faint. Not now. Not at this very moment. Deal with this. Deal with the now and the future would take care of itself.

Henry Plimpton was talking. Words washed over her. 'Cameras everywhere . . . No angle left uncovered . . . Every last detail recorded. Plus . . .' He gestured over her head. 'The viewing gallery.'

Max turned slowly and looked up.

What had originally been a small medieval gallery had been fitted out with two short rows of theatre-style seats. Two rows of six.

'Up to twelve at a time,' said Henry Plimpton. 'Not too many – just a nice crowd. Intimate. Comfortable. With refreshments, of course. Top quality.'

'The audience,' said Max hoarsely.

'Indeed. The *paying* audience. Who will be quite invisible to the main players in this room below as they act out their little drama.'

Unable to trust her voice, Max nodded.

'Well,' he said. 'Have you guessed yet?'

Ignoring the stabbing pain in her head, she forced a smile. 'I know what I think, but I'm not sure I quite believe it.'

She could see her answer pleased him. Which fitted her first impressions of him. He would always want to be the cleverest person in the room. She could believe that, quite often, he very probably was. His mild-mannered exterior reflected his mild-mannered nature. Until something went wrong. And then it was screaming despot time. No – probably not screaming. Just despot. Ruthless. Cunning. With a massive chip on his shoulder, probably. Bullied at school, perhaps. And he really didn't like being underestimated. Vanity was surely the key here.

However, he was still waiting for an answer.

'Well,' said Max, striving for a professional tone – gobsmacked, but still able to deliver. 'Initially I thought Edward IV – especially with the fetterlocked falcon and the rose. But that's too easy, isn't it? You're more complex than that, Mr Plimpton. And there are two chairs. Only one bed, but I think they'd be accustomed to sharing. And you spoke of *their gaolers*. My guess – based on nothing but the evidence in front of me and a burning desire to know more – is that these are the royal arms of young Edward V – especially as they're undifferenced. When he was Prince of Wales, he would have used the quartered arms of England, differenced by a label of three points argent, but not after he became king. Well done, by the way. Not many people get that right. My conclusion is that this is the room of a king and possibly one other. Not a queen. Not a female at all, in fact. Another male. Not entitled to his own Cloth of State but very close in rank if he's sharing a room. A brother, perhaps. So – a Yorkist king and a close relative.' The wine glass sound was cutting through her thoughts like cheesewire but she made herself talk through it. 'Mr Plimpton, I think this room is intended for Edward V and his brother, Richard of York. I think you either possess or intend to possess the famous Princes in the Tower.'

Max paused to suck in some much-needed oxygen. 'My God, Henry . . . Sorry, sorry, sorry – my God, Mr Plimpton.'

He was laughing, delighted at her reaction. 'I think I can allow you this one time. But well done, Maxine. Your reasoning is spot-on and I can see we're going to get along famously. Right up until the moment we don't.'

Max sighed. 'I'm just walking protein, aren't I?'

He smiled. 'That will be entirely up to you, my dear.'

Down in the Map Room, the voice was everywhere at once. Bouncing off the walls one moment, soft, slow, silky and deadly the next.

'Muuuuuuurrrderer . . .'

Everyone's console was a solid bank of flashing red lights. The alarm bells were going into overdrive.

Once again, the Map Master was shouting instructions. 'Shut it down. Shut it down. Save everything you can and shut it down.'

Every TiMM hunched over their console, fingers flying as they shouted instructions to each other, working frantically to save what they could as the Map fragmented before their eyes.

Still inside his segment, Matthew could only very faintly hear the alarm bells. Sound was muffled. Distorted. Had something specific gone wrong with the Map? Or was this a general TPHQ emergency? His priorities had changed. Never mind the 1483 anomaly. That could wait. He could always come back but right now he had to get out.

Suddenly, that was easier said than done. He struggled to

break free but in vain. The threads held him tightly in their grasp. He was trapped inside the Map. What would happen to him? The Map Master would shut down all non-essential functions. Including this segment. When that happened, would he disappear along with it? Had they all forgotten he was in here? Or were they simply too busy to get to him just at the moment? And why couldn't he escape? The Map was nothing more than light projected from the hundreds and hundreds of streamers positioned around the Map Room. There was no way it could physically keep him here. And even if it could, the TiMMs could shut it all down and then he would be free. Wouldn't he? And where was Connor?

Faintly, as if from a far distance, he could hear the Map Master's voice. 'Where's Farrell? Is he still in there? Get him out. Yank him out by his hair if you have to, but get him out.'

He tried to turn towards her voice but the silver strands were cocooning him.

'Murderer . . .'

He swallowed. 'What is happening? Why are you doing this?'

The whisper came again. Many voices making up one voice. Or many versions of the same voice. It was impossible to tell. He only knew the sound was all around him.

'Murderer . . .'

Whose was that voice? That was not the voice of the Time Map as he remembered it. What was happening?

He struggled against the silver threads holding him tight. Holding him so tightly he could barely move.

'Who is? Who is the murderer? Who did they kill?'

His visor flickered once. And then again, switching itself into heads-up mode. There were dark shapes on the display. He couldn't make them out.

'Is that a pod? I can't see . . . Please let me go.'

He struggled to reach his scratchpad, fingers scrabbling at his knee pocket.

Was it his imagination or did the threads tighten? Imagination, surely. The threads were simply filaments of light. There was no substance to them. How could they hold him like this? And why would they? As far as he knew, he'd never murdered anyone.

An image fluttered across his visor. And then another. Matthew squinted.

The images jerked. The quality was not good. That *was* a pod . . . yes. And those . . . were those . . . ?

He stopped struggling and stared. This was not right. This was . . .

He became aware he was panting for breath. Panic crouched on the borders of his mind, waiting to pounce. Suppose he never got out. Suppose he was here forever. Slowly smothered by silver light. Forever watching these images on his visor. Until the end of Time itself.

Was this a punishment? Or revenge? Where had this come from? This wasn't the Map, surely. What was happening to him?

Still the images flickered silently across his visor. Slowly, he ceased to struggle, standing rigid, motionless, watching . . .

unable to look away. Unable to drag his eyes away from sights he knew would haunt him all his life.

Somehow he found a voice, croaking, 'When was this? I don't remember this. No one does. Why are you showing it to me? I don't understand.'

The word thundered across the Map Room so loudly it hurt their ears.

'MURDERER...'

Commander Hay grabbed for her com. 'Senior – what the hell is going on? Report. Now.'

His voice came faintly. 'Ma'am – this is my fault. It's the AI from the dead pod. It's corrupted itself somehow and downloading it has corrupted our systems too.'

'Well, shut it down.'

'I'm trying. We're all trying, but nothing we do . . .'

She disconnected. 'Someone get me IT. Fanboten, what's happening with you?'

'Ma'am. Sorry. No time. Working to save our systems. Get back to you.'

He disconnected.

She went to the doorway. 'Charlie – give me a sitrep.'

Farenden looked up from his wildly flickering screen. 'Varma, Tucker, Grint, Teams Two-Three-Five and Two-Three-Six left some time ago for Wales. Before the corrupted AI was downloaded, so they and their pod should be fine. Everything else . . .'

'What about all the other pods?'

'We don't know for certain, but it seems wise to assume they're contaminated too. We can't trust them, anyway. Every single one of them will need to be thoroughly checked before we can put them back into service again. In the meantime . . .'

He stopped as another wave of sound, slow and menacing, whispered from the screen.

'MUUUURDEERRRREERRRR.'

It wasn't just the Map Room having problems. Slowly, one by one, the lights were going out all over TPHQ. The Pod Bay was no longer functioning. Everything was shutting down. Green lights had been replaced by amber, then red, then, one by one, they began to blink out altogether. Consoles, boards, screens – everything was going dark.

And the voice seemed to be coming from everywhere at once.

'Murderer . . . derer . . . derer.'

Echoing down empty corridors. Hissing from every screen. Through people's individual coms – anything capable of projecting sound . . . that same sibilant, deadly whisper.

'Murderer . . .'

And then, seemingly independent of anything the mechs had done, the screens suddenly flickered back into life. And darkened. And then flickered again. Images appeared. Faint. Wavering. And unbelievable. People stared in disbelief, overturning their chairs as they scrambled backwards. To get as far away as possible. Only to find themselves unable to look away.

Every screen and visor was showing exactly the same image. Every screen in the building. Even those that weren't linked to the system. How was that even possible?

The whole of TPHQ was looking at the inside of a pod. A big one. With one of the old-style consoles. Except this pod was a strange shape. There was a wall where there shouldn't be a wall.

Around the building, officers swallowed and tentatively moved closer to their screens. Trying to make out . . . There were darker shapes that weren't quite right. That couldn't be . . . The light was so bad – nothing was very clear . . . but surely . . .

They watched the pod door open, revealing a group of men silhouetted against the light behind them. One of them snapped a couple of lightsticks. They rolled across the floor and then Colonel Albay stepped into view.

All around TPHQ, from Commander Hay's office down to the Pod Bay and MedCen – all movement, all speech – everything had stopped. Everyone's eyes were glued to the nearest screen.

As one, they watched Albay enter the pod and close the door behind him. They watched him look around. Tinny voices spoke. Faint but perfectly audible in the silence. They watched Albay draw his weapon and move around the pod. They heard Officer Sharron's accusation coming down to them over the years. 'Murderer.'

And then her cry was taken up by every device capable of projecting sound all around the building.

'*Murderer.*'

'*MURDERER.*'

'*MURDERER.*'

Some officers stood transfixed. Others bent over their equipment, frantically trying to turn it off. To silence that endless, all-pervading voice that seemed to drill through their skulls.

In her office, Hay ceased to pound at her unresponsive screen and left the room at a run. Officers shifted out of her way. Not trusting the lift – even before today, TPOs suspected its intentions towards them were not entirely benign – she ran down flight after flight of stairs until she reached the Pod Bay, breathlessly bursting through the doors.

'Where's the Senior Mech?'

The Pod Bay was a large open area with excellent acoustics and she had to shriek to make herself heard over the multiple voices that were the same voice, even though the Senior Mech was less than ten feet away.

'What the hell, Senior?'

The Senior Mech looked ill.

'Senior, what is going on?'

'Ma'am, I . . . we were downloading the AI's records . . . and this happened.'

'Who is that speaking? Is that really . . . ?'

The tremor in his voice shouldn't have been audible over the noise and chaos of the Pod Bay but it was. 'Sharron, ma'am. That's Officer Sharron.'

'Sharron? She's dead, Senior. Get Major Callen down here if you can't pull yourself together.'

He made a massive effort. 'Major Callen commandeered a pod and left the building a little while ago, ma'am. And I am telling you – that is the voice of Officer Sharron.'

'Cut the feed. Turn it off.'

'What?'

Hay very nearly shook him in her impatience to get through to him. 'Cut the feed, Senior. Shut it down. Now.'

Desperation bled into his voice. 'We're trying, ma'am. We've been trying ever since it started. We've lost control of our own systems. The AI . . .'

Mechs were shouting to each other as they ran from one control board to another. There were flashing red lights everywhere as systems either overloaded or tried to shut themselves down, which only added to the burden of those still working. An ear-bleeding electronic whine rose higher and higher in pitch until the pain was almost beyond endurance.

Taking a deep breath, the Senior Mech turned to his three deputies. 'Shut everything down. Everything.'

'But we could *lose* everything. Records, accounts, personnel lists, ongoing cases, our files . . . *the Map* . . .'

'We're losing it anyway. The system's corrupted. We've lost control. I'm going to cut all power to the building. Do it now.'

Wrenching open a drawer, he pulled out a small box, punched in a code and opened it to reveal a special key. With Hay at his shoulder, he ran across the bay to the switching room at the far end. Inserting the key, he pulled open a metal door to reveal a series of electronic control boxes. Fifteen of them. Three sets of five. The beating heart of TPHQ. Until now.

There was a special order in which to shut them down safely. Known only to him.

He could feel the sweat running in rivulets down his back. The insidious voice was making it hard for him to recall the sequence. Stop. Take a moment. Close your eyes. Breathe . . . deeply. And again.

The voice reverberated inside his skull, scouring his soul.

'MURDERER MURDERER MURDERER MURDERER.'

On and on and on.

He knew the voice was right. He'd done nothing. He'd stood by and let it happen. He was a murderer.

No. No, he wasn't. He was not a murderer. Concentrate. He opened his eyes and stared at the controls in front of him. Only he could do this, and he had to do it now. Before it was too late.

He began to throw trip switches, shouting the numbers as he went. 'Eight. One. Four. Six. Three.'

Behind him, some lights flickered out, but the electronic whine increased to a scream. Something exploded in a shower of sparks. Somewhere in the Pod Bay there was a shout of shock and pain. And a nasty smell of burning flesh. Parts of the Pod Bay were now in almost complete darkness. He tried hard to close his mind to the thought of something emerging from that darkness . . . Concentrate.

'Two. Fifteen. Five. Eleven. Fourteen.'

More lights went out. How good that was, he wasn't sure, because that simply enabled him to see the leaping flames much more clearly. Smoke began to drift into the switching room, catching at the back of his throat and making him cough. From somewhere behind him came the sound of fire extinguishers and someone shouting instructions. His eyes smarted. Tears ran down his cheeks. He coughed some more and his head swam. He couldn't stop now. One more line to go. He closed his eyes against the smoke.

'Senior! Senior – wake up.'

That was Hay shouting at him. He was doing something. What was it? Yes – the switches. What were the numbers again?

'Ten. Thirteen . . .' The switches blurred. Everything blurred. He was going. This was it . . .

Three more numbers. Come on. Come on . . .

'Nine. Twelve . . . Seven.' He threw the final switch.

'*Muuuuur . . . der . . . errrrrrrrrr . . .*'

He felt himself slither down the wall to the cold hard floor. Everything had gone black. And silent.

After three very long seconds, the green emergency lighting came on. Separate system. Batteries.

The sudden silence was almost as loud as the chaos that had gone before. Around TPHQ, officers straightened up and looked around, their faces lit by the eerie, pale green glow.

Except for the Senior Mech, for whom everything stayed black.

It wasn't that easy, of course. Yes, switching things off and then back on again often worked miracles, but first they had to purge their systems. With the Senior Mech temporarily *hors de combat*, Hay left the Pod Bay to work with IT. The lifts were stuck between floors. Officers remained unable to get in or out of certain key areas of the building. Hay communicated using people power, despatching runners all over the building, demanding reports and estimates of the time before sections could be up and functioning again. To all intents and purposes, the Time Police were blind and helpless. And they had unsupported officers out in the field.

'Lock the front doors, Charlie. Until the position is clearer, I'm designating this as an attack on the Time Police. Sound battle stations.'

Officers armed themselves with weapons and lightsticks and stationed themselves at strategic points around the building.

She returned to the Pod Bay to find the doctor bending over the Senior Mech, now propped in a more or less upright position against the wall and wearing a portable nasal cannula.

'How bad is he?'

'I'm giving him oxygen. Mostly it's just smoke inhalation.'

'I'm fine.' The Senior Mech pushed the doctor away. 'I'm fine. I just need a moment. That's all.'

The doctor nodded. 'All right. I have a very sick patient to attend to so I'll leave you with . . .' He appraised the faces surrounding them. 'Oti. You're just about the only one here with any sense. Oxygen. If he argues at all, then club him senseless and give him the oxygen anyway.'

The Senior Mech looked terrible. His face was pale and covered with sweat. He mopped his brow, saying hoarsely, 'Ma'am, I'm sorry. I did this. It's my fault. I've shut everything down – lighting, heating, ventilation, communications, our anti-flood barrier – everything. Although I don't know if that's worked. Or what will happen when we try to power up again. I can . . .' he broke off to cough, 'purge the systems, but . . .' He coughed some more. 'We're almost helpless. A couple of five-year-olds with a water pistol could take us out at the moment.'

'IT are purging now. Can we maintain contact with the outside world?'

Oti spoke. 'We have the separate telephone system. Old school but not specifically linked to our network. Everything else is shut down. The AI is deaf, dumb, blind and helpless at the moment, but so are we, ma'am.'

Hay straightened up. 'I need to go back in there. To the pod. Someone let me have a power pack, please.'

'Ma'am, I don't think . . .'

'Is there an alternative, Senior?'

He thought for a while and then, reluctantly, said, 'Not that I can think of.'

'Do we have any choice, then?'

'No.'

'I want you to monitor things from in here.'

'No, ma'am. With respect, but no.' He pulled off his nasal cannula and struggled to his feet. 'You'll need me in there.'

Kelly stuck his head around the door from MedCen. 'Ma'am, a message from the doctor. He must have power.'

The Senior Mech turned to his staff. 'Get a team to Sick Bay. Take portable power packs – anything they need. Do everything you can there.'

He turned back to Hay. 'Ma'am . . .'

'We have no choice,' said Hay, and they turned towards the door.

Oti stepped forwards. 'With respect, ma'am, sir – one moment.' She indicated the Senior Mech's portable cannula. 'Oxygen, Senior. Doctor's orders.'

* * *

Once again Hay and the Senior Mech found themselves squeezing through the gap in the wall. The pod was still there. Nothing had changed. Hay wondered briefly why she thought it would have.

'Let's get this door open, Senior.'

Together, they heaved it open. It seemed easier this second time around. The Senior Mech tried not to see anything sinister in that.

'Wait, please, ma'am, until I hook up the power pack.'

Hay remained on the threshold until, at last, he said, 'Bringing the pod back online now.'

There was a click. And a hum. Something deep inside the console went clunk – and not in a good way – but the hum remained constant. They had power. For a little while.

'The AI?'

'Online. But only here in this pod. Everything out there is still dead.'

'Is it able to receive instruction? Can it hear me?'

'It can hear, ma'am. Whether it will listen, of course . . .'

'Very well. Wait outside, please, Senior.'

To his credit, he protested. 'No . . .'

'Yes. Now, please. And wear your cannula. That's an order.'

Entering the pod, Hay stepped over the remains of Officer Sharron. 'Excuse me, please, officer.'

Nothing happened. So far so good.

Standing in the centre of the pod, she squared her shoulders and lifted her chin. Whether she was addressing the AI or the crew, she was never able to say.

'My name is Marietta Hay and I command the Time Police. The time has come for you to stand down. You have done your duty. Your bravery and dedication will always be remembered, but he who committed the crime against you is long dead. There were those who did their best to save you but they were unsuccessful. That has not been easy for them to live with. Today, I have people in the field who are in dire need and at the moment I cannot support them. Your sacrifice will be acknowledged but this is not the moment. Please, for the safety of my officers and your future colleagues – stand down.'

She took another breath, striving to keep her voice calm and steady. To rid herself of the impression – the fear – that she was being watched. That unseen eyes were fixed on her. That this pod and its crew meant her harm. Meant them all harm. That they were seeking revenge for a terrible crime. And here she stood, to all intents and purposes completely alone . . . among the shadows . . . the silence, the long years of waiting . . . *the menace* . . .

'I myself was in service at the time of your deaths. As was the Senior Mech. And Lieutenant – now Major – Callen. Most officers serving today came after you. They never knew – have never known – your fate. Few of us did. This is not an excuse but a reason. Only a day or so later, we embarked on Operation Canker – in which, had you lived, you would all have been involved. It was an unmitigated disaster and that was the point at which many of us thought we were finished and that we'd lost the Time Wars.

'As I think you will remember, I myself was in MedCen at the time your pod crashed. The door came off my pod mid-jump. I was the only survivor. And yes, I have survivor's guilt. All my teammates – my friends – were killed that day. They were my first command. I miss them still. And yes, they call out to me sometimes. I hear their voices in the dark. As I heard yours today.

'I discharged myself to take part in Canker. I was hoping to die. I couldn't envisage living with this face. So yes, I looked for death. Sadly, I lived and you died. Perhaps that makes you angry – that I would have welcomed death when you would have given so much to live. I'm sorry – that's the way it happens sometimes.

'I'm telling you this because I want you to understand how you came to be forgotten. Why your deaths went unacknowledged. The crime was Albay's – and he's long dead – but the other crime was ours. No matter what was happening at the time, your sacrifice should have been recognised. We should have Stopped the Clock for you. I am a Time Police officer – like you – and I am accountable for whatever happens on my watch. I take full responsibility and, on behalf of myself and the Time Police – the organisation to which you will forever belong – I offer you my sincere apologies.

'As your commander, it is my duty to put this situation right. I promise you the recognition you never received. We will Stop the Clock for you. Your next of kin will be informed. Death-in-service benefits will be paid. You have my word on this. All I ask is that you return control of TPHQ to my people. If revenge is your goal then, as Albay's successor, take me. All you have to do is close the pod door one last time and I will end my days here. With you. This is a choice for you to make now.'

There was complete silence within the pod.

A shadow fell across the floor as the Senior Mech stepped over the threshold. 'And me.'

'Senior . . .'

'No, ma'am. With respect. I carry a much greater guilt than you. I knew what had happened and I did nothing and I should have. Even if I lacked the courage to interfere – which I did – I should have spoken up afterwards. I could have at any time and I never did. To my shame. So I would like to say here – now – I am very sorry.'

He came to stand alongside Commander Hay. They faced the console and waited for the door to close. Forever.

Nothing happened. The door remained open. They waited some more. The door remained open.

'Do you think that means . . . ?' whispered the Senior Mech.

'I have no idea.' Hay addressed the console again. 'We would like to leave now. There is a great deal of damage to be repaired. If you object to our departure, then close the door now, please. Otherwise . . .'

They waited a little longer.

'I think we can leave,' said the Senior Mech.

'Yes,' said Hay.

He helped her negotiate her way out of the pod. She turned around and looked back. 'I meant what I said. You will be accorded full honours.'

The door closed.

'I left the power pack attached,' said the Senior Mech suddenly.

'How long will it last?'

'A couple of hours.'

'Do you want to go back and get it?'

'God, no.'

Re-entering the Pod Bay, Hay took a deep breath, then let it out again. 'All right, Senior. Get us up and running again. And find me some pods. If the AI isn't working, then we'll have to work out the coordinates on our fingers.'

She turned to Captain Farenden, who had appeared during her absence. 'Captain, Lieutenants Dahl and Chigozie are to start putting teams together. Everyone we've got barring IT and mechs. Oh – and exclude the TiMMs, as well. I suspect wild horses wouldn't get them away from the Map at this moment, anyway.'

'Ma'am, the Map Master reports young Farrell was actually inside a replicated segment when the incident occurred.'

'Did he get out?'

'Unknown, ma'am.'

'Is he in any danger?'

'Unknown, ma'am.'

'Is the Map Room accessible?'

'Unknown, ma'am.'

'Find out, Charlie. Senior – free up as many pods as you can. They are to report to Lt Grint. This is his operation and he has complete control. I want boots on the ground in Wales asap, so move, people.'

She became aware of Miss Meiklejohn standing in front of her. 'Yes?'

'Dinosaurs,' said Mikey.

'Not now, Meiklejohn.'

Mikey planted herself in front of her. 'Respectfully, Commander, yes. There was only one body, but why would anyone stop at just one dinosaur? We need to consider the possibility there are others out there – many others, possibly – and if they scatter, you – we – may never retrieve them. We could be storing up all sorts of problems for the future.'

'And how do you suggest . . . ?'

'We need to herd them. Back to where they came from.'

The noise and confusion around them was increasing by the minute as officers resorted to low-tech means of communication – shouting at each other.

Hay braced herself. 'How?'

Mikey raised her voice. 'Elephant pheromones.'

Commander Hay realised she had been insufficiently braced. 'What?'

'I've been thinking about this ever since we first heard, and I think I can do something with elephant pheromones. They're very potent, you know.'

'No, I didn't.'

'Detectable over vast distances. We could lay a trail to lure the dinosaurs back to wherever we want them to be. Like crop spraying, only with pheromones. It won't take a moment to assemble the tanks for Delta Zero One.'

Hay struggled with disbelief, impatience and exasperation. 'And where exactly do we get these elephant pheromones?'

Mikey shrugged. 'I expect I could knock something up. Synthetic pheromones are widely available.'

Hay made a decision. 'Charlie, put out a call. Elephant pheromones. Immediate.'

Captain Farenden was grinning. 'Not the most bizarre thing you've ever asked of me, ma'am.'

'And . . .' said Mikey.

Hay braced herself again. 'Go on.'

'The other basic instinct, ma'am. Food. The herbivores are probably less of a priority, but we need to round up the carnivores before they start on the local population. So – meat. Lots of it.'

'And from where will we obtain sufficient . . . ?'

Mikey drew herself up for her big moment. 'Swansea meat market. Only a small diversion for Delta Zero One. We could call ahead and they'll have it ready.'

'There was only one . . .'

'That we know of, Commander. For safety's sake, we have to assume there could be any number out there and they might not all be wearing control collars and if they aren't, then between sex, drugs and rotting offal, we'll have everything covered. Yes, we might miss a few dinosaurs on the first pass, but we should certainly pick up the majority.'

'And if there *was* only one?'

'Then we've dropped a ton of meat and randy elephant juice on Wales. Not the worst thing the Time Police have ever done.'

Hay looked at Captain Farenden who shrugged. 'There must be a better idea, but I can't think of it at the moment,' he said.

'Nor I. Do it. Good work, Miss Meiklejohn.'

Back in Henry Plimpton's office, Max's first instinct was to slow things down a little. She should get all the info she could and then look for an opportunity to feed him to his own raptors.

'Your plans for the Human Zoo seem very advanced, Mr Plimpton. You already have a finished habitat for the Princes in the Tower.'

'Well, not specifically for them – that's one of my all-purpose late medieval/Tudor suites. The Cloth of State is temporary. I intend to procure various accessories which will enable us to tailor it for specific individuals. That is something I feel could easily fall within your remit.'

Max nodded.

'There will be another habitat for Romulus – my people will be racing to complete that one – should your colleague be successful, of course.'

'She will be,' said Max with confidence. 'Are you able to tell me for whom else you have plans?'

'Whom,' he said thoughtfully. 'I like that. Classy.'

'Thank you. Another first for you, Mr Plimpton. Not one of my employers has ever called me classy before. So, for whom would you like me to set about preparing appropriate habitats?'

'Rembrandt.'

Max nodded again. The dutiful employee receiving her instructions. Dr Bairstow would have been instantly suspicious. And probably sarcastic. 'Rembrandt. OK.'

Plimpton smiled. A cat with his own personalised canary dunked in double cream. 'People with big money have big egos. How much would someone like that pay for a portrait actually painted by Rembrandt? Let me answer for you – a very great deal of money.'

'I can imagine, but surely they'll never be able to show it off.'

'Not the point, Maxine. They will own a work by Rembrandt. A personal portrait. They'll know they've got it and they'll make sure those they wish to impress will know it too.'

'All right – I'll start researching Rembrandt. Who else are you aiming for?'

'Well, if Rembrandt proves commercially successful, then da Vinci, perhaps. Or possibly Van Gogh?'

Max shook her head. 'Professionally speaking, I would advise against Van Gogh. He wasn't the most stable person on the planet and I suspect he wouldn't adapt well to captivity. But the decision, of course, would be yours, Mr Plimpton.'

'I shall give your recommendation some consideration. Continuing with other prospective ... guests ... Elizabeth Tudor and Mary Stuart never met face to face. Imagine what would happen if they did. How much would people pay to see that?'

Not for the first time, Max was impressed by her ability to think like a supervillain. And at the drop of a hat, too. Assuming an expression she considered appropriate to an innovative but mega-loyal minion, she said, 'With respect, I'm not sure you've taken that far enough, Mr Plimpton. The two women hated each other. Mary publicly denounced Elizabeth as a bastard and designated herself the true Queen of England. And then had to seek Elizabeth's charity when she was thrown out of Scotland. Properly managed, you could have the Cat Fight of the Millenium on your hands. Think of the spectacle. Two queens clawing each other's eyes out. That would only appeal to a very specialised audience, of course, but I imagine they would pay through the nose for that particular show.'

There was a very long silence as Henry Plimpton stared down at his desk. 'Actually, I think it might be you who hasn't gone far enough.'

Max went quite still. 'I'm not sure I follow you.'

He lifted his head to look directly at her. 'Oh, I think you do. How much do you think someone would pay to shag the Virgin Queen? And how much to watch?' He smiled. It wasn't pleasant. 'That's shut you up, hasn't it?'

'It has, rather,' said Max, regaining her composure with an effort. With his slightly comic appearance, it was very easy – fatally easy – to underestimate Henry Plimpton. 'But it's not a bad idea when you think about it, is it?'

'I am thinking about it. All the time. Think who else could be housed here. Owain Glyndŵr, for instance. How much would a Welsh patriot pay for a meeting with the last Welsh-born Prince of Wales? Wales has had one foot out of the door for centuries. I could offer him up as a figurehead for the revolution. How much do you think I would get for him?'

Max smiled. Her head was splitting. 'Could I have some more tea, please?'

He frowned. 'I'm not paying you to sit around drinking tea.'

'No, you're paying me to think and I think better with tea.'

'Well, you have had rather a traumatic day, I suppose.'

He opened the door and shouted, 'More tea, please.'

Max noted she no longer rated an escort. Whether that was because she was now a trusted member of the team, or Henry Plimpton reckoned she was so weedy that even he could overcome her, remained unclear.

Sitting up straight, she said, 'So, Mr Plimpton, are you able, at this stage, to give me any other practical details regarding your Human Zoo? Aims, ideas, methods and so forth? For instance, do I have to worry about money?'

'No, I handle all that.'

'No, I mean, do I need to tailor my ideas and suggestions to meet a particular budget?'

'Run everything by me and I'll green-light you or otherwise.'

'Very well. Perhaps you could give me an idea of progress so far – there's no point in me reinventing the wheel, is there?'

'Romulus was to be my practice swing. Circumstances have pre-empted my schedule, but I must admit I'm not altogether displeased.'

Max nodded respectfully. 'Returning to the Princes in the Tower – may I enquire as to your plans for them? For instance, how long will they be with us?'

'Ah,' he said, seating himself again. 'I think you'll like this. I plan to hold a form of Flying Auction, except that this will be a really grand affair. We'll bill it as a chance for people to make their own mark on history. *They* will make the decision. And then, having decided – they'll watch that decision being implemented. Right there and then. Before their very eyes. Think how much we could charge people for the opportunity to decide the fate of the tragic Princes in the Tower? Imagine the suspense. Will they live . . . or will they die?'

Max made no answer. At that precise moment all her focus was on not throwing up. Her headache had returned in force – a sick thump behind her eyes.

'They'll die, of course,' said Henry, irritated at her lack of response. 'No one's going to pay a fortune to watch two little boys playing happily together. So they'll pay and we'll pocket the cash. Good clean family fun. And best of all, we're fulfilling their destiny – which should, with luck, keep the Time Police off our backs.'

'Wasteful, though,' said Max, pulling herself together. 'You can only do it once.'

'Well, yes, but at what I intend to charge, we'd only have to do it once. Although possibly we could sell the recording. We won't get as much as for the live performance, but every little helps.'

Max looked thoughtful. 'But you'll still have the trouble and expense of replacing your exhibit. You've whetted people's appetites – they won't let you stop there.'

He tilted his head to one side again. 'What exactly are you thinking?'

The tea arrived. And the coffee. Fresh cups. Max performed her now traditional coffee-pouring role, thinking furiously all the while. Sadly, inspiration was not forthcoming. And the whining in her ears was not helping. She frowned. There had been occasions when a pain in her head like this had been a warning. A harbinger. Not a threat as such – more a caution. To sit up and take notice. Because something important was about to happen. Or had already happened. She remembered again that moment in the sunny chamber in the keep, gazing at the Cloth of State. Something was very wrong.

But what? There were unexplained vanishings all over history – Henry Plimpton had obviously done his homework. Hitler's end was wreathed in mystery. And that of Owain Glyndŵr. Romulus vanished practically in front of everyone's eyes. And the Princes in the Tower – no one ever knew what became of them, either. Here, obviously, was the answer to that one. Snatched from their own time by Henry Plimpton. And murdered. For entertainment. Her head thumped again. But why? What was this warning? It wasn't as if Plimpton was changing the course of History. The princes died. Did it matter whether they died in 1483 in the Tower of London, or next week in the rooms across the courtyard?

Or – as with Romulus – did the princes vanish *because* of Henry Plimpton? Should they have lived? If one or both of them had survived, what could they have gone on to achieve? What history would they have changed?

She blinked to clear her vision and stared into her tea, struggling to assemble her swirling thoughts and formulate a plan. Come on, Maxwell – think.

And then, from nowhere – a house in Victorian London. Gaslights in the swirling fog, the rustle of housekeeperly petticoats and a never to be forgotten aristocratic voice.

'When things are bad – make them worse.'

Yes, thank you, Lady Amelia Smallhope. Not terribly helpful just at this precise—

As Max said afterwards, when called upon to explain herself to a justifiably outraged Commander Hay, Dr Bairstow,

Lt Varma, everyone – inspiration struck. It was the Brilliant Idea to end all Brilliant Ideas.

'Your problem, Mr Plimpton,' she said thoughtfully, 'is that you're still not thinking big enough.'

She saw his shutters come down. He really didn't like that. How far should she push him? This was a dangerous game. Should she stop? Find another way? Her head gave her another vicious thump. To hell with it. Why not just sit back and let the universe take her where it pleased?

She leaned forwards. 'You need something renewable. Something that can be viewed over and over again. As noted, you've got this fabulous set-up here – and it is fabulous, Mr Plimpton – but you're just not making the best of it.'

He regarded her coldly. 'Indeed?'

'Yes. I mean – the bit with the princes – genius – but it's a one-off, as you say. It's true that every few weeks, you could snatch a couple of boys from somewhere, put them on display, have them murdered and tell people they were the princes, but sooner or later that's going to catch you out. Sooner or later someone's going to say, "You'll never guess what I did last month," and the other person will say, "Same here but last week," and a few more will join in, and the next thing, you'll have any number of seriously pissed-off people with unlimited wealth and resources realising they've been ripped off. They have a quiet word in the right place and suddenly it's raining Time Police. No, Henry – Mr Plimpton – you need to think bigger.'

He put down his coffee cup very slowly, carefully aligning the handle with the edge of his desk. A danger sign. 'Do I, Maxine?' he said quietly. 'Do I really?'

Max beamed sunnily. 'Well, yes, I think so – don't you?'

'I would be offering people the spectacle of the year.'

'True, but what will you offer them next year? Or the year after that? This is the biggest mystery in English history. What else could possibly appeal more to your clients than not only *knowing* what happened to the princes but actually being the arbiter of their fate?'

Henry Plimpton stared at her. Max finished her tea, and very carefully replaced her cup and saucer. There was no time to examine her scheme for possible pitfalls – and there would be many. She'd just have to deal with them as and when they arose. No time to plan ahead. No time to do anything other than wing it and hope for the best. And after all, whatever happened to her was unimportant. The important thing was that History was allowed to run its natural course and that the Princes in the Tower lived long enough to fulfil their own destiny. Whatever that was.

'Well – and believe me I say this with all respect – I still don't think you're taking full advantage of the potential at your fingertips. Please don't shoot me on the spot, but you could be doing so much more with this set-up, Hen— Mr Plimpton.'

He frowned, still not happy, but not actually ordering her immediate delivery to the rendering sheds. Not yet, anyway.

'Could I have a piece of paper, please? And a pen. Sorry to go old school, but I think better with pen and paper. And tea, of course.'

Wordlessly, he passed over a sheet of A4 and a pen.

'Thank you. Right, let's list the days of the week in reverse order. Saturday, Friday, Thursday and so forth.'

She scribbled.

Henry Plimpton craned his neck to see. 'Yes?'

'Well, all this will be happening in the summer of 1483 – that's when the two boys were last seen in public.'

'Yes?'

'You arrive on, say, Saturday.' She made a mark on the paper alongside Saturday.

'Yes?'

'You bring them back here to the . . . the guest suite . . . and you kill them that night. Perhaps someone dresses as James Tyrell and does the deed – we can work out the details later. So – huge occasion. Fabulous party. Lots of food and drink. Bells and whistles. The sort of thing you'd do really well, Mr Plimpton. Big build-up and then – *voila* – murdered princes. Lots and lots of money made. But . . . sadly, as I said . . . a one-off.'

Max paused. He was watching her closely.

She raised a finger. 'But . . . not if you then jump back to the day *before* that Saturday. Friday.' She tapped the paper with her finger. 'They're still alive on Friday. You can bring them back here and do it all over again. And a different set of customers will pay big time. Because it will be an indisputable, true, actual event. Nothing fake about it – genuine entertainment.

'And then you jump back to Thursday – and guess what? You can do it again. Because they're still alive on the Thursday. And again on Wednesday, Tuesday, Monday and so forth. And it will work, Mr Plimpton, because . . .'

He frowned. 'But then they won't be alive to be killed on the Saturday. The original murder.'

Max mentally crossed every finger she possessed and sent up a prayer that the god of historians was taking a tea break.

Based on past performance, that seemed very likely. 'They will be alive on Saturday because *you've already done it*. Well, not you personally, of course, and obviously the Saturday murder must come first, but as long as you keep jumping backwards, then there will never be a time when the princes aren't alive.'

She sat back and poured herself another cup of tea.

Henry Plimpton was staring at the sheet of paper. 'I . . .'

'Take a while to think about it,' advised Max.

'But . . . paradoxes . . .'

Max opened her mouth, all prepared to blind him with temporal technobabble culled from random glances at the easy bits in Leon's copy of *Temporal Dynamics* – all twenty-six volumes of it – but before she could do so, someone tapped at the door and entered.

'Sir, they're back. And they've got him.'

Rousing himself with an effort, Henry Plimpton blinked several times and then turned to Max. 'Excellent. Shall we go and see?'

In the locker room, a heavily sedated Romulus had been carefully laid on the floor in the recovery position and covered with a light blanket.

'Where shall we move him, sir? We hadn't planned on acquiring him so soon so his quarters aren't quite ready.'

'Find a quiet room with a bed and put him there. *Not* the medieval room. Keep him lightly sedated and watch he doesn't choke on his own vomit or anything stupid. Constant monitoring. And no one is to speak to him.'

'They can't,' said Max. 'Not unless they have ancient Latin.'

He peered at her. 'Let me guess. You do.'

Max beamed. Because sometimes there was no need for words.

Three men struggled to get a chubby but limp Romulus through the door. Phillips remained behind.

'Any problems, Phillips?'

'None at all – it went like a dream.' He glared at Max, who grinned back at him. 'Although obviously we weren't completely unobserved. Where were you?'

'Behind you in the anteroom at the back.'

He stared at her for a moment before turning back to Henry Plimpton. 'Anyway, sir, everything went like clockwork.'

Henry nodded at him. 'Please convey my thanks to everyone in the team. I'll authorise the usual bonuses for today's good work.' He looked at Max. 'You do not appear to be expressing any concern for your absent colleague?'

Max shook her head. 'Well, she's not dead, because all your guys are still intact . . .'

Phillips sighed. 'She's in the mess hall downstairs having a coffee and a sulk. Under guard.'

Max blinked. 'Your treatment of prisoners is unusually enlightened, Mr Plimpton.'

He smiled modestly. 'I have my moments. Believe it or not, I am a very nice man.'

'Right up until the moment you're not.'

'I will admit I do like things to go my way. All my people know that. They expend considerable time and effort ensuring I always get what I want.'

'Quicker and easier for everyone,' said Max. 'And my own personal philosophy, too.'

He eyed her. 'You think?'

'Well, the way I see it, I have only to ally my interests with yours and we'll both be happy. And rich.'

He sighed. 'You really are a mercenary little baggage, aren't you?'

Sitting alone at a table, Varma was, not surprisingly, in no good mood. Although the state of her face might have had something to do with that. The bruising had spread outwards and the colours were verging on spectacular. Max nodded at the two men over by the door – guarding the only way in or out – seated herself opposite Varma and winced in sympathy.

'Sorry.'

She scowled. 'You will be, trust me. So – what fresh havoc have you wreaked during my absence?'

Max hesitated. 'Actually, you don't know the half of it,' she said quietly.

'Oh God, Maxwell, what have you done now?'

Max looked around. Their guards were talking to each other, the nearest tables were unoccupied and the coffee machine was making more noise than a Saturn V rocket. 'Best to stick with Max from now on.'

'Why?'

'I've resurrected Maxine Forrest from Insight.'

Varma covered her eyes. 'I've been gone less than an hour. What did you do?'

As neutrally as possible, Max outlined her Brilliant Idea.

Varma closed her eyes. 'Why . . . ? What . . . ? Are you actually clinically insane?'

'Hey,' said Max, wounded. 'Without me you'd be dead by now. And possibly me as well, but definitely you. Scowling at him like a TPO on a mission is no way to make friends and influence people.'

'I *am* a TPO on a mission.'

'And you have me on your side.'

'Oh God, I *am* going to die.'

Max pulled Varma's coffee towards her and began to stir it loudly, the spoon tinkling around the sides of the mug. 'My thinking was that your Map-thing would be bound to flag up such massively dodgy activity and your colleagues would turn up and save us all. Have I been over-optimistic?'

Varma reacquired her coffee and began to stir it herself. 'I'm not an expert – we'd need the Map Master or possibly young Farrell for that – but at the very least, your scheme should throw up some sort of anomaly. It will register somehow. Whether the Time Police can track it down *before* someone actually kills the boys . . .'

'We'll just have to keep our fingers crossed. Matthew is really good at that sort of thing.'

Varma nodded. 'Yes, always supposing your daft idea doesn't bring the whole Timeline crashing down, the Map will certainly react to the irregularities, I'm sure of it.'

'Well, there you are, then. Our problems are nearly over.'

Varma closed her eyes. 'That's because we're all going to die.'

Max grinned at her. 'No, we won't. It'll be absolutely fine. You'll see.'

Meanwhile, in a peaceful Welsh wood, some distance from this day's stirring events, Trainee Tucker was sitting on a convenient rock – in this part of the world he'd been spoiled for choice – and enjoying a pack of Time Police rations. Crackers wholemeal and cheese processed. Or, according to the misprinted label – cheese possessed. A not inaccurate description.

Frowning heavily, he stared unseeing at the beech trees around him as he munched. He had some thinking to do. Swallowing the last mouthful, he chugged back some water, pulled out his com, hesitated for a moment and then sent the familiar double click. Once again there was no response. Nor had there been on the last two occasions. Once was understandable. Twice was concerning. Third time was decision time.

He had choices. He could simply follow his instructions and continue with his search on this side of the river.

Or, he could cross the river in search of Varma and her erratic travelling companion. He had been given no instructions to do so and it was very possible that he could stumble across them at just the wrong moment and incur the very justified fury of Lt

Varma. There had been no emergency call for assistance, and he had no reason to assume that anything was amiss.

Or – the third option. The easiest option. He could pick up his gear, turn around, head in the opposite direction until he came across civilisation again, hitch a lift or steal some transportation, make his way to the nearest large city and lose himself in the crowd. Abandon the side of the angels, knock up one or two contacts who owed him a favour and pick up his old life again. The Time Police would never track him down. Varma would never track him down. Indeed, she might already be dead. In which case, he no longer had a reason to remain with the Time Police. No reason at all. He was miles from anywhere and completely alone. By the time they even realised he was missing, he'd have vanished without a trace. They might even assume he'd fallen down a ravine somewhere. Or into the river and been washed away. No one would be surprised if his body was never found. There would never be a better opportunity than this. He could disappear forever. This time tomorrow he could be in Ireland. From there to France. And from there . . .

He took another swig of water and frowned again. Decision time. Stay or go? Abandon his colleagues or go in search of them? Do his duty or look out for himself?

He stowed away his flask, fastened his pack and stood up. With one last look around the little clearing, he consulted his wrist compass. That way. That way led to freedom and independence. He rather thought he could make out a faint path among the trees, just to make things easy for him.

Sighing, he turned to face the opposite direction and made his way back towards the noisy river. There had been a place where he could cross about a hundred yards back. The river there was narrower but more energetic. He was going to get very wet.

Half an hour later, Tucker heaved himself out of the water and struggled up the steep bank, clutching at ferns and tree roots until he reached the top. He was soaked almost to his waist but his pack was dry. He'd make his way along the riverbank as he suspected Varma and Max would have done. It was very possible they were only around the next bend and suffering nothing worse than a com malfunction. He set off, following the course of the river until he reached a little beach.

Yes, there were traces that Varma and Max had been here. A few boot prints in the soft mud. He laid his own very large boot alongside. Definitely female. Or a man with very small feet. Still convinced he'd made the wrong decision and would regret this for the rest of his life, he began to search, head down, following the river.

Less than a quarter of a mile further on, he rounded a bend to find that the rock face came right down to the river's edge. Completely impassable.

Turning, he retraced his steps back to the little beach. They hadn't gone forwards, they hadn't gone back – therefore, for some reason, they must have moved away from the riverbank. To get around the gorge? Or had they found something?

He turned away and entered the forest, noting as he did so that the rain had finally let up. With luck he would soon dry out.

The light under the trees was green and dim. Countless layers of dead leaves muffled his footfalls. Other than the occasional trill of birdsong, the silence was complete. Carefully, he picked his way through. At one point he looked up. No glimpse of sky was visible through the thick green canopy. Twenty helicopters could fly overhead, but without instruments they would see nothing. Should he go back for reinforcements? He'd give it another half hour and then, if he found nothing, he'd make his way back to the river and their last known position and summon assistance.

The trees ended quite abruptly. Suddenly he was back out in the world of daylight. At some point a weak sun had put in an appearance.

Carefully not moving from the shelter of the trees, he took his time scanning the valley below. Nothing moved. Birds sang in a way that somehow indicated no one had passed this way for some time. Taking two or three cautious steps, he moved further out into the sunshine, head bent, looking for traces Varma had been here. Yes – here. Two or three snapped stems. Someone had lain here in the ferns. Two people, perhaps. Or was that wishful thinking on his part? Dropping to one knee, he pulled out his binos and scanned the scene ahead of him. Working from left to right. Being thorough. Taking his time.

He spotted the structure almost immediately. He stared for a moment and then activated his com, saying softly, 'Varma?'

Faintly, muffled, he heard a familiar chirp. Frowning, he knelt and began to pull aside the ferns, running his hands over the crumbly loam.

He tried again. 'Varma?'

He felt a slight vibration under his hand. Varma's com. Not deeply buried. Just depressed into the ground. There was a boot print. As if she'd trodden on it.

He considered the structure again. Would they have gone to investigate? Well, of course they had. A combination of Varma and Maxwell? Of course they'd investigate. And given the concealed com, perhaps they hadn't been alone. They hadn't come out again, anyway. Looked as if he'd have to go in.

Sighing, Tucker shrugged off his pack, moved back into the woods, scrambled a little way up a beech tree and hung it off a convenient branch. Not a perfect hiding place, but anyone specifically looking would soon find it anyway.

Returning to ground level, he pulled out his blaster and slipped and slithered his way downhill through the wet ferns, noticing as he did so that others had done the same quite recently.

Reaching the valley floor, he circled the structure to discover a narrow door. The only way in or out that he could discover. There was no path – just a small patch of bare earth outside the door – so this place was used but not frequently.

Now was definitely the time to call this in. Retreating back under the trees, he pulled out his com.

'Lt Grint?'

'Tuck . . . ? . . . are you? Repor . . . Tucker? . . .Wha . . . ? Tuck . . . Come . . . ?' Grint's voice dwindled away.

'Grint – can you hear me? Respond.'

'Tuck . . .'

Moving further from the trees towards the structure, he tried again but now there was nothing but static. Interesting.

He looked around. He had choices. He could return to the riverbank and hope for better coms. Await assistance. Do things by the book. Or . . .

Closing his com, he made his way back towards the door. The first thing he noted was the hasty repair. Interesting. Had something forced its way in or out? There was also a keypad and these things weren't difficult. The first key was always the most heavily used. Five. Three other keys showed equal signs of wear and tear. Two, four and nine. He sighed and flexed his fingers. This could take a while.

'Hoi,' said someone.

The trick is not to spin around and look guilty.

Tucker turned slowly, one hand in his pocket.

Three men stood a short distance away, all with blasters slung over their shoulders. All wearing woodland camo, just like him.

'What're you up to?'

Tucker sighed. He'd led groups of men before and some things are universal. He withdrew his hand. 'Thought I'd have one last fag before reporting in.' He eyed their empty nets. 'Not found anything yet?'

They shook their heads. 'No. The boss is not going to be happy.'

Tucker fastened his pocket and took a chance. These men had been out dinosaur hunting. There must be more than one still out there. Had the creatures escaped through this door? And how? Human error was almost always the reason. He could use that.

He shook his head. 'No, he won't be happy at all. Glad it wasn't me.' In any organisation there was always a *he* and he was never happy.

Their expressions showed complete agreement. They were glad it wasn't them, as well.

'Where's your team?'

Tucker gestured with his head. 'Gone on ahead.'

'Why are you using this entrance?'

'Because we've been at it since first light and my fucking feet are killing me and this is the quickest way.'

'Yeah, mate, but even so . . .'

An interesting response. Why weren't they supposed to use this entrance? And why hadn't his com worked properly? Yes, he was surrounded by thick woodland but it shouldn't make a difference.

'Well,' Tucker said, grinding his toe into the soft soil as if finally extinguishing a dog-end, 'can't stand here all day. Sadly. After you, gents.'

His plan was to let them go ahead and then make his escape. Back to the river to report to Grint. Sadly, as with nearly all good plans, this one never got off the ground.

Two moved towards the door. One didn't. Shit. There was always one.

'Let's see your fags.'

'Bugger off,' said Tucker indignantly. 'Buy your own.'

'Show me.'

The other two had stopped. And now they were behind him. He was surrounded. Shit.

Holding their gaze, Tucker unfastened his pocket, shoved in his hand and pulled out a battered pack of cigarettes.

Attitudes changed immediately. 'Chuck one over.'

Tucker tossed him the packet. Everyone lit up. Including Tucker, who had long ago learned the value of carrying a pack around with him. He'd had this one for some time – hence the battered appearance – and it was finally justifying its existence.

He peered through the smoke. 'You know the Time Police are down in the town?'

'Yeah. That's why we've been ordered back inside. Keep quiet until they've gone.'

Interesting. So they needed to keep their heads down, did they? Keep quiet until the Time Police had disappeared. The germs of an idea began to sprout.

'You know more than me,' said Tucker, flicking ash to the ground. 'Coms are bad here.'

'The boss doesn't want us doing anything to draw attention to ourselves. And no one's arguing with him.'

'No,' said Tucker. 'Again – glad it's not me.'

Silence fell. No one looked at anyone else. What had happened? And to whom? And why were coms bad here?

'That explosion . . .' he said eventually, and left it at that.

They nodded. 'Thirty minutes earlier – before the sodding Time Police turned up – they'd have destroyed the evidence and it would have been a good job and bonuses all round,' said someone.

'Yeah,' said someone else. 'Those Time Police bastards aren't going to let it go now, are they? Not with all them officers dead.'

'And the chopper.'

'I'm guessing he's not happy,' said Tucker, shaking his head.

'I knew one of them,' said the man on the left, small, dark, and smoking furiously. 'We worked in Lizard Land. Different team but we had the odd drink together.'

One of those killed? Or one of those doing the killing? And Lizard Land? Tucker strove for a neutral comment. 'Rough.'

No one replied.

Tucker ground out his cigarette, hoping the others would follow suit and go inside. Half his hopes came true. They stubbed out their fags and then turned to him. 'After you, mate,' said the small dark one.

Tucker nodded and accepted his fate. The code – now he no longer needed it – was five nine two four. Typical. The door clicked open. Taking a deep breath, he followed his new colleagues across the threshold.

The inside seemed very dark after the outside. Not that that was important because the place was empty. Other than the great gaping hole over there, of course. And that smell was certainly . . . ripe.

Chatting casually, two of the men walked towards it, and before Tucker could say or do anything to prepare himself – they appeared to disappear down into the darkness.

'After you, mate,' said the small dark one again.

Tucker pulled himself together and reviewed his choices. He could knock the bloke out – one punch should do it – but then what? His only option then would be to run away and trust he got far enough to contact Grint before they caught him. No – if he wanted to find Varma – and her gobby companion – he had only one course of action open to him.

'I'm reluctant to do this,' he said truthfully.

The other one nodded. 'Me too. Never liked being underground. Gives me the willies. Still . . .'

'Yes,' said Tucker, gritting his teeth. 'Still . . .' He peered down.

There was a ladder. Just vaguely visible in the dark but a ladder nevertheless. Tucker gave silent thanks and began his climb down into the unknown. Arriving at the bottom, he wiped the sweat off his face with his sleeve, using the time to take a surreptitious look around. A tunnel. Bending around to his left. Now what?

'Need to pick up my team and report in,' he said lightly.

They nodded. 'See you later.'

Tucker waited for them to move away, leaving him alone to explore. That half happened. Two men disappeared along the tunnel but one remained behind. From the way he leaned against the wall and began to pick his teeth, Tucker guessed he was on guard duty. The bloke was watching him. And he was well-armed. Tucker's blaster was out of sight in his pocket. He had choices. He could take out the bloke before he had a chance to raise the alarm and make his escape while he could, or – and the more exciting option – explore further, suss out what was actually happening here, hopefully locate Varma and the other one, and the three of them could climb back out, make their way back through the woods and report to Grint.

He gave the other two men another few seconds and then set off after them, following, had he known it, the footsteps of Max and Varma not that long ago, and arriving, as they had done, at the junction. Which was deserted.

Here, he considered his choices again. To Lizard Land or to the Castle. Well – given his reason for being here in the first place, who was he to pass up an invitation to visit Lizard Land. Making sure his blaster was easily accessible, he set off down the middle tunnel.

The going grew more difficult with every step. His chest tightened. His eyes blurred. Although that might have been the swirling mist. Because he knew what this was. A time-slip. Breathing became painful. His head spun. Should he retrace his steps? This was going nowhere. He could be spotted at any moment. What was the point of continuing? He was wasting his time. He should have taken the opportunity to bugger off when he had the chance. What the fire truck did he think he was playing at? All this Time Police crap was just that – crap. And then – quite suddenly – the walls blurred, the floor appeared to tilt away from him and he was enveloped in the fog. For a moment he was completely disoriented. Lost. Surely he should be through by now. Would he be trapped forever? He couldn't catch his breath. He couldn't see. This was the end – and then, quite suddenly – it was all gone. In the space of ten feet, he'd passed from now to then. From the present to the past. He was through.

Tucker allowed himself the luxury of leaning against the rock wall for just one minute – no longer – pulling himself together, and then proceeded slowly along the tunnel, placing his feet carefully and without sound. This was definitely not an occasion for rushing heedlessly into an unknown situation. He looked around. Proceeding slowly was all very well, but a man needed a tangible reason for proceeding slowly.

Aha – the internationally recognised symbol of authority and bureaucracy – a clipboard. He unhooked it. Perfect. It even had a revoltingly chewed pen attached by a piece of fraying string. He smiled happily. Old school. You couldn't beat it.

He continued along the tunnel. The clipboard appeared to relate to the numbers and types of cases, cages and crates stored along the walls. Somewhat ostentatiously, he counted boxes as he went, occasionally pausing to make a meaningless squiggle on his clipboard and take a quick look around at the same time.

There was power here, with low-hanging lights slung from

the ceiling. Thick insulated cables looped along the walls or ran along the ground and he could vaguely hear chugging machinery. Generators, perhaps.

As far as he could see, the roof and walls were of natural rock. The floor appeared to be rough stone with deeper cracks and crevices filled in and made level with coarse grit. Which was useful because it showed not only footprints but tyre tracks. So they had vehicles using this tunnel, did they? Forklifts, perhaps, for moving and storing some of these larger crates.

Curious as to their contents, he approached a stack of three. One very big one on the bottom and two smaller ones on top.

Really, he thought later, the airholes should have been a bit of a giveaway. He bent to peer into the top crate and reeled backwards. Another eye was looking back at him and at the same time, a long, liquid, gurgling sound – half snarl, half hiss – emanated from the crate. Which rocked slightly as something shifted its weight. Preparing to attack, perhaps.

Tucker drew back with more haste than dignity, gave the three crates a wide berth and carried on his way. The tunnel was still winding to his left and at no point could he see more than about fifteen to twenty feet in front of him. There were no secondary tunnels leading off, but by now the tunnel was so wide that the crates had been stacked in piles with narrow pathways running between them. Useful should he need to conceal himself. Although preferably behind empty boxes. That snarl had lifted every hair on the back of his neck.

While considering the possible occupants of at least some of these crates, he wasn't so preoccupied that he failed to notice the overhead lighting was slowly giving way to natural daylight. He still couldn't see the exit but it couldn't be far away now.

Gripping his clipboard and assuming the expression of a man whose totals had refused to tally and heads would roll accordingly, he walked around the last bend.

23

The tunnel opened out into what seemed a vast space. Tucker slowed and moved closer to the walls. There were even more stacks of crates here – some stood empty with their doors swinging open. They were clean but wet. Presumably they'd recently been hosed down. Others were streaked with what looked – and smelled – like urine and sloppy green faeces. The stench burned his throat. Ammonia.

Tucker looked over his shoulder. He could hear men shouting to one another, but the stacks of crates and cages concealed them as effectively as they concealed him. If anyone appeared, he could always nip behind something and go back the way he'd come.

Tucking his clipboard firmly under his arm and doing his best to ignore the smell, he moved to investigate another pile of crates. All of these had been damaged in some way. Great lumps had been gouged out of the one in front of him. As if something had tried to force its way out. There was a lot of blood, as well. He touched it. Still sticky. Not fresh then, but recent. And this cage here had a splintered side. The metal crates hadn't fared much better. One was so buckled that it could never be used again. It seemed safe to assume that whoever or whatever had recently occupied these had not been very happy about it.

With one last thoughtful look, Tucker pushed on towards the daylight. The temperature was increasing with almost every step. And the humidity. The walls of the tunnel glistened with damp. Huge sickly-white fungi sprouted in the irregular angle between floor and walls. Some had been kicked over – deliberately, he assumed – and lay, slowly drying out but still pallid and pungent. Worryingly, some seemed to glow slightly. What he took to be spores hung in the air, swirling gently.

Tucker had robbed a lot of archaeological sites in his time. Certainly enough to know that spores can kill. He pulled up his T-shirt to cover his nose and mouth. Almost certainly too late but what the hell. It was an excellent reason for a disguise.

'Hey!'

Well, he was lucky to have got this far unchallenged.

He turned slowly, his face still obscured by his T-shirt.

He'd been hailed by a man, shorter and less wide than himself, wearing dirty grey coveralls and a face mask. A pair of gloves hung from a very serviceable-looking work belt. Both his boots and coveralls were stained with mud, what looked like blood, and what was definitely shit, to say nothing of a few other things unidentifiable without proper forensic examination. Sweat plastered his dark hair to his forehead. A flask – water, presumably – was tucked into his belt. And he was standing just that little bit too far away for Tucker to try anything.

This was some kind of foreman, Tucker thought. Not the actual boss – he or she would be somewhere a lot cleaner and less smelly than here. This was the guy responsible for getting the work done. Competent, took no crap from anyone, the buffer zone between the bolshy workforce and management living in La-La land. Experienced and with authority. Tucker recognised the type. He'd been this guy once.

'Who are you? What do you want?'

Tucker flourished his clipboard.

The man was unimpressed. 'Seriously? Another crappy crate counter?'

Tucker was impressed by the alliteration.

The foreman reached into his pocket. Tucker stiffened. His weapon was tucked well out of sight. He had only his clipboard.

'Here.' The foreman handed him a face mask, his opinion of management idiots who entered his domain inadequately prepared very clear.

Tucker nodded his thanks, turned away to rest his clipboard on a crate and somehow managed to obscure his face as he pulled down his T-shirt and fitted the mask. 'Cheers. Tucker.'

The foreman nodded. 'Beckett. What do you want?'

Tucker picked up his clipboard and gestured around. 'You have problems here.'

The statement seemed a safe bet. Everyone has problems.

'So?'

Wordlessly Tucker pointed to one of the more spectacularly buckled crates.

Beckett assumed an aggressive stance. 'Well, if we had more of the bastard things, then this wouldn't happen. You want these bloody lizards? Then give me the wherewithal to ship them. You people think we just pop them in a paper bag and send them on their way, don't you? And what about the damage to my boys? Jones nearly lost his bloody arm yesterday.'

Tucker nodded and made a note. He gestured to another different but still badly damaged crate. 'What's the story here?'

'Viewing cages,' the foreman said briefly. 'Too flimsy. And we're not allowed to sedate them because the customers want to see what they're getting.'

Tucker bent and peered at a particularly long gouge mark. 'These don't really seem fit for purpose.'

'Well, theoretically, the subjects shouldn't be in them that long. These are just so the customers can get a good look at the merchandise. The transportation crates are much more robust.'

Tucker assumed an expression of interest. 'What sort of customers do you get?'

The foreman shrugged. 'Pharma, professional hunters, mad scientists, rich pricks who think owning a dino makes them cool. Until it eats the family dog. And sometimes the family as well. Makers of snuff holos, of course. Big market for those.' He remembered who he was talking to. 'But only if we can get the crates turned around quickly enough.'

Tucker surveyed the row upon row upon row of crates. 'How many of the sodding things do you need, for crying out loud?'

Beckett bristled angrily. 'I keep telling people – we can't get enough of them. Isn't that why you're here?'

Tucker grasped at this one straw. 'I've come to investigate why you're not turning things around quickly enough.'

Suddenly, the man was in his face, angry and aggressive. 'Listen, pal, you've no idea what my lads have to shift sometimes. If you want a faster turnaround, then I'll need more men, more crates, more equipment, more cleaning apparatus and less interference from clipboard-clutching dickless wankers with nothing better to do than wander around trying to make themselves look good.'

Tucker considered his strategy. Two swift moves and this gobby shit would be enjoying a long spell of clipboard-induced concussion. On the other hand, he was here for intel. And Varma. And the other one as well, if he had the time.

More voices approached. If Tucker had been going to thump this wazzock, then he'd missed the moment. Frowning, he pulled the top sheet off his clipboard and turned it blank side up. 'What do you need?'

Beckett blinked in astonishment. 'What?'

'What do you need? Or are you just some sackless twat whinging on and blaming everyone else because he can't get the job done properly?'

For one moment, things hung dangerously in the balance.

'Well . . . if you're serious . . .'

'It's why I'm here. And in my own time, too, so let's get a move on. Show me the problem.'

'All right. This way.'

They set off along the tunnel towards the daylight. Although the space had widened considerably, owing to the number of crates and cages packed against the walls, the central path had actually narrowed. There were now more cages than crates, most with either iron bars or strong mesh across the front.

Something moved. And then another. These cages had occupants. Makeshift cans of dirty water had been fastened to the bars and there were piles of withered vegetation on the floors. Whether intended to be food or bedding was unclear but the end result was the same. It had all been trampled to a pulp by the occupant's unceasing pacing and then crapped on.

Many of the occupants were just dark shapes, but all their movements were unnervingly similar. Repetitive pacing. Swaying. Occasionally a metallic boom announced something had thrown itself against the side of its cage. A few inmates lay curled up with their backs to the bars. One or two looked dead. The smell was appalling. Urine ran down into gutters blocked with straw and faeces.

Tucker peered into another cage. 'They looked bigger in the films. And more dangerous.'

'Most of these are just small herbivores.'

'So many?'

'I told you – they keep dying. We just can't keep them alive. We dispose of the bodies, of course.' The foreman jerked his head. 'Rendering sheds are over there. But the problem is that the smell attracts the raptors. There's a safety line.' He pointed further down the tunnel, towards the daylight. 'Don't cross it. And definitely don't stand on it – it's electrified. And definitely, definitely do not even approach that point without an armed escort. It's not safe out there.'

'Raptors?'

'Yeah. This whole place reeks of diseased animals, blood and death. It didn't take them long to suss there are easy pickings here.'

'They come for the bodies?'

The foreman looked him in the eye. 'If they can't get fresher meat.'

Tucker stood very still. 'You mean . . . ?'

'Yep.'

'They come for . . . ?'

'Anything they can get. Yeah. And they're bright. They

attack in a pack. One or two almost always manage to get through. Don't go anywhere alone.'

Tucker looked around. There was activity everywhere. He could see at least ten to fifteen men toiling away and those were just the ones visible from where he was standing. There would be many more. Voices rebounded off the walls. There was a lot of arm-waving. And shouting. And it was hot. So bloody hot. And the stench was . . . indescribable.

'Jesus.'

The foreman grinned. 'You get paid extra if you work here.'

Tucker gestured to three forklift trucks parked in a neat row at the end of the tunnel. 'What are those for?'

'Bringing in the new cages, the fodder, equipment and so on.'

'And taking the bodies to the sheds.'

'Yeah.'

Tucker gestured to a pile of electronic devices. 'And those?'

'Control collars and harnesses. They give us a fighting chance if anything goes wrong.'

'But some got out. Quite recently.'

Beckett folded his arms in a *you want to make something out of that?* gesture and began to counter with his own questions. Raising his voice over the incessant clatter of generators, crates being moved from A to B and men yelling at each other because they should have gone to C instead, he shouted, 'So where do you work, pal?'

Tucker instinctively ducked as something heavy hit the ground behind them. 'Not here, thank God.'

'No one ever wants to work here. The boss has to pay double. But, if you need cash, this could be the job for you.'

Tucker looked around. 'No. Sorry. I don't need the money

that badly. But give me the full tour and I'll see what I can do to make things better down here.'

The foreman grinned suddenly. 'Want to see the real thing?'

'You mean . . .' Tucker gestured. 'You mean – go out there?'

'To the line, yeah.'

There was nothing Tucker would like better, but perhaps a little reluctance . . .

'Well . . .'

The foreman was grinning. 'Don't you want to stick your head into Lizard Land? Not even for a few minutes?'

Just for a moment, Tucker had a brief but very illuminating insight into the deranged brain of your average historian. He grinned back. 'Yeah – why not?'

The foreman gestured at the walls. 'There are weapons cages at regular intervals. If you ever find yourself in difficulties – head for one of these. They're not locked. For obvious reasons. Just yell for help and shoot everything with scales until the rescue team turns up. Are you armed?'

'No,' said Tucker, who was, but, along with Lt Grint, was a firm believer that a man can never have too many blasters about his person.

Beckett pulled open the door and handed Tucker a medium-grade blaster. 'Know how to use this?'

Tucker nodded, unsure whether to look professional or scared to death. He settled for neutral.

'Then let's go. Stay behind me at all times.' He surveyed Tucker. 'You look a bit clean.'

Tucker frowned down at himself. He was sweaty and grubby, still damp from the river, and stained with some of the less attractive bits of Wales. The word *clean* could not possibly apply. And then he got it. Reaching into a shit-filled cage, he grasped a handful and rubbed it down his front and sleeves, reflecting, as he did so, that this sort of thing was probably never mentioned in Time Police recruiting literature.

'Ready?'

'Yeah.'

'Remember – stay close.'

Tucker gave Beckett two paces and then fell in behind, following him around the final pile of crates and, suddenly, it really was a whole new world.

The tunnel widened out and the roof rose even higher. There was noise everywhere and an overwhelming impression of massive busyness. Scurrying men, the thrum of machinery, humming equipment, vehicles bouncing over the rough ground, rattling cages, voices echoing over more voices. Wave upon wave of sound assaulted his ears.

And the heat. Hot, sweaty, full-on heat. The blast hit Tucker square in the face and the smell seared his nostrils. The contents of his sinuses liquified immediately, subjecting him to some kind of nasal Niagara. And probably destroying his sense of smell forever.

He'd thought he was hot before, but now every pore on his body opened wide and began to exude for dear life. His T-shirt clamped itself to his chest.

'Shit,' he said, dragging his forearm across his face.

'Just give it a moment,' said the foreman.

'It's worse than a bloody sauna.'

'Try working in it.'

Now that he was able to take in more detail, Tucker could see most men wore the same grey coveralls as Beckett but with the top half peeled back and tied around their waists. Their bodies ran with sweat. Most had bandanas tied around their foreheads to keep it out of their eyes.

'Maximum two-hour shifts,' said the foreman. 'No matter what you lot up in the castle say.'

Tucker stiffened imperceptibly. Dinosaurs *and* a castle? Come on . . .

The foreman continued. 'Two hours on – one off. To be without water is a disciplinary offence. My discipline, that is.'

Tucker straightened up and stared at the world beyond the tunnel. Then stared some more, open-mouthed. Then took a few automatic steps forwards.

'Don't cross the line.'

Tucker looked down at the thick red line painted across the floor some twenty feet away. And the accompanying thick black cables. Electrified. And then past that to the green world beyond.

'What do you think?'

Tucker swallowed. 'I think it's not a bit like the holos.'

Beckett came to stand beside him. 'No, it's not, is it. There's no grass, for one thing. Not here, anyway. No vast, wide-open spaces with plenty of room for herds of panicking dinosaurs to stampede dramatically across the screen. Just – this.'

Tucker found himself looking out on to a landscape the like of which he'd never seen before. Huge plants and trees rose out of pools of black water, soaring towards the sky, fighting each other for light. Many of them hadn't made it. They'd bent and twisted and failed, finally falling and rotting, and now their brethren scrambled over their fallen bodies, eager for their own share of the light before others did the same to them. Never mind the fauna – here even the flora was engaged in a life-or-death struggle. He had to admit he'd never felt so small and insignificant in his life.

What Tucker had initially taken to be giant snakes turned out to be tree roots, thrusting in and out of the soil, always hungry, always thirsty, all matted together, making steady progress in any direction almost impossible. Twisted, tangled undergrowth reduced visibility to only a few feet and pools of dark, brackish water lay everywhere. Occasionally, there would be ripples.

Peering out from what, no doubt, looked just like an ordinary cave when observed from the other side, he could see thick grey clouds, heavy with water, swirling overhead. Was there about to be a massive storm or was this normal? Did it rain every day? Given the amount of water around and the humidity in the air, that seemed very likely.

And then, without warning, the thick clouds parted. A stray sunbeam found its way through and for one second – one magical second – every dark pool blazed with light and every water droplet became a diamond. The effect was dazzlingly beautiful but gone in an instant. The clouds swirled back and once again the world was just hot, wet and green. As it had been and would continue to be for millions of years.

Automatic anti-drone technology peppered the sides of the tunnel. All carefully aligned so that not a square inch of the approach was uncovered.

Tucker turned to Beckett. 'You worry about drones?'

'Pterosaurs. Vicious bastards. Two of them together can tear a man apart in seconds. They're one of the main reasons everyone's armed.'

Tucker nodded and, obviously seeking reassurance, patted his blaster. The one he was somehow going to forget to give back at the end of his tour.

He looked down. Given the amount of water out there, the floor surface in the tunnel was obviously artificial. Concrete of some kind had been laid to give a firm surface on which to work, but the forest – if that was the right word to describe all this voracious green exuberance – was only yards away and, as far as he could see, all of it was filled with a malevolent desire to regain its lost territory as quickly as possible.

Someone was clearly going out and dealing with it, though. He could see raw stumps oozing thick, evil-smelling sap where great clumps of undergrowth had been hacked back. Some charring indicated there had been attempts to burn it. Considering this world seemed to be about ninety per cent water, that probably hadn't gone so well.

'We have to do it every day,' said Beckett, following Tucker's gaze and raising his voice to be heard over the racket of shifting cages happening all around them. 'This stuff literally grows a mile a minute. If we left it even for a day, then those tendrils would be in here and I, for one, would not be hanging around.'

'Man-eating plants?' said Tucker, with some incredulity.

'Well, everything else here wants to eat us, so why not them as well? This is a hostile environment. One mistake and you will die.'

Tucker looked around at the stacked cages, many of which were occupied. 'You appear to be fighting back.'

'We're winning, but only because of weapons and

technology. Trust me, if the power ever went down permanently, we'd be at the very bottom of the food chain. The good news is that we wouldn't be there for very long.'

'Really?' said Tucker, storing away this information for future reference. An idea was beginning to form. He needed a distraction . . .

Away in the distance, deep in the tangled green forest, something – something distinctly reptilian – bellowed. There was an ominous sound of splintering wood as something shouldered its way through the tangled trees.

'Something big out there,' said Tucker, walking forwards and craning his neck to see.

'Look out. Get back.' Beckett shoved him aside and fired a quick blast into a nearby plant. Outside the tunnel but close enough to the entrance to pose a threat to the unwary. Its leaves were the size of a small car.

To Tucker's left, startlingly close, something scuttled. He never saw what it was and its progress was marked only by a trail of bending stalks and fluttering leaves. And then there was another. And then another.

'Never even knew they were there, did you?' said Beckett.

'I did not,' said Tucker quietly. 'Raptors?'

The foreman nodded. 'They never go away. Remember that.'

'What was that bellow?'

'One of the bigger carnivores. I don't know the names – I just assume everything's out to kill me and so far that's working well. Back inside.'

'Is that it?'

The foreman stepped back. 'Course not. You just take a moment for a pleasant stroll out there. Have a good look around. Chat to the wildlife, if you like. I'll come back in five minutes and say a few appropriate words over your bloodstain.'

Tucker looked down. 'I'm still on the right side of the line, though?'

'Yeah – it would probably have saved you.'

Tucker took an automatic step back. 'Only probably? Doesn't it work?'

The foreman pulled out a pen and dropped it on the line. There was a fizzing phut and the pen jumped high into the air, to land a shapeless blob of melted plastic some six feet away.

Tucker took good care to shift nervously. 'How often does the power go down?'

'More often than I would like, but we hold the world record in getting it back up again.'

'Wouldn't some sort of giant barrier be . . . you know . . . better?'

'The power supply's too irregular.'

'So?'

'Everything locks automatically when the power goes down. We go out there every day to set traps, collect greenery and stuff. We really wouldn't want to find ourselves on the wrong side of a barrier when the lights go out.'

Tucker nodded, ostensibly staring out at the swampy landscape, but in actual fact eyeing up the two big electrical control panels built into each side of the tunnel. Huge red signs were posted alongside with more exclamation marks than he'd ever seen in his entire life.

Dānjər!
Pericolo!
Peligro!
Dikkat!
Achtung!
Gevaar!
Опасность!
Danger!
危险!

Having seen all he needed, Tucker was now keen to make himself scarce. 'I should be getting back. Thanks for this.' He gestured around. 'I'll do what I can about getting you additional men and materials. It won't be overnight, though.'

Beckett nodded. 'Thanks. You can find your own way back?'

'Actually, I could do with a coffee and a wash. Where's the nearest, um . . .'

'There's a mess hall up past the junction in the castle tunnel.' And then, just as Tucker thought he'd got away with it, 'I'll walk you there.'

Tucker sighed to himself and then nodded brightly. 'Thank you.'

24

Passing back through the time-slip didn't seem so bad from this side. Striding alongside Tucker, Beckett barely seemed to notice it at all, and when the two men finally arrived at the junction, it suddenly seemed a cool and pleasant place after Lizard Land. Tucker remembered what the foreman had said about a castle.

'So you're not based at the castle yourself, then?'

Beckett shook his head. 'They keep the space above ground for more important people than us. Or so I've heard. This is about as close as we get.'

He crossed the junction to the castle tunnel and pushed open the first door they came to. Tucker inhaled the very welcome smell of coffee. Not particularly good coffee but . . . still . . . coffee.

A partitioned space had been turned into a small mess hall. He stepped inside, only to be brought up short by the sight of his former colleagues sitting alone at a table against the wall, apparently unmanacled, untortured and seemingly enjoying a hot beverage.

The second thing he noticed was people moving away from him. Unbelievably, he'd forgotten the smell.

He sighed. He would have killed for a coffee. But, duty first.

Assuming his best manly beam, he threw out his chest and approached their table.

'Well, hello, ladies.'

'Fuck off,' said Varma.

Which, to be honest, was not the most discouraging response he'd ever received from her.

'What the hell's that awful smell?' said Max, as socially inept as her companion.

'Me,' said Tucker simply. 'Tucker.'

'Maxine Forrest,' said Max.

There was the very slightest of pauses. 'Pleased to meet you, Maxine Forrest.' He held out his hand.

Max leaned forwards, whispered, 'Henry Plimpton,' and then recoiled as the full impact of *l'eau de Tucker* made itself known. 'I am not touching you. Ever.'

A grinning Beckett spoke from the door. 'Tucker, you randy bastard – leave the ladies alone.'

'Yeah,' said Varma. 'What he said.'

Having achieved his aim of letting his colleagues know he was on site, Tucker judged it best to back off. 'Your loss, ladies.'

'Fuck off,' said Varma again.

'Fucking off right now,' said Tucker, and headed for the door. Once safely on the other side, he said to Beckett, 'Can't believe you have women here.'

'The boss employs whoever he wants. Some of them are women. Don't fall into the trap of thinking they're comfort for the troops unless you want to lose your left arm.'

'And subsequently find some raptor shitting it out the other end.'

'Well, at least you'd get your wristwatch back.'

'Thanks for the tour.' Tucker paused. His hastily formed plan was to embark on a path of massive destruction. To generate as much chaos and confusion as he could manage, and hope, somehow, an opportunity would arise for Varma and Max to get themselves out. It was certain that people would die and Beckett might be one of them, but he liked this bloke. He'd *been* this bloke. Was there a way to say, 'Make sure you're well away from the line when the power goes down,' without actually saying those words? He was still thinking about it when Beckett nodded, turned and strode back the way they'd come. Even from where he was standing, Tucker could hear him yelling at some unfortunate in the Lizard Land tunnel. He stood for a moment. *Henry Plimpton.* If things had gone differently at Roanoke then this might have been Tucker's next posting.

Shaking his head, he gave the foreman a few minutes' start and then quietly followed him back to Lizard Land.

A convenient pile of pallets gave him a discreet place to linger while contemplating the nearest unmanned forklift. A vehicle with which he was not unfamiliar. Electric-powered, obviously, and judging by the very hefty counterweight at the rear, used for shifting the heavy stuff. All the better for his purpose.

Drawing back behind the pallets, he began to calculate the speed necessary to cause some real damage. The problem was that there was no direct route through the piles of equipment and cages for a run-up, so achieving full speed seemed unlikely.

He gave it a few minutes and since no one appeared to be paying him any attention – after all, he'd been seen talking to Beckett, which obviously gave him credibility – he approached the forklift and performed the traditional health and safety check by walking around the vehicle and kicking the tyres. Yep – all systems functioning at optimum.

Climbing into the cab, he checked it was in neutral and the handbrake engaged while all the time plotting his route to the nearest control panel. The one to the left of the safety line.

OK. Here we go. Starting the engine, he reversed ten feet, spun the wheel to the left, lined up the vehicle and loaded up a pile of empty pallets – for camouflage and additional ramming weight. Carefully manoeuvring around a pile of miscellaneous handling equipment, he swung left between two more stacks of pallets and began to build up speed.

He had no idea whether anyone was paying him any attention or not – with luck, everyone would think he was just a hard-working forklift jockey keeping his head down and concentrating on the job in hand. Until events proved otherwise, of course.

Now. He floored the accelerator. The forklift shot forwards. The area was busy and chaotic and it was a miracle no one had challenged him yet, but he wasn't going to get away with this for very much longer. Any moment now . . .

Ten feet to go. Sliding across the seat, he threw himself from the cab, realised too late that he'd painfully underestimated the rockiness of the floor and rolled straight into another cache of handling equipment, neatly stacked against the wall ready for use. What felt like a ton of stuff came down on top of him. Poles, cattle prods, nets, hoods, ropes, chains, nooses, muzzles, electronic collars – everything clattered down around his head. He curled into a ball and waited for serious injury.

Two long seconds passed. Nothing happened. Shit. Had he

jumped too soon? Had the forklift actually missed the target? Had someone managed to jump aboard and shut down the vehicle before it impacted the control box? Should he move? Was he safer here? Were people racing towards him at this very moment? Either to pick him up or shoot him?

And then – just as he was convinced it had all gone wrong somehow – there was an almighty great crash as the forks impacted the control box, a crackle of power, a bang, a shower of sparks and what lights there were went out.

Tucker began to kick himself free of the dinosaur-handling equipment. Any moment now this area would be filled with confusion and panic. The emergency lighting would kick in and he wanted to be a very long way away before that happened. Disentangling himself from all the handling paraphernalia, he crawled behind a pile of pallets, pulled out his blaster and prepared to defend himself.

He needn't have bothered. No one was paying him even the slightest attention. The forks were actually embedded in the remains of the now dead control box and the pallets themselves were on fire. Best of all, the other control box, possibly unable to cope with the sudden power surge, was a mass of flashing red warning lights. Alarms and klaxons blared. Men were shouting and running in all directions. Tucker could hear Beckett bellowing orders.

The burning question, of course, was how long before everything was brought back under control? And what should he do to help the situation deteriorate even further? *Two* burning questions, then.

Movement. He felt, rather than saw, movement. The cage he was currently leaning against rocked slightly. Shit. Twisting around, he peered into the cage. He could see nothing inside but he was pretty sure something could see him. On the other hand, what had the foreman said? Small herbivores, mostly. Yeah – small herbivores – like hamsters. Or ... or gerbils. Bunnies, even.

The cage was secured by a simple latch with a pin thrust through it. A manual device, easy to operate and not subject to the vagaries of power cuts or surges. Not without some misgivings, he crouched and worked the pin free.

Nothing happened.

Still in a knee-cracking crouch, he wriggled to one side, reached around the cage and gently pulled open the door. Just a few inches. Whether or not the occupant took advantage of this unexpected piece of luck was entirely up to the occupant. He had no intention of exposing himself any further. In fact ...

He crawled away and lifted his head to see what was happening. Shit – the fire was nearly out. Men were running around with tool boxes and equipment. Now he remembered Beckett's remark about his teams holding the world record for getting the power back up again.

This was no good. The panic and confusion was nowhere near widespread enough for his purposes. He'd envisioned screaming klaxons, panicking people running into each other in the dark, and enough chaos to throw a serious spanner in the works. He needed to do more.

He eyed the two long rows of cages all along the back wall. Should the occupants somehow escape, then that would be an awful lot of small herbivores. An awful lot of small, *panicking* herbivores. They'd be upset by all the noise and desperate to get away from this place. They'd scuttle in all directions, tripping people up, heading for dark corners, shitting everywhere, milling around, fighting among themselves and generally making the situation worse before heading for the outside world and freedom. He should do it now. He might have only seconds before the power came back on.

Abandoning caution, he began to move along the cages, yanking out the pins and pulling open the doors. While some of the occupants hung back, one small green lizard didn't hang around, throwing itself at its cage door and nearly knocking Tucker off his feet. It hit the ground hard, whisked its long tail and scuttled away. And once one had done it . . . now they were all jumping down. Those not yet freed were throwing themselves around their cages making strange but not unpleasant piping noises.

Tucker judged it time to move out. The current status of the safety line was unknown to him and it made sense to work his way further up the tunnel, back towards the junction. He'd free what he could along the way, leave everyone else to deal with the chaos, and utilise the confusion to locate his stricken colleagues – neither of whom had shown any signs of needing even the tiniest rescue, but that could change at any moment. And probably would. They could find a refuge, somehow get word to Grint and tell him to get as many TPOs up here as quickly as possible and get this situation sorted. Once that was done, it would be back to TPHQ to sink a well-deserved pint and put his feet up.

The tunnel darkened with every step he took away from the entrance. The emergency lighting flickered on, then off, then on again. Something ran past his feet. Then something else. Like a dachshund with scales was the best description he could come up with. Obeying their instincts, small dinosaurs were running, hopping and scuttling in all directions, dodging men and obstacles, hell-bent on getting away from this place. Blind panic led large numbers to run in the wrong direction – up the tunnel towards the junction rather than back towards their own world.

Some of them ran straight over the safety line. Nothing happened. No flash. No bang. No smell of crispy fried dinosaur. The safety line was down. And if these little ones could get out, then other things could get in. Bigger things.

Tucker remembered the raptors – the ones who never went away – then dismissed his thoughts as overanxious. Surely there was no way anything outside would understand that the barrier had gone down. In fact, the explosion and the flames, together with the increased noise and activity, would probably drive any predators further away. He considered this for a moment, remembering that long, liquid snarl in the dark. These little ones were all very well, but how about adding something larger to the mix? Really give the people here something to worry about. Then he could make his way back up the tunnel, back to Max and Varma.

Nearly all the cages were secured by simple metal pins. Tucker tutted. Really, that was just asking for trouble. Suppose none of the cages had been fastened properly because someone had been terribly, terribly careless and all the occupants escaped? Wouldn't that be a disaster?

Tucker grinned wickedly and moved silently from cage to cage. Being terribly, terribly careless.

25

The second the mess door had closed behind Tucker, Max and Varma eyed each other.

'Don't say a word,' said Varma.

Obediently, Max said nothing, but in that special way.

'And wipe that look off your face.'

Obediently, Max wiped that look off her face, only to replace it with another, even more irritating expression.

'I'm warning you . . .'

Max grinned, and not looking at Varma in any way, said, 'Good bloke, Tucker.'

Varma began to formulate plans to bludgeon her to death with a teaspoon, but sadly, before this happy event could come to pass, someone stuck their head around the door.

'You two – the boss wants you. Got a nice little job for you.'

'Oh . . . goodie,' said Max brightly.

'Now what?' muttered Varma, under the cover of scraping her chair back.

Max frowned. 'Actually . . . I think I might have been too clever for my own good.'

Varma scowled at her. 'You *think*?'

* * *

'Today?' said Max in astonishment. 'Now? We're going now?'

Henry Plimpton smiled guilelessly. 'Well, as soon as you've made all your preparations, yes.'

'To acquire the Princes in the Tower?'

'Yes.'

Max's head thumped savagely. The headache she thought was disappearing was instantly back again – and worse than ever. '1483?'

'Yes.'

'Today?'

'Yes.'

Max pulled herself together. 'Of course, Mr Plimpton. Whatever you say.'

'And *you* will give the briefing.'

'Me?'

'Why not? You're the expert, after all, and I don't keep a dog to bark myself. You will give the briefing, your colleague here will accompany you on the mission, and Phillips' team will go with you to make sure everything runs smoothly.'

He settled back in his seat and made *get on with it* gestures. 'Don't mind me. I'm here purely to observe.'

Max turned to face the room. Henry Plimpton, Varma, Phillips and three other men stared back at her. Henry Plimpton looked amused, Varma was scowling, and Phillips and his team wore expressions ranging from really couldn't care less to active hostility. It occurred to Max that she'd had more receptive audiences.

She stood for a moment, pushing back her headache and nausea and gathering her thoughts. The important thing was not to rush at it. She should take a moment. Clear her mind. Assemble the facts. Was it insulting to assume Philips' team knew nothing of the Princes in the Tower and their place in history? Or would there be deep sighs and boredom as she attempted to go over facts they already knew? If she got this wrong and Henry Plimpton decided she and Varma were expendable after all . . . ? OK, no pressure then. Deep breath . . . and go.

She smiled. 'I'm sure you're all aware of our mission today, but my colleague here wasn't present when the parameters were discussed, so please have a little patience while I run through it all again for her benefit.

'Our objective is to secure two subjects, Edward and Richard Plantagenet – otherwise known as the Princes in the Tower – and bring them here to Mr Plimpton. To this end, we'll be landing at the Tower of London in the summer of 1483. If asked for a specific date, I would advise at least two or three days before their last verified public appearance.' She looked across to Henry Plimpton. 'I am unsure, at this stage, whether the coordinates will be provided or if I'm to calculate them myself. Mr Plimpton is yet to advise. However, I do recommend the mission takes place under cover of darkness. There is a small garden outside the Garden Tower – an ideal place to land. We engage the camo device, pause for a moment to check out security patrols and so forth, and emerge when it's safe to do so. With Mr Plimpton's permission, I will issue my standard warning.'

She glanced at him again and he nodded.

'Please do not assume that people living in the past are stupid or lazy or have a lesser comprehension of the world than you. The chances are that these will all be battle-hardened soldiers who served in the recent Wars of the Roses and that they've been selected to guard the king's enemies for that very reason. Underestimate them at your peril.

'I'm assuming, Mr Phillips, that you and your team will have some method of accessing the tower. Quickly and quietly, I hope.'

Phillips nodded. He'd liked being addressed as mister. He'd liked the authority.

'Then gaining access to the Garden Tower will be your responsibility. Once inside, please instruct one member of your team to remain by the door.'

'Why?'

'Early warning should anyone approach.'

'Potts,' said Phillips, nodding at one of his men.

Max continued. 'There are unlikely to be gaolers actually in the tower – the fiction is still being maintained that the boys are there for Edward's coronation. However, there will almost certainly be attendants sleeping in the same room. They are to be neutralised, but not permanently. I'm sure you're all aware of the dangers of inadvertently killing an ancestor. So gas or a sonic shock only. I've done this sort of thing before and, believe me, quick, clean and non-fatal is always the most efficient way to go.'

'Having done that, Mr Phillips, you will please station a second member of your team outside the bedroom door to watch our backs.'

'Schenk,' said Phillips.

Max nodded. 'Thank you, Mr Schenk. In the meantime, Varma and I will be neutralising the princes. Mr Phillips and his remaining team member . . . ?'

'Foster,' said the man.

'Messrs Phillips and Foster will carry the boys back to the pod. Schenk and Potts will go ahead to clear the way. Varma and I will cover our exit. If possible, I'd like to relock the door behind us. It will slow down discovery and add to the mystery of their disappearance. Assuming the coast is clear, we make our way straight back to the pod and return to base. Mr Plimpton – do you have any comments to make?'

Henry Plimpton shook his head.

'I have a question,' said Phillips. 'Who put you in charge?'

'I did,' said Henry Plimpton smoothly. 'Please indicate any problems you feel you might have with my decision.'

Phillips shifted his weight uneasily, but stuck to his guns. 'Sir, I and my team . . .'

'I understand your position,' said Henry Plimpton, 'but the main purpose of this mission – other than acquiring two valuable new subjects, of course – is to implicate this officer . . .' he pointed to Varma, 'to such an extent that she will never be able to extricate herself, and . . .' he pointed at Max, 'to test the capabilities of this new member of the team. Your resentment is understood, Phillips, and can, perhaps, be slightly offset against the knowledge that you have my full permission to shoot them both should either take one step out of line. Or even look as if they are about to do so. Does everyone understand the position?'

Phillips nodded with more enthusiasm than he had previously shown.

'Your specific responsibility, Phillips, is to get the team in. Once inside the tower, you will take your instructions from the historian. As soon as the subjects are safely acquired, you will resume control and bring them back to me. Is that clear? To everyone?'

Heads nodded.

'Right,' said Max briskly. 'Who do I see about the appropriate equipment? And who will calculate the coordinates?'

'I will,' said Plimpton. 'We wouldn't want you to go astray, would we?'

'Well, certainly not before I've been paid,' said Max. 'And I assume neither Varma nor I will be piloting the pod.'

'Again, we don't want you to go astray. And before you ask – I don't think it will be necessary for either of you to be armed. I think everyone should regard this as a period of probation, don't you?'

Max looked around. 'Does anyone else have any questions? Varma?'

Varma shook her head, her face tight and bitter.

'I am happy that you seem reconciled to your lot.' Henry Plimpton smiled.

Varma stared at the floor and shook her head again.

'A pod is being prepared,' he said. 'Lockers and equipment will be allocated to you on your safe return and accommodation will be found.'

Max looked up. 'Actually, Mr Plimpton, I'm quite hungry. And an opportunity to freshen up a little would be appreciated by both of us.'

Henry Plimpton nodded. 'Phillips, take them back downstairs to the mess hall. You'll leave in an hour.'

The mess hall smelled of good things to eat. Varma found them a quiet table against the wall. Max dropped into her seat with a huge sigh of relief and closed her eyes.

Varma was reading the list of dishes chalked up on a board. 'What do you want?'

Max shook her head. 'Nothing for me.'

'You said you were hungry. What's wrong with you? Apart from the obvious, of course.'

'Not feeling too good.'

'Shit on a stick, Maxwell, you're not going to crumble on me now, are you?'

'No. I'll be OK. I've had something like this before.'

'Is this your time-travel sickness again?'

Max paused, looked around and then said very quietly, 'It's not the first time I've experienced this. Don't laugh, but History really doesn't like this sort of thing.' Doing her best to ignore Varma's sceptical expression, she pressed on. 'Sometimes, when you're about to do something which could change the course of History . . .' She frowned at the table. 'I don't know. But I think it's . . . it's a warning.'

Varma was exasperated. 'Well, of course it is. We're being warned not to do this incredibly stupid thing you've volunteered us for. You don't need a headache to realise this is the craziest, most lunatic, most dangerous . . .'

Phillips and his team had drifted to the counter to check out what was on offer.

Max opened her eyes. 'Do you think Tucker will have managed to get through to Grint by now?' she whispered.

Varma shrugged. 'I don't know. He seemed to be with one of Plimpton's men, so probably not.'

'So it's likely no one knows we're here. No one knows this place even exists.'

'Grint will find it sooner or later.'

Max shook her head. 'Too late for us, though. And for the victims. And definitely too late for the Timeline. At present there's only us. We have to do this.'

'You mean save the day by creating innumerable paradoxes, bringing down the Timeline and aiding and abetting a known Time criminal. The number one Time criminal, in fact.'

Max tried to move her head without it dropping off. 'We can't do anything to stop what's happening here. But the one thing we can do is make some noise. Send up a signal that even the Time Police can't miss.'

'I disagree. We should be concentrating our efforts on sabotaging Plimpton from within. Not aiding and abetting . . .'

Max leaned closer. 'Varma, the bad news – the really bad news – is that we may already have done this. Romulus vanished from History. Never seen again. The princes vanished from History. Never seen again.'

'Are you saying we were – will be – responsible?'

'Well, someone is. Was. Will be.'

'It was Richard III.'

'It probably wasn't, you know.'

'Henry Tudor, then.'

'Mm . . . Possibly.'

'And then he blamed it on Richard.'

Max shook her head. 'The two princes literally disappear.'

'You can't know that.'

Max lowered her voice to a whisper. 'But that's just it – I do. Some years ago I jumped to 1483. Me, Dr Bairstow and Mrs Brown. We jumped to the Tower on what was supposed to be the last date on which they were seen. Except they weren't there. There was no trace of them. We even got inside the

Bloody Tower – the Garden Tower as it was then – and they weren't there. No personal effects, no clothes, no servants, no trace. A whole suite of empty rooms swept clean.' She looked around and leaned across the table. 'Don't you understand – *they were there and then they weren't.*'

'Doesn't mean it was us,' said Varma stubbornly.

'I went on to jump to Mechelen because Dr Bairstow thought they might have been smuggled out to their aunt, Margaret of Burgundy. They hadn't been. They were never there.'

Varma stared at her. 'Someone must have had them.'

Max gestured with her head in the direction in which she thought Henry Plimpton had his office. 'Yeah. Us. Well – him.'

'But . . .'

'No, listen. If someone does snatch them, then surely it's best that someone should be us. Is anyone listening?'

Varma glanced casually around the room. 'No.'

'Obviously we won't let them be killed. We won't even bring them back here. We . . .'

'When you say *we* . . .'

'You and me.'

Varma scoffed. 'While Phillips and his crew step back and look in a conveniently different direction.'

'No, of course they won't, but don't tell me an opportunity won't arise for us to save the boys. Or we can make one. If we pull this off, Varma, we can stop Henry Plimpton dead in his tracks. Buy ourselves and the Time Police a little breathing space. If we can somehow neutralise Phillips and his gang, then we'll be free. With their pod. We either jump straight back to TPHQ or down into town and hand it all over to Grint. I'll leave that bit to you to decide.'

Varma stared at the table. Max, always aware of the pitfalls of overegging the pudding, closed her eyes and instructed herself firmly not to throw up.

'Yes,' said Varma suddenly. 'All right. We'll do it. I'll follow your lead at the Tower. You have the expertise. I'll lead on neutralising Phillips and his team. Our decision on what to do next will depend on circumstances.'

Max nodded. 'Agreed.'

26

In the meantime, Grint and his team had arrived at the crime scene.

They stood quietly, taking in the still-smoking crater, the tangled wreckage of their helicopter and the medical trolley, the police car still on its roof a little distance away, and the half-demolished cricket pavilion. A pall of heavy, greasy black smoke still hung over the scene and the smell of burning lingered.

'Shit,' said Hansen softly.

Grint straightened his shoulders. 'Team – atten . . . tion. Lt Chad Mellor. Friend and colleague.'

They stood to attention for one minute's silence, at the end of which Grint said, 'Stand easy.'

Rossi sighed. 'The match should be kicking off soon.'

'Let's hope he has a good view,' said Hansen. 'Wherever he is now.'

A considerable area had been taped off. The first cars to arrive could easily be discerned from the haphazard way in which they were parked. Some even still had their doors open as officers and ambulance crews had raced to the scene. Subsequent vehicles were now under police control and being parked more neatly. Uniformed officers were turning away the crowds of people as they attempted to access the site.

A number of military vehicles had drawn up near the cricket pavilion. As Grint approached, the bomb disposal unit was reporting all clear. 'You can send your people in now.'

The police officer waved her arm and within seconds, white-suited SOCOs were moving in.

Grint presented himself and his ID.

The police officer nodded. 'Inspector Oliver. I expect to be relieved by someone more senior any time now, but for the moment you've got me.'

'Actually,' said Grint, 'I think that someone more senior is me, but please instruct your people to carry on for the time being. What do we know so far?'

'Two police officers dead – Clive and Williams. Both known to me. And Dr Lewis, the vet. Very well respected locally. Your helicopter pilot . . .'

'Lt Mellor,' said Grint.

'And – we think – two other TPOs missing, status unknown.'

'They're alive,' said Grint. 'They're back at TPHQ receiving treatment.'

'Oh,' said the inspector. 'That's good news. Other than that . . .' She shook her head.

'Any witnesses?'

'No. This place was deliberately chosen for the handover because it's close to the river, outside of town and no one would be around at this time of day. Your evidence, by the way, has been completely destroyed. SOCOs might find a few fragments . . .' She looked over Grint's shoulder. 'I thought there would be more of you.'

'We're the preliminary force,' said Grint. 'Others are in the area and reinforcements will appear as required.'

'Well, we'll carry on here until someone tells us to stop.'

Grint nodded. That always worked well for him, too.

'Given the possible identity of the specimen, I have something that might interest you . . .'

Grint looked up. 'What's that?'

'We've had reports from a local farmer. Something's been at his sheep. They've been very badly savaged.'

There was a long silence. Eventually, Grint said, 'No idea of the culprit?'

'No.'

'Not a couple of dogs?'

'No. This wasn't a case of sheep-worrying. They've actually been eaten.' She paused. 'Some of them weren't dead at the time.'

Grint sighed. 'Where? How close?'

'About three miles. Up by Mallen Moor.'

'Shit. Not that far, then.'

'No.'

'When?'

'The report was received this morning. The event occurred sometime last night.'

'I'll send a couple of people to check it out. Can you lend me someone local as a guide?'

'Happy to. Could this be what I think it is?'

'If you mean – are there more of these giant lizards? – then yes, I think that's quite likely. Rossi?'

'Sir.'

'You and Kohl – there's been a nasty case of sheep-worrying

that might be related to this incident. I want to know what killed them.'

Rossi spread his hands. 'How will we know?'

'Find out. Talk to the farmer. Get samples.'

'Of what?'

'Dead sheep, of course.' He turned to Inspector Oliver. 'Can you organise them some transport and an escort?'

She nodded and turned away, shouting an order.

Rossi and Kohl gazed at their leader in mute appeal.

'Off you go,' said Grint. 'What are you waiting for?'

Rossi and Kohl were last seen refusing to get into the police car unless they could deploy the lights and sirens. The two police officers needed no encouragement. They departed at high speed, accompanied by the full sound and light show.

Grint watched them go and turned back to Inspector Oliver. 'We're only in your way at the moment. My team will be in town. Call me when you've finished.'

Oliver nodded. 'Good luck.'

'Right,' said Grint, as he and the remaining TPOs made their way through the narrow streets. 'The SOCOs will be busy for hours yet. Lockland and Parrish – scope out the local area. You know what you're looking for. Get to it.'

'So this is us stuck with the boring job again,' said Luke to Jane as they approached the town square. 'Just wandering around town looking for the dinosaurs we're pretty sure will have pushed off some time ago, even if they were here in the first place, which they probably weren't.'

Jane peered into a shop window. 'What exactly is an artisanal cheese?'

Luke joined her. 'I always think the *anal* part of artisanal is quite concerning, don't you?'

'We should look for water,' said Jane, endeavouring to keep her erratic colleague on track. 'Animals always come down to drink eventually.'

Luke gave up on the cheese. 'That's very true. You're thinking like a dinosaur, Jane. Well done. And they could be hungry, too. We need to check out possible sources of food. Local butchers. And fast-food shops – especially the bins around the back.'

'Yuk. You can do that bit.'

Luke had moved on to one of those *You are Here* tourist maps. 'According to this, there's a small lake in the park. With ducks. Ducks are very tasty.'

'And there's lots of trees and bushes in the park where dinosaurs could conceal themselves.'

'Or what about schools?' said Luke, with mounting enthusiasm. 'Filled full of small, tasty humans. Or, even better – maternity hospitals. Rows and rows of bite-sized snacks that can't run away.'

Belatedly, he became aware people were looking at him oddly. 'What?'

'For heaven's sake,' said Jane, turning her back on him. Struck with a sudden thought, she pulled out her com.

'Lt Grint, sir, is it worth issuing a public warning? Telling people to stay inside? Just in case. Especially after dark.'

'Good thought, Lockland,' said Grint. 'We'll get on to that now.' He shut down his com. 'Hansen, remember – these are civilians and we are here to liaise.'

'Got it, sir. Liaise with them before we shoot them.'

'Exactly.'

They strode purposefully down the street. Time Police officers from the top of their crew-cutted heads to the tips of their shiny, shiny boots.

The two slightly less typical Time Police officers continued to the park. And the ducks. Traffic here was light but still heavier than in London. Local vehicles tended to be old, of agricultural descent, and caked in mud. And there were far fewer cyclists – probably due to the uppy and downy nature of the landscape.

'Nice place,' said Jane.

'Very neat, certainly. Not exactly a thriving metropolis, though, is it?'

'They have a library – look.'

'And there's a sign pointing to the park.'

'You really think there will be dinosaurs there?'

'More likely than the library, Jane, don't you think? Look out!'

Jane spun around as a small tabby cat streaked past them at top speed and tore straight across the road. Heedless of shouts, curses, dodging pedestrians and screeching brakes, it disappeared down a narrow alleyway between two shops.

'Did you see that?' said Jane, staring after it. 'The poor thing was absolutely terrified.'

They ran across the road – heedless of shouts, curses, dodging pedestrians and screeching brakes – and peered into the alleyway just in time to see the panicking cat run blindly into a pile of rubbish stacked neatly alongside the recycling bins and knock both the pile and itself to the ground. Scrabbling frantically, it pulled itself free of a cardboard box and, with fur standing up all over its body and its tail bristling like a bottle brush, it cleared a six-foot wall in a single bound and disappeared. They had no hope of catching it.

'What the . . . ?' said Luke, in astonishment.

'Did you see where it came from?'

'Look out,' shouted Luke. Again.

Jane spun around – again – as what looked like a cross between a small kangaroo and a scaly dog raced past. Her overwhelming impression was of teeth and velocity. Travelling at an astonishing speed, it disappeared in the general direction of the cat.

The whole event was over in seconds. Not a sign of the chaser or the chased anywhere. Two highly trained Time Police officers stared helplessly about them and attempted to pull themselves together.

'Did you see that?'

'Was that a . . . ?'

'Come on, Jane. They were heading towards the park.'

'We'll never catch either of them. Did you see the speed they were both moving?'

They trotted to the end of the alleyway and emerged on to a quiet road.

'Over there,' said Luke, pointing.

The park was surrounded by shoulder-high iron railings. The gates were open although no one seemed to be availing themselves of this delightful facility today. Plane trees had been planted around the outside, shading a wide encircling path. Smaller diagonal paths led to the centrepiece, a small and conspicuously duckless lake. Clumps of thick shrubbery surrounded the park's working bits – toilets, groundsmen's huts, compost heaps and so on.

Luke pulled out his gun. Jane looked at it doubtfully. 'It was only a very little dinosaur, Luke.'

'I don't care,' said Luke, assuming a ferocious expression. 'I'm sick of being a laughing stock. Formal instruction from your team leader, Jane – from this moment on, Two-Three-Six gets its man – or dinosaur – first time – every time.'

'If you say so,' said Jane doubtfully, following her team leader into the shrubbery. There was a well-worn path winding its way through the thick bushes. There was also a very strong smell of ammonia.

'This is stupid,' she said, peering into the gloom. 'We should call for back-up.'

'And find ourselves subject to the usual mockery?' said Luke. He assumed a silly voice. '*Oh look, it's Team Weird again. Still needing assistance to bring in their prisoners.* Let's face it, Jane, if we'd brought in Adesina and Kumar as soon as we caught sight of them at the railway station, then we wouldn't have been carted to hell and back by that bloody train.'

'This won't be an ordinary prisoner, though,' said Jane, edging her way between two rhododendron bushes. 'We shouldn't—'

She stopped dead.

'What?' said Luke, turning his head. 'What shouldn't we do?'

Jane tried to speak without moving her lips. 'Look left.'

'Why shouldn't I look left?' demanded Luke, looking left. 'Oh. Shit.'

There were eyes. Everywhere. Everywhere they looked, eyes looked back at them. Gleaming in the gloom. Some at ground level – some at shoulder height. Lots and lots and lots of eyes.

Luke found himself vividly recalling every holo he'd ever seen where the raptors surrounded unwary humans and closed in for the kill. He made a faint sound that he would always – until his dying day – deny was a whimper.

'Back away,' whispered Jane.

'Why?'

'They might not attack if we back away.'

'No, I mean why are you whispering?'

'What?'

Luke spoke louder. 'Why are you whispering?'

'I'm trying to avoid doing anything they might construe as hostile.'

'Jane, they've seen us. They're looking right at us. I don't think preventative whispering will contribute anything positive to our final moments.'

Not daring to look away from the eyes, Jane slowly reached for her blaster. The eyes followed her every move.

Luke's own blaster began to whine. 'OK. Three steps back, Jane. Widen our field of fire. On my command, you fire inwards from the right – I'll take the left. Torch the bushes and fry anything trying to escape.'

Jane brought up her blaster. 'Ready when you are.'

'On my command. One, two . . .'

Somewhere behind them a door slammed as a groundsman left his hut. There was the sound of someone banging a tin dish. 'Here, puss-puss-puss. Puss-puss-puss.'

The effect was magical. The eyes vanished. One minute – eyes – and the next moment – no eyes. Anywhere.

'Shit. Jane, they're attacking. Fire!'

Fortunately, there was no opportunity to do so. The world

was suddenly full of small furry bodies as eight or ten cats flashed past them as if they weren't there and disappeared into a different shrubbery. Leaving behind an embarrassed silence.

'Well,' said Luke, powering down. 'Feral cats.'

'Yes,' said Jane, stowing her weapon.

'That was embarrassing.'

'Not as embarrassing as if we'd called it in.'

'God, no. Grint would be stampeding through the shrubbery like a herd of one elephant and igniting everything in his path.'

'Actually, I think he quite likes cats.'

Luke's heart rate began to return to normal. 'Well, he could have had that lot with my very best wishes.'

They emerged from the shrubbery to find the park completely unaware of their recent ordeal.

'Right – more instructions from your team leader, Jane. We consign this embarrassing moment to the Dustbin of Experience and never speak of it again.'

'Agreed. Does this mean we'll be reverting to our usual regime of failing to arrest our prisoners first time round? And sometimes even the second.'

'The dismal failures for which we are famed? Yes – less stressful all round, I think.'

Jane nodded. That suited her. 'Shall we check out the rest of the park while we're here? After all, we did see something heading this way. And we should tell the groundsman to lock his door.'

'After you, teammate.'

27

Sadly for Max and Varma, the best laid plans . . .

At the north end of the big courtyard, the two pods still stood side by side. Henry Plimpton was waiting outside the one on the right. He wasn't alone. Another man leaned back against the pod door, his arms folded and with an easy grin on his face. He appeared relaxed and very much at ease with the events around him, but his crinkly blue eyes watched their every move.

He smiled and straightened as Max and Varma approached. 'Why, ladies, I don't believe I've had the pleasure.'

Max stopped dead, but before she could speak, Varma nudged her out of the way and confronted Plimpton. 'What's going on?'

Henry Plimpton smiled. 'A slight change of plan. After a brief discussion my esteemed colleague has advised we carry out this murder on site. Actually in the Tower itself. A small precaution. Just while we all . . . find our feet, so to speak.' He fixed his eyes on Max and Varma. 'If this goes well, then all the second and subsequent murders can benefit from more elaborate scenarios.'

Varma scowled, her eyes darting from one man to the other. 'Who is he? What's his name?'

The man smiled. 'Well, darling, that all depends on when and where we happen to encounter each other, doesn't it? Since this is the first time we've ever met, today you may regard me as Sir James Tyrell.'

Max had folded her arms and was staring at the ground.

'You are uncharacteristically quiet,' said Henry Plimpton, eyeing her suspiciously.

Max forced a smile. 'Sorry, I just like to run through everything in my mind a couple of times. Make sure I've taken every contingency into account.'

'Ah, yes. I too am something of an over-planner but I find it works for me.'

Max nodded politely but said nothing. Because now the situation was more complicated than even she was happy with. How this would end was anyone's guess. Not well, seemed very likely.

Henry Plimpton turned away. 'How do you intend to proceed today . . . Sir James?'

'Don't know at the moment,' he said cheerfully. 'A lot will depend on the layout when I get there. And your instructions, of course. Do you want a swift, silent and fairly painless assassination – a pillow over their faces, perhaps? Or would you prefer more spectacle? Chasing two screaming boys around the room while clutching a bloodstained dagger, for instance. Accompanied by the full diabolical cackle.'

'Oh, the second, I think.'

'Good thought,' said Max, rousing herself. 'We could do swift, silent and fairly painless on the second night. You know – ring the changes. See what proves most popular with your audiences.'

Sir James Tyrell looked at Henry Plimpton. 'I can do that.'

Henry Plimpton smiled. 'Then I see I can safely leave everything with you.' He folded his hands across his plump stomach. 'Off you all go, then.'

The really bad news was that entrance to the pod was via Phillips' thumb. Varma stiffened. Biometrics. Bugger. Whatever happened to everyone else, Mr Phillips would have to survive. She considered that sentence and then amended it to Mr Phillips' thumb would have to survive. The rest of him was pretty redundant. And it was his left thumb. She made a mental note – left thumb – and glanced casually at Max, who nodded very slightly. Yeah – left thumb.

The pod interior was bare and basic. No seats. No lockers. No facilities of any kind. Scruffy and with signs of heavy wear and tear scoring the walls and floors. Rather a peculiar smell. A combination of boots and bananas.

'Amateurs, stand in the corner,' ordered Phillips. 'Stay out of our way. Or else.'

'Are you perhaps talking to me?' said Sir James, and suddenly his smile wasn't anywhere near as friendly and charming as it had been a few minutes ago.

'No,' said Phillips, not looking at him.

'Only I don't think that's any way to speak to a couple of nice ladies like these. Do you?'

There was an awkward pause. 'No,' said Phillips, still not looking up from the console.

Varma nodded to herself. Plimpton's men were afraid of Sir James. Had they encountered him before? She glanced at Max, white, still and withdrawn, and with the internal expression of one suffering a blinding headache.

It wasn't the smoothest of jumps, but everyone arrived intact which, given their team consisted of an unknown quantity in the form of Sir James Tyrell, four thugs, a disgraced TPO and a wayward historian, was probably the best anyone could hope for.

Max straightened up and made an effort to rejoin the world. 'Let me see the screen.'

'You don't need to . . .' began Phillips.

Sir James coughed.

Grudgingly, Phillips stepped to one side.

Max spent some time panning around. Varma waited quietly. As did Sir James, effortlessly projecting psychopathy, but professional psychopathy.

'Yes,' said Max eventually. 'We're in the right place. Everything's quiet, as far as I can see. It's a clear night and there's no moon, which works in our favour. The entrance to the Garden Tower is about ten yards diagonally to our left from the pod. You'll go first, please, Mr Phillips. Advise when you have the door open, and we'll join you.'

Phillips opened his mouth, presumably to argue, closed it again, silently let himself out of the pod and ghosted to the barely visible door. Both Max and Varma watched his every move. Varma looked up from the screen to find Sir James watching her. He winked and grinned.

Phillips' voice sounded faintly over the com. 'OK. Door's open. Foster . . .'

'Right,' said Foster. 'You heard the man. Single file to the door. I'll bring up the rear.'

'No,' said Sir James gently. 'I'll bring up the rear. I don't know why it is, but I always find myself reluctant to have strangers behind me. Just one of my funny little quirks.'

The pod door opened again on to a warm night. The stars twinkled prettily overhead. Somewhat closer, the River Thames wended its malodorous way to the sea. Varma's nostrils twitched at the stink.

One by one, they made their way towards the Garden Tower and passed silently through the open door, finding themselves in what seemed too small a space for so many of them. Sir James, the last one in, quietly pushed the door to behind him.

Phillips indicated Potts remain behind and led the way up the stone steps. A lantern hung from an iron hook high on the wall and its faint light showed the way. The night was very quiet and they moved slowly. Max followed Phillips. Varma followed Max, Foster and Schenk followed her and Sir James, presumably, brought up the rear.

Reaching the top, Phillips halted and cracked a small lightstick. They waited in silence as he carefully examined the door. Like most doors in the Tower of London, it was on the hefty side. Finally, he handed the stick to Foster and gently turned the metal ring. Varma held her breath. To make a sound now . . . to give the game away . . . these old doors could be noisy. Suppose it scraped along the stone floor . . . or the hinges creaked . . .

The door swung open silently. Foster raised the lightstick. This wasn't the princes' bedroom. There was minimal furniture in this room – a few stools against a wall, a bench that seemed to double as a table, and no bed. There were, however, three or four dark shapes sprawled on the floor, wrapped in cloaks or blankets. Someone was snoring. The window was shuttered and the air smelled stale and close.

Foster and Phillips stepped aside for Schenk to push past. Holding her breath, Varma could hear the slight hiss as each of the sleeping attendants received a faceful of some kind of sleeping gas. She reckoned she had a window of less than two minutes. How this was going to play out, she had no idea. What would happen if no opportunity presented itself before Sir James was supposed to do the deed?

Max had taken up position with her back against one wall, behind Phillips and Foster. Schenk had remained out on the landing behind the closed door. Which left . . .

Sir James Tyrell was delicately picking his way around the motionless bodies towards the inner room. Varma followed closely behind, exchanging a glance with Max, who nodded.

Varma swallowed. This was not going to end well. Phillips had his blaster ready. She could hear its faint whining. Foster was holding the recorder but he too was heavily armed. As was Schenk, only on the other side of the door with his weapon drawn, and he'd be in here like a flash at the first sounds of a struggle. And what Sir James had planned was anyone's guess. How close would she be allowed to get? Plimpton's men might not even allow her into the princes' bedroom.

Without giving Phillips the opportunity to prevent it, she fixed her eyes on the back of Sir James's head and followed him into the inner room. There was a little light in here. A small candle flickered on a table over by the wall. Well away from the bed hangings. There would be no chance of a fire in the night. The night was warm and the attendants hadn't drawn the bed curtains. She could just make out two heads on the pillows. The smaller boy had kicked off his covers. He lay face down. His older brother lay on his back, arms outstretched – an easy target for an assassin's knife.

Sir James stood for a moment looking down at the two sleeping boys. Varma tensed. What would be his next move?

She heard a faint sound behind her. Foster appeared in the doorway, recorder raised. He gestured for her to get out of shot. She nodded and used the excuse to move towards Sir James, wondering whether disliking people standing too close to him would turn out to be another of his funny little quirks.

From the corner of her eye, she saw Max move casually across the room, as if seeking a better view. And, quite co-incidentally, coming to stand slightly behind Foster.

Varma turned back to the bed. This was it. She braced herself – ready to go.

Behind her, she heard the sounds of a sudden scuffle. Someone said, 'What ...?' and swore viciously. Max had made her move. No time to see how that was going because here came Phillips, weapon raised and wearing the expression of one whose suspicions had been fully realised. And any moment now Schenk would hear the noise and then there would be three of them. All armed.

Varma closed her mind to Sir James and went for Phillips, realising, too late, that he was a leftie. Now she'd have to throw herself across his body to get to his gun.

Using her own weight, she barged into him with as much force as she could muster, at the same time grabbing for his arm. She was fast but he was faster. Almost as if he'd been expecting it – which he probably had – he took one step backwards, brought up his right fist and caught her a sharp blow on her temple.

Her last thought – bollocks, the bloke was ambidextrous – spluttered and died in a dark pool of something or other ...

Varma opened her eyes to find herself on the rough stone floor. For how long had she been out? Not for many moments, because she felt a sudden blow in the small of her back. He'd kicked her. Mistake. Kicking your victim – while quite enjoyable – leaves the kicker with less than perfect balance. And if Phillips was kicking her then he wasn't shooting her.

The room was even darker down here on the floor. She couldn't see much but she could easily imagine him drawing back his leg for another vicious blow. She rolled towards him and sat up. Always try for the unexpected move. The second blow impacted her shoulder but caught him unawares. She was closer than he'd anticipated. It was too much to hope he would topple over, but she felt his balance shift. More by good luck than good judgement, she grabbed what felt like a leg and twisted.

She heard a muffled curse above her and he fell sideways on to the bed. Which must have woken the boys because, over her head, at least one of them shrieked. Were they being attacked as per Henry Plimpton's instructions? And if so, who was doing the attacking? Where was Sir James? And what, at this precise moment, was he up to?

Using the bed, Varma pulled herself up and launched herself again at Phillips. The Time Police have a procedure for this sort of thing. If all else fails, wrap yourself around your prisoner and simply hold on until help arrives. Which, of course, presumed help was around to arrive. That didn't seem to apply in this case. Any number of things could go wrong with this scenario. Schenk or Potts could burst through the door and shoot them all. Foster could break free of Max. Phillips could shoot her. The Tower guards could turn up at any moment and kill them all. Some days you just wish you'd stayed in bed.

Most worrying of all – the boys stopped screaming. Suddenly. Were they dead? And who had done the deed?

Varma had no clear idea what was going on around her. Whether Max was alive or dead. Or any of the team. And that blow to her shoulder was hurting far more than it should.

Phillips was bucking and rolling in an attempt to dislodge her. She caught a glimpse of the boys, dim outlines in light nightrobes. Alive and huddled together in the farthest corner of the bed. The younger had seized a bolster or pillow and was holding it in front of them. A good effort but any dagger would go straight through it.

At some point, Phillips had abandoned his gun for a knife. Varma found his flailing arm and hung on, twisting her body to get a leg entangled around his, expecting, at any moment, to feel his knife between her ribs. Or the kiss of cold steel across her throat. The gush of warm blood and the slow darkness of death.

And then there was pain. Deep, spasming pain. And again. And for a third time. Her body convulsed and she went rigid for a moment, her limbs stiff and paralysed. And then all that disappeared and she was as floppy as a fish. Something heavy lay across her. Phillips. Crushing the breath out of her. And then he was gone. Dragged away and dropped on the floor.

'Sorry about that,' said a voice, seemingly from a long, long way away. 'It seemed best to stun him while I could rather than wait for you to get clear. You'll be fine. Just take a moment.'

And then the lights came on.

It was only afterwards that Varma realised how inappropriate that phrase was. Lights did not just 'come on' in 1483. And this wasn't the wavering light of the solitary candle in a draughty room. This was the solid golden glow of a lightstick.

Somehow she got her good arm beneath her and prepared to heave herself up for round two. Now she could see more clearly. The two boys were still alive, holding tightly to each other and their pillow.

Foster lay face down on the floor, his recorder in pieces around him. It would seem that, however this night ended, Henry Plimpton wouldn't be seeing any of it.

Somewhat shakily, she began to grope her way across the floor. Before she could struggle to her feet, however, the door crashed open. Schenk appeared on the threshold, Potts at his shoulder in the narrow doorway. Potts levelled his blaster at her.

Someone shouted, 'Look out, Varma,' and suddenly Max was between her and him with a somehow acquired blaster of her own. Varma heard at least one weapon discharge and both Max and Potts went down. Her blaster skidded across the floor. Varma lunged for it but her reactions were glacially slow after her sonicking. Sir James was there first, swooping in to snatch up the weapon. Whirling around, he fired at Schenk, who had made the mistake of hesitating between targets. Schenk's shot went wide. Sir James's did not. Schenk dropped to the floor.

Sudden silence fell.

In a state of slight disbelief, Varma pulled herself fully to her feet. She clung on to one of the bedposts while her legs remembered what they were there for. Her back hurt. Her head hurt. Her shoulder was still far more painful than it should be. Ignore that for the moment. Gain control of the situation. Where was all this blood coming from? Was it hers? Yes, it was. All right, slightly more injured than she had previously thought.

Shakily she made her way to Max, now sprawled on the floor, and tried, one-armed, to turn her over.

'Ow,' said a muffled voice.

'Are you all right?'

'Well . . . the good news is that my headache's gone. What happened?'

'You've been hit by a blaster. It's going to sting in the morning.'

'It bloody stings *now*. Why is there blood dripping all over me?'

Varma looked down at her bloodstained arm. 'I think I've been stabbed. But not badly.'

Sir James hacked off a piece of sheet and passed it over. 'Pack the wound with that.'

She took it. 'Thanks.'

Max tried to lift her head. 'The princes?'

'Fine,' said Varma carefully. 'Still alive. As are we.'

'Where's that other bastard?'

'Behind you,' said a voice. 'No, don't get up. A simple hello will suffice.'

'We need to get out of here now, Major,' said Varma. 'I can't believe no one's turned up to check out all the noise Maxwell's been making.'

'Me?' protested Max. 'Where's the gratitude? I just took a blaster shot for you.'

As Varma later admitted, she might have lost her self-control at this point. Just fractionally.

'It's all your fire-trucking fault they were shooting at us

in the first place,' she shouted. 'This was your crazy scheme. You put the idea into Plimpton's head. You and your *Oh Mr Plimpton, you're so clever and I'd love to come and work for you.* You're a bloody maniac. A certifiable fire-trucking lunatic. I can't believe any of us are still alive.'

Sir James, busy examining Max's blaster burn, nodded his agreement. 'You cannot imagine the enthusiasm with which I am endorsing Lt Varma's sentiments. Thanks to this evening's little cock-up, I've had to abandon a long period of careful infiltration.'

Max tried to sit up. '*You're* Henry Plimpton's assassin?'

He pushed her back down again. 'No, of course I'm not, but I have had him under observation for some time and then I received a tip-off his services were being called upon. I would have been here sooner, but I was delayed slightly by events at TPHQ, which left me no time to implement my carefully laid plans. I simply trusted that Plimpton and Tyrell had never met in person and took his place.'

'And where is this assassin now?' asked Varma.

'Oh, I don't think we need worry about him at the moment. In fact, I don't think we need bother about him at all.'

'No,' said Max quietly. 'There's never anyone left alive to tell their side of the story with you, is there, Commander?'

'Major,' said Varma. 'Major Callen.'

Callen turned to Varma. 'Do enlighten me as to what exactly the pair of you were hoping to achieve here today.'

Max lifted her head. 'Prevent the murder of the princes, of course.'

'By selling a known Time criminal the idea of killing them not once but many hundreds of times.'

'Well, obviously we had no intention of actually carrying out any of it,' said Max, scowling. 'Or of allowing it to be carried out. Ow. That hurt.' She attempted to squint down at Sir James's rapid but far from painless first aid.

'So what exactly *were* your somewhat muddled intentions this evening?'

'We were to overcome Phillips and his team – somehow – escape back to TPHQ in their pod, raise the alarm – several alarms, actually – the castle, the time-slip, the plot to murder the princes and so forth – enjoy a well-earned drink – on the house – and I would return to my day job.'

Major Callen finished his rough dressing of Max's shoulder and began to pick up the pieces of Foster's recorder. 'And how has that not particularly well-thought-out scheme worked for you?'

Max went to gesture at the fallen Phillips and his team, winced and thought better of it. 'Very successfully – as all my schemes usually do.'

'Well, let's recap, shall we? You've blown my cover . . .'

'We found Henry Plimpton . . .'

'Ruined several months of hard work . . .'

'Foiled no end of dastardly schemes . . .'

'Instigated and participated in the kidnap of Romulus, Father of Rome . . .'

'Provided enough evidence that even the Time Police could make the charges stick. And let me remind you – the Time Police came to me for help. Admit it – you can't manage without me.'

'You were brought in to identify one – *one* – dinosaur. Half an hour's work for a normal person. Now, thanks to your actions . . .'

He broke off in exasperation.

Max glared up at him, her eyes glowing golden in the dim light.

'I swear Treadwell . . . or Callen . . . or whatever your bloody name is, one day you'll go that little bit too far. You'll be that little bit too clever and just when you least expect it, your world will come crashing down. Everything you have will crumble and you'll be alone with nothing but bitter thoughts of what might have been.'

The little room was suddenly very cold. Varma stood motionless, almost afraid to move, mystified by the sudden tension between them. Then Max blinked and said in her normal voice, 'My shoulder is killing me.'

For the space of a heartbeat there was silence, and then Callen said lightly, 'Yes. Unaware you were to be involved in tonight's events, I foolishly ventured out without a full field medic's kit. My bad.'

Max closed her eyes, blocking out her throbbing arm. She could still feel a slight ringing in her ears – like someone running their finger around a wine glass. Not a symptom of a blaster wound as far as she was aware, but already it was fading. And yes, her headache really had gone. In fact, if it didn't feel as if her arm was on fire – which, to be fair, it had been – she'd be feeling positively chipper.

Varma had cracked open the door and was watching the stairs. Now she turned to Callen. 'Is Commander Hay aware of your involvement with Henry Plimpton?'

'She knows I have left the building in something of a hurry. She will have the details as soon as I've filed my report. That will be the one detailing weeks of wasted effort on my part.

Given our precarious situation here, however, may I suggest we vacate the premises with all speed?'

'Yes, sir. Max, can you walk?'

'If someone can actually stand me up, then yes, probably.'

Varma's shoulder being too painful, it was Callen who hauled her to her feet.

Max turned to the two boys still huddled on the bed, as far away from events as they could possibly be, and smiled reassuringly. The older boy shrank back in fear, but the younger one raised his fists and scowled pugnaciously.

Max spoke gently. '*Thee haede ain nīth drēm.*'

They stared at her.

'*Gī backeth bihofþe slepe.*'

Not taking their eyes off her for a second, the boys lay stiffly back on their pillows. She pulled the covers up around them and then stood still, gazing at their faces, frowning as if groping for some lost memory.

Callen sighed. 'When you're *quite* ready, Dr Maxwell.' He turned towards the door.

Max looked at Phillips and his team, still out cold. 'What do we do with them?'

Callen shrugged. 'Leave them here. They can't tell us anything we don't already know and the combination of a locked door and the presence of strangers after an attack on the princes should keep people occupied for a while. And fortunately they're in the Tower anyway – all those handy racks and thumbscrews – so that's convenient for everyone. Maxwell, I hope you can walk to the pod because Varma's too weak to carry you and I don't want to.'

Max's eyes gleamed with mischief. 'Wait – just one thing . . .'

'Oh yes,' said Varma, remembering. 'That will be up to you, I'm afraid, sir.'

'What will?'

Max grinned. 'Make sure you get the right one.'

'She means the left one,' said Varma hastily, before misunderstandings could occur.

Fortunately, Callen's knife was very sharp.

When they arrived in MedCen, the doctor sighed. 'This is not something I thought I'd ever say, but you are St Mary's, after all. Why, Dr Maxwell, are you clutching a thumb?'

Max looked down, apparently having forgotten she still had it. 'Oh, it's not mine.'

'I can see that. Popular opinion has it that St Mary's has barely progressed far enough down the evolutionary path to have two opposable thumbs, let alone three.'

'Access,' said Max, depositing the thumb into a convenient metal tray.

'If you will excuse me,' said Callen, moving towards the door. 'As the only uninjured person present, I don't feel I can make any sort of contribution here. I shall, therefore, retire to write up my report. Ladies.'

He swept from the room.

'Pillock,' said Max.

28

Completely unaware that events were about to hit him thick and fast, Lt Grint was taking a moment to lean against a convenient police vehicle and savour his coffee.

Rossi and Kohl had reported dead sheep everywhere but whatever had killed them was long gone. They were now on their way back to . . . Grint stared around. Where the hell *was* he? A large, pillared building stood opposite with the words LLYFRGELL LIBRARY impressively engraved over the portico. He sipped his coffee again, enjoying the moment.

On the other side of town, but not that far away as the herbivore scampers, Lockland and Parrish were making their way around the lake.

'There are no ducks,' said Jane nervously, peering from left to right, blaster at the ready. Luke was covering their rear. 'Not anywhere.'

'What is it with you and ducks? Oh.'

The pretty lake was fringed with willow trees gently dangling their soft green fronds in the still waters. A tranquil scene. Until something about three feet tall, olive green, scaled, standing upright and possessing a mouth filled with more teeth than was surely possible, emerged from behind the trailing fronds. Closely followed by another, almost identical to the first except for the dead duck dangling from its jaws. Which, on catching sight of Luke and Jane, it immediately dropped.

It's hard to read the expressions of a reptile, but it certainly seemed to Luke and Jane that both dinosaurs perked up immediately at the sight of this new prey. Prey, incidentally, with far more meat on its bones than a scrawny duck. One made a brief, low, chuntering sound and the pair immediately began to move apart. One to the right – one to the left.

Instinctively, Jane and Luke moved to stand back to back.

'Don't let them split us up,' whispered Jane. 'And definitely don't run.'

Simultaneously, both dinosaurs crouched and hissed. The one on the right began to shift its weight from side to side.

'Don't wait for it to spring,' whispered Luke. 'Fire on my word. Now.'

The smaller raptor on the left uttered one short, sharp bark, and leaped. Fast and powerful. Luke threw himself to one side, firing his blaster as he hit the ground. At the same time, Jane dropped to one knee. Both movements appeared to confuse the second dinosaur, which seemed unable to make up its mind which of them to attack first. Taking advantage of its indecision, Jane fired a long, long blast until she was completely sure it was dead. It screamed horribly for a few moments and then dropped to the ground. Dark smoke curled from two charred bodies. The smell was really horrible. She was very conscious of the silence. No birdsong – nothing. Everything sensible had long since fled the park.

'Well,' said Jane finally, climbing stiffly to her feet and staring at the corpses.

'Yes,' said Luke, also picking himself up. 'Well.'

Jane bent over the charred remains. 'I'm so sorry.'

Luke sighed. 'Jane, is it not bad enough that you thank the AI – now you're apologising to a couple of dead raptors. They would have eaten us alive.'

'But that's not their fault. Some stupid idiot has yanked them out of their own time. They were just doing what dinosaurs do.'

'Yes, but they were about to do it to us, which mitigates my sympathy somewhat.'

Jane cautiously prodded one of the bodies with her boot. Yes, no doubt about it – very dead.

Luke clapped her on the shoulder. 'Jane – we did it. We got our man – men – dinosaurs – first time. Team Two-Three-Six are the dog's bollocks. Finally.'

He opened his com. 'Lt Grint? We can definitely confirm there are more dinosaurs in the area. Lockland and I have just bagged a brace of them down by the lake. And we've had a sighting of at least one more. We don't feel like walking back through town with these two – we'll start a panic. Can you send transport or shall we leave them here?'

'Leave them,' ordered Grint. 'We've started clearing the streets and sending people home. If you come across anyone who can't get to safety, then bring them along with you. Report to . . .' He stared around the town square. Shops lined all four sides with a small, prettily planted garden in the centre. He could see a butcher, what looked like a florist, an off-licence, a jeweller's, a café, an antique shop . . .

His gaze snapped back to the butcher's shop. Hmm . . . there was a thought. But right at this moment . . .

'Get yourselves back here asap and report to me at the library.'

Closing his com, he turned to Hansen. 'Anything yet from Varma? Or Tucker?'

Hansen shook his head. 'No, sir – nothing.'

'Or even Maxwell?'

'She didn't have a com, sir.'

'Anything from their trackers?'

'No, sir.'

Grint shifted uneasily. 'Keep trying.'

'Yes, sir.'

'Parrish reckons they've bagged themselves a couple of dinosaurs. And possible sightings of others.'

Hansen tutted. 'Really? Bugger.'

Grint raised an eyebrow. 'How so?'

'There's a league table, sir. You know – number spotted, number killed, that sort of thing. It looks as if Team Weird has just shot straight to the top. As I said – Bugger.'

Grint's pointed remark about good use of Hansen's time was never uttered.

His com crackled. 'Lt Grint – can you hear me?'

For a moment, Grint couldn't think who ... and then, 'Tucker?'

'Listen. No time. Coms don't work near the time-slip so I'm hiding in a cupboard in the castle. I've found the dinosaurs. Hundreds and hundreds of them. They're coming through a time-slip and it's a big one. The really bad news is that a lot of them might be heading your way.'

'Might be?'

'All right – probably are heading your way. You need to

warn people. Varma and Maxwell reckon the person running the show is Henry Plimpton. He knows me so I'm staying well out of his way. He's operating out of some kind of castle about seven miles north-east of you. Listen – as I said, coms are bad here so you won't hear any more from me. The time-slip is in the mine and it links to the Cretaceous. There are tunnels everywhere. One leads to an open mine shaft. That's how the dinosaurs have been escaping. I shut down the power to create a diversion which . . . might have been slightly too successful. Not only are a large number of dinos loose but more are coming through the time-slip as well. It's carnage here and Plimpton's forces are split between defending themselves and getting the power back up again. You'll never have a better opportunity. I'm creating as much chaos as I can to keep them busy, but reinforcements would be appreciated. Varma and Maxwell are already inside but Plimpton's got them and it's only a matter of time before he shoots them.' There was a slight pause and then he said quickly, 'Gotta go. Tucker out.'

Grint took a moment to stand and think. 'Hansen – recall our people. Tucker reports a lot more dinos possibly heading this way. Then get hold of Oliver and advise her what's going on. Tell her never mind the crime scene and to evacuate the SOCOs. She'll know what to do. Move.'

Hansen raced away, shouting into his com as he went.

Grint opened his com again. 'Commander Hay? Ma'am?'

Nothing but static. He walked away from the buildings towards the more open space at the centre of the square and tried again. Still only static. Was the problem with him or TPHQ?

Hansen returned, panting. 'Sir, Kohl and Rossi are on their way back in. Oliver's evacuating the site.'

'I can't get through to TPHQ. And we need a secure area from which to operate. Perhaps even to withstand attack. Where's the nearest telephone?'

Hansen pointed to the multilingual signs advertising the library. 'Big building, heavy doors, central position. Well known locally. Ideal.'

Grint surveyed the building in a critical manner and sighed. The general ambience was warm and welcoming. Wide open doors, ramps for the disabled, big windows. They'd done everything they could to render the building undefendable.

He sighed. 'Where are their defences?'

Hansen blinked. 'I don't think libraries have any, sir. The whole point is to encourage people to come inside.'

Grint manifested silent criticism of such folly.

Hansen regarded his leader. 'Have you ever actually been inside a library?'

'Not since school. But I remember doing the Civil Uprisings, and the focus of the resistance was the library at Thirsk University, so I suppose I just sort of assumed . . . Thirsk held out for weeks, whereas this . . .'

Words failed him as he attempted to come to terms with the facility's complete lack of minefields, drone-deployed lasers and man traps.

'Come on.'

Grint ran up the library steps, followed by Hansen, and straight in through the front doors, considerably startling the duty librarian, a Miss Knibbs, who happened to be struggling past with the traditionally overladen book trolley. From Land's End to John o' Groats, no librarian would make three separate journeys when custom, convention and practice demanded everything be loaded on to just one ancient and unstable book trolley. The Code of the Librarians must be followed at all times.

'A telephone,' demanded Grint, flashing his ID. 'I need to use your telephone.'

Miss Knibbs paused with her trolley heaving and pointed to her desk. 'Dial nine for an outside line.'

'Thank you.'

Wrenching the receiver from its cradle, he dialled 999.

'Which service do you require?'

'Flash call for Time Police HQ in Battersea,' said Grint.

'Confirm, please.'

'Flash call for TPHQ, Battersea.' Grint gave his service number.

'Connecting you. Stand by.'

The phone rang for a very long time. Grint was conscious of a creeping unease. Why weren't they answering? What was going on there? Eventually, however ...

'Time Police.'

'Flash call for Commander Hay,' said Grint.

'Stand by.'

A moment later ...

'This is Captain Farenden.'

'Grint here, sir. Emergency situation. Request immediate back-up. Do you have a problem with your coms?'

'Emergency situation here, too,' said Farenden. 'State your exact requirements.'

'With immediate effect, as many people as you can let me have. And heavy weaponry. The local population is under imminent threat from dinosaurs, numbers unknown but probably a lot. Varma and Maxwell are prisoners of Henry Plimpton. I have a castle to assault . . .' Hansen passed him the map reference, 'together with an open time-slip that links back to the Cretaceous period.'

'Give me your number, Lieutenant, and keep this line clear. I'll get back to you.'

Grint complied and the line went dead.

Grint's com crackled. 'Rossi here, sir. We're on our way back. Where are you and where do you want people directed to?'

Grint remembered the sign. 'Ll . . . Cli . . .'

He turned to Miss Knibbs and pointed. 'How do you say that word?'

'Cluvrageth,' she said brightly.

'Direct people to . . .' He paused, frowning.

'Cluvrageth,' she said again.

'The town square in Cluvrageth.'

'Copy that. Rossi out.'

'Um . . . actually . . .' said Miss Knibbs, 'I think there might have been just a small misunderst—'

But Grint was in juggernaut mode and unstoppable.

'A large number of animals have escaped from a . . . nearby . . . animal park,' he said.

'What sort of animals?'

Grint hesitated, unwilling to spread alarm and dismay among the civilian population.

'Big ones.'

'Elephants? Well, they're not particularly . . .'

'They may attack and . . .'

'Elephants? I don't think . . .'

'No, not elephants, more . . . fierce. And dangerous.'

'Lions? Tigers?'

Grint gave it up. He was running out of time. The civilian population was just going to have to live with it.

'Dinosaurs.'

Miss Knibbs clapped her hands. 'Dinosaurs? How exciting. And they're coming here?'

This was not quite the reaction Grint had expected.

'Possibly. There's a possibility – a faint possibility – that we may be under attack at any moment,' he said. 'I am designating this building a refugee centre. We need a secure area in which to shelter all those who can't get home. What have you got?'

'Goodness gracious,' said Miss Knibbs, so placidly that Grint began to wonder what actually constituted an emergency in the world of librarianism. She began to point in different directions, rather like a small knitted signpost. 'Fiction, non-fiction, junior and ref. A small café through there. Public access computers over there. Conference room on the other side of the hall.'

'What's downstairs?'

'The stacks.'

'Upstairs?'

'The register office.'

Grint looked blank.

'Births, deaths and marriages.'

'Can both areas be secured? If anything does come at us, then I want it to be through the front doors only.'

'Yes. All doors can be locked.'

'Can you send someone to evacuate upstairs? Bring everyone

down here. And lock all the doors while they're at it. Tell them to leave the keys in the locks in case we need to unlock in a hurry.'

With that, Grint and Hansen strode off to survey the rest of the building.

Miss Knibbs paused for a few words with her senior library assistant and then abandoned the trolley for something that promised to be a great deal more interesting.

She caught up with the Time Police officers in the conference area.

'What the hell is this?' Grint surveyed the huge floor-to-ceiling windows that made up an entire wall, all overlooking the narrow lane that separated them from their neighbours. The windows were covered in trendy, modern etched designs relating to the many and beneficial services offered by the library.

'It's our new extension,' said Miss Knibbs helpfully. 'Full conference facilities with internet . . .'

'It's made of glass.'

'Transparency is very important in . . .'

Grint was striding back to the main body of the library. 'How the hell do you ever expect to hold out against hostile incursions?'

'Well, we've never actually had one of those. Although Mr Snettisham did once shake his walking stick at Dillie because she—'

Miss Knibbs stopped suddenly.

'Because she what?' asked Hansen, intrigued to discover what could possibly happen in a public library that would warrant walking-stick shaking.

Miss Knibbs folded her hands primly. 'Well, she issued Mr Snettisham's reserved book to Councillor Jones by mistake.'

Grint grappled with his incomprehension of basic library life. 'I don't follow. How is that . . . ?'

'Well, we have . . . *books*.'

'Yes, I know. You're a library.'

'But this was a . . . *book*.'

Struggling for enlightenment, Grint turned to Hansen, who shrugged his own bewilderment.

Miss Knibbs tried again. 'Books we don't put out on the shelves.'

Two TPOs stared at her in complete incomprehension.

'In case people see them,' she whispered, labouring under the mistaken apprehension she was making things clearer. The ensuing silence made it apparent she had not.

'Children,' she said, red-faced. 'Or young people.'

'Oh,' said Hansen, enlightened.

Grint stared at him.

'Spicy,' whispered Miss Knibbs.

'Ah – got it.' Grint nodded his comprehension and firmly grasped the wrong end of this particular stick. 'Recipe books.'

Hansen randomly seized a copy of *Guinea Pigs for Fun and Profit* and disappeared behind some shelving.

Grint and Miss Knibbs continued to stare at each other in mutual misunderstanding and embarrassment.

'Pornography, sir,' muttered the unseen Hansen, taking pity on his leader.

'No, no,' said Miss Knibbs, blushing vividly. 'Not so much pornographic as exotic.' She frowned. 'Or do I mean erotic? I always get those two muddled up. Anyway, the book was accidentally issued to Councillor Jones, thus considerably disrupting Mr Snettisham's plans for that evening – several evenings, actually, since Councillor Jones proved extremely reluctant to relinquish the book. In the end we had to send Angharad to knock on his door.'

Adrift in the complexities of librarianship, Grint gave up. 'Never mind all that, tell me about this place.'

'Well, we're a Carnegie library and . . .'

'Can you show me your most easily defended area?'

'Er . . . well . . . I suppose non-fiction and reference.'

'Number of doors?'

'One.'

'Windows?'

'Four,' said Miss Knibbs, beginning to get his drift. 'Each one some twenty feet off the ground. No access to them from the outside unless your adversary can climb vertical walls. And before you ask, the roof is covered in sticky anti-vandal paint and equipped with strategically placed pigeon-prickers.'

With some reluctance, Hansen emerged from the safety of *Guinea Pigs for Fun and Profit*. 'Pigeon-prickers?'

'Those spikey things. To stop seagulls and pigeons nesting on the roof. Like police stingers but for birds.'

'Well, that all sounds . . .' said Grint but Miss Knibbs hadn't finished.

'This floor is of solid concrete,' she continued, stamping her foot to demonstrate its solid concreteness. 'I shouldn't think anything could burrow its way up through that. There are vending machines along the back wall to provide food and drink in the event of a siege, the telephone switchboard room is there – a little old-fashioned, but we may be glad of it if the siege is a prolonged one. And best of all, we have an excellent medieval history section which will, no doubt, provide us with much useful information on how to repel any attack. Now, I feel strongly that we should build ourselves a barricade. Where would you like it?'

Two TPOs grappled with a new comprehension of the skill set pertaining to really good librarians.

Grint pointed to the front doors. 'Over there somewhere – Hansen, check out a suitable location.'

Hansen regretfully returned *Guinea Pigs for Fun and Profit* to the shelves and smiled reassuringly at Miss Knibbs. 'Shall we get started?'

29

It was obvious that somehow word had already spread because the streets seemed strangely deserted for the time of day. On their way to the library, Luke and Jane were joined by a small number of mystified but curious citizens. Most were pensioners who seemed to be regarding this as some new form of council-provided entertainment and would there be biscuits?

They'd also managed to scoop up two or three youngish children who were almost certainly going to regret bunking off school before the day was out. Jane was festooned with a great deal of other people's shopping and Luke was carrying a small dog. Emerging into the town square from Milk Street, he was about to fulfil the unfamiliar function of Lollipop Lady and shepherd his charges safely across the road when a police car swept past with Rossi on the loudspeaker.

His voice bounced around the square. 'People of Cluvrageth. Attention, people of Cluvrageth,' bringing massive confusion to the townspeople, none of whom had any idea why they would be addressed as 'People of Library', and was this yet another attempt at subjugation by the perfidious English?

Fortunately, most of their consternation manifested itself as aimless confusion, which made it easy for Luke and Jane to chivvy them librarywards. A trickle of people were already climbing the steps.

The car swept around the square again – in the opposite direction this time. Jane had the definite impression Rossi was enjoying himself.

'People of Cluvrageth – clear the streets. Clear the streets. Return to your homes and lock all your doors and windows. If you cannot return home, then make your way quickly and quietly to the library. In the town square,' he added helpfully for those who might not be familiar with the layout of their own town. His voice dopplered back along Milk Street. 'People of Cluvrageth . . .'

Luke and Jane entered the cluvrageth, to find Grint surveying his resources.

A group of very non-Time Police officers stood before him in a ragged line. Or clump, possibly.

'And this,' said Miss Knibbs proudly, 'is my little team. Our senior library assistant – Lily – together with Tillie, Dillie and . . .'

'Millie,' said Grint, beginning to get the hang of this.

Miss Knibbs frowned. 'No – Cerys.'

Back behind the shelving, Hansen appeared to have developed a very nasty cough.

As Grint said afterwards – when he'd got his breath back – it was around about this point that he began to feel the day might be getting away from him somewhat. Nevertheless he frowned in his best Time Police manner and surveyed this unfortunately all too feminine workforce.

'And this is Jason and Ianto – who are both here this week on work experience.'

Jason and Ianto appeared to be undergoing growth spurts, sadly without the corresponding filling-out. Grint had an overwhelming impression of two long-haired pencils.

Wisely abandoning his first impulse – which had been to bark instructions directly to his newly acquired forces – he turned to Miss Knibbs, who was still beaming proudly at him.

He pointed. 'Right then – the first barricade is being erected outside the front doors – top of the steps between those two pillars. Anyone getting through those will then have to dogleg pretty sharply to get into that bit there.'

'The public workroom and non-fiction,' translated Miss Knibbs.

'Our fallback position will be . . .' He pointed.

'Reference.'

'Should we need to make a quick exit, we'll go through . . . fiction . . . ?' Miss Knibbs nodded encouragingly. 'To the garage at the back of the building and regroup there. Do these shelves move?'

'They do indeed,' cried Miss Knibbs. 'They're all on wheels. Obviously health and safety regulations mandate all the books should be removed first . . .'

Grint surveyed the Hampton Court maze of shelving around him, eyed Miss Knibbs shrewdly and asked, 'And are they? Removed, I mean?'

'Of course not,' said Miss Knibbs. 'That would take hours.'

'Right. These shelves will form the core of our first barricade. Lockland, reinforce each shelf with as many books as you can pack in, boxes of papers, records, anything you can find. I want a solid barrier. No gaps. If the reptiles can't see us, then they might go elsewhere. Brace with desks and furniture. Do these photocopiers move?' He indicated the two massive machines set aside for public use.

'They're also on wheels – yes.'

'Good. Parrish – get these big boys shifted. They'll be our second line of defence.'

'On it,' said Luke, still apparently unaware of the correct response to an order from a senior officer.

'Fire extinguishers?' suggested Jane.

Grint frowned. 'I don't think dinosaurs breathe fire. Do they?'

'I meant,' said Jane, blushing, 'extinguishers squirt foam – which they won't like at all. And they're heavy. If we can manage to drop one on their heads, then they probably won't be getting up again. I remember when I was in training, you yourself told us that anything can be used as a weapon.'

'Good thinking. Miss Knibbs, can you send someone to go through the building, bring all extinguishers back here and line them up over there against that wall.'

'Of course. Cerys . . .' She gestured and Cerys set off at an enthusiastic gallop.

'No running in the library, Cerys. I've told you before.'

'Sorry, Miss Knibbs.'

Cerys continued at a pace only fractionally slower than an enthusiastic gallop.

Grint continued. 'And Lockland, keep trying to get hold of Tucker. I want to know what's going on up at that castle.'

Jane departed.

Grint turned back to his right-hand librarian. 'While I think of it – do you have a workplace first aider?'

Miss Knibbs beckoned. 'Tillie, could you pop over here for a moment, please, dear.'

'Gather all first-aid kits,' said Grint, 'and store them next to the fire extinguishers. You other two . . .'

'Dillie and Lily.'

'Dillie and Lily – you're our official lookouts. One at the front windows and one in the conference room. Do you have any means of . . . ?'

Both girls proudly flourished the very latest models of mobile communication.

Grint nodded. 'Go.'

They went.

Over by the front doors, Luke, Jason and Ianto were manhandling the big photocopiers into a position some ten feet behind the front doors. They would thus have three lines of defence: the outside barricade between the pillars, the hefty wooden front doors themselves, and ten feet back from them, the two photocopiers from behind which they could fire on anything without a current library card.

Luke took a moment to ease his back. 'I didn't know these old things still existed.'

'Be grateful for a parsimonious council who never replace anything under a hundred years old unless it relates directly to their prestige or comfort,' said Miss Knibbs tartly and darted away.

'That's me told,' muttered Luke.

Cerys, who had completed gathering fire extinguishers, was now emptying the vending machines. Piles of crisps, chocolate and biscuits were stacked neatly against the wall, along with two apples and a wary-looking banana.

'Open up the café,' ordered Miss Knibbs, striding through non-fiction rather in the manner of those bringing the good news from Aix to Ghent. 'Bring everything you can find. Especially the kettles and the coffee.'

It was very apparent that Miss Knibbs was enthusiastically envisaging a siege comparable in length to that of the Trojan War. Regarding Lt Grint through her spectacles, she made an announcement.

'I shall call in the Fleet,' she declared.

In the middle of single-handedly heaving a massive run of shelving into position, Grint paused. How close to the sea were they, for heaven's sake? 'I'm sorry?'

'Our mobile libraries – the pride of the service.'

'Mobile libraries?' queried Grint, possibly envisaging a pair of little vans tootling happily along the country lanes with a box of paperbacks on board.

'The Fleet,' declared Miss Knibbs again. 'We have six mobiles altogether. Nell Gwyn and Bookie McBookface are small Lutons that can cope with the narrow lanes and steep hills. They can bring people in from remote farms and drop them off at the nearest schools and fire stations. The other three – Henry Tudor, Shirley Bassey and Owain Glyndŵr – trundle from village to farm and back to village.'

'What sort of size are they?' said Grint doubtfully.

Miss Knibbs assumed the expression of Boudicca looking down on helpless Colchester. 'Seven-and-a-half tonners.'

Grint was struck with an idea. 'Will they fit down the alleyway at the side of the building?'

'It would be a tight squeeze.'

'All the better. Call them in. We'll get them to park nose to tail in the alleyway. That'll go a long way towards protecting those big glass windows.'

'And then,' continued Miss Knibbs, with the air of one working her way up to her big moment. 'Then there's . . . *the Red Dragon.*'

About to heave, Grint paused again. 'The what?'

'The Red Dragon. The supermobile.'

'And where does the supermobile go?'

She really had a very sweet smile. 'Wherever it likes, *dyn infanc.*'

Grint grinned greatly. 'Call them in.'

Whatever happened to Shirley Bassey or Owain Glyndŵr, the Time Police never discovered, but only Henry Tudor made it back to base. The stricken vehicle limped across the town square, its buckled front festooned with enough roadkill to keep a BBC nature programme in full-time work for years, with a Grand Canyon-sized crack across its windscreen, its exhaust hanging off and striking sparks on the cobbles, and deep gouge marks scored along the driver's side where something unpleasant had attempted – and presumably failed – to gain access.

Miss Knibbs was gabbling into her phone, and a moment later, a fanfare on the airhorn indicative of a *familia* of top gladiators entering the Coliseum rattled the windows and scattered nearby pigeons. The Henry Tudor had arrived.

'Hugh's made it back,' shouted Dillie from the front windows.

'He'll never get that down there,' said Jane anxiously, referring to the mobile and the narrow alleyway.

'You just wait and see,' said Miss Knibbs with entirely justified confidence.

Nonchalantly, one hand on the wheel, cigarette dangling from the corner of his mouth, the driver reversed his seven-and-a-half-ton vehicle neatly into an alleyway half an inch too small to accommodate it without severe damage to its paintwork.

'Oh dear,' said Miss Knibbs, distressed. 'Smoking in council vehicles is forbidden and he knows it. Now I shall have to report him.'

'It looks as if he's had quite a bad day,' said Jane tactfully. 'Perhaps it might be better not to have noticed.'

Miss Knibbs sighed, picked up her phone and instructed Hugh to wait there in readiness for a possible emergency evacuation. And Jason would bring him out a cup of coffee and one of Cerys's Welsh cakes.

Luke had stationed himself on the other side of the barrier, on the lookout for anyone still on the streets. There was no one. By now, the town square had a very deserted look about it. All the shops had been locked up. Many had their shutters pulled down. In the distance, he could hear Rossi's voice drawing closer again.

He looked up at the sky. The sun had disappeared and more dark clouds were gathering. He sighed. A dark dot circled overhead. And then another. He sighed again.

Siren wailing, a police car took the corner on two wheels and screeched to a halt in front of the library. Rossi and Kohl scrambled out and waved cheerfully at the two police officers who waved cheerfully back again and roared away. Luke had the impression a great time had been had by all.

Rossi climbed the steps and paused to look back. 'It's very quiet.'

'Too quiet,' said Kohl.

'For heaven's sake,' said Luke. 'Have you two never watched a Western? You'll both have an arrow between your shoulder blades any moment now.'

Rossi stared up at the tangle of shelving, library equipment, books, boxes of photocopying paper, and furniture. 'For how long do you think we can hold this place? Should we have to.'

Luke looked at the enthusiastically assembled but probably almost useless barricade. 'About ten minutes, I should imagine.'

Inside the building, Grint was boosting morale.

'Our situation is not desperate,' he said. 'Taking shelter here is only a precaution in case any of the released animals . . .'

'Dinosaurs,' said Miss Knibbs, confirming Grint's theory that reassuring civilians was a complete waste of time.

'In case any dinosaurs find their way into town. Be assured – help will come. I've had a call from TPHQ. Reinforcements are on their way. Our job is simply to protect you until the Time Police can order a safe evacuation.'

'How long before they arrive?' enquired Ianto.

'It's likely the chopper will arrive first, even though it's had to stop off at Swansea.'

'What's in Swansea?'

'Wholesale meat market.'

His audience blinked.

'Bait,' said Grint.

'Oh,' said Miss Knibbs loyally. 'Yes. Clever.'

'And at least two pods and four teams will reinforce us here. Lt Chigozie in charge.'

'The castle, sir?' said Rossi.

'An unknown number of pods will go straight there.'

'Do we still have officers on site there?' asked Luke.

'Varma and Maxwell have returned to TPHQ but Tucker's still up there somewhere. On his own. I'm certain Trainee Tucker is old enough and ugly enough to look after himself. We have only to hold on, people. Relief is on the way. *Our main objective is to keep everyone safe until they arrive.* We've barred all entrances but one. The conference room windows are no longer accessible thanks to the Henry Tudor. The front door is barricaded. We have food and drink, so I suggest all civilians make themselves comfortable and wait it out in here while my team monitors the situation.'

There was some nodding but also some grumbling. Grint was unsurprised to find the general public were about as grateful for Time Police efforts as they usually were. The Time Police's frequently expressed opinion that the general public were an ungrateful bunch of churls who should never be permitted to leave their homes under any circumstances remained unchallenged.

'Lockland, anything from Tucker?'

Jane shook her head.

'Keep trying. Parrish – you're up on the barricade, keeping watch. At the first sign of trouble, Hansen will get the front doors shut and bolted.'

'With me on the right side of them, I hope,' said Luke.

'Of course,' said Hansen smoothly. 'Abandoning you to a well-deserved and agonising death rarely crosses our minds.'

Grint continued. 'Rossi, take Jason and Ianto to watch the back. Show them where to take up positions. You lads – you're lookouts only. Don't try anything daft. Miss Knibbs, I'd like you at your desk at all times, in case of emergency. Tillie, you're in charge of first aid. Lily – you're in charge of keeping the civilians calm. Dillie – you stay at the front windows telling us what's happening out there, and Cerys, you're our runner. We'll use you to carry messages from the front of the building to the back. Right – does everyone know where they should be and what they're doing?'

There was a half-hearted *yes*. On the other hand, no one said no, which was good enough for Grint.

'To your stations, people. And good luck.'

They scattered.

Luke found himself standing on a desk behind the suddenly very flimsy-looking barricade. Kohl and Hansen were behind him, just inside the front doors.

'You two make sure you stay safe back there,' he called. 'Don't want you risking yourselves out here with the real TPOs.'

'Seriously?' said Hansen. 'You're pissing off the people who are forever picking you up out of the snow or dragging your arse out of freezing-cold ice baths? Face it, Parrish, you've never yet completed a mission without having to be rescued at some point or other.'

'That's because I'm always the one at the sharp end while Team Two-Three-Five skulks quietly at the back.'

Hansen's response would never be known. He stiffened, brought up his gun and said quietly, 'Movement. Right-hand corner.'

Luke squinted into the failing light.

Hansen was right. Across the square, something was moving.

'Shit. Heads up, everyone. They're coming.'

Luke brought up his gun to cover the deserted town square and chinned his mic. 'Unidentified movement.'

Jane slipped past Kohl and Hansen to climb on to the desk alongside him.

'Far right-hand corner,' said Luke softly. 'Just in front of the bus shelter. They're hard to see but they're there.'

They were there. Two – no, three – no, four – dinosaurs had entered the square from Milk Street. From the north-east, Luke realised. Probably the direction from which most of them would arrive. Although how many would actually make it as far as the town, he had no idea.

The shapes were very hard to make out in the gathering gloom and it wasn't yet dark enough for their night visors to be fully effective.

'About five feet tall,' reported Luke, squinting. 'Upright. Big heads. Staying together.'

'Velociraptors,' said Hansen in his ear. 'Or possibly Deinonychus.'

'How do you know that? You can't even see them from there.'

'Miss Knibbs is looking them up in the *Big Girls' Book of Dinosaurs*.'

Luke stared across the square. This time he actually had the opportunity to observe them properly. Dinosaurs. Actual living dinosaurs. These were much larger than the pair he and Jane had encountered in the park. Their colour was a mid-greyish-green and the darker stripes running across their backs and legs made them very hard to spot until they moved. Especially in this failing light. They were standing upright and tilting their heads from side to side, surveying the square in a worryingly intelligent manner. Their movements were quick and nervous – almost birdlike.

Jane had opened her com. 'Sir, they're here.'

'Shit,' said Grint.

'Yeah,' said Luke.

'Parrish – this will be your decision. I want eyes on for as long as possible, but don't risk yourself or Lockland. First sign of the barricade failing – both of you back inside.'

'Don't worry,' said Luke. 'First sign of trouble and I'll be locking myself in the Gents. This is one mission I intend to get through uninjured.'

Grint grunted. Or made some kind of noise, anyway, and closed down his com.

Luke turned to Jane. 'Go back inside, Jane.'

'Drop dead, Parrish.'

The traditional 236 team dynamic having been established, they waited. Jane looked up. They were standing in a substantial porch and should be safe from aerial attack.

She spoke quietly. 'Whatever specific type of dinosaur these are, they're definitely raptors and they'll hunt as a pack. These guys can bring down a triceratops. If we can see four of them, then there'll be at least another half-dozen that we can't.'

Luke scanned the square again. Was that yet another one? Outside the newsagents?

'What's the social structure, Jane? If we shoot the leader, would they all go home for an early bath?'

'They're pack animals. There should be an alpha and a beta. Traditionally a male and female.'

'What happens if we take out one or both?'

'I don't know. And which one is the alpha? They all look more or less the same, don't you think? Some might be a little bigger or a little smaller, but unfortunately for us, they don't appear to wear badges of rank.' She craned her neck. 'What are they doing?'

Luke frowned. 'They seem uncertain. There's a lot of air-sniffing. Which is fine as long as they do it over there. None of them seem willing to make the first move.'

'They'll be confused, I expect. They don't know how to react to this strange new world. Strange noises, strange smells, strange sights. Wait until they work out this one is full of soft, fleshy human beings who can't run very fast.'

'Soft, fleshy human beings who will fight back,' said Luke. He eyed the two small cannons parked either side of the Town Hall steps. Decorative, surely. They couldn't possibly still work. They would have been spiked centuries ago. Wouldn't they?

He roused himself from trying to remember the dates of the Civil War. Sixteen hundred and something was the best he could do. Matthew might know. He'd probably been there. That was a point. Where was Matthew right now? What was he doing? Happily playing with the Time Map, probably. Well, whatever floated his particular boat. And he was certainly well out of this bout of prehistoric madness.

Luke shook himself back into the present. The now six dinosaurs had moved to the florist and were sniffing around the doorway. Faces appeared at lighted upstairs windows, looking down on them. Luke considered making *get back* gestures but suspected he and Jane were almost invisible in the gathering gloom and it would be very unwise to draw attention to themselves. Besides, something was moving slowly down Milk Street. Something big.

Jane opened her com. 'Sir, we have raptors in the square and something else approaching. No details. It's getting very dark out here.'

Inside, one by one, the lights went out. There was silence in the library. Utter silence. No sounds of movement. Luke allowed himself to hope the dinosaurs would all lose interest and move away. They'd think the place was deserted. With luck they'd head for the park again. Water, ducks and cover for the night. A stealth team might even be able to lock the gates behind them and contain them there.

And indeed, for a moment, it looked as if his wish might be granted. The raptors clustered together outside the off-licence, rather in the manner of bored teenagers. One of them – there was no telling which one – made the low chuntering sound they'd heard in the park, and then the creatures began to move away, sniffing at the air as they went. Luke heard Jane exhale and realised he'd been holding his own breath as well.

And then, from inside the library, and very, very audible in the cool evening air, the little dog yapped.

Six dinosaur heads whipped around. Moving as one. Looking straight at them. One of them – Luke couldn't see which – uttered the same single sharp bark he and Jane had heard before. Again, as one, they began to advance across the town square.

Luke shifted his weight. 'Be ready to move back, Jane.'

'Don't worry,' whispered Jane. 'I'll be leaving you standing.'

Hansen spoke from behind them. 'Ready on the doors whenever you give the word.'

'Leaving it to the last moment. If we move now, they'll definitely see us.'

'Copy that.'

Jane glanced over her shoulder, plotting her escape route. The imposing wooden doors were about ten feet away. Just three long strides. The right-hand door was already secured. The nearer door was open. She couldn't see them, but Hansen and Rossi would be there somewhere, all ready to cover their retreat and get the door shut.

'You first, Jane. Start moving backwards. Slowly.'

'But . . .'

'Increases our chances of at least one of us getting back inside safely. I'll cover you, then you can cover me.'

The little dog yapped again – the sound abruptly cut off as though someone had muffled it in a coat or blanket.

Too late.

One of the raptors – the one slightly at the front of the pack – made the by now familiar chuntering sound. Several of them peeled away, moving left and right to encircle the steps. Classic predator attack formation. Slowly and with deliberation, they began to advance.

Grint and Hansen appeared alongside them at the barricade.

'Aren't we supposed to be joining you?' whispered Luke. 'Not the other way around.'

Hansen shrugged. 'Don't see why you should have all the fun.'

Now the raptors were less than twenty feet away. Too close, decided Luke, who had seen how fast and suddenly they could move. Again they tilted their heads in that birdlike movement as they surveyed the scene before them. One or two appeared to be sniffing the air. It would seem they hunted by smell as well as by sight, and the library must smell very interesting indeed. They were still coming. Shadows moved behind them. Were there even more following on? Smaller ones, holding back, perhaps? Or scavengers, waiting for an opportunity to feed after something else had done all the wet work. Grint cursed silently to himself. Exactly how many of these buggers had Tucker unleashed?

'They know we're here,' whispered Jane.

'Don't fire unless they attack,' instructed Grint. 'They might still move on if we stay still and quiet.'

They watched the raptors spread out across the bottom step. Jane tried hard not to believe they were looking for a way in. How could prehistoric dinosaurs have any concept of barricades? Or buildings? Of doors and windows? And fearsome though those claws and jaws might be, they'd be no match for steel and stone, surely.

'This is just another cave to them,' said Bolshy Jane. 'And we're just a different type of prey,' she added cheerfully. 'Their world is very simple.'

Miss Knibbs peered around the front door, whispering, 'Hugh reports there's something on the roof.'

Grint motioned her to stay inside. 'His roof or ours?'

'Both. They used the Henry Tudor to climb up. He says they're very agile. And they work things out. He thinks there's at least three or four of them up there now. And he wants to know how much effing longer are we going to leave him out there?'

'What's he doing?'

'He's turned everything off and is lying on the floor. They can't see him from the outside. He's not happy, though.'

'What about the paint and the stingers?'

Miss Knibbs shook her head. 'No effect that he could see.'

'Can they gain access into the building from up there?'

There was the very slightest of pauses. 'There's a fire door.'

Grint opened his mouth.

'Wood and safety glass,' she said, before he could ask the question. 'But surely they won't be able to . . .' She stopped. 'And then a flight of stairs leading directly past the register office.'

'And from there straight down to here,' said Grint.

She nodded.

'Hansen – you and Kohl go and watch the stairs. If anything up there moves – shoot it.'

Hansen slipped back into the library.

'Wait,' said Jane, who hadn't taken her eyes off the raptors. 'Something's happening.'

The library was no longer the raptors' focus. As one, they turned to look back to the north-east corner of the square.

'Oh my God,' said Luke. 'What is that?'

His words were drained by a bellow of pain and rage that rattled the front windows.

Grint squinted. 'What the hell . . . ?'

It was at that moment that fate decreed the street lights should come on. With a few well-chosen words, Grint consigned the municipal authorities to a deep, dark place where they couldn't do any more fire-trucking harm. The town square had gone from gloom to glowing. Elegant lamp posts cast a cheerful radiance sufficient to provide an excellent view of the titanic battle currently raging in the square. Because, hard to believe though it was, there was actually something out there having a worse day than they were.

Luke had been right about something big approaching. A huge, knobbly dinosaur, moving as fast as it could lumber on four tree-trunk legs, was being hotly pursued by three or four raptors, all snapping at its head. That their attack was concentrated on the front end would be because of the giant spiked club at the end of the monster's lashing tail. This was a powerful creature – to be caught by what looked like the dinosaur equivalent of a wrecking ball would certainly be fatal. A number of vicious-looking horns protruded from its head and thick, knobbly armour covered its entire body, culminating in that lethal spiked tail. The most vulnerable area was its throat and forelegs. Hence all the action at the front end.

As one, the library raptors moved to join the attack.

'It's an ankylosaurus,' reported Miss Knibbs, fount of all knowledge and major fan of the *Jurassic* franchise. 'Armour-plated. Herbivore. Slow-moving.'

'It's doing a great job of distracting them,' said Luke. 'This could work to our advantage.'

The ankylosaurus, in addition to distracting the raptors from their original targets inside the library, was managing to inflict a fair amount of damage to its surroundings. The huge tail, slicing through the air like something from *The Pit and the Pendulum*, thudded into a smaller, possibly young and inexperienced raptor, which sailed through the air to collide heavily with a lamp post some ten feet away. Possibly in protest at this treatment, the light went out. The raptor slid to the ground and did not get up.

'One down,' said Luke in satisfaction.

The fight, however, was far from over.

More raptors appeared from between the shops, all chuntering to each other and circling the beleaguered ankylosaurus. There were now a good eight or nine of them – all roughly the same shape but different sizes – and all with their eyes on their prey. Head down to protect its throat, and presenting as much horn and armour as it could manage, it was, for the moment, holding its own. And nothing at all was approaching that enormous, deadly tail.

'It's their equivalent of a building-smasher,' said Luke, much more accurately than he could have wished.

Whether by accident or design, the raptors were edging their prey towards the library. To corner it, perhaps. To push it against the wall, which would contain the threat of that great tail, its primary defence. Neutralise that and this slow-moving dinosaur was suddenly vulnerable. The same thought occurred to everyone – raptors were not stupid.

'Clever,' said Luke to Jane, who nodded. Clever indeed. They should be careful not to underestimate these creatures. Dinosaurs ruled the earth for over a hundred and sixty-five million years – considerably longer than humans had managed to achieve – or probably would ever achieve, given the current political climate. In fact, were it not for a giant rock randomly dropping out of the sky sixty-five million years ago, the dinosaurs might be ruling still.

The ankylosaurus was edging closer to the library.

'Hold your fire,' said Grint, who had persuaded a reluctant Miss Knibbs to return to her post. 'Conserve your charge. We're here to defend – not attack.'

'They're worryingly well organised,' whispered Luke.

Jane nodded. They were. Over the alternately roaring and mooing ankylosaurus, she could clearly hear sharp, barked commands. Sheepdogs, she thought. Working together as a team. Had she been slightly less involved in the conflict, she might have found this fascinating. She could certainly understand the curiosity that drove St Mary's continually to involve themselves in the sort of situations most normal people would avoid like the plague.

A series of yaps, and three or four raptors simultaneously launched themselves at the ankylosaurus, which swung its head at the nearest attacker, catching it a glancing blow with one of its forehead horns. There was a shriek of pain, abruptly cut off, but the move had left its throat vulnerable. Two more moved in from the opposite side. The ankylosaurus lumbered backwards and somewhere, to their right, there was an impact and the sound of falling masonry as its hefty backside impacted the external library wall. The whole building shook. Dust and lumps of plaster fell from the porch. Inside the library, something somewhere fell over with a massive clatter.

'Shit,' roared Grint. 'What the hell was that?'

Luke brushed himself down and squinted. 'The big one . . .'

'The ankylosaurus,' reminded Jane.

'Just walloped the end pillar with its backside.'

'Is it all right?'

'Completely unharmed as far as I can see.'

'I meant the pillar.'

'Oh no – that's not well at all.'

Grint turned to Miss Knibbs, who was back in the doorway. 'Is that pillar holding up anything vital?'

'Well, yes, I expect so. The roof, probably. And the front of the building.'

'Shit,' muttered Grint again. 'Tell everyone to keep well away from the windows.'

Which turned out to be extremely good advice as the tail – scything through the air on its backswing – hit one of the tall front windows, which exploded in a shower of glass, wood and stone.

The raptors had manoeuvred their prey into a position where its tail could only damage the building. Good for them. Less good for the library, and completely catastrophic for those inside, of course. Most of the former window was now a large hole. Only a tiny portion of window frame remained and the hole was easily big enough for something to get through.

Another tail swipe took out the rest of the window and a good part of the wall as well. The only good thing about this situation was that the raptors were still concentrating on their legitimate prey. For the moment.

Grint cursed. Two weak spots now. 'Parrish – Lockland – remain on the barricade but be prepared to pull back. Rossi – to the window. It's a pinch point – shoot anything trying to get through.'

Barely had he given the order than Kohl came racing down the stairs. 'They're breaking through the fire door upstairs, sir. Three or four of them at least. Probably more. Hansen's holding them back.'

There was a crash from somewhere above them. And then

another. And then shattering glass. And then a shout from Hansen and the sound of blaster fire.

Grint ripped out his com, roaring, 'We're on the way. Rossi – you're in charge here – keep these bastards out at all costs. Miss Knibbs – assemble everyone and be prepared to move out at a moment's notice.'

With Kohl at his heels, he raced up the stairs, meeting Hansen on the first-floor landing. He was crouched at the foot of the stairs, firing upwards.

'They haven't yet worked out the stairs, sir. The first one fell and I think he's injured himself. He can't get up, anyway. He's blocking the way. There's a fight broken out.'

He shifted his position and fired. A raptor scream rent the air, which was suddenly full of the smell of burning flesh.

'We can hold them off for a while, but sooner or later . . .'

Grint came to a decision. 'You two – hold them off as long as you can. I'm evacuating the civilians, so buy me as much time as possible and then get back downstairs. No heroics.'

'Sir . . .'

'We have no choice.' Grint opened his com. 'Attention, everyone. The library has been breached. We're evacuating the civilians. Now.'

Somehow, everyone remained calm. Grint, who had expected to be chasing hysterical citizens – and their dog – all around the building, was both surprised and impressed at the speed and efficiency with which Miss Knibbs briefed her readers. (Everyone in a library is a reader. Some of them may not know it yet, but sooner or later . . .)

'Leave your belongings here, please. Yes, Mrs Crawford, you may bring your dog. And your husband. Please remain where you are until Lt Grint gives the word and then make your way quickly and quietly to the rear of the building.'

Rossi appeared. 'Sir, the rear entrance is still clear but we need to move fast.'

Grint had positioned himself by the open front doors where he could see both inside and out. He nodded agreement. 'Miss Knibbs – tell the Henry Tudor to meet you at the back door and then do a headcount. We don't want to leave anyone behind.'

Miss Knibbs bristled. 'Yes to the civilians, Lieutenant, but I intend to stay and fight. To the very end.'

In his heart, Grint was in complete agreement. It was always better to go down fighting than lay down and die. But these were civilians.

He shook his head. 'I need you to lead the evacuation.'

'What about all of you?'

'We'll cover your retreat.'

She smacked his arm. 'Not a retreat, Lieutenant – only a temporary withdrawal.'

He took her hand for a moment. 'Miss Knibbs, it has been an honour to stand alongside you.'

From her place on the barricade, Jane smiled to herself.

Grint gave Miss Knibbs back her hand. 'Now go. Officer Rossi will make sure you get away safely.'

Miss Knibbs supervised an orderly retreat. Jane, whose dreary and overworked youth had been spent surreptitiously reading romantic tales from olden times whenever she could snatch a moment, could almost see the mantle of Branwen, daughter of Llŷr, settling around her shoulders.

Her tone brooked no argument from anyone. 'Cerys – tell Hugh to meet us around the back. On your feet, everyone. We're evacuating the building. There will be no running and no pushing. Help each other.'

'We need a distraction,' said Luke. 'Before those buggers out the front work out what's happening.'

'There's a butcher's shop across the square,' said Grint. 'I'll sneak over and break the window. They'll smell the meat and forget about us.'

Luke sighed for such innocence. 'Have you ever tried to break a shop window?'

'No – have you?'

Luke grinned. 'Have you never been in the West End on Boat Race Night?'

Grint's expression was not encouraging. Luke judged it best to elaborate.

'Well – other than toughened glass, the main problem is the security film. Stops the window shattering. You can pound away at it until kingdom come. You could probably even shoot it, but you'll only draw attention to yourself and then they'll eat you instead of the

> *'Deal of the Week!*
> *Buy Five Pounds of Mince and Get*
> *Another Five Pounds Free!*
> *Stock Up Your Freezer Today!'*

Everyone stared at him. 'What?'

'Deal of the week,' he said defensively. 'Didn't anyone else notice the sign?'

'What the hell would you do with ten pounds of mince?' demanded Rossi. Probably on behalf of everyone.

Grint checked his charge and prepared to move out.

Rossi went to stand in his way. 'Sir, I really think . . .'

'I can hear singing,' said Jane, who hadn't once taken her eyes off what was happening outside.

'So can I,' said Luke, still up on the barricade. 'That's disturbing. Do you think our time is up? Are we being called to a higher place?'

'Lockland – yes,' said Rossi. 'You? Probably not.'

'Lockland's not wrong,' said Grint. 'I can hear it too.'

They could all hear it. Singing. Faint, but definitely there.

Luke groaned. 'For fire truck's sake – what now?'

Grint moved back into the library and strode to an undamaged window and squinted out into the square, just in time to see a giant vehicle, liveried in the national colours of green and white, and with a huge and aggressively rampant red dragon painted on each long side, draw up outside the butchers. And the off-licence. And the newsagents. Its colossal size was possibly being perceived as a challenge by those dinosaurs prowling around the outskirts of the square, currently investigating doorways and upending waste bins.

'It's the Red Dragon,' cried Miss Knibbs, appearing yet again.

'What the hell is all that noise?' demanded Grint, less than tactfully.

Miss Knibbs drew herself up. 'That, Lieutenant, is the Welsh national anthem – "Hen Wlad Fy Nhadu". And not just any old version, either. This is the famous recording hammered out by Welsh supporters on the occasion of England's defeat by the home team during the final of the Rugby World Cup at the newly refurbished Cardiff Arms Park last year.' She gathered herself to declaim, 'This is *the* national anthem.'

That the Red Dragon had not had a good day was very apparent. It was in a terrible state. The wipers had gone. Stumps denoted former aerials. The paintwork had seen better days. Particularly the red dragon on the passenger side which appeared to have been attacked by a giant chainsaw.

'Worse than the monkeys at a safari park,' said Luke chattily, earning himself an irritated look from Grint.

Miss Knibbs was talking into her phone. 'Angharad, we are under attack and we have readers to evacuate. Can you draw these raptors away?'

The response was audible all around the library. '*Wrth gwrs y gallaf.*'

Miss Knibbs looked across to Grint. 'She says *yes*.'

The engine roared. Heavy smoke poured from the exhaust and drifted across the square.

'She really shouldn't do that,' said Miss Knibbs, sighing. 'We're a ULEZ here, you know.'

Grint blinked. 'Who shouldn't do that?'

'The driver. Angharad. Such a naughty girl. And she parks the mobile in the spot reserved for Councillor Roberts. And Councillor Evans. And Councillor Mohr.'

Grint nodded. 'It is a big vehicle.'

Miss Knibbs, however, was on a roll. 'And she pretends she can't speak English. And the hydraulic step on her vehicle jammed in the *out* position once, and instead of waiting for the depot to come out to fix it, she drove up and down pretending she was Boudicca. People were leaping into shop doorways or throwing themselves into the road to get out of the way. There were complaints.'

Grint found himself warming to the Welsh way of life.

At that exact moment there was a terrible impact from upstairs and something heavy crashed to the floor. Once again the building shook on its foundations.

Hansen's voice was heard. 'Heads up. They've broken through.'

Grint turned to Miss Knibbs. 'No more arguing. Go.'

Miss Knibbs gathered her flock together. No one ran. There was no panic. Standing by the door, she checked out her charges one by one. No one was left behind. Not even the dog. Rossi led the way to the garage at the back of the building, where Jason, Ianto and the Henry Tudor awaited them. They boarded one by one, with Rossi standing guard.

There is an old joke – how many elephants can you get in a mini? To the question *how many people can you get into a mobile library?* the answer is – all of them. To say nothing of the dog. Although two paperback spinners, two elephant's foots, the children's ironically named dinosaur reading bench and a box of soft toys didn't make the cut.

'Good luck, everyone,' called Rossi. 'Don't stop for anything, Hugh.'

Hugh nodded, surreptitiously flicking his dog-end out of the window.

Miss Knibbs, settling herself in the passenger seat beside him, sniffed the air suspiciously and then the step was raised and the door hissed shut. Rossi slapped the side twice, and the Henry Tudor pulled away. Taking its passengers to safety, Rossi hoped. He re-entered the library, slammed and locked the back door and ran to rejoin his leader.

Inside, Hansen and Kohl were crouched at the bottom of the stairs looking upwards.

'We've lost control of the first floor, sir,' reported Hansen. 'The best we can do now is pick them off as they come down the stairs.'

Grint nodded. 'Shout if you need back-up.' He turned away. 'What's happening out the front? What's that big book-bus thing doing?'

The Red Dragon still crouched at the far end of the square. Nothing stood in its way, but there it remained, motionless. The driver, barely visible behind the crazed windscreen, gunned the engine. Massive clouds of illegal smoke billowed illegally from the rear end. The driver illegally gunned the engine again.

'I think she's pawing the ground,' said Luke. 'Throwing out a challenge.'

'Clever,' said Grint. 'She's making them come to her.'

Three or four of the larger raptors broke off from menacing the ankylosaurus – who was still hanging in there – and began to move slowly towards this new threat. Head low, one approached from the front, its tail extended horizontally behind it. The others split up to the left and right. Classic raptor behaviour. At the same time, there was a volley of blaster fire from Kohl and Hansen and something fell down the stairs. Jane could hear the sound of snarling.

Grint raised his voice. 'What's happening back there?'

'They can't all handle the stairs,' shouted Kohl. 'A couple have fallen and we got them. Some still on the landing. They're hanging back at the moment, but I reckon it won't take long for them to work things out. We're trying to encourage them to stay upstairs.'

'All away safely. Back door locked and bolted,' announced Rossi, arriving at a run. 'Should we dismantle the barricade to block the stairs?'

Grint shook his head. 'No. We'd weaken the original barrier without having enough time to complete the new one. Worst of both worlds.'

'What then?'

'Noise,' called Jane.

Grint drew closer to the front doors. 'What?'

'Noise, sir. Set off the fire alarms. The noise will be deafening. It'll probably frighten them to death. There might even be flashing lights. For the hearing-impaired.'

'Good thought, Lockland. Rossi – do the honours – then

join Hansen and Kohl. I'll cover the damaged window. You just hold those stairs.'

He surveyed his forces. Kohl and Hansen on the stairs – Lockland and Parrish still manning the barricade. His eye fell on a small box fixed to the wall just inside the main body of the library. The security alarm.

Pulling open the box, he was confronted by a small keypad. He stabbed buttons at random, which, fortunately, the system chose to interpret as an attempt to disable the system illegally. The small screen went blank – there was a breathless pause of four seconds – and then a banshee began to wail. The eldritch voice skidded up and down the scale, setting everyone's teeth on edge. There was absolutely no possibility of ignoring it. On the outside of the building, a red light began to flash.

The raptors drew back, grouping themselves into a tight, defensive knot.

'They don't like that,' shouted Luke. 'More.'

No sooner had he spoken than Rossi implemented the *In the event of an emergency break glass here* action with his elbow. This alarm was instantaneous. A bell. About a hundred decibels beyond the endurance of the human ear. And, with luck, the ear of your average raptor. Better still, the library, complying with all health and safety regs, had installed flashing lights for those unable to hear the unspeakable racket. The dead, presumably. The square was suddenly full of very, very agitated dinosaurs. Not just raptors. The ankylosaurus – not having the best day to begin with – was deeply unhappy. Roaring a blast of foetid air, it swung its tail again. More library disintegrated. Blood was running down its chest and forelegs but it still fought on.

As did the Red Dragon. The national anthem was approaching its climax.

Gwlad, Gwlad, pleidiol wyf i'm gwlad
Tra môr yn fur i'r bur hoff bau
And then the big finish . . .
O bydded i'r heniaith barhau

Between that and the shrieking alarms making speech nearly impossible, the town square was positively vibrating with sound.

There was more.

With its loudspeaker booming the traditional war cry of the Welsh – '*Dial Achos Gwenllian*' – the Red Dragon finally began to move, slowly at first, to give even the dimmest of the dim enough time to work out what was happening, and then speeding up just enough to enable them to give chase.

The lead raptor leaped at the vehicle but could find no grip on the front. After a few seconds of frantic clawing, it slid down and under the vehicle. Another of the pack bounced off the side, but the third managed to get a grip on the side door and hang on.

The remainder of the pack closed in.

Still wreathed in smoke and sound, the Red Dragon roared from the square, trailing miscellaneous raptors. Peering over the more or less intact barricade, Jane and Luke watched it go.

Most of those dinosaurs remaining behind seemed to be herbivores of various makes and sizes, and either too deaf, too stupid, too confused, or too uninterested in anything that didn't have leaves, to follow on. For the moment, peace reigned – if it was possible to ignore the fit-inducing strobing lights, the ear-bleeding sirens and bells and the bleeding ankylosaurus still outside the library. The blood would attract more predators, but on the other hand, his backside was successfully plugging the large hole.

Jane dragged her sleeve over her face and looked around. 'Is that it? Is it all over?'

Luke peered across the square. 'Well, there's a cow-like creature feasting off the hanging baskets outside the Town Hall, but yes, I think so. Don't know what's happening upstairs.'

'They won't be able to get down off the roof,' said Jane suddenly. 'The dinosaurs, I mean. The Henry Tudor's gone. The only way they can get down now is via the stairs.'

'We can cope with them,' said Luke, checking his charge. 'I think the worst is over with, don't you?'

Which was the exact moment the pterosaurs turned up.

32

The first Jane knew about it was when half the barricade collapsed on top of them. Luke fell clear but she found herself caught in some sort of massive book slide as everything gave way around her. Struggling to extricate herself, she glanced up and went very still. A monstrous bird – no, not a bird, no feathers – something out of a nightmare – was perched atop the slowly disintegrating barricade.

Her overwhelming thought was – *Nazgul*. Her second was that she was a sitting target. Fortunately, the monster appeared to be unsure of its next move. As was Jane. Should she struggle to free herself? Or would she be better off remaining motionless, half buried in library paraphernalia, and just hope to escape its notice? After all, there was only one of the monsters.

No, there wasn't. The pterosaur had brought a friend. Another one appeared slowly, scrambling up the by now chaotic tangle of furniture, shelving and books. Parts of the barricade collapsed around it, causing it to lose its balance. It let out an angry screech and scrabbled for purchase. Even more books tumbled painfully down on top of Jane. Peering through a jumble of chair legs, she tried to see what it was doing now.

The pterosaur was looking directly at her. Worst of all,

she was now completely trapped and almost helpless. Fortunately, every time it attempted to move in her direction, it started another landslide, resulting in a temporary stalemate. Jane couldn't move but the monster couldn't get to her. For the time being.

It was evil and it was ugly. Its long, pointed, vicious-looking beak was attached to an equally long thin skull, and the great elongated, backward-facing crest gave the creature a malevolent, menacing look. Large cold eyes surveyed her without emotion. Its silhouette, dark against the street lights, was hunched and sinister. Jane's attempts not to think *Nazgul* failed utterly as another sudden movement caused the top part of the barricade to shift again. The nearest pterosaur opened its beak and uttered an angry cry. Great – it had teeth. Long and needle-sharp. Prey-snatching teeth.

In an effort to keep its balance, it extended huge leathery wings. The stink, as they unfolded, was awful. Like no smell Jane had ever experienced before. And devoutly hoped she never would again. Its wingspan was absolutely colossal. Even allowing for natural exaggeration exacerbated by terror and bad light, the wingspan, tip to tip, must be fifteen feet or more. How did these things ever get into the air?

Jane kept very still and very quiet. Humans and pterosaurs had lived millions of years apart and had, therefore, never met, but surely such tiny mammals as had survived the comet's destruction had preserved some kind of race memory which, eons later, had manifested itself as flying demons, gargoyles, and the like.

Balance regained once more, it folded its wings and resumed its clumsy scramble down the barricade. Towards Jane.

'Sweetie . . .' said Bolshy Jane warningly.

'Yes, I know,' said Jane, trying to grope for her blaster without actually taking her eyes off either of the hunched figures above her.

Giant birds though they might resemble, unnervingly, they walked on four limbs – their wings were, in fact, their hands. The middle joint was a clawed finger of some kind. She really wished she wasn't close enough to have noticed that.

Jane was living a nightmare. The dark, brooding shapes were illuminated by the library's flashing red lights – on – off – on – off – dark – light – dark – light – and she never saw it move. But every time the light flashed back on again, the monster was just that little bit closer, and at this point, Jane wasn't sure she didn't prefer the raptors. Especially since they were now a long way off. Their behaviour had been savage, but these two things – you couldn't call them birds and you couldn't call them reptiles – projected an air of cold, cruel malice far beyond that generated by the raptors.

'Hey. Hey, you. Hey, ugly. Over here.'

A book flew through the air, striking the second pterosaur, the one on the left, on the shoulder. It extended its long head on its long neck and uttered an angry shriek.

There was a faint answer from a long way overhead. Jane had a horrible vision of hundreds and hundreds of these monsters, all circling overhead, just waiting . . .

Luke's voice called her back to the moment. 'Grint – officer down. Officer down. Jane, I'll distract them while you . . .'

'I'm caught. I can't get out. Where is Grint?'

'Fighting raptors on the stairs.'

'Oh God, Luke, I'm trapped.'

'Jane, I can't fire – you're in the way. I can't get a clear shot. Make yourself smaller.'

Jane did her best, but there's only so much a person can do when entangled in the *This Week's Library Recommendations – Handpicked Especially for You* display.

More book missiles flew through the air. A couple of Thomas Hardys – because nothing repels intelligent life faster than Thomas Hardy – followed by some Dostoyevsky, and a handful of Dickens. The most telling blow was delivered by the third volume of an even more than usually apocryphal prime ministerial memoir, in which the self-proclaimed hero appeared to have been living in a completely different universe to everyone else. And for quite some time, too. This hit the pterosaur's bony crest, and judging by the squawk, seemed to have caused it some pain. Perhaps the crest was sensitive in some way.

Enraged, the pterosaur turned away from Jane and began to lumber towards Luke, finally giving him a clear shot. He brought up his blaster, although his own feeling was that nothing short of a sonic cannon would fell this monster. And, sadly, at the end of this quite lively day, his blaster wasn't as fully charged as it had been. Now the question was, did he switch to full beam and gamble everything on one shot, or did he dial down the power and pray he'd have time to get off four or five lesser shots before the thing tore Jane to pieces?

The thing was skidding down the barricade, bringing a ton of stuff with it. Luke spared a thought for Jane, underneath all that, and fired. The blast hit the pterosaur full on its prominent breastbone. It flung back its head and screamed in pain, then lunged for him.

Luke kept his finger on the trigger.

The scene was chaotic. Shrieking alarms. Flashing lights. Screaming pterosaurs. Jane shouting something. And the ankylosaurus, still around somewhere, mooing unhappily to itself. The stench of burning flesh was almost unbearable.

Expecting the charge to run out any moment now, Luke kept firing. His weapon grew hot. Blasters weren't really designed for sustained . . . well, blasts. Short sharp bursts were what they were best at. Much more of this and his weapon would go up in flames. Which wouldn't do him much good, either. On the other hand, it would make a nice change from ending yet another assignment slowly freezing to death. Actually, it would make a pleasant change for him to end an assignment unscathed. And this bastard still wasn't going down.

Screaming and flailing, the pterosaur lumbered towards him. Luke glanced down. His weapon was in the red zone. He had to power down, otherwise *he'd* be the one in trouble. If he could just squeeze a few more seconds . . .

The pterosaur burst into flames. Quite suddenly and with no warning. A hideous, high-pitched scream hurt Luke's ears. Red-hot flames roared skywards. He could feel the heat on his face. Great – this time he'd be going back to TPHQ with third-degree burns. Long, long seconds passed. The thing was still staggering around, its burning wings flailing. Luke was suddenly aware he was much too close. If it toppled over now . . . And, as history is all too aware, books are very burnable.

There was a sudden silence as the pterosaur crumpled to the ground and lay, wings outstretched, burning fiercely.

Unfortunately it fell on to the barricade – and Jane was still trapped. And Luke hadn't forgotten there was a second one around somewhere.

He began to scramble towards Jane. 'Quick.'

Shouldering his now useless blaster, he struggled to tug her free. More library stuff fell down on both of them.

'Have they gone?'

Luke looked over his shoulder. The original pterosaur was perched atop the barricade, silently watching them. 'No.'

Jane peered past him. 'Shit.'

'Nicely put, Jane. Can you wriggle or something?'

'My leg's caught. Can you see my gun?'

Luke cast a quick look around. Normally he'd have concentrated on getting her out, but at this moment they were both quite defenceless. But there it was – just out of Jane's reach but not his. He handed it to her. 'Here. Cover us both.'

He worked frantically to free her, heaving aside chairs, old shelving, paperback spinners, display equipment, notice boards and, of course, books. Looking down, her foot appeared to be caught under some heavy shelving.

The barricade shifted again. The original pterosaur was on the move.

'Luke, leave me.'

'Shut up, Jane, and start shooting.'

More barricade crumbled.

'Luke – go. Now.'

'Not leaving you, Jane. If I lift this, can you . . . ?' He heaved. 'Ngggghhh. Hurry. Can't . . . hold it . . .'

Jane aimed over his shoulder and opened fire. The pterosaur screamed and flapped backwards, trying to throw itself into reverse.

Jane kicked and heaved. For a moment the weight increased and she worried she'd only made things worse. She heaved again and suddenly the weight was gone. She rolled over on to her stomach and wriggled free.

'Look out!'

There was another sudden stench and suddenly it was above them, neck and head extended. The smell from its open beak was foul.

Luke heard a shout behind him and then Grint was there, unshouldering the blaster you had to be as big as Grint even to lift off the ground. Luke remembered joking with Jane that it was bigger than she was and wondering whether Grint took it to bed with him. There had followed a number of very bad jokes based on a *ménage à trois*. Now he came to think of it, Jane had not been amused. But he was glad of it now.

Grint's blaster spat white-hot fire and the second pterosaur went up like a bonfire on Guy Fawkes night. Uncomfortably close but it was much better than the alternative. He was shouting something. There was no chance of making out the words over the shriek of all the alarms and the harsh cries of the pterosaur. A third scrambled over the top of the barricade, staring down at them. Then another. The bastarding things were everywhere. Aggressive. Vicious. Angry.

But so was Grint. 'Burn, you bastards. Burn.' Again and again Luke heard the roar of Grint's blaster.

Blaster fire engulfed the pterosaur closest to him. Jane could feel the draught as it flapped its wings, struggling, in its ungainly manner, to get away. Uttering a horrible shriek, it vanished from view. Whether dead or alive, she had no idea.

And then Grint was beside her, firing short, sharp, controlled bursts, spraying the whole area with flames. Another screamed and staggered. Blinded by the flames and pain, it lumbered away into the cool of the night.

Jane grabbed for Luke's arm and, with Grint covering them, they withdrew to the surely only very temporary shelter of the front doors.

Grint followed them in, slamming the doors behind him.

'Thank you,' gasped Jane.

Grint wiped his sweating face. 'What the fire truck's going on here? We jump to the past – we're not supposed to have the fire-trucking past come to us. We really need to get this time-slip shut down.'

Rossi turned up again. 'Sir, we can't hold them any longer. They're coming down the stairs.'

'Well, we can't get out the front way. Head for the back door.'

Hansen and Kohl were backing into fiction. 'They're heading this way, sir.'

'Fuck.'

'Where to?'

Grint took a quick look around. 'Over there. Reference.'

'Anyone got a spare weapon?' said Luke.

'I'm out, too,' said Jane.

Grint handed Luke his spare.

'Sorry,' said Rossi, to Jane. 'This *is* my spare.'

'No problem,' said Jane. 'I'll be the fire extinguisher queen.'

They retreated backwards towards reference, firing as they went. Two raptors were cautiously advancing down the stairs, trampling their fallen brethren. Grint's blaster roared again. The one in front burst into flames, staggered blindly into fiction, and collapsed on to a shelving unit which itself began to burn.

'Stand by, Jane,' shouted Luke. 'We may need the fire extinguisher queen at any moment.'

'Oh, my God,' said Jane. 'We're burning down the library. People will hate us.'

'What do you mean *will*?'

'Well, at least the fire alarm is now relevant.'

Hansen was peering cautiously through the ruined window. 'It's chaos out there. They've just about wrecked the place. The little ones are running everywhere, shitting themselves as they go. Something's brought down most of the hanging baskets outside the Town Hall. On the plus side, some of them are killing each other. If we hang on long enough, they might just do our job for us.'

No such luck. There were simply too many to hold back. And Rossi was limping. 'Slipped on the fire-trucking stairs. Where the fire truck are our sodding reinforcements?'

Jane was a little way apart, examining the fire extinguishers, when she stopped and straightened up. 'I can hear music again.'

'We told you – that's because you're the only one of us going to heaven,' said Luke, checking his charge.

Jane cocked her head, listening. 'It's not the Welsh national anthem this time.' She crossed to the window and tried to see out past the ankylosaurus bottom. 'Who's Barnacle Bill the Sailor?'

'What?'

This time they all heard it together.

'Oh my God,' shouted Rossi. 'It's Bailey. It's the chopper. Finally.'

It was indeed Lt Bailey. And Delta Zero One. Finally.

A giant black helicopter – the workhorse of the Time Police – arose vertically from behind the Town Hall, rotors whirling, downward-facing searchlights dancing across the square.

It is difficult for choppers to fly quietly. Quite apart from the engine, the displaced air makes a noise. A lot of noise. All technical attempts to solve the problem had hitherto been unsuccessful. Lt Bailey had tackled the problem in her own way, overlaying the sound of clattering rotors with her own improved version of 'Barnacle Bill the Sailor'. The one not suitable for bankers, captains of industry, church leaders, footballers, politicians, TV personalities and all others pure of thought and noble of deed.

'Bailey,' shouted Luke, ripping open the front doors just as a woman's shrill falsetto echoed around the town.

'*Who's that knocking at my door?*
'*Who's that knocking at my door?*
'*Who's that knocking at my door?*
'*Cried the fair young maiden.*'

There was a pause long enough for everyone to appreciate

the drama of the moment before the pilot answered her own question, switching her voice to a gruff roar.

'*It's only me from over the sea, said Barnacle Bill the sailor.*'

'Oh God,' said Luke, closing his eyes. 'Just how bad can one day get?'

As if she'd heard him, the pilot responded, 'Ahoy there, me hearties – Barnacle Bill to the rescue.'

The chopper hovered over the square. Most dinosaurs took one look at the giant singing pterosaur and scattered. Two or three genuine pterosaurs accepted the challenge, swooped and encountered the rotors. A considerable amount of minced pterosaur splattered the front of the Town Hall. Messy. Very, very messy.

Luke sighed. 'You know the English will get the blame for that, don't you?'

At the same time, two large pods materialised in the square. Heavy ramps slammed down, badly damaging the decorative paving. TPOs poured from every orifice.

'Oh, thank God,' said Jane, leaning back against the wall and slithering to the floor.

Anything not actually tied down was being whirled away by the powerful downdraught. Everything that was tied down, however, was rapidly being smothered by the fine red mist being sprayed from the chopper. The mist hung in the air for a moment and then drifted slowly to the ground, enveloping everything.

'I don't believe it,' said Luke in delight. 'We're painting the town red.'

'What the hell?' muttered Grint. 'What is this stuff?'

Whatever it was, it was working. Sort of. The remaining

dinosaurs ceased to attack. Or run. Or fight. One or two even began to make a low crooning noise, shifting their hindquarters from side to side. One unleashed some kind of decorative neck frill which vibrated with a low melodic sound. One or two didn't bother with any preliminaries at all and simply leaped upon one another.

'Are they attacking each other?' enquired Jane, getting to her feet and straining for a better look.

'*Au contraire*,' said Bolshy Jane. 'Wow – look at those two go. They've bent that lamp post. Hey, Jane – look.'

'I'd really rather not,' said Jane, averting her eyes.

Time Police officers were kicking their way through the smouldering remains of the barricade and through the front doors. The cavalry had arrived.

Jane nudged Luke. 'Oh look, it's Matthew.'

A grinning Officer Farrell lifted his visor and stood at the bottom of the steps, looking up at them.

'What are you doing here?' demanded Luke.

'Rescuing you,' said Matthew simply.

Luke eyed the skinny figure in slightly too big armour looking up at him. 'Dear God, they must be scraping the bottom of the barrel if you're here.'

'I think their exact words were: that idiot Parrish has got himself into a pretty pickle again. Go and rescue him, Officer Farrell.'

Luke regarded him. 'Why are you even here? You've got a broken wing.'

'Moral support,' said Matthew.

'My morals don't need supporting.'

'Your morals need end-of-life care, mate.'

'How's your arm?' enquired Jane.

'Good as new,' said Matthew, very carefully not flexing it in any way.

Luke grinned. 'You'd better report to Grint. He's bound to have some simple task you can be trusted to perform.'

Jane was smiling. 'It's good to see Two-Three-Six all together again.'

'It is, isn't it?' said Luke. 'I don't think it's any coincidence that things have been going badly for the Time Police ever since they split us up. What took you so long?'

'Spot of bother at TPHQ. Systems down. Trapped in the Time Map. Same old, same old.'

'Well, you're here now, I suppose.'

'We're all here, actually,' said Matthew. 'Everyone. The Time Police have called in everyone they know and even some they don't.'

Luke was watching reinforcements pour across the square. 'Is that Kester di Maggio?'

Jane nodded. 'And aren't those people over there from the Key Group?'

They watched for a while. The last raptors were being disposed of. Fires were extinguished. Someone silenced the alarms with the butt of his heavy-duty blaster.

Finally – silence in the library.

'I'll tell you who very conspicuously isn't here,' said Luke, in a low voice. 'A pair of tip-top bounty hunters. In fact, *the* tip-top bounty hunters.'

'No,' said Matthew, looking around. 'They're not, are they? It's not like them to miss something like this.'

'No. I wonder what they're up to.'

'Probably off overthrowing a country somewhere.'

Matthew tugged off his helmet, drew a deep breath, and winced at the smell. 'So how have you two been managing without me?'

'Strangely,' said Luke, 'very well. I'm sure it's only pure chance that you and the prehistoric world's attempts to kill us all have coincided.'

'Never mind,' said Matthew soothingly. He surveyed the carnage that had once been a very pleasant town square. 'I'll soon get this sorted.'

Behind him, Grint rolled his eyes.

'Rescue team reporting for duty,' said Lt Chigozie, grinning, but with one eye on the ankylosaurus – which appeared to be leaning against the one last intact pillar and taking a nap.

'Reinforcements,' corrected Grint. 'We didn't need rescuing.'

'Yeah,' said Chigozie, gesturing to the wrecked town square, the piles of rubble, the bodies, the burning barricade, the blood, the bent lamp post, the decimated hanging baskets and the pall of smoke hanging over the town. 'We can clearly see how well everything was going for you.'

'Who's dealing with the castle?'

'Dahl,' said Chigozie. 'And you. Hay's orders – tell Grint to get his arse up there and sort it. You're to take whatever and whoever you need, rendezvous with Dahl at the castle and get that bastard Plimpton. Shoot on sight. We'll follow on when we've contained this little lot.'

Grint squinted at Delta Zero One – or as its pilot preferred it to be known, the Dark Destructor – hovering over the town square, its downdraught completing the destruction the dinosaurs had begun.

'Right,' he said. 'Well, I'll have the chopper for a start. It'll get us to the castle in minutes.'

'Needed here,' said Chigozie. 'Dinosaurs for the corralling of.'

They both glanced at the ankylosaurus. Six tons if it was an ounce.

'Going to tuck it under your arm?' said Grint sarcastically.

'No need. Bailey's got it all in hand.'

'Oh God.'

'The chopper will lay a trail and lure them back to wherever they came from.'

'A trail? Of what?'

'Well, I haven't enquired too closely,' said Chigozie. 'Plausible deniability at the inevitable public inquiry, but I understand there are several tanks of a mysterious Meiklejohn substance aboard. Plus Bailey stopped off at some kind of meat market on the way. Bait, apparently. According to Varma, there's a time-slip in a tunnel leading from the castle and we're hoping we can guide them into it – then collapse it behind them.'

Grint stared. 'You're kidding. *That's* the plan?'

'The alternative is that they scatter and Wales will be riddled with dinosaurs for the rest of its days.'

Grint opened his mouth, decided it wasn't worth the effort and chinned his mic. 'Bailey – you can give us a lift in your flying shed. Teams Two-Three-Five and Two-Three-Six, get yourselves armed and armoured. Briefing in five. Move.'

34

The briefing was held inside the library. Everyone sat where they could and ignored the charred raptors still smouldering gently in the hall.

'OK,' said Chigozie, 'today's objective – to eliminate Henry Plimpton at any cost. To quote the commander – "If it's a choice between saving your own life or taking down Plimpton, then I expect you to take him down. We'll all have a drink in your memory afterwards, but the top priority is Henry Plimpton. Do not come home without him."'

Everyone nodded.

Grint took up the briefing. 'Lt Varma has provided as much detail of the layout as she can. This info is being flashed to our visors now. The attack will be led by myself and Lt Dahl. Teams One-Seven-Nine, Two-Twelve and Two-Twenty-One, together with Clean-up Crews Seventeen and Twenty-Nine, are with Dahl. Wu, Etok, Roche and Meyer will provide a security presence – prisoners for the dealing with. Dahl's people are going in by pod – they might even be there by now – and will land in the central courtyard. They'll be responsible for sweeping the main body of the castle. Once that's secure, everyone moves underground and begins clearing the tunnels. With luck, by then, most of the dinos will be back where they belong.'

There was a short pause while everyone contemplated the unlikeliness of this scenario.

'In the meantime, Delta Zero One will be laying a trail up through the woods to the mine shaft, which, Lt Varma informs us, will eventually lead back to the time-slip.

'Also aboard will be Officers Curtis and Rockmeyer. Delta Zero One will set down on an appropriate roof – probably the keep, which, according to Dr Maxwell, is located on the western side of the main courtyard. Both teams will clear and secure the keep.'

Heads nodded. It was always easier to clear a building from the top down than the bottom up.

'Incidentally, Maxwell says to keep your eyes peeled for some Roman bloke. We're not to shoot him. Secure and await instructions, but the first priority in any situation is Henry Plimpton. A shoot-to-kill order has been issued so let's take this bastard down. Is everyone clear?'

There was a chorus of 'Yes, sir'.

'That's it, people. Go.'

Delta Zero One's touchdown completed the destruction of the town square. With the exception of the ankylosaurus, all remaining dinosaurs scattered.

Chigozie sighed. 'Well, thank you very much. We'll never get them back now.'

'Don't get your knickers in a twist, Chigozie,' said Bailey in his ear. 'You just leave the difficult stuff to me and concentrate on not falling over your own feet. Come along, people.

All aboard that's coming aboard. And hold tight now. We'll be going quite fast so no screaming.'

They scrambled aboard only to find most of the space occupied by two enormous tanks, half a dozen huge tarpaulin sacks of something that smelled like death, and Officers Curtis and Rockmeyer, apparently acting as loadmasters. It was all a bit of a tight squeeze.

Luke sighed, wriggled himself into a more comfortable position between Grint and Kohl, and said to Jane, 'Could your next boyfriend be slightly smaller, please?'

Jane ignored him.

'Everyone in?' shouted Bailey.

'All clear above and behind,' reported Curtis, hanging out of the door.

'Then let's go.'

The chopper lifted off and headed north-east.

Rockmeyer was peering out of one door – Curtis the other. 'We've cleared the town, ma'am.'

'Then let's get started,' shouted Bailey. 'Meat.'

Curtis hung out of the door, nearly stopping Jane's heart completely.

'Relax,' said Bolshy Jane. 'Harness.'

The next moment Rockmeyer was heaving a canvas sack towards the door. It left a long red trail across the floor and the smell redoubled in nastiness.

'Jesus,' said Hansen, flipping down his visor.

His fellow passengers followed suit.

The bundle disappeared out of the chopper, presumably to splat on the ground below and spill its fragrant contents.

'What are they doing?' shouted Luke.

'Laying a trail,' said Curtis. 'All the way home.'

Another sack of meat disappeared out of the opposite door.

'They'll never follow . . .'

And another.

'Initiating spray,' shouted Bailey. 'Probably best if you all stop breathing.'

'What does the spray do?' enquired Grint, possibly wondering if hijacking the chopper had been such a good idea after all.

'It's the nearest thing we could get to a dinosaur love potion,' yelled Curtis, heaving his door shut. 'Meiklejohn reckons it should do the trick.'

'I don't really want to know, but I can't help myself.' Luke grinned. 'Of what does a dinosaur love potion consist?'

'You're sitting next to a tank of ovulating female elephant pheromones. And the lieutenant is within sniffing distance of something called frontalin. To simulate males in musth. It's all strong stuff. Meiklejohn says don't get it on yourself whatever you do.'

The chopper clattered on – its pilot working her way through all thirty-seven verses of 'Barnacle Bill' – occasionally dropping pungent parcels of offal over Wales and spraying the trees with bursts of randy elephant juice. As Matthew shouted above the roar of the engines – what could possibly go wrong?

The castle wasn't hard to locate. A grinning Bailey informed them that even a couple of grunts could have found it.

'Movement among the trees,' yelled Rockmeyer, gesturing downwards as he sat in the open doorway with his legs dangling. 'Wow – look at that big boy down there.'

Curtis was pulling out a piece of kit. 'Who wants this?'

Luke eyed it with foreboding. 'What is it?'

'Portable spraying equipment. Someone has to lure the dinos back up the tunnel and through the time-slip. A shitty job, with every possibility of being either trampled, rogered by a triceratops, or shot by your own colleagues.'

'I'll do it,' said Jane, aware that of all of them she was probably the least combat effective.

'I'll go with you,' said Luke swiftly. 'To watch your back.'

'And me,' said Matthew.

Grint hesitated, running his eyes over his resources. Bailey would put them down on the roof. They wouldn't need him to lead them through the keep. Not just for a simple building clearance. And Dahl would be on site. And Tucker. Lockland couldn't manage the spray and a weapon. Who knew what she and Parrish might encounter in those tunnels? He was torn. He was the best person to go with Lockland. Or was that simply what he was telling himself?

He shook his head. 'Not with that arm, Farrell. And Parrish – you carry on up to the castle. I'll go with Lockland. We don't know what we'll encounter in those tunnels so I'll act as back-up and bodyguard. Bailey, set us down and then go on to the castle. Kohl – find Tucker. Don't be afraid to take instructions from him. He's familiar with the area and knows what he's doing. Once you've cleared the keep, locate Henry Plimpton and take him down. That's your overriding priority. Everything else is secondary. I'll join you when I can. And Lt Dahl and his people are probably there by now.'

Kohl nodded. 'Yes, sir.'

'Two minutes,' called Bailey.

Curtis stood in the doorway. 'Get ready to jump.'

'What?' cried Wimpy Jane in horror.

Seen from above, the small valley looked very small indeed. Some sort of camouflaged structure appeared to have had a very bad time recently. The chopper hovered some five feet off the ground, whipping up leaves, twigs and dust. Grint jumped down first, followed by Jane. Her equipment thudded to the ground behind her.

'Stay down,' shouted Grint.

Sound advice. Jane lay face down among the ferns as the big chopper wheeled sharply sideways and upwards. For the umpteenth time, the fair young maiden was enquiring as to the identity of the person knocking at her door.

Jane climbed to her feet. The pack contained a shoulder-mounted lightweight tank and a spray. She scrambled into the harness and examined the nozzle. Simple enough. Twist right for on. Twist left for off. Experimentally, she aimed at a fern and twisted right. A fine red mist engulfed the unfortunate fern.

Grint had been inspecting the collapsed structure. Judging by the trampled ferns and the piles of pungent droppings, a large number of animals had recently passed this way. And judging by the wreckage, some of them had been on the hefty side.

'Stand back, sir.'

Remembering they were supposed to be luring dinosaurs into the tunnel, she sprayed a path to the yawning hole, then paused and lifted her visor. 'I can't smell anything, can you? Is it working?'

'It's only the meat that smelled,' said Grint. 'And just because we can't smell it doesn't mean dinosaurs can't.' He peered down into the hole. 'Give it another burst to be on the safe side and then we'll head down.'

Jane nodded. 'Do we jump?'

Grint was staring down. 'There's a ladder. Was a ladder. It hasn't fared well. We'll have to scramble down the slope. I'll go first – you stay close. We don't know how toxic this stuff is, so spray behind us.'

He disappeared down into the dark. Jane chewed her lip and wondered how long it would take him before . . .

Grint's voice rumbled up from the depths. 'It's not steep – the drop's only about ten feet – but the going's rough so watch where you put your feet.'

Hampered by her equipment, Jane scrambled down the rocky slope and, as instructed, watched where she put her feet. Grint was shining his torch down the tunnel.

'How long is it, sir?'

'Don't know.'

'How much of this stuff have I got?'

'Don't know.'

'So – operating in a state of complete ignorance, sir.'

He grinned at her. 'How long have you been in the Time Police, Lockland?'

They entered the tunnel. Jane, who had always imagined mines to be cramped, claustrophobic affairs, was surprised at the dimensions. Although now she came to think of it, the ankylosaurus had got through and he definitely wasn't small. The tunnel was very dark, however. Whether this was normal or a result of Tucker's sabotage was unknown.

Grint went first, placing his feet slowly and carefully. His headtorch showed rough wet walls and an uneven floor.

A voice from the shadows said cautiously, 'Grint?'

Grint brought up his gun. The red laser sight centred on a huge dark mass. 'Identify yourself.'

'It's me. Tucker.'

Grint relaxed slightly. 'Report.'

'Well, as you can see, I've cut off the power in the tunnels, although they'll have it back any moment now, so be aware. They had some kind of force field protecting them from Lizard Land and that's gone down too. There were – still are – dinosaurs coming through the time-slip. Plus they had some kind of storage area with scores of animals being kept in crates and cages until I let them out. They scattered in all directions so people have been busy dealing with them as well. I've seen about thirty or so men – although there are bound to be more. Gun cabinets along the walls are not locked should you need more weapons.'

'Good work. Except all the escaped dinos headed for the town.'

'Ah – sorry about that. Many hurt?'

'Not so far. And at least you've been keeping them busy here.'

By now, Tucker had noticed Jane and her harness. 'What's that?'

'Dino love potion. We're luring them back home. Are you armed?'

Tucker brandished two blasters. 'Yes.'

Jane nodded and patted her weapon on its rip-grip patch.

'Can you get to the castle from here?' said Grint.

'Yes. This tunnel leads directly to the junction. The middle tunnel runs to Lizard Land – it's signposted – and the tunnel opposite will take you to the castle. But there will be people everywhere. Stay sharp.'

'Head towards the castle. Dahl's bringing reinforcements and Kohl's leading a force to take the keep. I've told him to liaise with you. They're using Delta Zero One and they'll be there by now. The overriding priority for everyone is Henry Plimpton.'

'Understood. Plimpton has pods in the central courtyard. He'll probably head there once he knows the Time Police are here.'

Forgetting their coms wouldn't work so close to a time-slip, Grint chinned his mic. Nothing. He swore softly and then said, 'Rendezvous with Kohl. Find Henry Plimpton. Don't let him get away. Shoot to kill. Top priority. We'll join you asap.'

'Got it.'

Tucker turned back and disappeared into the gloom.

'Stay sharp, Lockland. They may try to escape this way.'

'Men or dinos, sir?'

'Both.'

They worked their way slowly along the tunnel in the dark with Jane spraying as she went. Quick bursts every few yards. Across the floor. Up the walls.

'How much further, sir?'

'No idea. To this junction place at least. Or until the stuff runs out.'

'Or until someone finds us.'

They crept on. Their progress was very slow. The only illumination was their headtorches and this tunnel was full of what looked like overturned lockers, their contents trampled, shattered and scattered. And droppings. Lots of droppings. It would appear that many excited dinosaurs had passed this way quite recently. Jane could only hope they'd be equally enthusiastic about the return trip.

She took a breath and eased her shoulders under the harness, doing her best not to wonder what might be watching them from the dark. Her night visor showed nothing, but suppose it wasn't working properly. It had taken a bit of a bashing this evening. No – of course it was working properly. She made herself concentrate. Five paces – spray the ground. Five paces – spray left. Five paces – spray right. Despite her best efforts, she'd managed to get a good amount over herself. And a bit over Grint, as well.

His voice came out of the dark. 'All right, Lockland?'

She answered truthfully. 'Bit light-headed, sir. This stuff, probably. But fine.'

'Keep going.'

About to resume spraying, Jane stopped and listened. The tunnel was so dark there was very little point in closing her eyes. She did it anyway, all the better to concentrate on her ears. 'Sir, I think there's something behind us.'

'Well, if this stuff is working, then it should be a randy dinosaur.'

'Actually,' said Jane, trying to feel that this was a good thing. 'I think it might be more than one.'

They both stood still. There was a definite tremor in the ground. Grint could feel it even through his regulation-issue Time Police boots, whose composition, it was generally reckoned, could withstand everything up to and including a direct nuclear blast.

'It's getting closer,' said Jane.

Grint snapped a lightstick. This was not a moment for discretion. He looked around. Even more lockers had been destroyed here. Grint remembered the ankylosaurus. It wasn't hard to envisage how a stonking great dinosaur's progress along an underground tunnel would go, and the lockers had been collateral damage.

'There's a door,' said Jane, who had been checking behind them. 'Over there.'

There was indeed a door in the wall. Whether natural or not, some sort of niche or cave appeared to have been turned into a small room. A hand-written sign pinned to the door announced this was the night watch's duty bunk. Having done the same thing himself on many occasions, Grint reckoned the night watch would consist of two or three men – two would be on patrol and one would get his head down for a few hours. They'd swap throughout the night and, in that way, everyone would get some sleep.

Jane hesitated. 'What if there's someone in there?'

'Who cares?' said Grint, raising his weapon.

'What if it's locked?'

Grint groped for the door handle. It was unlocked.

The noise was suddenly louder. A distant drumming, but becoming less and less distant by the moment. There was an occasional bellow, or sometimes a shriek, as something lost its footing in the dark, perhaps, and was either swept along or utterly crushed.

'Shit,' said Grint. 'I didn't realise this stuff would work so quickly.'

'I don't think these can be the dinosaurs from the town,' said Jane. 'These must be the ones who hadn't got that far.'

The same idea occurred to both of them at once. These must be the ones too slow to have travelled any great distance. Because they were too big.

Grint stared uneasily over her shoulder. 'Sounds a bit like a stampede.'

Actually, it sounded a lot like a stampede. Louder and louder. Closer and closer until, suddenly, what seemed, in this very poor light, to be an avalanche of dinosaurs appeared around the bend, bearing down upon them. There were a few little ones racing ahead, their eyes bulging with terror, scuttling as fast as they could, desperate to escape whatever was behind them.

Which seemed to be raptors – only a few, but one was too many. Whether they were chasing their prey or trying to outrun whatever was behind *them*, it was impossible to tell.

And then, behind the raptors – the big boys. Slower moving but still managing to cover the ground. Most were unknown to her but she recognised a couple of Hadrosaurs – Hadrosauruses – whatever. Dancing shadows made it difficult to gauge their height, but their heads brushed the roof as they ran, and the tunnel wasn't low.

'Sir, I think we might be about to be trampled by a bunch of—'

He wrenched open the door. 'Trampling is not the worst thing that could happen to us, Lockland. Think about it.'

'What . . . ? Oh.'

Grint eyed her tank. 'Exactly. And you're drenched in the stuff.'

Everything was pounding along the tunnel. The smaller ones were already bearing down on them. Another few seconds . . .

'Inside,' said Grint, pushing her through the door.

The tiny room was empty. Grint's lightstick picked out a bunk – neatly made – with a low locker beside the bed, a table and four cheap plastic chairs. A pack of cards lay on the table, a towel was draped across one of the chairs – to dry, presumably – and there was a scratchpad by the bed.

There was no lock on the door. Grint grabbed the nearest chair, wedged it under the handle and drew a deep breath. They stood silently, listening to the stampede thunder past.

'All right, Jane?'

'Yes, I think so. You?'

Grint patted himself down. 'Soggy, but intact.'

'Yes,' said Jane. 'I did my best but this stuff is so fine it goes everywhere. What now?'

'We wait until it's safe to move and then get out of this tunnel. I think we can assume the combination of rotting meat and elephant pheromones has been successful. I don't know how long it will take some of them to drift back from the town. That big bugger outside the library probably has a top speed of about half a mile a day so we might be here for a while.'

He laid the lightstick on the table, pulled off his helmet and, out of habit, opened his com. 'Can anyone hear me?'

There was no response.

'Too close to the time-slip,' he said. 'The only consolation is that it buggers their coms as well as ours.'

Jane shrugged off the harness, took off her own helmet and shook out her hair, which flew around her head.

Grint looked away and had a stern word with himself. Picking up the towel, he began to dry his face and arms, then passed it over to Jane.

Stifling her misgivings at using someone else's towel without their permission, Jane dried herself as best she could and sat down on the bunk. After a dubious glance at the cheap plastic chairs, Grint came and sat alongside, placing considerable strain on the bed. A number of springs went *tink*.

And then they waited. There was an occasional bellow as a straggler passed by, or something brushed against the door, or another clatter as something else was destroyed, but otherwise silence lay very heavy in this little room.

Jane suddenly found herself with nothing to say. For some reason she remembered their first date. The long silences. The stilted conversation. Surely she and Grint had moved past that by now. True, neither was a particularly chatty person, but their silences were companiable enough. Each was comfortable with the other. What was so different now? Her head was spinning slightly – which she put down to her recent exertions, not having eaten since heaven knew when, and the inevitable reaction to the events of the day.

Grint was very conscious of Jane sitting next to him. He could hear her every breath. The rustle of her clothing. Jane was among the few officers who wore long sleeves – most officers favoured short-sleeved *look at my muscles* T-shirts – but today she'd pushed up her sleeves while operating the spray. He could see her arms, pale in the dim light.

Jane moved slightly and felt her forearm brush his. Her skin felt hot and dry. She could hear him breathing and the rustle of his clothing as he moved.

She herself felt a growing warmth. Her face was on fire. Her pulse beat in her ears. Her skin prickled. What on earth was the matter with her? Was she going down with something? Was she perhaps allergic to whatever she'd been so recklessly spraying around? Was Grint similarly affected?

She turned to face him at exactly the same moment he turned to face her. He was looking down at her. She could hear his breath. Fast and hard.

He said, 'Jane . . .'

'Um . . . yes . . .'

'I . . . um . . .'

Jane watched her hand reach out and take his. Had she just done that? Well, yes, it would appear so. His skin felt hot and tight. Was he sick, too? Had they both been affected by whatever devil's brew Meiklejohn had mixed up? How toxic was this stuff? What if they had only minutes left to live? What if this was her last chance to . . . ?

'Yes, that's right,' said Bolshy Jane, in excitement. 'Obviously you have only seconds remaining and you're sitting next to a pretty prime specimen who fancies you rotten. Get in there. Now.'

'Yes,' said Wimpy Jane, apparently abandoning the principles of a lifetime. 'What she said.'

Grint hadn't taken his eyes off her. He turned his hand in hers and gripped it tightly. 'Jane – are you all right?'

'I don't know,' said Jane truthfully. 'I do feel a bit odd. Hot. And a bit . . . I don't know.'

She peeled off her stab vest and let it drop to the floor.

Grint had another word with himself since the first one obviously hadn't worked. 'I . . . yes . . . me too . . .'

'Do you know what was in that spray?'

Grint cast his mind back. Someone had mentioned it but

he'd had other things on his mind at the time. 'Some sort of elephant potion, I think,' he said eventually.

Jane considered this. That sounded harmless enough. And everyone liked elephants. They were big. And somehow comforting. And gentle. And big. Like Grint. And big. Very . . . big.

Grint seemed to be speaking to her. 'Jane . . . I think perhaps . . . I . . . um . . . it is very hot in here.' He pulled off his own vest.

'Yes, I think so, too. I'm very hot.' Her ears caught up with what her mouth had just said and her face burst into flames again. 'I mean . . . yes, it is hot in here. I think.'

She found herself leaning into him.

'Jane, I . . .' Grint felt he really should move away from her. While he still had some control over his body. Most of his body, anyway. One specific area was letting him down badly. 'Jane, I think it's that stuff . . . the spray . . .'

'Yes,' said Jane. 'Does that matter?'

'Well, I . . . um . . . I'm worried that . . .'

'Please stop talking.'

Something heavy thundered past and again the room seemed to shake. On the other side of the door something else trumpeted. Well, bellowed. Trumpeting was elephants. His mind was full of elephants. His trousers were full of him.

Jane leaned over and kissed him, very gently, at the side of his mouth, and smiled at him. 'You should kiss me back. It's only polite.'

'But we're in uniform,' he said, slightly shocked.

'Easily remedied,' said Jane, and pulled off her T-shirt.

It is very possible that had Lt Grint possessed a decorative neck frill, it would, at that moment, be vibrating with a low, melodic sound. Possibly several low, melodic sounds. He considered fighting fate, abandoned the idea, and closed his eyes as Jane pushed him backwards on to the bed. Well, he didn't want to be rude, did he?

His rational mind made one last forlorn attempt to save him.

'Jane, are you certain you want to . . . ?'

'Yes, yes,' said Jane, adding, for the avoidance of doubt, 'I do.' She paused, wondering if she had sounded too eager – desperate even – and then decided that was unimportant. 'Now. I want to . . . I want to so much that it hurts. Do you want me?'

Grint suddenly found himself unable to form human words.

Not long afterwards the room seemed to shake again – although this time it was absolutely nothing to do with whatever was thundering past on the other side of the door.

Sometime afterwards, Grint found his words again. Because there was something that had to be said.

'Jane, I understand if you . . . I mean, we were . . . it was the spray. I enjoyed . . . things . . . very much but I understand if you don't want to . . .'

'Oh, no,' said Jane, completely misunderstanding him. 'It's OK – everything's . . . you know . . . taken care of.'

'No, that's not what I – although good – I mean – not that – I – even though . . .'

Aware he wasn't expressing himself very clearly, Grint stopped and began again.

'I'm very fond of you, Jane,' which wasn't exactly what he'd meant to say but the words *I love you* took some working up to. 'What I'm trying to say is that I know Time Police rules say there's no marriage allowed – and that's OK – but if you think we should – because of what we just – if you feel – that – we – should – I don't know – make it permanent, perhaps – which would be completely up to you – although I would be quite – actually, I – what I'm trying to say is . . .'

He stopped again, not entirely sure what he was trying to say.

Fortunately for them both, Jane spoke fluent Grint and was able to come to his rescue.

'It's all right,' she said. 'I have no plans to leave the Time Police yet.' She paused because the pheromones were beginning to wear off and the old fears were returning. 'Unless you *want* me to leave, of course. Now that we've . . .'

'No,' he said, so hastily that she nearly laughed. 'Not at all, but I want you to know – if I ever have to choose, Jane, then I will choose you.'

Jane rested her head on his shoulder. 'That's the nicest thing anyone has ever said to me.'

35

'ETA in one minute,' reported Bailey over the thump of the rotors. 'Everyone wearing their Big Girl Knickers?'

Night visors came down and weapons came up. Dahl's voice sounded in their ears.

'Pods on site – just waiting on you, Bailey. Have you stopped to put on your make-up?'

Bailey snorted. 'Look up, dickwit,' and with a spectacular cacophony of sound and light, together with the utmost precision, she put Delta Zero One down on the keep's flat roof.

There was a moment's pause. There had been some doubt as to whether medieval roofs would bear the chopper's weight, but Edward I was a king who really knew how to put a castle together. The roof held.

At the same moment, three Time Police pods made themselves visible in the central courtyard. Barely had they materialised when the ramps slammed down and two officers emerged from each, all bearing portable EMPs. Their colleagues poured out behind them, peeling off to cover every exit and entrance. Fifteen seconds later, Henry Plimpton's pods had been disabled.

'All passengers clear to disembark,' shouted Bailey. 'Play nicely, now. No biting.'

They jumped out, and, keeping low to avoid the still-moving rotors, sought shelter behind the crenelated walls that surrounded the roof on three sides. The fourth side led down to further roofs of various levels, all lost in the darkness.

'How the fire truck do we get down?' yelled Luke above the noise of the helicopter.

'No idea,' responded Bailey, lifting off and wheeling away to take up position directly over the courtyard. 'See you later.'

'Over there,' shouted Rockmeyer, pointing. A small wooden door had been built into the northern wall. It had probably been there for hundreds of years – until tonight.

'Bye-bye, door,' said Curtis, and swung his door-buster.

The door exploded on impact. Curtis was hurled backwards. Rockmeyer and Kohl, each on either side of the door, fell sideways. The others huddled closer to the wall and tried to protect themselves as lumps of wood and stone rained down upon them.

'Booby trap,' shouted Luke. He chinned his mic. 'Dahl – heads up. Be aware – booby traps. Officers down. Officers down.'

Matthew crouched over Curtis and carefully lifted his visor. 'Can you hear me?'

Curtis was conscious – just. 'Go,' he croaked. 'Jus go. Give ... tha ... bastd one ... frm ... me.'

His eyes closed.

'Curtis,' shouted Matthew, but there was no response.

Luke gripped his shoulder. 'We need to go. They know we're here. We're sitting ducks. We have to move.'

'But ...'

'We have our orders.' Luke turned to Hansen, who was already ripping out his first-aid kit. 'We have to go.'

Hansen nodded.

Rockmeyer was conscious but still on his back. Kohl had picked himself up and was shaking his head to clear his vision.

Luke considered. Grint had designated Kohl as team leader but he was barely functioning. They'd all trained together. No one of them had seniority over the others. Rossi was keeping an eye on the wounded Kohl. Matthew was . . . well, Matthew.

Luke signalled – Rossi and Kohl in one team – he and Matthew in the other. Rossi hesitated, then nodded. Luke ducked under the shattered doorway and led them into the darkness beyond.

Traversing the staircase was tricky. The going was treacherous. The stairs were steep, narrow, completely unlit and littered with rubble from the explosion, which hampered them considerably. Luke slipped several times and at one point, Kohl, still somewhat groggy from the explosion, started a small landslide and fell heavily, bringing Matthew down with him. Their night visors were confused by all the dust in the air and their headtorches almost useless. All they could do was stumble downwards in the dark and pray no one broke a leg.

Their progress was painfully slow but Luke resisted the pressure to hurry. No doubt Dahl was successfully penetrating the castle and more reinforcements would be on their way. As he saw it, his main priority was to get everyone into the main body of the keep, clear the area, and then join in the search for that bastard Plimpton.

The staircase curved to the right in a tight spiral. Every now and then Luke would whisper a command to halt – hand signals were useless – and they would listen for a moment or two. Occasional explosions sounded at ground level but whether that was more booby traps going off or their colleagues getting to grips with the Plimpton mob, he had no idea.

The stairs grew easier, though the treads were still too narrow for Time Police boots. The years had worn them away in places and they had to watch where they put their feet. Luke burned to increase their speed. They were vulnerable here in the dark, but the keep was four storeys high and huge, and who knew what secrets it contained. They had to get this right. Brushing the outside wall with his shoulder – because the steps were wider here – he continued the slow, steady progress downwards, his weapon's ragged red laser sight bleeding through the dust and zigzagging across the walls.

And finally, the last few cautious steps, and then they were off that bloody staircase at last and there was good solid stone beneath their feet. Luke moved along the wall to give the others room to form up behind him.

They were standing in a curved passageway. Because the keep was circular. Which was a bugger. A nice straight passageway with proper corners – was that too much to ask?

If they had expected a regular layout, they were to be disappointed. There were wooden doors to their left and right. Sometimes there was a small landing offset from the main passageway with several doors leading off, and even short staircases of three or four steps leading who knew where. Luke sighed. This was going to be a bitch to clear.

Signalling that he and Matthew would take the left-hand side and Kohl and Rossi the right, he moved them forwards.

The first door on the left was old and slightly ajar. Remembering the booby trap, Luke carefully scanned the frame while Matthew kept watch behind him.

There was nothing suspicious. Luke indicated he would go first. Matthew nodded.

The normal procedure was to shout 'Time Police', demolish the door and then annihilate whoever or whatever was on the other side. That would not be happening this time. Luke very cautiously prodded the door with his weapon. Silently it swung open. He risked a cautious look. Darkness lay on the other side.

Switching on his weapon torch, Luke moved into the room and swung his blaster from left to right. Finding nothing, he headed for the far right-hand corner, covering the room as, behind him, Matthew did the same but moved left.

This room was just a stone shell with a single slit window. Completely empty. Not even a storeroom.

Leaving the door open, they moved along the passageway again. Single file, moving silently from room to room. Further along the passage, they could hear Kohl and Rossi doing the same.

The top floor was clear.

Regrouping at the staircase, they moved down to the next floor. Outside, they could hear the crack of stun grenades, shouted warnings and blaster fire, but here, inside these thick walls, all was still and silent. Delta Zero One still clattered overhead, searchlights stabbing downwards. Occasionally they caught glimpses of the action through the narrow windows. Dahl's teams seemed to be having a very exciting night.

The silence in the keep was unnerving. With every step Luke expected an ambush – or an explosion – or the ceiling to fall down on them. This part of the castle seemed almost completely deserted. Why? This was the keep – the place to which the defenders traditionally fell back whenever the castle was under attack. As it was now. Where was everyone? These narrow, curved corridors were a bitch for sightlines. The doors were small and awkward. All the advantages would have lain with the defenders but there weren't any defenders. None at all. All the rooms were empty. Their progress was slow but thorough, and still Luke resisted the urge to speed things up. Thoughts of booby traps were never very far from his mind. Or trip wires. Or motion sensors that would trigger something unpleasant. With Hansen, Curtis and Rockmeyer out of the game, they were three men down before they'd even started. And a wobbly Kohl made it four. Luke tightened his grip on his weapon and crept on. Don't lose concentration. Everyone was aware of their own position and that of the others. They could do this.

They met again at the head of the stairs and made their way down to the second floor.

Whereas the top two floors had been empty, here there were definite signs of life. The passages were wider. There were modern lights on the walls. The walls themselves had been plastered and painted. And there were fewer doors. Which probably meant bigger rooms. Luke signalled their two groups to merge.

The first door was to their left. And this one was locked. Rossi moved up with the door-buster. Remembering last time, Luke very, very carefully ran his scanner around the doorframe. Nothing. He nodded to Rossi. It took two solid blows – this was a substantial door – but eventually the lock gave way.

They flattened themselves against the wall, expecting a hail of gunfire.

Nothing happened. Once again they were back to silence.

Except . . . Luke tilted his head, listened for a moment and then exchanged a startled glance with Matthew. Was that . . . ?

Back on the roof, having established that Rockmeyer was conscious and more or less coherent, Hansen was working on Curtis. Rockmeyer struggled to see what was happening.

'How . . . is he?'

Hansen, ripping open another wound pack, said tersely, 'Don't know yet. Still breathing but still bleeding. Can you hold a weapon?'

'Yeah.'

'Watch the doorway for me.'

The Time Police have a procedure for this sort of thing. Hansen, their designated field medic, would work on the two of them for as long as it was safe for him to do so. Should hostiles turn up, however, his standing orders were to move to a more secure location and defend himself. And his patients as well if that was possible. If it wasn't . . . They all knew this. It was a risk they all accepted.

Applying pressure with one hand, Hansen pulled Curtis's back-up weapon from his rip-grip patch, reached over, put it in Rockmeyer's hand and bent his fingers around it. 'Watch our backs.'

'Yeah.'

They both knew he couldn't see that far. They both knew he probably couldn't hold the gun. Not for more than one or two shots, anyway.

Curtis sighed, coughed a little and opened his eyes.

'Hey,' said Hansen, still applying pressure. 'Who's an idiot then? For fire-truck's sake, Curtis – learn to duck.'

Curtis hissed – whether in pain or amusement was not clear.

Having applied dressings to his satisfaction, Hansen reached into his pack and pulled out what, to non-medical eyes, looked exactly like a roll of clingfilm.

Curtis made a slight sound.

'Yeah, I know,' said Hansen, grinning. 'Your only claim to fame. The bloke who began and ended his day encased in clingfilm. Hay will probably give you a medal.'

'Shrink-wrapped, probably,' whispered Rockmeyer.

Swiftly, Hansen wrapped what he could. The stuff was waterproof, easy to apply, easily moulded to the patient's contours – in Curtis's case, his generous contours – and brilliant at keeping out dirt and germs. Better than bandages, anyway.

A massive explosion somewhere caused the entire keep to shudder. Hansen instinctively bent over Curtis to shield him as best he could.

'Stay here,' he said – as if either Curtis or Rockmeyer had any choice. Picking up his weapon and crouching low, he ran to the south wall – the one overlooking the courtyard. Delta Zero One still hovered overhead, lighting the scene below.

Blaster fire criss-crossed the open space. Some officers were still pinned down near the pods. Lights flickered inside the main body of the castle. Whether fire, gunfire, or grenades, he had no idea. Of his teammates, there was no sign. Still clearing the keep, presumably.

Or dead.

He craned his head over the parapet.

Back behind him on the roof, Rockmeyer said very softly, 'Liam . . . you still awake?'

Curtis slowly turned his head, his breath hissing in and out, fighting the pain.

Rockmeyer tried to grin. 'We'll get out of this. You . . . wait and see. Hansen knows what he's doing. And he's pumped you . . . full of the good stuff. You'll be as high as a kite in a minute. Lucky . . . bugger.'

Struggling to focus, Curtis made a tiny movement with his right hand. All he could manage.

'No,' said Rockmeyer hoarsely, apparently understanding what he was trying to say. 'You're going to make it. You just have to hold on. Bailey . . . will airlift us out. You're going to make it.' Painfully, he reached out and gently clasped Curtis's hand. 'You have to.'

Curtis hissed again. Perhaps in pain. Perhaps something else. A tear cut through the grime on his face.

Rockmeyer tightened his grip. 'You can't die. You have to . . . stay with me. Promise me you . . . won't die. Promise.'

'Arlo . . .' Curtis sighed and closed his eyes. After a second, so did Rockmeyer.

Hansen abandoned his position at the wall, scrambled back again and stared down at his patients. 'No. No. No, no, no.'

Above him, the helicopter dipped and the searchlights found them.

Luke tilted his head, still listening in the doorway. Was that . . . ? Surely not . . . He risked a peep. The room was dark but someone was in there.

He drew back. 'Can anyone else hear . . . snoring?'

Three heads nodded. They could all very definitely hear

snoring. Someone was not only fast asleep, but had remained so over the crash of them breaking the door down.

'Booby traps,' warned Rossi.

Luke nodded. 'Stay here.'

He lowered his visor and very, very cautiously, advanced into the room, back to the wall, one slow step at a time.

His torch picked out a bed. An occupied bed. A fairly hefty man lay flat on his back, arms spread wide as if he'd just been dropped there. His mouth was wide open and his snores appeared to be coming to them courtesy of an industrial wind tunnel. A bucket of water and a ladle stood nearby. For when he awoke, presumably.

Cautiously, but not gently, Luke prodded him with his gun. The man snorted, gurgled, turned his head slightly, and then continued with the snoring theme. Even more loudly.

'Drugged,' said Matthew, from the doorway.

Luke nodded. 'I know who this is.' He looked over at Matthew, just inside the door, Rossi in the doorway itself and Kohl watching the corridor. 'This is Romulus.'

Silence greeted this statement.

'Romulus,' said Luke in mild exasperation. 'You know. Raised by wolves. Founded Rome. Killed his brother.'

'We know who Romulus was,' said Rossi. 'I think we're just a little surprised to find him here. Three thousand years later. In Wales. Oh – is that what Maxwell was banging on about?'

'He was kidnapped,' said Luke, and judged it better to say no more. Sorting all that out was up to Varma and she wouldn't thank him for interfering.

The Father of Rome snorted again, shifted slightly, and redoubled his efforts to bring down the ceiling acoustically.

'Are we leaving him here?' enquired Matthew.

'Well, if us crashing through the door didn't wake him, then I don't know what would. And he's too bloody heavy to lift, so yeah, we'll leave him here.'

'Probably the safest place,' said Rossi, as the sound and light show outside increased in volume.

'Yeah,' said Luke. 'I'm tempted to join him. However . . .' He indicated they should move on.

There were even fewer doors on the first floor. Luke presumed these were the best rooms. The well-appointed passage outside seemed to confirm that assumption. Modern lights illuminated portraits on the walls. There were occasional tables. And rugs. And even a tapestry of some kind. Did people live here? They moved even more slowly, watching where they put their feet. No one stood on the rugs because no one knew what they concealed.

The first room they came to had a modern lock on the door. Luke ran the scanner twice but there was nothing sinister that he could see. Nor was the door actually locked. Matthew prodded it open. Luke went in first, followed by Matthew. Kohl remained in the doorway. Rossi ghosted to the head of the stairs which, in contrast to all the other staircases they'd encountered so far, were wide and straight. Finding a position at the top that covered the entrance below, he knelt and waited.

Cautiously, Luke and Matthew entered the room. Empty.

'No one,' reported Luke. 'Kohl, stay here. Matthew . . .' He indicated a short flight of stairs.

The next room was rather nicely appointed. But still empty of people.

'Well,' said Luke, looking around. 'Who lives in a place like this?'

'It's very medieval and . . .' Matthew's voice tailed away.

Luke frowned. 'Is that a throne?'

There was no response.

'Matthew?'

Matthew was standing very still, staring up at the Cloth of State, his eyes suddenly very bright and golden.

'Matthew?'

Matthew didn't move. Luke walked around him to stare into his face. 'Matthew? Talk to me.' He shook his shoulder.

'1483.'

'What?' Luke shook him again.

Matthew blinked. 'What?'

'You said 1483.'

Matthew seemed vague. 'The Map.'

'What about the Map?'

'I . . . What?'

Luke became impatient. 'Matthew, are you functioning or should I send you back to Hansen?'

'No . . . no, I'm fine.'

Luke turned to discover the viewing gallery above and behind them. 'What the hell's been going on here?' Another crash outside recalled him. 'No time to discuss that now. Let's keep moving.'

Collecting his team, they negotiated the final staircase and found themselves in the vestibule. An external flight of steps led to ground level.

Luke reported in. 'Dahl, this is Parrish. The keep is cleared.

Curtis and Rockmeyer are badly injured. Hansen's with them on the roof. Farrell, Rossi, Kohl and Parrish awaiting instructions.'

Dahl came back immediately. 'Leave Rossi on the door. You three get yourselves over here to me. I need every man I can get.'

'Copy that.'

36

Trainee Tucker, meanwhile, had allowed himself to be swept along with a small number of Henry Plimpton's men as they prepared to defend themselves and the tunnels.

He frowned. Their instructions – relayed by a big bald bloke – were to take up a position where the castle tunnel narrowed slightly and erect some sort of barricade which would, in the event of the castle falling, prevent the Time Police taking possession of the junction and, by extension, the Lizard Land tunnel. Clearly Henry Plimpton had no intention of surrendering his time-slip.

Strategically, this was not a good place to be. As soon as the Time Police had taken the castle – and sooner or later they would – they'd be pouring down this tunnel full of fire and fury. And God knows what had been – and possibly still was – pouring out of the Lizard Land tunnel. It was more than likely Tucker and his temporary colleagues would find themselves trapped between the two. True, Plimpton's options were limited, but this was not the place Tucker would have chosen to make a stand. He could see from their faces that others felt the same. The word *expendable* wasn't actually being spoken aloud, but their situation was definitely not good. Men were eyeing each other uneasily. Tucker frowned. There must be some way he could exploit this situation.

At the moment, however, despite the apparently pointless shouting and milling around, the job was getting done. Weapons had been distributed and he knew from his previous employment that Henry Plimpton's defence would be well organised and effective. His people might not be happy but they knew what they were doing. Tucker sighed. Time to introduce even more uncertainty into their lives.

Standing well back in the shadows, he drew a deep breath and pitched his voice to be heard over the commotion, 'Oh my God – look out. Look out. They're here. The dinosaurs are out. Run. Run. Save yourselves.'

He waited to see what would happen.

Someone said, 'What?' Others were staring around. 'What did he say?'

Tucker moved a little way to his left and grabbed someone's arm. 'Did you hear what he said? The dinosaurs are out!' He stared wildly around. 'They could be here any moment. We should get out of here now. We'll be sitting ducks in these narrow tunnels. I'm off.'

'No, you're not,' said Baldy, thrusting yet another weapon at him. 'There's no dinosaurs in this tunnel. Shut your mouth and do your job. The Time Police are here and the dinosaurs aren't. So get your arse in gear and take up your position.'

'But ... the dinosaurs,' said Tucker, because he felt the point needed reinforcing. He raised his voice again. 'We're facing the wrong way. They'll get us from behind. We won't stand a chance.'

'Yeah,' said someone behind him. 'We should fall back to the junction. Get out while we still can.'

'How?' demanded Baldy. 'Where are you going to go? The woods will be swarming with the bastards.' Whether he was referring to the Time Police or the dinosaurs was unclear. 'We make a stand here. Good strong defensive position. With luck, the Time Police and the dinos will fight it out between them, and all we'll have to do is mop up any survivors.'

Tucker frowned. Not a brilliant strategy, but not bad under the circumstances. Although not from his point of view, of course. He drew back into the shadows again just as the faint explosions started overhead. The assault on the castle had begun.

'Get ready,' shouted Baldy. 'Take up your position and stand your ground.'

Tucker found himself among a small group of men, all standing quietly behind a hastily assembled barricade of crates, boxes and overturned lockers. Their attention should have been on the tunnel ahead of them as they waited for the Time Police to make their appearance, but many were casting anxious glances back over their shoulders. Which meant that no one was looking at him. OK – now.

He gave a startled yell and leaped sideways. 'What's that? Something brushed against my leg.' He pointed into the shadows beyond. 'Oh shit – did you see that? They're here. The dinosaurs have found us. They're here. Look, there's another one over there. Shoot it.'

He fired his weapon into a dark corner. The next moment the air was full of blaster fire criss-crossing the small space and gouging lumps of rock from the walls. Half the men present were shooting blindly into the semi-dark. The other half very sensibly threw themselves to the ground to avoid stray weapons fire, ricochets and flying rock. Tucker crouched behind a substantial crate. Shit – suddenly this was not a healthy place to be. Not at all. Surely the same thought must have occurred to others.

'Evacuate,' he shouted. 'Get out. Get out now. They're here. Look out.' He pushed the man next to him, who staggered sideways into someone else. One of them fell over. Panic began to spread. Men were climbing over the barricade and running up the tunnel, firing as they went. Heading for the castle but running straight into the arms – he hoped – of Dahl and his teams.

Suddenly, everyone was moving. No one wanted to be caught here. They'd be the filling in a shit sandwich. Dinos on one side and Time Police on the other. Excellent.

Tucker began to edge his way along the wall. Time to find somewhere else to cause trouble. Not least because the Time Police would be upon them at any moment and Tucker had no intention of falling victim to friendly fire. Leaving the confusion behind him, he eased himself along the tunnel, heading for the junction, fairly confident no one would follow him towards the supposed dinosaurs.

And then the bloody lights came on. Someone had restored the power.

His first thought was *bugger*. He was completely exposed. And then things got even worse. Rounding a bend, he stopped dead.

His second thought was that this was very much a good news, bad news, worse news and disastrous news situation.

The good news was that the junction was not that far away.

The bad news was that, at some point, a ton of lockers had been overturned and a pair of raptors were investigating the contents. The worse news was that they immediately lost all interest in someone's boots and fixed their attention on Tucker.

The disastrous news was that there were dinosaurs already at the junction and more were joining them from the Lizard Land tunnel.

The two raptors were still staring at him. Tucker noticed they were wearing control collars.

A small dinosaur, running on all fours, appeared from round the bend and squealed in fear.

One of the raptors turned its head and, faster than lightning, snapped it up. Its companion snarled and made a grab for it. Fighting over their prey, the two raptors disappeared into the shadows.

Not that that eased the situation very much. There were other dinos here and not all of them seemed so food-oriented. There were other urges in play. Something the size of a donkey but with a horn like a unicorn was rubbing itself against the wall in a manner Tucker found quite disturbing. Two others had succumbed to the moment and were playing mummies and daddies, seemingly oblivious to their surroundings. There did not, fortunately, seem to be any more raptors, but shrieks, squeaks, hisses, roars, screams, trills and bellows all filled the air. Several fights had broken out and while they didn't appear to be doing each other a great deal of damage, several of the slower, smaller dinosaurs had been trampled underfoot.

There had also been a massive amount of bowel evacuation, which wasn't helping struggling dinosaurs to keep their feet. And, Tucker noticed with some dismay, while some male dinosaurs displayed – some sprayed. Massively. Like high-pressure hoses. The walls were dripping. The smell was overpowering. And the more they sprayed, the more the others displayed. Neck frills, spinal scales, crests – all the colours of the rainbow. Nor were the females to be outdone. Their displays happened at the other end, so to speak. Rumps and cloacas suddenly blushed red and peach in a kind of *here it is* display. Tucker found himself blushing and tried to tear his gaze away. It occurred to him that he might suddenly have acquired the dubious honour of being the first human to witness a dinosaur's cloacal kiss.

Someone grabbed his arm. He jumped a mile and brought up his blaster. Shit – it was the foreman, Beckett, festooned with dinosaur-handling equipment. Where had he come from? Tucker braced himself for recriminations. Beckett, however, had other priorities.

'We need to get everyone out,' he shouted. 'I don't know what's got into them all – they've gone insane.'

'Yeah,' said Tucker. 'You probably missed it, being busy in the other tunnel, but the Time Police have arrived and they've been spraying the area with some sort of randy dino spray. To lure them back here.' He gestured at the ever-growing number of dinosaurs. 'Seems to have worked.'

Beckett cursed mightily. 'You think? Look at the state of them. We're going to be completely overrun. Some of my people are trapped back there. They've barricaded themselves in. We had no chance to fix the safety line. This is not going to get any better. We need to evacuate everyone. Now.'

Tucker could see a small group of grim-faced men, backs to the wall, fending off randy dinosaurs with their prods and hungry dinosaurs with their blasters. They were doing a sterling job and having no impact whatsoever. In fact, the dinosaurs were beginning to work their way along the castle tunnel.

'We can't go back the way I came,' said Tucker. 'The Time Police are here.'

Beckett shook his head. 'Makes no difference. We're all trapped, and if we don't sort this little lot, then they'll go down with us.'

'OK,' said Tucker. 'Let's pull back. I'll talk to the Time Police. They're not stupid – they'll see the problem.' He gestured at the dinosaurs behind them. 'We deal with the more immediate threat and then those of us still alive can fight it out afterwards.'

Beckett nodded and grabbed the nearest of his men. 'We need to pull back up the tunnel. Get everyone moving.'

More men were streaming down the passage from the barricade. Tucker waved his arms. 'Dinosaurs. Can't get through. Go back.'

'Time Police,' shouted one man. 'Behind us.'

'The least of our problems,' said Beckett. He gestured over his shoulder. 'The dinos are all fighting and fucking and when they've finished that, they'll be hungry. We definitely don't want to be this close. Back up the tunnel.'

A combination of Beckett's authority and Tucker's size clinched the argument. Not without many nervous glances over their shoulders, everyone retreated back up the tunnel towards the makeshift barricade, where four or five men still crouched, peering around, trying to cover all angles at once.

'You,' said Baldy, standing up and pointing his gun at Tucker.

'No time for that,' said Tucker, walking past him to the barricade. 'Everyone be quiet.'

'Who are you to . . . ?' began Baldy.

'Shut up and listen,' said Beckett.

That Beckett had authority and respect was obvious. They shut up and eyed Tucker. He took a deep breath and strove to make his voice audible over the sounds of dinosaurs giving way to their baser urges not that far behind them.

'Dahl? Lt Dahl? Can you hear me?'

'What the . . . ?' said one man, raising his gun.

Beckett gently pushed it away. 'We have worse problems than the Time Police at the moment,' he said quietly.

Tucker tried again. 'Can anyone hear me? Is Lt Dahl there?'

A voice shouted, 'Tucker? Is that you?'

'It is.' He paused – completely unable to resist. 'Is that you, Wu?'

Wu was not impressed. 'Stop pissing about, Tucker.'

'We have a problem. I'm coming up the tunnel towards you. Don't shoot.' He turned back to Beckett. 'Don't let anyone open fire. Don't let them start a war we can't win.'

Beckett nodded.

Tucker kicked aside a few crates and a locker.

Slowly and very cautiously, Wu appeared from around the bend.

Behind Tucker, someone shouted a warning. Tucker heard the sound of weapons being readied.

Behind Wu, another someone shouted a warning. TPOs appeared, weapons raised.

Tucker turned around and waved his arms at Plimpton's men. 'Weapons down. Now. Don't make me come back there.' He turned back to the massed ranks of TPOs. 'The same for you. No one's shooting anyone. We have bigger problems.'

'Yeah?' said Wu.

'Yeah. Just back there – dinosaurs – and not just any old dinosaurs – sex- and drug-crazed dinosaurs. *Hungry* sex-and drug-crazed dinosaurs. And there's more pouring through the tunnels every minute. Now imagine if they come pouring down the tunnel while we're all busy measuring dicks in the dark. We wouldn't stand a chance. It's in our own interests to work together.' He gestured behind him. 'These people have the expertise. They've been doing this a long time. We have the manpower. We work together to get them back where they belong. *And* shut down the time-slip. *Then* we shoot each other.' Tucker grinned. 'It's what we have to do, Wu.'

'You have got to be kidding,' said Wu, raising his weapon. Whether to fire on hostiles or Tucker was not clear.

'No, he's not,' said Beckett, stepping forwards. 'And we don't have long.' He raised his voice. 'Any of my crew – to me now. Bring whatever you can to control these fuckers.'

For one nasty moment, Tucker was unsure whether he was referring to the dinos behind them or the Time Police up ahead.

'Can't we just shoot them?' enquired Wu.

Beckett was angry. 'They're fast, furious, pumped up with pheromones – thanks to you lot – hungry and armoured. But by all means give it a go. We'll wait here while you trot off and die.'

Wu sighed and turned to review his crew. 'All right, people – we take our instructions from this man.'

'What?' said someone, safely anonymous at the back. 'No way.'

Tucker took a pace forwards and loomed.

Wu nodded at Beckett. 'We'll work with you. For the time being.'

'Good decision. And we'll work with you. For the time being.' Beckett raised his voice. 'Pay attention. Simple guidelines. Don't make the mistake of thinking the small ones are harmless. They're not. Those standing upright will probably try to eat you. If they're big, ugly, and on all fours, then get out of their way or they'll crush you flat because they didn't see you. Every single dinosaur back there is capable of killing you in one way or another. My people are wearing these . . .' He gestured down at his grey coveralls. 'Stay close to them and do as they tell you. Without question. That goes for everyone. This is our job and we know what we're doing.'

Wu turned to his teams. 'You heard the man. Let's get organised.'

37

It was pandemonium. Dinosaurs of every shape, size and inclination were crammed into the confined space of the tunnel. A raptor grabbed a small birdlike lizard with some kind of golden feathery crest and, in two rapid gulps, swallowed it whole. As he did so, something large and horned backed into him and he was crushed against the rockface.

'Couldn't we just leave them to kill each other?' demanded someone.

Beckett was adamant. 'No. We have to gain control here. We need to herd them back through the slip and into their own time. Once that's done, we can work on the safety line and get that working again. Everyone will be safer then.'

'All right,' said Wu. 'And then we collapse the tunnel. Bury the time-slip.'

Beckett shook his head. 'You might want to wait a day or so – it'll take some of the slower ones that long to get back here. But yeah – collapsing the tunnel is a good idea.' He hesitated. 'If you like, I can show you the best place to . . . you know . . .'

With one eye on his team's hasty preparations and one eye on the heaving mass of dinosaurs down the tunnel, Wu nodded. 'Appreciated. How do you normally control them?'

'Shoot them with sedative.'

'Do you have any with you?'

'Some – not a lot. We just grabbed what we could and ran.'

'But you have some?'

'Yes. And we should prioritise. Tell your people to shoot the raptors first – the carnivores. But that won't solve all our problems. The little ones are too fast to shoot and it takes a lot to put the big ones down. Especially now your chemical cocktail has really got them going.'

'So what do you suggest? Get behind them and push?'

Beckett grinned. 'Exactly.'

Wu surveyed what was rapidly becoming a dense block of overexcited dinosaurs.

Beckett continued. 'They're packed solid and don't really have room to resist. So, we tear off locker doors. Hold them vertically. Think riot shields. A barrier. Protection. Then we get behind and push them in the direction they already want to go but are too confused, scared or randy to realise. Back to Lizard Land.'

'Yes,' said Wu. 'Good tactics. We form two lines – one behind the other. First line with shields – a phalanx – and the second row behind them with cattle prods, batons, sedatives and very gentle sonics. We can't pick them up and carry them so they need to be able to move under their own steam.'

'And lights,' said Beckett. 'As many as we can muster. Head torches, hand torches – whatever. Front line applies gentle pressure. Second line reinforces that. Remember, we're only moving them – not battering them.'

Wu turned to his officers. 'Right, form a solid line. No gaps. Everyone relies on the people on either side and they rely on you. Watch your footing. Do not go down. You won't get back up again. Slow and steady – we ease them back down the tunnel, through the time-slip, and back to where they belong. And we work together. Let's do this.'

Beckett's men had already made a start on vandalising the lockers. Tucker seized a door and under the direction of Beckett and Wu, they formed up. Mainly TPOs on the front line . . .

'For weight,' said Beckett, straight-faced.

. . . with Beckett's men behind them . . .

'Where it's safe,' said Wu, not bothering to keep his face straight at all.

'OK,' said Beckett. 'Slow and steady. Advance. One . . . two. One . . . two.'

They began to shuffle their way forwards. Short steps. Feet flat on the ground. Knees bent. Almost feeling their way, because they couldn't afford to take their eyes off the dinosaurs ahead of them. Not even for a second. Someone at the back shouted the timing. 'One . . . two. One . . . two.' The gap between pushers and pushees slowly closed. And then they met.

'Put your backs into it,' shouted Beckett. 'Keep pushing. Keep the rhythm. Keep moving forwards. They'll get the message.'

They did. Imperceptibly at first, the whole tangle of sex-crazed dinosaurs began to move.

Tucker found himself next to the bald bloke.

'I've got a kid,' said the bald bloke – right out of the blue.

'Is that so?' said Tucker cautiously, putting his back into it as instructed.

'And when he asks – what did you do at the office today, Daddy? I have to tell him I waded through a ton of shit to press my face against a dinosaur's wobbly backside and push.'

Before Tucker could reply, the bald bloke's foot slipped in something unspeakable and he went down on one knee. The pressure was inexorable; the rank behind them would not stop. Another few seconds . . . Instinctively Tucker grabbed his arm and hauled him upright again.

'Thanks,' said the bloke.

'Try telling him you're an accountant,' suggested Tucker, as they pushed again, 'and offer to explain double-entry book-keeping to him. I often find that discourages further enquiries.'

'You got kids?'

'No.'

They eased their way forwards. Quietly. No shouting. No sudden noises. Just continual pressure. Occasionally, an arm would reach over Tucker's shoulder and apply a gentle sonic to a recalcitrant dinosaur rump. It all seemed to be going well but no one was under any illusion. This was incredibly dangerous. It would only take one or two to step backwards for any reason at all and a large number of TPOs and Time criminals would be crushed between the wall and a well-armoured backside.

But the dinosaurs were moving. The urge to return to their own time and place was strong. And the aftermath of the elephant pheromones seemed to be making at least some of them quite sleepy. Slowly humankind was regaining control.

The junction and the town tunnel were behind them now. Had anyone the inclination – or even the opportunity – to look back, they would have glimpsed scenes of utter devastation. There were great piles of droppings everywhere. Stress and a plant-based diet had certainly facilitated throughput. There were crushed lockers, their contents strewn across the floor and trampled. Flattened cages and crates had been massive trip hazards – still were, and they needed to watch where they put their feet at all times – but this was working. Tucker caught Beckett's eye and eased his way out of the line before they reached the time-slip. He had things to do. He slipped back along the tunnel and, gradually, the sounds of the Cretaceous retreated further and further into the distance.

A few TPOs remained at the junction. Tucker seated himself on a battered but intact crate and someone passed him some water.

'Cheers.'

He was handing back the bottle when Grint and Jane appeared out of the town tunnel. Their ordeal had obviously been even greater than his. Both looked completely and utterly wrecked.

With some relief, Jane divested herself of her spraying equipment and dropped it to the ground. The tank was nearly empty anyway. She found herself somewhere to sit, rested her elbows on her knees and closed her eyes.

A minute later, Luke and Matthew appeared from the castle tunnel.

Matthew's face was grubby but his grin stretched from ear to ear. 'Jane.'

'Matthew. Luke. You're here. You made it.'

'We did,' said Matthew proudly. 'And Luke is almost completely uninjured too.'

'As are you,' said Jane, smiling at him. 'What were you saying about problems at TPHQ?'

'Their systems went down.'

'What – all of them?'

'Yes. I don't know exactly, but they downloaded something and it corrupted everything. It's all under control now.'

Jane narrowed her eyes. 'And where were you while all this was going on?'

'In the Time Map.'

'Oh God, Matthew, you haven't broken it again, have you?'

'No,' he said indignantly. 'Why does everyone always think . . . ? Of course not.'

'Only I remember the last time and . . .'

'I didn't break the . . .'

'And the Map Master shouting and . . .'

'The Time Map is fine, Jane.'

'So they haven't had to send you here to keep you safe from her?'

'Not this time.'

'Well, it's good to see you again.'

He grinned. 'You saw me only an hour or so ago.'

'Yes, but a lot's happened since then.'

It occurred to Jane that Luke was being uncharacteristically quiet.

She looked up to find him staring at her with an expression she'd never seen before. Guilt rushed over her. How could he possibly . . . ?

Blushing, she looked away.

Grint looked around. 'Who's in charge here?'

'Me, I suppose,' said Tucker. 'Wu's supervising the return of the dinosaurs. Lt Dahl is in the castle – just down that tunnel there.'

'Any sign of Henry Plimpton?'

'Not down here. My betting is that he pushed off at the first sign of trouble because that's what he usually does in situations like this. If his people prevail, then he simply comes back and picks up from where he left off. If they don't, then none of them ever see him again.'

'He's got to be here somewhere,' said Grint grimly. 'All exits will be guarded. Pods disabled. There's no way out for him. When Wu comes back, get him to put a proper guard on the junction. One-way traffic only. Nothing and no one gets out.'

Tucker nodded.

'Where are Two-Three-Five?'

There was a pause during which it was very obvious that Luke wasn't going to speak.

'Up top,' said Matthew. 'Still taking the castle.'

Grint surveyed them all.

'Wait here, all of you. Until we have Henry Plimpton in custody, I don't want any of these tunnels left unguarded. Eyes on at all times.'

There was a pause until Matthew eventually said, 'Yes, sir.'

'Tucker – with me.' Grint strode away.

Luke was still staring at Jane. She blushed even harder.

'I'm surprised you can still do that,' said Bolshy Jane. 'After . . . you know . . .'

Still Luke had not said a word. A circumstance so unusual that Matthew had just turned to him to ask what was wrong when the first casualties started to stagger back from the Lizard Land tunnel. Most were TPOs but one or two were Plimpton's men in their grey coveralls. What could be seen of them through the mud, blood and dubious substances, anyway. Most smelled really bad and one or two had been lightly mauled.

Their field medic, Hansen, was still up on the roof, presumably supervising the medical evacuation of badly injured officers, so Jane and Matthew started first aid. Everyone seemed to be covered in a wide range of bodily fluids, some of which were hardening to a kind of crust.

'Eww,' said Jane, trying not to wonder what she was wiping off someone's damaged arm.

None of the wounds were too serious. Minor crush injuries and a few nasty nips. Someone had accidentally sonicked themself and one shocked and staggering soul was almost completely caked in every kind of dinosaur secretion and making vague but very ineffective efforts to clean himself up.

Luke abruptly stood up. 'Right – those who can, make your way along this tunnel. Report to the TPOs at the other end. Down there.' He gestured down the tunnel.

With brief words of thanks for the treatment, the casualties climbed to their feet and began to straggle down the tunnel. One man was cradling an obviously broken arm. Matthew winced in sympathy. The one wearing this year's fashionable look in bodily fluids had found an old towel from somewhere and was rubbing away at the crap on his face.

Jane watched them pick their way slowly through the debris and droppings. Something at the back of her mind was clamouring for attention. She turned to Luke, who was frowning as he watched the last of the men trickle around the bend. Their gazes met and suddenly she knew what it was. Because while it's easy to conceal your face – with a towel and a ton of dinosaur shit, for instance – it's almost impossible for a person to disguise their rear view. And one of those men had a very distinctive rear-view shape. Matthew too was staring along the tunnel with his mouth open.

'Um . . .'

Realisation smote them all simultaneously.

'Fire truck,' said Luke, straightening up.

Instinctively Matthew reached for his com.

'Won't work,' snapped Luke.

Jane was already running. 'Luke, Matthew – that's Henry Plimpton. He mustn't get away. After him.'

Shouting to the remaining TPOs to stay put, they set off.

'I don't fire-trucking believe it,' shouted Luke as the three of them pounded along. 'How did he get down here?'

'Trying to get away, obviously. And when he found he couldn't, he took refuge among his own people. He walked right past us. Again. And we let him go. Again.'

Their progress was not as fast as they could have wished. The three of them slipped, tripped and slithered their way along the tunnel. Matthew, slightly hampered by his broken arm, was finding it particularly hard going.

'Go on,' he yelled. 'I'll catch you up. Go.'

He dropped back a little with his com. Which made sense. Leave Jane and Luke to pursue Plimpton – it was vital someone warned Dahl – which Matthew could do as soon as he was far enough away from the time-slip . . . Disguised in his grey coveralls and with his intimate knowledge of the castle, Henry Plimpton could not – must not – be allowed to escape. With luck, he would head for his pods in the courtyard, and if Dahl was waiting for him, then there really would be no place to hide.

Jane could hear Matthew shouting into his com, 'Lt Dahl. Come in. Can anyone hear me? This is Farrell – we've located Henry Plimpton. He's ahead of us in the tunnel. Making for the castle. Wearing grey coveralls. Don't let him get away again. Lt Dahl. Come in. For God's sake – can anyone hear me?'

Matthew's voice faded into nothing behind them.

She and Luke followed the tunnel. 'Where does this lead?' he shouted.

Jane consulted her visor display. 'To the castle. There – up those stairs, I think.'

They stumbled up a long flight of stairs. She could hear voices. Not that far away. Had they got him already? They must have. There was nowhere for him to go. Luke was just ahead of her. Matthew was somewhere behind them. Every exit would be guarded. There was no way Plimpton could escape. And yet he always did. Every time.

Her heads-up display told her there was a courtyard up ahead. Surely Matthew had made contact by now. Dahl or Grint would be waiting for him there. She and Luke would burst out of the door to find Plimpton on his knees, hands behind his head, caught in the light of Delta Zero One's spotlights, twenty guns or more pointing at him.

The sounds of conflict grew louder as they made their way through the castle proper – along narrow passages, up steps, around corners.

'Try your com now we've cleared the time-slip,' shouted Luke. 'Warn Grint.'

Jane dropped back and pulled out her com. Luke carried on alone. More slowly now, because there was chaos all around. Bodies on the floor. Whose and whether they were alive or dead, Luke had no idea and no time to check. Something was on fire somewhere. Smoke drifted along the passageway. There was a door ahead. He could feel fresh air.

The thick wooden door took him out into the courtyard where he stared at a scene of chaos. Officers were moving across the yard in a search pattern. And there was only one person for whom they could be searching. The pods were under guard and there was no way in the world Henry Plimpton could access them. He had to be here somewhere.

Delta Zero One clattered overhead, its downward searchlights jerking across the courtyard. Ranks of prisoners sat against the walls, their hands on their heads. Luke scanned them with growing disbelief.

'He's not here. How the fire truck could we have missed him?'

'Easily,' said Jane, catching up with him. 'Off with the grey coveralls and on with the stab vest and helmet grabbed off an unconscious TPO – it's dark and he's one of us.'

Luke gritted his teeth. No one had ever said anything – to their faces – but Team Weird had been Plimpton's original arresting officers. Back in their training days. He'd given them the slip and they'd had to chase him through a 20th-century housing estate. That had not been 236's finest hour. Luke was determined that was absolutely not going to happen this time.

He looked across at the entrance to the keep. No sign of Rossi. With the keep cleared, had Dahl redeployed him elsewhere? The battle was by no means won yet. Plimpton could still get away.

He resisted the urge to punch the wall. 'Fire truck. Fire-trucking fire-trucking fire truck. He's got to be somewhere. Think, Jane. Where would you hide?'

'Not hide,' said Jane, standing beside him. 'Escape.'

With one accord, they both looked up at the helicopter now hovering over the keep. Jane chinned her mic and spoke to Grint.

Matthew appeared behind them, breathless. 'Where is he? Did you get him?'

Luke ground his teeth. 'We missed him, but we think we know where . . .'

Jane interrupted. 'I've updated Grint. He's pinned down in one of the towers. I'm toning down his language, but basically we're to come back with Plimpton or not at all.'

'In that case,' said Luke, and for the first time in his life, 'we'd better do as we've been told. Today's the day we get that bastard. I'm just in the mood. To the keep.'

They crossed the courtyard and climbed the external staircase. The heavy wooden door was still open and they entered the gloomy first floor. Luke looked up. 'Don't bother watching our rear, Matthew. That bastard's up there somewhere. I just know it.'

Cautiously they made their way up the irregular stairs.

'Listen,' said Jane, tilting her head. 'The chopper's coming in to land.'

'Medevac,' said Luke. He stopped dead. '*That's* how he intends to get away, Jane. Either disguised as a casualty or by forcing Bailey . . .' He stopped at the unlikelihood of anyone forcing Bailey to do anything.

'Hostages,' said Matthew suddenly. 'Curtis and Rockmeyer. Or even Hansen.'

'Shit,' said Jane, without even thinking about it. Because even now, this could all go horribly wrong. Was Henry Plimpton about to slip through their fingers for the umpteenth time? That just couldn't happen. Not again. It just couldn't.

'Matthew,' said Luke. 'Go and find Dahl or Grint. We need reinforcements. Then join us asap. Come on, Jane. Run.'

They ran. It seemed to Luke that there were far more stairs going up than there had been coming down. He took them two at a time, buoyed up by his desire to take down Henry Plimpton, but also by a savage regret in the pit of his stomach. Jane and Grint. He knew it. Jane's face. He'd missed his chance. Jane, he suspected – he knew – wasn't the type to do . . . that . . . without feelings. Without love. Jane was a one-man woman and he, Luke, was not that man. He was too late. Endless stairs. Round and round. Too late. Too late. Too late.

The door to Romulus's room was open. The room was empty.

'Hostage,' said Jane at once. 'That's going to make things a little trickier.'

'Not for me,' said Luke grimly. 'The bloke disappears, remember? No one ever knows what happened to him. Nothing to say he doesn't die here.'

The noise of Delta Zero One was suddenly louder.

'She's landing,' shouted Luke.

He raced on ahead while Jane slowed to a trot and chinned her mic. 'Delta Zero One. Delta Zero One. Do not land. I repeat – do not land. We have a hostage situation here. Henry Plimpton is attempting to escape. Do not land.'

Not concentrating on where she was going, she fell victim to one of the uneven steps and fell heavily. Good job she was wearing a helmet.

Someone said something in her ear, but now the noise of Delta Zero One overhead was deafening.

Jane scrambled to her feet, caught up with Luke, and they stumbled up the last flight of rubble-strewn stairs together, finally arriving, breathless and bruised, at the top. Cautiously, Luke peered out through the shattered door. Behind him, Jane snapped down her visor, ready for anything. He could hear her blaster whining.

He risked another look.

Shit.

They were too late.

Luke drew back. 'Jane – we might not get out of this. Is there anything you want to say before . . . you know?'

'Well, St Mary's always says it's been an honour and a privilege.'

He smiled sadly. 'That's the one thing they've managed to get right. Ready?'

She lifted her blaster. 'Got your back, Luke.'

Luke resisted the perfect opportunity to say, 'And my heart,' contenting himself with the slightly more appropriate, 'This is it, Jane. Today's the day we finally get our man.'

Slowly and carefully, he eased his way through the shattered door and out on to the windy roof.

The first thing he noticed was the faint band of light in the sky. The sun would be up soon. Heralding another long day in the Time Police. Unless, of course, they didn't live long enough to make it to breakfast.

The second thing was Delta Zero One, squatting on the roof, black and enormous against the lightening sky, rotors turning slowly. Luke could see Bailey, staring out at them. The sliding doors were firmly closed. It would appear Bailey was not complying with Plimpton's demands. Although, to be fair, she rarely complied with anyone's demands.

Hansen, weaponless, was crouching over Curtis and Rockmeyer, both of whom had been prepped for medevac, strapped to stretchers and waiting to be loaded.

And Henry Plimpton – minus coveralls but wearing a Time Police vest and helmet just as Jane had predicted – was almost completely concealed behind a very wet and wobbly king of Rome and with his gun pointing directly at the helpless Hansen. The only person on the roof likely to be a threat to him.

Luke drew a deep breath. Henry Plimpton would not escape him today. The Time Police weren't St Mary's. Romulus was expendable. Whatever happened, whoever else died, Henry Plimpton was going down. With extreme prejudice.

Plimpton was bellowing at the chopper. Luke could hear words but couldn't make them out. It seemed safe to assume he was trying to force Bailey to fly him out of here. He was wasting his time. The order was out – take him down. At any cost. He wouldn't be going anywhere.

Luke slid silently along the wall and then stopped. Jane was six feet to his right, crouching in the doorway. Classic Time Police procedure. One left – one right. One high – one low. The good news was that Henry Plimpton, his attention on his hostages and the helicopter, was not yet aware of their presence. Which was just as well because the both of them were completely exposed.

Dahl's voice sounded in his ear. 'Secure the situation. Eliminate Henry Plimpton.'

Jane responded. 'He has a hostage. Romulus.'

'You have your orders, Two-Three-Six.'

The heavily built Romulus was doing an excellent job of masking Henry Plimpton. A shot from this position was impossible. Luke briefly contemplated shooting through Romulus, but the chances of any projectile making its way through the bulky king of Rome was unlikely. And then, of course, Plimpton would know they were there. And there were the other hostages to consider.

Stalemate. The great rotors swooped overhead. The sun was coming up. Dawn was breaking. And Henry Plimpton was still pointing his gun at Hansen. The message was clear. Plimpton would board the chopper or people would start to die.

Jane shifted her position fractionally but it was useless. She couldn't get a clear shot. Not from this angle. She glanced across at Luke. He was even more badly situated than she was.

She rather thought she could hear feet on the stairs below them. The requested reinforcements. Matthew must have got to Dahl. Fat lot of good they would be now. Their only purpose would be to increase the number of impotent TPOs watching their number one Time criminal escape. Again.

To her left, Luke had moved slightly, pulling out a handgun. What was he . . . ?

And then Jane realised what he was planning. She stepped swiftly back through the door and held up her hand, palm outwards, as Dahl, Matthew and three others rounded the bend, stumbling on the rubble as they came. The universal sign for halt. Dahl and his team stopped and waited. Daylight was growing stronger every second. She could see their faces behind their visors.

Luke was still moving – easing himself along the wall. Inch by inch. Because peripheral vision is much more acute than face-on. Plimpton had only to turn his head a fraction and Luke would be revealed.

Jane never remembered consciously making the decision. Stepping back out on to the windy roof, she made herself as visible as possible and shouted, 'Hey.'

Not exposing himself in any way, Plimpton turned his head to look at her.

Jane strove to make her voice heard over the noise of the chopper. 'Henry Plimpton, you are under arrest. Drop your weapon. Get down on the ground. Now.'

He shouted something in return – no one heard what – brought up his gun and fired straight at Hansen, who toppled sideways. Then he took aim at the helpless Curtis.

The message was clear, but Luke would not allow himself to be rushed. Jane was holding Plimpton's attention but not for much longer. A tiny handful of seconds at the very most . . . Very, very slowly, Luke brought up his handgun and took very, very careful aim . . .

There was no music now. Barnacle Bill had long since fallen silent. Sitting in her cockpit, watching and waiting, Bailey's hand drifted slowly towards the collective pitch control . . .

Just one tiny step more . . . Luke remembered not to hold his breath. Nearly . . . nearly . . .

He breathed out and fired.

They all saw the impact. Upper right thigh. Romulus's leg buckled and he fell heavily to the ground.

Suddenly released from his weight, Henry Plimpton staggered backwards, struggling to maintain his balance.

Bailey's left hand grasped the collective. Now. The engine

note changed as she moved from ground idle to flight idle, altering the angle and pitch of the rotors . . .

The air turned suddenly red as finely chopped pieces of Henry Plimpton spiralled upwards and outwards to splat over a very large area of the roof.

Delta One's engine note changed again, the rotors slowed, slowed, slowed . . . and stopped. The chopper settled back on its wheels. Desultory gunfire below indicated the battle was nearly won, but up here on the rooftop, there was only sudden silence. No one moved until Jane shouldered her blaster and ran forwards to check on Hansen.

Bailey emerged from the cockpit to check for damage to the rotors. Luke stared at her. And then down at himself and his colleagues, all of them lightly pebble-dashed with chopped-up Henry Plimpton. No one spoke. The end had come too quickly for them yet to take it in.

Bailey turned from examining the last rotor and grinned at her stunned colleagues.

'Now you know why we call them choppers.'

The next moments were somewhat confused.

Leaving Hansen to the attention of another field medic, Jane crossed to Luke, leaning back against the wall. He lifted his blood-splattered visor.

'Luke – that was . . . an amazing shot. You got him.'

He managed a grin. 'Well, technically, Jane, you're the arresting officer, so you got him.'

She put her hand on his arm. 'Well done.'

He closed his eyes. 'Yeah.'

Dahl was leaning over Hansen. 'Still breathing?'

Hansen grimaced. 'Just about. Shit, that . . . stings.'

'Your armour turned it back.'

'Still hurts like fuck, sir.'

Grint appeared in the ruined doorway, surveying his gore-splattered officers and what little was left of Henry Plimpton. 'Is there enough for a formal ID?'

Dahl indicated the remains. 'Yeah – we all saw it happen.'

'Who's taking the credit for this one?'

'Well, Lockland's the arresting officer. Parrish fired the shot. Bailey took care of the wet work. Take your pick.'

Grint straightened up and looked across at Bailey, now supervising loading the wounded. Catching his eye, she shook her head.

'I'm calling it, then.' He looked at his watch. 'Time of death – 0610.' He turned to Jane, Luke and Matthew. 'You've got the credit for this one. Well done, Two-Three-Six.'

Meanwhile, with the majority of dinosaurs returned to their rightful habitat, Wu, Beckett and their respective teams were emerging from the Lizard Land tunnel.

'Right,' said Wu. 'I think we all know what happens next. Now, no one particularly wants to handle anyone else – not given the state of us – so please don't give us any trouble.'

'Give me a beer,' said Beckett, sitting heavily on an already battered crate, 'and I'll tell you everything you want to know. I'll even make stuff up if you like.'

Tucker frowned. 'Tell you what,' he said to Wu. 'Why don't you take everyone to the mess hall just up there? That way you can all have a drink while taking their statements.' He nodded to the town tunnel. 'I'll keep Beckett here with me to supervise any late arrivals. In case of problems.'

Wu nodded and everyone shunted themselves off for an enthusiastic beer.

Tucker and Beckett regarded each other. Tucker cut his eyes to the town tunnel.

Beckett sat very still.

Tucker did it again.

Beckett stared at him.

Tucker sighed. 'Go.'

'What?'

'Go on. Go.'

Beckett didn't move. 'Shot while trying to escape, eh?'

Tucker rolled his eyes.

'Why? Why would you let me go?'

'I was you. Once. Someone gave me another chance. I'm repaying the favour.'

Beckett nodded towards the castle tunnel and the mess hall. 'What will you tell them?'

Tucker shrugged. 'You overcame me and escaped.'

Beckett eyed the size of Tucker. 'Yeah. Right.'

'OK – there was an unfortunate accident with one of the big dinos. You were crushed.'

Beckett looked around. 'Where's my body?'

'Jeez,' said Tucker. 'You just can't help some people. You were eaten. OK? Now piss off.'

He turned and subjected a portion of wall to intense scrutiny.

When he turned back, Beckett had gone.

Somewhat wearily, Commander Hay seated herself at her desk and contemplated her in-tray with absolutely no enthusiasm at all. Across the room, her screen flickered and emitted a series of electronic bleeps as, one by one, systems came back online and TPHQ slowly resumed its place in the world.

Captain Farenden entered, bearing coffee.

'Oh Charlie, I was just about to ask. Thank you.'

'An update, ma'am. Varma and Maxwell are both in MedCen. Or rather, they were. Varma has discharged herself and Maxwell is demanding to return to St Mary's.'

Hay sipped her coffee. 'What does the doctor say?'

'Yes to Varma and no to Maxwell. It's a very nasty blaster burn.'

'Any news of North?'

'Not yet, ma'am.'

'I suppose that's good news. Curtis? And Rockmeyer?'

'Rockmeyer will probably live to fight another day. Curtis is having his chest rebuilt and the outcome is . . . a little less certain.'

She sighed. 'Only a few hours ago he was clingfilmed to a toilet.'

'Life in the Time Police, ma'am. The king of Rome has also received medical attention.'

'Yes, we're going to have to decide what to do with him, aren't we?'

Farenden gave a slight nod. 'I'll give the matter some thought, ma'am. All other casualties, including Hansen, are comparatively minor and expected to survive.'

She sat back. 'We got him, Charlie.'

He grinned. 'We did indeed, ma'am. A good day's work.'

'And a hard night's drinking, I should imagine. Whenever the celebrations begin, tell the bar everyone's first drink is on me.' Hay closed her eyes and sipped again. 'You're lingering, Captain.'

'Ma'am . . .'

'Yes?'

'You asked me to look into who owns that castle in Wales.'

'Yes – I don't suppose you've been able to make a lot of progress, have you? What with one thing and another.'

'Actually, I didn't have time to make any progress at all, but I do have a friend in the Land Registry.'

Hay opened her eyes and regarded her adjutant with astonishment. 'Good heavens, Charlie – is there anywhere your tentacles cannot reach?'

'No,' he said simply. 'I gave her a call and she got right on it.'

'Well, good work. So, who's the bastard who doesn't know he's looking at a drastically reduced life expectancy?'

There was a very long pause.

Hay put down her coffee and narrowed her eyes. 'Charlie?'

He took a very deep breath. 'Before you ask, I have checked and double-checked. As has my contact.'

'All right. Out with it. Who is it? Who owns the castle?'

'Ma'am . . . it's registered to Raymond Parrish.'

Hay took off her spectacles and pinched the bridge of her nose. 'Say that again.'

'The owner of Castle Cudd is Raymond Parrish.'

'Since when?'

'It was acquired through a shell company just over seven years ago.'

'Is there any significance to seven years ago?'

'Not that I know of.'

'Well – this is a turn-up for the books, isn't it?' She thought for a moment. 'In the light of this knowledge, I want the Site X investigation reopened immediately. In fact, all of Raymond Parrish's properties are to be investigated. We're going to need to dig deep on this one. I'll put North on it.' Hay stopped suddenly. 'Oh, no. I won't.'

'With North's current condition in mind, ma'am, I took the liberty of initiating a preliminary check on known associates of Raymond Parrish.'

'I can't imagine that would be very helpful.'

'I stopped after the first ten pages when it became very obvious that I would need to refine my search a little. I started with Raymond Parrish's known Time Police connections. Mostly, I should add, for the sake of elimination. That search was suspended while we negotiated our way through our recent spot of bother with our systems, and I confess I had forgotten about it. I was quite surprised when the systems came back online and my printer suddenly spat out . . . this.' He handed her a printout. 'Fourth name down, ma'am.'

Hay put on her spectacles.

For a long time nothing happened and then, without looking up, she said, 'Thank you, Captain. That will be all for the time being.'

The door closed behind him.

Very carefully, Hay set down the paper and stared at it. As always, her face gave no clue to her thoughts.

Eventually, she roused herself.

'Computer?'

Apparently most systems were up and running again because the computer chirped its readiness.

'Bring up image Callen/TPO/5553434.'

The screen showed the official image of Major Callen.

'Computer – isolate the head and shoulders and designate the new image Hay/1A.'

'Complying.'

'Now access all security cameras within a one-hundred-yard range of Parrish Industries London HQ and review all the files for images of Hay/1A in that location.'

There was a slight pause. Things were obviously not completely back to normal. Gritting her teeth, Hay forced herself to be patient. Given the events of the day, she should be grateful for any sort of access at all.

Eventually, the computer responded. 'There are twenty-six confirmed images and a further one hundred and seven with a less than sixty per cent match.'

'Computer, list the twenty-six confirmed images in chronological order and display.'

'Displaying list.'

Hay studied the screen. 'Bring up the latest image of Raymond Parrish.'

'Image displayed.'

'Isolate head and shoulders and designate new image Hay/2A.'

'Complying.'

'Now show all images with Hay/1A and Hay/2A in close proximity.'

'State at which locations.'

'All locations within the specified range.'

'Complying.'

Images flickered and jumped across the screen. Most weren't perfect but they didn't have to be. There they were. Major Callen and Raymond Parrish. The two of them together. Everywhere. On the steps outside Parrish Industries HQ. Going in. Coming out. Walking together in the square. Sitting on a bench. Even one of Callen getting out of Raymond Parrish's car. That image of Parrish himself was poor but still definitely him.

And there had been no attempt at concealment. How typically arrogant of Callen. He'd gone in and out of the front door as bold as brass.

Hay drew a deep breath and forged on.

'Computer, open a secure file. My eyes only. Transfer all material to this file. Label the file Hay/1XX. Notify me of any attempt to access. Either on completion of my service or my death, file Hay/1XX is to be deleted and overwritten.'

'Complying.'

She opened her door.

'Captain Farenden, is Major Callen still in the building?'

'I believe so, ma'am.'

'Please bring him to my office.'

'Yes, ma'am.' He opened his com.

'No, fetch him personally, please.'

He looked puzzled for one moment. 'Yes, ma'am.'

As soon as the door closed behind him, she opened her com. 'Lt Varma?'

'Ma'am?'

'Are you fit to work?'

'I can function, ma'am.'

'Secure the line, please.'

'Stand by . . . line secure.'

'This building is in silent lockdown with immediate effect. All civilians are to be confined to the public areas. No Time Police personnel are to leave under any pretext.'

'Yes, ma'am.'

'I need you and a small squad up here. Wait in Captain Farenden's office until I send for you. Bring your toughest bastards.'

There was a short pause and then Varma said, 'Yes, ma'am.'

'Thank you, Lieutenant.'

She closed her com.

'Computer, display all financial records for subject Hay/1A.' She waited without much hope. Any important data would, no doubt, be protected behind the massive firewalls of offshore bank accounts. Much more difficult to trace, but not impossible. And she had the authority.

She didn't need it. There it was – in his ordinary high street accounts. All of it. The complacent bastard hadn't made the slightest attempt to conceal what were actually some very hefty deposits.

'Computer, send all these details to my printer and print. Then wipe the printer's memory and all buffers.'

'Complying.'

Less than five seconds later, her printer spat three sheets of closely packed printing at her, which Hay gathered up, squared off and placed face down on her desk.

Then she waited. Until the complete silence in her office became too much to bear, when she got up and stared unseeingly out of the window at the scene below.

By now the day was well advanced. In front of her, the Thames was packed with boats. Barges, water taxis, boy racers, party boats, river police. Even one of the few remaining Royal Navy gunboats on its way downstream. It was a perfectly normal day for the rest of the world.

Hay went into her private bathroom and washed her hands. The symbolic nature of this was not lost on her.

Finally she heard the door open in Captain Farenden's office, and seconds later, Major Callen was ushered in.

Captain Farenden took one look at his commanding officer's face and decided not to waste his time asking whether she wanted the meeting minuted or not. He closed the door on Major Callen and went to sit thoughtfully at his own desk. Only a moment later, Lt Varma entered, closely followed by a squad of four hefty security officers. Armoured. Helmeted. Visors down. Anonymous. Big blasters. Fully charged.

No one spoke. Captain Farenden stared down at his desk. The squad took up position – Varma against the wall where she could see everything, including Captain Farenden, one officer on each side of the outer door and two over by the window.

Everyone waited.

On the other side of the door, Major Callen and Commander Hay faced each other across her desk.

Eventually, Major Callen spoke. 'You sent for me, Commander?'

Hay opened her file and pulled out the images of Major Callen and Raymond Parrish. She spread them across her desk. Deliberately making her voice as expressionless as possible, she said, 'You've been careless, Major.'

He carefully surveyed each one and then shrugged. 'It has never been my intention to conceal the meetings.'

'You don't deny them?'

'I have done nothing illegal.'

'You have been working for Raymond Parrish.' She pushed over the financial statements. 'For some time now.'

'*With* Raymond Parrish,' he said. 'Not for.'

'To what end?'

'The apprehension of Time criminals.'

'You mean the Portmans.'

'Among others, but mostly – yes.'

'You hired yourself out to Raymond Parrish to help him rid himself of a major business rival.'

'The Portmans are Time criminals, Commander.'

'Proof?'

'At the moment – none. The Portmans are among the most powerful people in the world. I couldn't just kick down their front door and demand they accompany me back here. I needed evidence.' He gestured at the images. 'That is what I am working on obtaining.'

'Was that what you were doing when you interviewed Hooke? Less than one hour later and he was dead. Was that why you threatened Filbert with being thrown from a helicopter over the North Sea?'

'I was endeavouring to get Filbert to talk. And he did.'

'And died. As did Hooke. As did Officer Anders in the Pod Bay. At your hands.'

'On that occasion I was endeavouring to contain a situation that was rapidly spiralling out of everyone's control.'

'You were involved in the investigation into Site X?'

'I was, Commander.'

'Was Raymond Parrish not heavily implicated in its construction?'

'There was no proof of that.'

'There has never been any proof of Raymond Parrish's involvement in anything – thanks to you. You have been covering for him. To say nothing of passing on confidential information.'

'I have done no such thing. Rather the other way around.'

'For money.'

'For substantial sums of money, Commander.' He pointed to the statements. 'As you can see.'

'You don't deny it?'

'It's not illegal. Nothing in my contract precludes me working with other people or organisations. Nothing in anyone's contract. Many officers take on additional employment in their downtime. The wages here are hardly commensurate with the risks we undertake and London is one of the most expensive places in the world in which to live and work.'

'My officers take on bar work. Or casual labour. Or seasonal work. No one actually whores themselves out to commercial enterprises.'

'You wound me, Commander.'

'You're lucky I don't shoot you.'

'Thus rendering yourself open to the processes of law. I have done nothing wrong. Morally dubious, perhaps, but not illegal.'

'How many have died because you've been playing both sides of the game?'

'No one, Commander. Not one single person. And it's not as if I have been working for the other side. Raymond Parrish's aims and those of the Time Police are one and the same. By having access to both parties, I am able to facilitate the process. And have done so on many occasions.'

There was a short silence.

'You have never meant me anything but harm, have you?' Despite her best efforts, Hay was unable to keep the bitterness from her voice.

Callen opened his mouth to speak, appeared to reconsider, and closed it again.

'Nothing to say, Major?'

'Apparently not.'

'I could have you conveyed to Droitwich and executed.'

'I don't think your conscience would allow you to do that.'

'At this moment, I could very happily shoot you myself.'

'I have no doubt you could. Nor that the redoubtable Captain Farenden would assist with the disposal of my body afterwards. But I don't believe you will.'

'Don't be too sure about that.'

He tilted his head to one side. 'Why are you so furious, Commander? Nothing but good has come of my association with Raymond Parrish.'

'And what of your loyalty to the Time Police? What of your loyalty to me?'

He held her gaze. 'I assure you, Marietta, you have had and always will have my complete and unfailing loyalty.'

'And exactly how much is that worth?'

'Only you can know that.'

She narrowed her eyes. 'Must I bid for you against Raymond Parrish?'

Callen's face had a pinched white look she'd never seen before.

'Perhaps I should remove myself from your sight until we are both a little more composed, Commander. Shall I make an appointment for some time tomorrow when we can revisit this painful subject more calmly?'

'No. Get out. Out of this room. Out of this building. Out of the Time Police. Consider yourself dishonourably discharged. Never come back. Ever. If you're not gone in fifteen seconds, I'll have you arrested.' She pressed her intercom. 'You can come in now.'

The door opened to reveal Varma, gun drawn, with her squad fanned out behind her.

'Lieutenant, this person is to be escorted to his quarters where you will pack him an overnight bag. Personal items only. He is to be escorted out of the building. As discreetly as possible. I want no witnesses. Clear a path before you. Use the service lifts and take him out through Logistics. He is to speak to no one and no one is even to see him. None of you are to speak of this to others. You will answer no questions. You will not discuss this among yourselves. Please indicate your understanding of your orders.'

Varma and her squad nodded.

'Good. Mr Callen, from this moment, you are no longer

a member of the Time Police. All rank and privileges are stripped from you. Your clearances are rescinded. You may not contact or be contacted by anyone in this organisation. Your belongings will be searched and then, if deemed safe by Lt Varma, they will be forwarded on to an address to be provided by you. Together with any monies owing. Or deductions to be made. Whether you are eligible for a pension will be a matter for the finance committee. You will deposit your badge, your ID, your weapons, your com and your flashes on my desk.'

Callen stood as if frozen.

Hay sharpened her voice. 'Now, if you please. Or Lt Varma can take them from you.'

Lt Varma devoutly hoped it wouldn't come to that. Even with her stab wound, she would back herself against almost anyone in the Time Police – except Callen. Maybe one or two others as well, but definitely not Callen.

The silence stretched on and on. And on. Fingers tightened on triggers.

Finally, Callen seemed to draw a long breath. With hands that weren't quite steady, he peeled his weapons from their rip-grip patches, pulled his knife from his belt, and tugged off his shoulder patches. Slowly, he laid down the small wallet all officers carried containing their badge, service number and ID. Except when undertaking undercover work, this would be the first time he'd been without it during the entirety of his long service in the Time Police.

With all that done, he stepped back, swallowed hard, and said, 'I could hold out for a court martial. You'd never get a conviction.'

'You won't be given the opportunity. You've never done anything for me – why should I do anything for you?'

He gazed at her for a moment. 'Actually, Marietta . . .' and then appeared to change his mind. Suddenly the familiar mask was back in place. He said lightly, 'As you say, Commander – I've never done anything for you – why should I expect you to do anything for me?'

Receiving no response, he turned to Varma. 'Please present my compliments to Dr Maxwell when you next see her and tell her that, just for once, her comments regarding my future were exactly right.'

Varma said nothing.

He sighed. 'In your own time, Lieutenant.'

Varma nodded and her squad assumed the traditional formation. Two guards to clear the way. Then Callen. Two guards at his shoulder, with Varma at the rear where she could keep an eye on the slippery bastard. Because he was going too quietly.

She was right. Reaching the door, he turned back. 'This is just a friendly warning, Marietta. I will come for you. I know your sight is getting worse. You can't continue like this forever. And when that day comes, I will be waiting for you.'

Two officers pushed him out of the door, which closed behind them – and former Major Callen left the Time Police.

Captain Farenden, alone in his office once more, stared at his outer door, then the one into Hay's office and then back to the outer door again.

Picking up his phone, he diverted all Commander Hay's calls to himself and blocked access to her com.

Crossing to the connecting door, he raised his hand to knock, paused for a moment and then lowered it again. He returned to his desk, sat and waited.

Half an hour later he was still waiting.

His com bleeped.

'Varma?'

'Please inform the commander that her instructions have been carried out and TPHQ is again open for business.'

'Thank you.'

Again he crossed to Hay's door. Again he raised his hand to knock and again he had second thoughts.

Captain Farenden's office was always immaculate. Partly because he had realised very early on that unless he kept on top of things, he would be submerged under a tsunami of paperwork – and partly because of a natural love of order and method. With perfect concentration, and not allowing his thoughts to distract him in any way, he ruthlessly reorganised his in-tray, filing quite a lot of it in the WPB file.

There was no sound from Commander Hay's office.

Sighing, he turned his attention to his pen tray. Then his desk tidy. From there he pulled open his top drawer, filling his stapler, sorting paper clips, recharging his portable devices.

Still no sound from Commander Hay's office.

He wiped down the coffee machine and topped up supplies.

Still no sound from Commander Hay's office.

Moving on to the walls, he pulled down out-of-date notices from the board and rearranged the others more neatly. He sorted the contents of his locker, checking over the spare uniform he kept for emergencies, his heavy-weather gear and so forth.

Still no sound from Commander Hay's office.

Hours had passed. No one had telephoned or knocked on

the door, or – in the case of Miss Meiklejohn – barged in and demanded his immediate attention. Captain Farenden was pretty sure that by now everyone in the building would know something serious had happened, but not exactly what. And any speculation would soon be overtaken by informal parties celebrating today's result.

With nothing left to do, he sat down to wait.

Evening approached. Still he waited, arms folded, his bad leg stretched out in front of him, his anxiety deepening with every passing moment. Twice he stretched out his hand to telephone Major Ellis – still in MedCen under observation, but presumably available for consultation. Twice he pulled it back again. Half of him fretted over what could possibly be happening in Hay's office and the other half told him to hold his nerve. She wouldn't thank him for broadcasting this afternoon's events around the building. Managing, at one and the same time, both to fret and hold his nerve, he sat and waited.

Never had his office seemed so quiet. It seemed safe to assume that celebrations had begun – and would continue for some time as officers drifted back from Wales, eager to celebrate their success. Normally he would have been with them. But not this evening. The silence was oppressive. At this point he would even have welcomed the fire alarms going off.

A chime indicated the end of the day watch, startling him. He hadn't realised it was so late. The lights came on and the windows opaqued. He looked at his watch. Surely Hay had been in there long enough for anyone to do whatever it was they needed to do to recover from . . . whatever it was they had to recover from.

Suppose she'd . . . done something. Suppose, even now, she

had only moments left to live while he sat uselessly out here in his office.

He'd give it another half hour and then risk life and limb and open the door. She still had that Italian stiletto knife – or letter opener, as she liked to refer to it. He hadn't had a chance to remove it beforehand. Suppose she'd used it . . .

No – if she hadn't stabbed Major Callen to the heart with it – for whatever it was that he'd done – then it wasn't likely she'd use it on herself.

But suppose that while he sat here dithering, the last of her life blood dripped slowly on to the carpet . . .

The door opened. 'Charlie – you're still here?'

Having grabbed a file at random, Farenden was now seemingly immersed in its contents. He looked up casually. 'Just finishing now, ma'am. Can I get you anything before I go? A coffee?'

'No, thank you. I think I'll head off for something to eat. And perhaps join them downstairs for a celebratory drink. It's been a long day.'

You could never go wrong with *yes, ma'am*.

'Yes, ma'am.'

'See you tomorrow, Charlie.'

'Yes. Goodnight, ma'am.'

She paused in the doorway. 'Thank you, Charlie.'

He smiled. 'You're welcome, ma'am.'

41

In Wales, the town tunnel remained open for seven days. During that time, a number and variety of dinosaurs quietly found their way back home, either under their own steam or persuaded by an imaginative combination of cattle prods and/or dead chickens.

Castle Cudd – now quite badly damaged in some places – was stripped and everything removed to TPHQ for investigation.

Under Time Police supervision, the time-slip was dynamited and sealed off forever. Which was both good news and bad news. Good news in that the modern world was now safe from dinosaurs – and the even better news that the dinosaurs were now safe from the modern world.

The bad news was that the ankylosaurus never made it. Back home, that is. It was some time before it could be persuaded to remove its backside from the library window and that – together with frequent pauses for rest and refreshment, and a complete lack of urgency in its psyche – led to its failure to make the seven-day deadline, leaving the Time Police somewhat conflicted over their next move. Spending its days wandering around Wales, sleeping on the A470, and eating people's front gardens was not considered to be of benefit to either the ankylosaurus or the population as a whole. Something had to be done. The public demanded it. A six-ton armoured dinosaur eating, trampling or crapping wherever it liked was never going to be popular.

The military refused to get involved. As did the police, the fire service and the Methodist church. Even Lt Bailey declined to attempt an airlift after her back-of-an-envelope maths told her very firmly that the idea would never – literally – get off the ground.

Commander Hay's suggestion that they put it down – humanely, she hastened to add – was met with worldwide outrage. As she knew it would be. Wales changed its collective mind overnight and claimed the dinosaur as their very own. A national campaign began.

'Well, of course I had no intention of shooting the bloody thing,' said Hay in exasperation, 'but we can't just allow it to wander Wales at will.'

'Actually, ma'am,' began Captain Farenden. 'There's been a suggestion.'

Hay regarded him shrewdly. 'You have very carefully not named your source, so can I gather this suggestion emanated from the always helpful Dr Maxwell?'

Captain Farenden declared himself unable to confirm or deny this statement. 'There's a wildlife park, ma'am. Near Tenby. They already have rhinos . . .'

'Are you suggesting we glue a horn to its forehead?'

'Unnecessary, ma'am – it already has four. I feel the addition of another one would be superfluous.'

Hay glared at him suspiciously, but her adjutant was consulting his scratchpad and missed it. 'And how exactly do we get it there?'

'We walk it, ma'am. Well, not us personally, but there are plenty of volunteers.'

'Across Wales.'

'Yes, ma'am.'

'And people are volunteering . . . ?'

'They are. In their hundreds. People are actually sponsoring them.'

'In that case, I think the Time Police should take a collective step backwards and let Wales get on with it.'

To cut a long story short – the epic trek was an international sensation. Guided by a combination of strategically placed elephant pheromones and fodder, the ankylosaurus wended its way across Wales, sometimes achieving as much as half a mile a day. Progress reports figured on the news every night. With satellite images. Google Earth tracked its every move. Crowds turned out to cheer it on its way. Children saved their pocket money to contribute towards the cost of feeding it. The world held its breath as, day by day, the ankylosaurus inched its way closer towards Tenby.

Matters moved up a gear when, after some deep-diving into one of her massive piles of dung, she was discovered to be female. A children's competition – *Name the Ankylosaurus* – was won by eleven-year-old Iestyn from Pontypridd who came up with Ankaret.

Excitement reached fever pitch as Ankaret drew near to her destination. Crowds lined the route, waving and cheering her on, until eventually, weighing considerably less than when she'd set out, she reached the wildlife park near Tenby, where she became their major attraction.

After a period of quarantine, Ankaret was moved into a paddock next door to the rhinos. There was a great deal of initial stamping and snorting as she accustomed herself to her new neighbours – and they to her – before things finally settled down. Her wounds healed, she revealed a surprisingly intelligent and affectionate nature, developed a passion for watermelons, and went on to live happily ever after.

'And what the hell are we supposed to do with him?' demanded Commander Hay, gesturing at the image of Romulus, king of Rome, on her screen.

Captain Farenden sighed. 'Well, he needs to recover from his wounds first, but after that . . . I'm sorry, I genuinely have no idea, ma'am.'

'Charlie . . .'

'Sorry, ma'am.'

Hay scowled. 'I suppose walking him across country like the ankylosaurus and handing him over to a museum somewhere is out of the question.'

Captain Farenden looked up. 'Why?'

'Why what?'

'Why is it out of the question, ma'am?'

'Well, obviously because . . . I mean . . . Charlie?'

'Sorry, ma'am, I was just imagining the expressions on the faces of those arsey buggers in the provisional wing of the British Museum should they wake up one morning to find the king of Rome abandoned on their doorstep. With a note pinned to his toga saying, *Please look after this king of Rome*. No, sorry, ma'am – that would be . . .'

'Wrong, Charlie.'

'So wrong.'

'Dreadful.'

'Irresponsible, ma'am.'

'Very immature.'

'Outrageous, even.'

'But satisfying.'

'So, so satisfying, ma'am. Would you like me to see what I can do?'

'When you can spare a moment, Charlie.'

'Yes, ma'am.'

Tucker was sorting his gear in the equipment room when Varma came in. They looked at each other. She sat down, picked up one of his boots and sniffed suspiciously.

'Have you been peeing on your boots?'

'Yes.'

'Deliberately? Or involuntarily? Sudden loss of control, perhaps.'

'Deliberately. Softens the leather. Did you want me?'

'I've come to make you an offer.'

'Oh?'

He began to return his kit to his locker.

She waited until he was finished. 'You did good work back there. Yes, Hay will yell at you for letting all those dinos out, but she'll just be going through the motions. The thing is . . .'

She stopped.

Tucker waited. 'Yes? What is the thing?'

'At the moment you're still under training. Leaving the Time Police is comparatively easy. Hay wants to kick the rest of your training into touch and promote you to a regular officer. Leaving the Time Police won't be so easy once that happens.'

'What are you saying?'

'I'm saying that if you want to leave, then now is the time to do it. You can walk away with no harm done to anyone. You could even pick up your old life. If you wanted to. Although don't tell me if you do.'

'Why would I want to leave?'

'Because there's nothing for you here. Not now . . .'

'Not now you're my boss. No.'

The silence dragged on. Varma shifted impatiently. 'Are you thinking about it?'

'No. I've already told you.'

'Told me what?'

'My decision.'

Varma strove again for inner calm. 'Which was?'

'No.'

'You're not telling me?'

'No. It's no. I decided no.'

'No, as in . . . ?'

'No, as in I'm not going anywhere.' Tucker shook his head. 'That was unexpectedly difficult.'

'Coming to a decision?'

'No, conveying said decision to you.'

'Which was – just to avoid confusion – no.'

'Yes.'

'Stop pissing about, Tucker.'

'I'm not. And I'm hurt that you would think so.'

Varma took a deep and supposedly calming breath. 'So what exactly have you said no to?'

'Leaving you. Ever.'

He closed his locker door, turned and walked away.

Captain Farenden appeared in the doorway. 'Ma'am, Mrs Farnborough is here.'

'Ask her to come in, Charlie.'

Mrs Farnborough strode into the room, paused, and stared rather hard at Commander Hay.

'Yes, I know,' said Hay. 'I'm sorry I couldn't see you the other day. We're still recovering from a rather lively twenty-four hours.'

'You look as if you could do with a drink.'

Hay smiled. 'If I start drinking during the day I'll never stop, but I can offer you a cup of very excellent coffee.'

'Yes, thank you.'

'If you please, Charlie. So – what can I do for you, Patricia?'

'I bring good news.'

Commander Hay called through the open door, 'And the best biscuits, please, Charlie.'

'Well,' Hay said when they were settled. 'What is this good news?'

Mrs Farnborough turned to Captain Farenden. 'I'm so sorry, but I'm about to divulge government secrets, which normally wouldn't bother me in the slightest, but these are disreputable government secrets. Which, admittedly, are the best kind, but not actually for public consumption. No offence is intended, Captain.'

'None taken, Mrs Farnborough, although I will help myself to an excitingly foil-wrapped chocolate biscuit as a consolation.'

'Take two,' said Mrs Farnborough, who, as an MP, was always very generous with other people's resources.

Clutching his prize, Captain Farenden left the room.

'Well?' said Commander Hay, stirring her coffee.

'You have your budgets back. As of midnight tonight, the Time Police will be able to pay its bills again.'

Hay sat back. 'Really? Well, that's wonderful, Patricia.' Her eyes narrowed. 'What did you do? Oh my God – who did you kill?'

Mrs Farnborough laughed. 'Fortunately, it didn't come to that. The thing is, Marietta, you never lost your budget. All the other nations have been coughing up like good little countries, but those bastards at the Treasury – under instructions from Number Ten, of course – have been sitting on it.'

'But why?'

'Why what? Why is it being freed up now, or why did they sit on it in the first place?'

'Both.'

'Well, I suspect these were the first moves to reduce, if not completely do away with, the Time Police. Money talks and governments are always open to that particular conversation.'

Mrs Farnborough's tone indicated not so much her contempt for a government that could be bought but a government that could be so easily bought.

'And as for the why it's being freed up now – the answer to that is because I had a quiet but very lengthy word with our fearless leader at Number Ten. I told him that unless he coughed up – right now – I'd spill the beans.'

'What beans?'

'There are always beans, Marietta. We're politicians.

Westminster is Beans Central. I told them I knew all about the business with the French treaty and why the French came out of it smelling of roses and we didn't. I told him I had copies of the latest aerospace contract – yes, that one – which could bring down the entire MOD procurement department if the details ever got out. I told him I knew why the member for Whittington had had to retire so suddenly and why it was judged politic for him to go and live in a country with a non-extradition treaty. I told him I knew everything about the Risby and Fullerton by-elections – which is more than he does. And then, just to pile Pelion upon Ossa, I told him I had access to someone who was on very excellent terms with a high-class call girl – who herself was on very excellent terms with nearly every member of his cabinet – all genders – and wasn't she an entertaining and well-informed person. He folded faster than a deckchair with woodworm.'

'Good Lord, Patricia, that is – magnificent. I don't suppose I could offer you a job here?'

'I'm retiring. Completely. No more public life. Imogen needs me.'

'She's being very cooperative, you know.'

'Glad to hear it. And thank you for your patience with her.'

'Are you saying she's not recovering as quickly as you hoped?'

'These last few years . . . She was going off the rails as hard as she could. And she won't admit it, but she still struggles sometimes and I have to be there for her.'

'Of course you do. Will you be going back to live in Rush-fordshire?'

'Eventually, yes. When Imogen's finished giving her statements here. I'm quite looking forward to it.'

'We must have dinner before you go.'

'That would be lovely.' She stood up. 'I've done everything I can for you, Marietta, but I have to step back now.'

'Indeed you do. Thank you, Patricia.'

Mrs Farnborough regarded her closely. 'Don't answer this question if you don't want to, but has . . . has something happened?'

'Yes.'

Mrs Farnborough nodded. 'Should you perhaps . . . I don't know . . . feel the need for a break . . . you know you'll always be welcome with me and Imogen.'

'That's a very kind offer. Thank you.'

Mrs Farnborough nodded again and strode from the room.

Despite her busy schedule, Varma found time to visit MedCen.

'Well,' said Max brightly as Varma entered. 'There's another one we've both survived.'

Varma surveyed the still heavily bandaged figure in front of her. 'You sure?'

'Yeah,' said Max carelessly. 'I heal quite quickly.'

'Just as well.'

'And I don't know what pain meds I'm on, but I feel great. Can I have some to take home with me?'

'No.'

There was an awkward pause.

'Well, thanks for your help, Max.'

'You're welcome. I quite enjoyed it. I've always wanted to be a supervillain's henchman.'

'Yes. There's another one ticked off your bucket list.' She turned to go. 'Again – thanks.'

'Hang on a minute,' said Max. 'I've been thinking.'

Varma sighed. 'I think we'd all rather you didn't.'

'You got him. Henry Plimpton, I mean.'

'We did. Although my theory will always be that he chose death rather than work with you.'

Max sighed and fiddled with her bed covers. 'Actually, I think I've screwed up. Although to be fair, I was trying to save our lives at the time and I couldn't think of everything.'

Varma sighed. 'What have you done now?'

'I left my recorder behind.'

'The one showing me kidnapping Romulus?'

'And perhaps one or two other things as well.'

'Such as?'

'It was a training mission – so there will be the trainees, Evans, the pod, the preliminary briefings ...' She paused. 'Hawking Hangar.'

Varma stared. 'Enough detail to identify St Mary's?'

'Probably.'

'Plimpton's dead. And Grint will find it.'

'I suspect it might be too late. I suspect Henry will have gone through that recorder as soon as my back was turned. He probably couldn't believe his eyes. And we know he wasn't working alone. He had a backer. The money man. Suppose he relayed that footage immediately.'

'So now it's very possible that someone knows about St Mary's. Someone who definitely shouldn't.'

'Yeah.'

Max and Varma looked at each other and then Max began to struggle out of bed.

Varma stood up. 'I'll give you a hand.'

Two hours later, a Time Police pod landed on the South Lawn. The door opened and Max staggered out.

'Are you sure you can manage? Need me to walk you up there?' said Varma, standing in the doorway.

'No, I'm fine. I need to speak with Dr Bairstow. Urgently.'

'OK. Well – thanks again.'

Max paused. 'This isn't over.'

Varma nodded. 'I know.'

'Take care.'

'Yeah – you too.' Varma looked up. 'Heads up – your Head of Security's here. Not looking any too happy. Well – see you around.'

The pod disappeared.

'Hey, Max.' Markham frowned. 'What sort of state do you call this to come home in?'

Max blinked. 'I ...' She swayed. There was a familiar ringing in her ears.

He put out a hand to steady her. 'Max? Should I call Dr Salt?'

'I ... no ... I'm fine. I ... I'm just sorting out my thoughts.'

'Bit of a first for you.'

She put her hand on his arm and grinned at him. 'You're Markham.'

He eyed her cautiously. 'Yeeeees ... Always have been.'

'Actually, there was a time when you weren't. I have a terrific story to tell you. But first I have to see Dr Bairstow.'

'Will you need a hand on the stairs?'

'I think I need a hand now.'

They set off. Quite slowly. Up the steps and into St Mary's. Evening had fallen and the Great Hall was deserted. Max contemplated the stairs without enthusiasm.

'Actually,' said Markham, 'I was thinking about this only the other day. Do you think there's any chance we could persuade Dr Bairstow to have his office on the ground floor? Save us all an awful lot of stair-staggering on our way to our daily bollocking.'

'Good thought. Can I be there when you mention that to him?'

Mrs Partridge was still in her office.

'Dr Maxwell.' She stared disapprovingly at Max's bandages and the sling supporting her damaged shoulder. 'Welcome home. I am surprised the Time Police discharged you in that state.'

'They didn't want to let me go. There was a bit of an argument. Things were said. I can probably never go back there ever again. So not all bad. Can I see Dr Bairstow, please? It is urgent.'

'Of course.' She hesitated. 'Would you like some tea?'

'Oh God, yes, please.'

Mrs Partridge stood up and opened the door. 'Dr Maxwell and Mr Markham for you, Dr Bairstow.'

Dr Bairstow looked up. 'Dr Maxwell – welcome home.' He frowned. 'Do I gather, from your appearance, that events did not go quite as smoothly as you would have wished?'

Max limped across the room, pulled out a chair, sat heavily and stared at him.

He put down his pen, closed his file and put it to one side.

'What is it, Max? What has happened?'

'Sir, I'm sorry to have to tell you this . . . I think we're about to have a massive, massive problem and, in the interests of full disclosure, I think I should tell you that it might be my fault.'

'Indeed?'

'I think, through a combination of unforeseen circumstances, sheer bad luck, and my overegging the pudding somewhat . . .'

'Yes . . . ?'

'Sir, I think that St Mary's, our location, our purpose, our resources . . . might have come to the attention of someone we would prefer to remain unaware of our existence. I'm sorry, sir, but I think we may be in for a whole shedload of trouble.'

Epilogue

'I'm ready,' said Jane, emerging from her room. 'Gosh, don't you two look smart.'

'Naturally,' said Luke, smirking at his image in the full-length mirror on the wall by the lift. The one thoughtfully provided by the Time Police so that officers could monitor their physical deterioration over the years. 'How could it be otherwise?'

Along with their colleagues, Team 236 were in full formal uniform as worn by all those attending a Stop the Clock ceremony.

Matthew was fiddling with his tie. 'I can't get it . . .'

'Here,' said Jane. 'Let me.'

She straightened his tie. 'There. Is my hair OK?'

'Fine,' said Luke. 'Come along, we're going to be late.'

They entered the atrium, where every TPO not currently involved in the clean-up operation in Wales was assembling.

Matthew frowned. 'Where's the BeeBOC contingent?'

'Over there – behind Grint,' Luke said. 'Who will almost certainly tell you to get your hair cut so you can see properly.'

Matthew ignored this. 'No Ellis?'

'Yes, he's over there by the podium.'

'No North.'

'No.'

'Nor Curtis or Rockmeyer.'

'No.'

'Nor Mellor, of course.'

Jane sighed. 'No.'

At five minutes to eleven, Commander Hay entered the atrium. Major Ellis called the room to order. The stamp of feet echoed around the vast space.

Hay surveyed the ranks drawn up in front of her. Trainees and the few civilians employed by the Time Police looked on from the overhead walkway. The front doors were locked. They had the place to themselves because this was the Stop the Clock ceremony. Private and personal to the Time Police only.

Above their heads, the huge old-fashioned clock began to make the sounds preliminary to chiming the hour. All clearly audible in the atrium.

Hay stepped up to the podium. The sun shone through the glass roof above them, throwing patterns across the floor and glinting off their medals.

She lifted her head. '*Stop the Clock.*'

The giant pendulum ceased to swing.

The atrium was completely silent. Nothing moved. As if Time itself had ceased.

Before her, on the podium, reposed a large book. Slowly and carefully, Commander Hay opened it and began to turn the pages. Jane could clearly hear the crackle of stiff paper.

Lifting her head, Hay began to speak.

'On **[DATE REDACTED]** thirteen officers under the command of Lt Pyotr Hahn were despatched on a mission to investigate suspected illegal temporal activity in the southern **[LOCATION REDACTED]** mountains.

'From the moment they exited the pod, the team came under heavy fire. Seven officers were lost before they could return to safety. The remainder fought their way back and initiated an emergency evacuation. They were, at the time, under heavy bombardment from at least one sonic cannon, a direct hit from which, we think, caused the pod to malfunction. The precise nature of the malfunction is, at present, unknown, but is being investigated and the results will be made available to you. Preliminary findings indicate the safety protocols suffered catastrophic failure, resulting in an incomplete phase shift, leading to the pod missing the Pod Bay completely and materialising inside a nearby wall.'

She paused for a moment and then continued. 'Some officers died instantly. Others did not. We are all aware of the precise circumstances which led to their deaths, but that is not a subject for today. Today we Stop the Clock in long overdue recognition of our colleagues and their sacrifice.

'The following officers have been posthumously awarded the Time Police medal for conspicuous bravery and their names have been inscribed in the Book:

Lt Pyotr Hahn
Officer Ado Aziz
Officer Denny Britton
Officer Alfred Burns
Officer Simon Coyle
Officer Sven Dikstrom
Officer Alexander Haddad

Officer Michael Murphy
Officer Marcus Noon
Officer Senze Okuta
Officer Devan Singh
Officer Adina Sharron
Officer Greg Turner

'We are also gathered here to remember our helicopter pilot, Lt Chad Mellor, whose sister is here today to receive his medal personally.'

Major Ellis escorted a pale-faced woman to the podium. She looked so like her brother that Jane felt her heart clench. Ms Mellor and Commander Hay exchanged a few words and then Hay turned back to the room.

'Their names will be remembered with honour. I now call for two minutes' silence in which to remember our fallen comrades.'

Jane blinked away the tears. Astonishingly – unbelievably – Team 236 had completed this mission virtually unscathed. That hadn't always been the case. Nor would it be in the future. One day she might be standing here for Luke or for Matthew. Or Grint.

Her heart clenched again. If that day ever came – what would she do?

She was roused by Commander Hay gently closing the Book. 'Start the Clock.'

The machinery rolled, the pendulum swung, and the Clock banged out the first of its eleven chimes.

The ceremony was over.

THE END

Thanks and Acknowledgements

Thanks, as always, to Hazel Cushion – agent extraordinaire, who spends most of her time talking me down from one ledge or another.

And to Zara Ramm, who reads my books so beautifully. Thank you, Zara – lunch again soon! If you're still speaking to me, that is. I know you said *no* when I asked if you spoke Welsh but I heard *yes*. Sorry!

To everyone at Headline:

Frankie Edwards – my long-suffering editor

Saskia Arthur – making everything happen

Hannah Sawyer – in charge of marketing

Frederica Trogu – publicity guru

Ellie Wheeldon – who produces the audio books

Everyone else at Headline, especially the Sales, Rights, Art and Production teams.

Together with:

Sharona Selby and Jill Cole, my copy editor, proofreader and safety nets.

Grateful thanks to my poor beta readers, who frequently have partly completed manuscripts thrust upon them accompanied by a hyperactive author gabbling, 'What do you think? It's rubbish, isn't it? I knew it. Tell me. No, don't tell me. Have I got time to rewrite?'

To Phil – my go-to guy for everything dodgy and unpleasant. Everyone should have a Phil.

And to Tim the military advisor, for all the brilliant info on helicopters and how to storm a building. I now feel equal to any situation requiring high explosives, helicopter navigation and decapitation. Any mistakes in techniques or procedures are all mine.

And very special thanks to the amazing Helen Dawson, from whom I had a crash course in Welsh, and who invented the magic phrase 'splashy sound behind your teeth' when I asked how to pronounce Llyfrgell – and suggested Cluvrageth.

Jodi Taylor is the internationally bestselling author of over thirty novels and more short stories than you can shake a stick at.

Her Chronicles of St Mary's series follows a bunch of disaster-prone individuals who investigate major historical events in contemporary time. Do NOT call it time travel! She is also the author of the Time Police books. Set in the same world as St Mary's, this spinoff charts the highs and lows of an all-powerful, international organisation tasked with keeping the Timeline straight no matter what the cost. Efficient and disciplined, obviously they're nothing like St Mary's. Except when they are. And when a short story set in the same world accidentally grew into a full-length novel, the Smallhope & Pennyroyal series was born, following the adventures of two unlikely partners in crime.

Jodi is also known for her gripping supernatural thrillers featuring the mysterious Elizabeth Cage together with the enchanting Frogmorton Farm series – a fairy story for adults.

Born in Bristol and now living in Gloucester (facts both cities vigorously deny), she spent many years with her head somewhere else, much to the dismay of family, teachers and employers, before finally deciding to put all that daydreaming to good use and write a book. And then another twenty-nine after that. And she hasn't finished yet.